# ALMOST
# INVINCIBLE

# ALMOST INVINCIBLE

A biographical novel of
## MARY SHELLEY
Author of Frankenstein

## SUZANNE BURDON

Criteria
PUBLISHING

ISBN: 978-0-9923540-0-8

Cover Design by R'tor John D. Maghuyop
Mary Shelley 1857 Reginald Easton
P.B. Shelley 1819 Alfred Clint
Claire Claremont 1819 Amelia Curry
Frankensstein 1922 playbill
Villa Diodati : *Finden's Landscape & Portrait Illustrations to the Life and Works of Lord Byron*, vol. 2 (London: John Murray, 1832).
CC-PD-MarkPD OldPD-Art (PD-old default)PD-Art (PD-old)

Criteria
PUBLISHING

She is singularly bold, somewhat imperious, and active of mind.
Her desire of knowledge is great, and her perseverance
in everything she undertakes, almost invincible.

*Letter from William Godwin (1813)*
*describing his daughter Mary, at fifteen.*

# Table of Contents

# PROLOGUE

Geneva July 1816

'The ghastly image of my fancy.'

*Introduction to Frankenstein,* Mary Shelley

It was barely five on a summer afternoon but already eerily dark. The candles were lit and shivered in response to the wind and rain pounding against the large panelled windows. Mary took up her scribbled pages and found her voice.

'With an anxiety that almost amounted to agony, I collected the instruments of life around me, that I might infuse a spark of being into the lifeless thing that lay at my feet. It was already one in the morning; the rain pattered dismally against the panes, and my candle was nearly burnt out, when, by the glimmer of the half-extinguished light, I saw the dull yellow eye of the creature open; it breathed hard, and a convulsive motion agitated its limbs ...'

She stopped reading to take a breath and took a quick glance around at the listeners in the cavernous and ornate Louis Quinze drawing room. They were too quiet. There should be interjections. None of this company was usually so silent. She cleared her throat and continued defiantly.

'How can I describe the wretch I had formed from foraged body parts with such infinite pains and care? I had selected his features as beautiful. Beautiful! Great God! His lustrous black hair and pearly white teeth only formed a more horrid contrast with his yellow skin and watery eyes in dun-white sockets, his shrivelled complexion and straight black lips. I had worked hard for nearly two years, for the sole purpose of infusing life into an inanimate body. For this I had deprived myself of rest and health, but now that I had finished, the beauty of the dream vanished, and breathless horror and disgust filled my heart. Unable to endure the aspect of the being I had created, I rushed out of the room ...'

Mary crumpled the edges of her paper and trailed off, feeling anxious in face of the serious silence. What did Shelley think of it? What did Albe think of it? She examined their faces and mentally prepared her defence, that it was merely the retelling of a strange dream. She hated the feeling that they saw her as a balloon filled with creative literary gases, distilled from talented parents, which had so far failed to rise.

Then Shelley was laughing and talking, his voice high with excitement.

'Mary, that's the most marvellous gothic story,' he said, coming over and coiling his tall frame to look over her shoulder, kissing the back of her neck in passing. 'The ambition to create life, to be God-like. I adore it ...'

'You would, Shiloh, you atheist,' interrupted Lord Byron, his baritone almost drowned out as the enormous mastiff curled at his feet leapt up and barked loudly to join in the excitement. 'Quiet, Mutz.' He snapped his fingers and stared commandingly at the dog, which subsided in the face of the blue-eyed gaze. Byron's attention shifted to the young girl with the high forehead and deep-set, serious eyes, sitting firmly upright, clutching Shelley's hand where it rested on her shoulder.

'Mary, it is brilliant, and it has so much of modern philosophy and natural science. You were thinking of galvanism of course, and the experiments to animate frogs with electricity that we were discussing last night ...'

'And Rousseau – the creature would vindicate his philosophy,' added Shelley. 'It would be his Natural Man, fully formed but child-like and uncorrupted by society.'

Mary blushed with pleasure at the enthusiasm in their voices. Polidori took longer to react, having watched Byron for his cue.

'I suppose you were thinking of my tales of grave-robbing when I was a medical student in Edinburgh?' he said slowly, looking, as usual, to where he could draw credit for himself.

She nodded at him distractedly, her eyes turned up to Shelley. His approval was always acclamation enough.

'I also thought about the story we heard when we were traveling up the Rhine and came across Castle Frankenstein. Do you remember, Shelley? We saw it from the river — the two great ruined gothic spires — and the boatman told the story of the scientist who lived there with a reputation for stealing bodies for experiments.'

'I do remember,' answered Shelley, thoughtfully. 'He was known as an heretic.'

The fifth person in the room, Claire, clapped slowly. She was arranged with her legs curled under her white muslin skirts, set to advantage in the frame of a formal striped sofa, a little back from the rest of the group. Nestled in her lap were two of Byron's Persian cats, purring gently. Looking towards Byron she said, with a sneer, 'Now Albe will have to concede that a woman has as much of a brain as a man.'

He glared back at her, angrily.

'When I suggested our little diversion of creating ghost stories, did I not say that hers should be published with mine? I have great confidence in Mary. The genius emerges.'

Mary felt herself glowing and hoped her excessive satisfaction wasn't too obvious. Even Claire had failed to find fault for once. Mary briefly wondered why.

'So, Maie, what happens next?' chuckled Shelley. He stood and staggered across the room, his long limbs contorted into an exaggerated stumbling gait, his fingers curled and his eyes wide and staring, his wild yellow hair completing the mime, so that Claire shrieked.

'What happens to the student's creation?' he continued, putting on a croaking voice. 'Or shall we call it Herr Frankenstein's creation? Does it fail to take root in this earthly abode? Is the student chastened? Does he try again?'

He flopped at Mary's feet, staring comically up at her, hands out in supplication, and she laughed and pushed him away. As he gave up his mime and sat down again, she answered thoughtfully. 'No. I think the creature stays alive and pursues his creator, and the student is never free of him. Think what it must be to be made new and then rejected as hideous. The creature will be physically strong but will have no way to learn human morality. I know you idolise Rousseau's philosophy, Shelley, and he thinks that man is naturally good, but I think this monster will want revenge on the creator who abandons him.'

She said the last words in low and menacing tones and, as she did so, there was a clap of thunder and lightning which illuminated the balcony and reflected on the darkness of Lake Geneva beyond. A shriek and a banging outside completed the gothic scene and Claire leapt to her feet, throwing off the cats, which then added their voices to the cacophony. She rushed, arms outstretched, towards Shelley's chair but on almost reaching it saw Mary watching her. She checked herself and huddled on a stool near his feet instead, trembling. The two monkeys on their perch in the corner ran back and forth in agitation, their chattering turning to thin screams and Byron got up languidly to soothe them and peer out into the rain.

'It is one of the guinea hens escaped and terrified,' he said, smiling. 'Tonight is not the night we will have our throats cut, Claire.'

Mary saw his look of slight disgust and wondered if he felt his liaison with her stepsister, Claire, to be worth it as the price of the company of Shelley and herself. There were plenty of other willing candidates for his attention, in particular among the dozens of young ladies who regularly jostled on the opposite bank of the Lake. They waited in all weathers with muddy feet and telescopes, hoping for a glimpse of him, the fashionable and notorious poet, whose wife had left him and accused him of unmentionable acts.

He pulled one of the thick bell-ropes which hung on either side of the marble fireplace.

'Rescue the fowl from the balcony, Braydon,' he said, as the servant bowed in. 'Or if it's dead, use it for the servants' supper. You'd better put the peacocks in the coach house too, and check on the badger and bring the other dogs inside. You may as well draw the curtains.'

'Yes, it could easily be night-time,' shivered Claire, as the butler drew the long silk curtains across each of the six casement windows, all of which were rattling as if part of a strange skeleton dance. 'It should still be light at this hour, but we've had only candles and firelight since noon. This weather,' she moaned, going back to her sofa for her shawl and drawing a straight backed chair closer to the fire. 'It's July and there has been no sun for weeks, just endless storms.'

Shelley went to the sideboard and poured himself a glass of water. He raised an eyebrow to Byron, who nodded, so he filled another glass with Vin de Grave and seltzer and took the drink across the room. Then he stopped to glance at some newspapers laid out on a side table.

'Look here, these papers that came from London yesterday are saying there are reports of spots on the sun causing all this strange weather, and mobs in France and England are predicting the end of the world.'

Byron took a swig of his drink, lit another cigar and said dreamily, 'Morn came and went — and came, and brought no day; and men forgot their passions in the dread of this their desolation; and ... and all hearts were chill'd into a selfish prayer for light.'

'That sounds like the beginnings of a tragic poem, Albe,' Shelley observed in a tone of genuine admiration.

'A few lines so far. I've been thinking about men's fear of this darkness. What would happen, Shiloh, if the darkness were to remain? If there were never again a sliver of sun or moon? How would people behave?'

'Not well, I think. The apocalypse would come not from Divine intervention, but from man's own nature, as with all things. There would be despair, riots, food would run out. The animals would die. People would need to keep warm, to make fires. They would have to burn everything.'

'They would fight tooth and nail over the dwindling resources of the earth.'

'I agree it would be bloody,' said Shelley sadly. 'Even my best hopes for human nature would be severely tested.' For a while the only sound was the still driving rain.

'Talking of blood, metaphorically, we also have the *Aeneid* magazine arrived from London,' said Mary, deliberately cracking the silence. She picked it up from the table beside her and held it up. 'It prints what it calls a '*Monstrous, Deformed, Titanic Rumour*,' saying we four are unbridled libertines, living in an incestuous foursome: Claire and me and Albe and you, Shelley.'

'Which annoys you most, Albe, the libertine or the deformed part of the libel?' giggled Claire.

Byron blushed, glancing down at his club foot disguised in its heavy boot, and slightly wide-ankled pantaloons. He reflexively crossed his unwithered calf over, pulled across his velvet smoking jacket and shot Claire a look of hatred. He had thought her handsome enough, with her flashing eyes, until she had proved to be not just outspoken but sarcastic and often hysterical as well. It didn't help that she saw his admiration of Mary, whom he pointedly referred to as a calm beauty. He would casually remark on her hazel eyes or the richness of her golden russet hair, and Claire would toss her own dark curls in frustration.

Mary knew he was still suspicious about why she and Shelley had taken Claire with them when they eloped. Even though Shelley had given Byron his word it was not a ménage, she saw that the underlying hostility between her and Claire made him wonder.

The butler called supper and they moved to the dining room, chilly in spite of a blazing fire, and sat to the usual plates of vegetables.

'You brought me here as your physician, so I think you should take my advice that your constitution would be better served if you ate meat occasionally,' commented Polidori to Byron, sighing.

'Nonsense, Polly Dolly, don't fuss,' responded Byron. 'Look at Shelley. He's been on the vegetable diet for years with no harm.'

Mary wanted to support Polidori's plea, but held her tongue. In her opinion, Shelley's frequent illnesses, his ethereal pallor, his too lean frame and his weak lungs was partly a result of this diet. But the vegetable diet was his passion, and Shelley's passion was part of what she admired in him. It was different from the obsessive anxiety about his weight that caused Byron to limit what he ate or purge it out after every meal. Shelley's commitment was based on belief, the belief that eating animals was wrong, and only the fruits of the earth were man's intended consumption.

She left her meal half finished. 'I must go and feed William,' she said, rising, feeling an irrational urge to hold her baby, not yet six months, to be reassured of his wellbeing by his newly learnt smile. She wondered if this was common to all mothers, or was it stronger in those, like her, who had lost a baby? She was only eighteen, and her own mother had died giving birth to her. There was no-one to ask.

She pretended not to notice Claire's little cough and mockingly raised eyebrows in Shelley's direction, implying that Mary was fussing. In this though, she knew Claire had it wrong. Shelley was gazing at Mary with admiration. Unlike most in European society, he believed that mothers should feed their babies themselves and not use a wet nurse. His first wife — still wife — Harriet had refused to breast-feed their daughter and he had never forgiven her.

'Bring the child down for me to kiss goodnight afterward, Dormouse,' he said with a fond smile, and Claire's lips tightened. 'I don't think his vaccination has had any adverse reaction, has it Polly?' he turned to the doctor.

'The child seems very well,' reassured Polidori assuming his professional voice. 'I ordered the best quality cowpox lymph for the vaccine. I think you are very wise. Smallpox has declined in the past twenty years and it is the vaccine that has done it, despite the scaremongering of the Anti-Vak movement. I have yet to see a person develop cow horns!' He drew a gold watch from his breast pocket as he spoke, tapped it and nodded to Shelley. 'And this is good payment for my services.'

Later, after dinner, over green tea in the music room, Polidori asked Shelley if he had thought of a ghost story.

'I have nothing more than the images that overcame me three days ago, when I almost fainted from the vision … the girl whose nipples became eyes. As to how this strange situation should come about, I have not yet found a story for her, or a meaning.' Shelley sounded faintly exasperated. 'It was probably just because we were sitting in the half dark reading *Christabel*. Coleridge's lines have a powerful resonance. But at least that made Albe throw out the challenge of ghost story making, and now we have Mary's wonderful idea. I will be a tyrant and make sure she writes it in full.' He smiled, turning to Mary next to him on the sofa and feigned a whip, which coiled into an embrace.

'You can't be any more of a tyrant than you are already. Perhaps now you'll give me a rest from learning Greek.' Mary laughed and wriggled free. 'Anyway, I'll start now. I will sit at the bureau by the window, with the thunder and lightning as my muse, and leave you two to continue your discussion of Plato and the Trinity.'

'Stay here, Mary, by the fire,' urged Byron, softly.

Mary laughed. 'I know your opinion of women philosophising, Albe. I have heard you say that you only need to give a woman a looking-glass and a few sugar plums to keep her happy. Well, tonight I will pander to your prejudices and absent myself – but not to sugarplums, to a sweeter labour.'

Claire moved towards the piano. 'Shall I sing, Shelley?' she asked, hesitantly.

Shelley contemplated her, nervously fiddling with the cameo at her throat. It was unlike Claire to ask. She knew her voice was good and that it always pleased him to hear her sing. She would normally just begin, but he also saw Byron's face become taut and he wanted to provoke no more tension. Claire needed to stay in the background. He had seen Byron getting more and more irritated with her. Shelley failed to understand how anyone could bed someone he so clearly disliked. He knew that he never could. For himself there had to be love — if not marriage. They needed to get Claire away from Byron for a while. Maybe a trip around the lake.

'I think, sadly, the noise of the storm is too loud tonight, Claire,' he said gently.

Claire moved on, towards Byron's side.

'Well then, is there more of your poem, *Childe Harold*, to copy, Albe?' she asked.

Why, Mary wondered, as she observed this exchange, was Claire being so unusually demure?

'Yes, on the pile there.' Byron, not turning to look at Claire, indicated the strewn sheets of manuscript on the chaise longue. Claire gathered them up and sighed as she glanced at the blotted and crossed lines, some spattered with wine or cigar ash. She took them to a little drum pedestal table in the corner, where there was fresh paper and an inkwell set out, and the room settled to the sounds of the scratching pens of the girls and the arguments and laughter of the young men.

It was two a.m. before Shelley, Mary and Claire wound their way down the rocky path to Maison Chapuis, their little cottage on the lakeside, wrapped in blankets against the night chill. Byron's Villa Diodati stood high above the lake, its three stories commanding a magnificent view but vulnerable to the icy winds of the past weeks. Maison Chapuis, because it was lower down on the lakeshore and surrounded by trees, was more sheltered, and they reached their porch with relief. Claire had not tried to hang back to be alone with Byron as she so often did, and he had made no attempt to detain her.

The rain had made the short descent to the cottage treacherous and they arrived cold and dishevelled. Claire took off her shoes by the door, the thin white leather and velvet trim clogged with mud.

'Ugh. These are ruined. I hate this weather.' She pulled on some slippers and tried to brush the dirt off the hem of her skirt.

Mary went to check on William, who had been brought back earlier and put to bed by the nurse, Elise. Claire drew Shelley into his study.

'I need to talk to you. I'm pregnant,' she said, unceremoniously.

Shelley staggered slightly, then managed a weak smile.

'That's wonderful, Claire. And Albe ... is the father?' He tried to keep the question out of his voice, but failed enough for Claire to step up close and poke him disgustedly in the chest.

'You, of all people, should know that it could only be his.'

'We must tell him. Have you told Mary?' As he said this, Mary came in, looking between the two, suspicious.

'What is it?'

Shelley told her, while Claire went to face out of the window, looking for light in the darkness, keeping her back to them.

Mary pulled Shelley to the far corner of the room and exploded, hissing into his ear. 'Oh yes, now she has it all. She has achieved her ambition to be just like me. She has the poet, and now the poet's child.' Her voice got louder, so that it became audible to Claire. 'Except that it won't be that poet,' — pointing back up towards the Villa Diodati — 'who takes responsibility for it, I'm sure of that,' she rasped. 'It will be this poet.' His already dishevelled shirt suffered another poke. 'The drain on our limited resources will not just be for my stepsister, as it is now, but for my stepsister's child as well, who everyone will say is yours, and our lives will be even more complicated and hateful.'

From the window came the sob of someone who was not prepared to allow herself to sob. Or someone who knows that a restrained sob can be more wrenching than an overt one.

'She is right in one thing,' said Claire, turning to face them. 'Albe won't want anything to do with the child, because he no longer wants anything to do with me. I will go away. I'll go to … I don't know, Russia, and earn my living as a governess, and leave the baby with a nursemaid. I don't want to be any more of a drain on you, Shelley, and I don't want to face Mama back in London. It was bad enough me refusing to go back home after running away with you both. This would kill her, and yes, she and everyone else will assume it's yours. What a mess! Ten minutes of happy passion, and it discomposes the rest of your life.'

Shelley looked at Mary, worry and appeal distorting his features. He was choosing to ignore her bitter and vindictive explosion. In a situation like this, she was resigned to knowing that compassion would be his strongest emotion. This man who could not comfortably walk past a beggar without tossing a coin, who sought out orphans to subsidise, this man could only see distress, not justice.

Yet again I must maintain the image of Mary that he has constructed, she thought tiredly, the calm and in control Mary who can soothe her distraught stepsister, hiding the angry and insecure Mary who more often finds her stepsister selfish and manipulative.

So she went to Claire and enfolded her, while Claire stared piteously at Shelley over her shoulder.

'I'm sorry, Claire, it was a shock. We will look after you, of course, and Shelley will talk to Albe for you.' Mary was conciliatory and Shelley nodded, vigorously.

'We will demand that he acknowledges the child and takes responsibility for it,' he said firmly.

'But he will not acknowledge me, so how is that to be managed? He has already said he wants me to leave.'

Mary was also wondering just how Byron was to be made to take responsibility for Claire's child. He would feel no compassion for Claire and would need to be assured that the child was his. Perhaps he could be appealed to as a potential father, since Lady Byron never allowed him to see his legitimate child. Perhaps he would do it out of friendship for Shelley. Shelley would be prepared to support Claire and her baby as much as he could, but, as things stood, his father barely gave him a decent allowance, and if he were thought to be responsible for a child by yet another woman he would be completely disowned.

'Not, of course that I would ever want to be married. Hateful institution,' Claire went on, defiantly.

Mary felt the surging hatred of Claire that ebbed and flowed, but whose peaks had become continually higher since they had allowed her to come with them when they eloped, two years ago. Shelley had adopted responsibility for her, since he and Mary were supposedly at fault in Claire's tumble from the rickety heights of respectability, but Mary constantly worried that it was not only duty that drove him. She saw that Shelley was drawn to Claire's freethinking attitudes, which were more extremely liberal and careless of what society thought than her own. It unsettled Mary that Claire knew her secret, that her true nature was essentially modest and conservative. And Claire knew just how to use that knowledge.

Since Mary had first met Shelley in the St. Pancras churchyard, in North London, she had learnt to share many of his passions and admired him for those she could not quite endorse. The problem was that he expected her, the daughter of two radical thinkers, to lead him in liberality, while in reality she felt she was desperately trying to keep pace. With Claire always on her heels, threatening to overtake and overcome.

# PART ONE

London 1814

# 1

'Is there such a feeling as love at first sight? And
if there be, in what does its nature differ from love
founded in long observation and slow growth?'

*The Last Man*, Mary Shelley

'Mary Godwin!'

She was sitting with a book of poetry in St. Pancras churchyard
by her mother's grave. It made her feel close to her mother, and she
loved it there – the peace, the willow trees, the lawns and crocuses,
the little pathways between the scattered graves. She imagined her
mother's care and wisdom emanating from the large memorial that
covered her remains.

The young man who had been calling to her came bounding
across, breathless, yellow hair wild, buttons on his striped waistcoat
carelessly undone, necktie loose. He barely brought himself up short
as he reached her side.

'Mr. Shelley?' she asked. She knew from her sisters' description
that this could only be Shelley, and couldn't help smiling at him and
his disarray.

'Mary Godwin?' panted Shelley, looking at her quizzically. 'I took
it to be you, here by Mary Wollstonecraft's grave. I've come with a
message from your stepmother, that you are needed back in Skinner
Street. What are you reading?'

She blushed and got up quickly, trying to conceal the slim volume
in her skirt, but as she did so, it slipped from her fingers and he
caught it deftly. The ground was wet from the morning rain, and the
embroidered hem of her dress was stained with damp. There was no
escaping his glance at the book he had rescued and he saw it was the
copy of his own work — *Queen Mab* — which he had given to her
father.

'Well, well,' he said, with a grin, looking at the slim volume, 'I see you spend your time idly!'

'You are too modest, Mr. Shelley.' She took the book from him and pointed to the verse she had been reading. 'See, these are some of my favourite lines, about the pure spirit:

*Custom, and Faith, and Power thou spurnest;*
*From hate and awe thy heart is free;*
*Ardent and pure as day thou burnest,*
*For dark and cold mortality*
*A living light, to cheer it long,*
*The watch-fires of the world among.*

'Are you trying to change the way the world thinks?'

The question was a hesitant compliment, one that Shelley dismissed with an airy wave of his hand.

'The haphazard ramblings of a young and naive mind. But I still think there is so much that can be done to achieve the perfectibility of humankind.'

'A great ambition, Mr. Shelley.' She looked up at him with a slightly sardonic smile.

'I don't mean to sound arrogant.' He was a little sheepish. 'I know only too well that one man can do very little. When I started writing to your father for advice last year, he warned me of the futility of practical action, and I found he was right. I went to Ireland to try to support Catholic emancipation and to help in the slums of Dublin. All failures.'

'But in your defence, at least you have a vision,' said Mary, carefully arranging some flowers which were lying on top of the memorial, that had seemed to Shelley already perfectly bunched. 'It seems to me the worst crime is to feel these things and not to try to do something about it.'

'My feelings exactly, Miss Godwin,' replied Shelley, surprised. 'But now ... now I believe that it is through poetry that I can try to bring about change. I think that poets are the unacknowledged legislators of the world.'

Mary looked thoughtful. 'And in poetry you can stir the soul as well as the reason.'

Shelley felt unaccountably drawn to this tall, slight, very young girl — what was she, sixteen her father had said? — with the strong and confident voice of one much older, who seemed to understand so well. Of course her father was a great political thinker, which was why he had chosen him as a mentor. His daughter would naturally be imbued with his ideas. He wondered if she was just parroting her father or if she thought for herself.

'Do you write poetry? While you were away in Scotland, when your father mentioned you, I think the words he used were something like … strong-minded and talented.'

Mary blushed again and felt embarrassed at her reaction. She did not want him to see her as simpering, but wasn't sure why it bothered her what he thought. She was not given to worrying about other people's opinion, so she replied sharply.

'I suspect that he mentioned strong-minded in front of my stepmother and stepsister, Claire, and talented when they were not there. On both counts he was wrong. Shall we set off to walk back?'

Ohh, thought Shelley, that is a topic to avoid. He had enough family politics of his own to cope with.

'Do you believe in spirits, Miss Godwin?' he asked as Mary turned to leave, trying to recapture some warmth.

'Yes, when I am here I believe I feel my mother's spirit,' replied Mary, softening. 'My father brought me here to remember her when I was a child. He taught me my letters by tracing the characters on this memorial.' She traced them now with her fingers. *'Mary Wollstonecraft, Author of A Vindication of the Rights of Women.'* But her real, lasting memorial is her writing. I wish I had even a small part of her courage and insight, let alone the ability to express it.'

They set off along the path out of the well-tended cemetery and he pulled open the heavy ironwork gate for her.

'And you, Mr. Shelley, do you believe in spirits?'

As they headed towards busy Euston Road, he glanced up at the old stone church, the dark eye of the bell tower glaring back in challenge.

'I do, though my friends say because I am an atheist it is a contradiction, but they don't understand me. I believe that there is a pervading Spirit, coeternal with the universe. There are many spiritual mysteries that we have yet to understand. I am only an atheist because I won't follow Christianity or any formal religion that demands obedience to a set of man-made rules that defy reason.' His tone was defensive, but Mary's reply was matter-of-fact.

'In our house we have certainly not been brought up to slavishly follow dogma. My father thinks that men should require no external help to behave as moral beings. I hope he is right, but surely history tells us we can't rely on people behaving well.'

They had reached Grays Inn Road and turned towards Holborn. With his long legs he unconsciously set a rapid pace, and she worked hard to keep up and to talk without seeming breathless.

'Tell me, Miss Godwin, have you read Rousseau?'

'I have read his novels, *Emile* and *Julie*. I think he underrates women by seeing them as naturally weaker than men.' She looked up briefly, challenging him before moving to safer ground. 'But I was reading *Julie* while I was in Scotland, and the sublime Swiss scenery he describes, well, it was easy to imagine, sitting among the mountains. And my friend Isabella was in tears for days over poor Julie and her thwarted love.'

'Yes, it made me want nothing more than to visit the mountains of Switzerland.' She thought he was going to ignore her daring comment about women, but he nodded thoughtfully and stopped walking to face her. 'I agree with you that girls' education in particular, is given no attention in *Emile*.' He continued, his voice rising, high-pitched with enthusiasm, his hands expressive. 'But Miss Godwin, you must read his *Social Contract*. He makes one see that man in his natural state is a glorious creature. With encouragement and education the power of good will always assert itself over evil.'

Even while she was embarrassed to be standing stock still in the middle of a busy thoroughfare apparently being harangued by a madman, she felt excited by his idealism. Shelley's passion and eloquence made him especially attractive, she decided. His ideals were not just an intellectual exercise. Compassion for the whole world lit his face when he talked about them. She smiled at him with sympathy and turned to walk on, so that he had to follow.

As they neared Skinner Street, they were swept up in the crowds flocking towards Newgate prison. It seemed there was to be an execution that afternoon. Italian merchants with brightly coloured barrows were selling ginger pop and ice cream. Fathers carried children on their shoulders. There was an air of festivity and soon they were pushing through the throng. Shelley was beside himself with anger.

'Governments that exert control by showing contempt for human life are not only morally deficient, they encourage the same contempt in their subjects.'

'As we see from the joy of this rabble,' answered Mary, equally disgusted, but a little distracted by Shelley's need to circle his arm around her, to shield her from the jostling crowd.

'All these self-righteous people seeing themselves as morally superior,' he said. 'Jesus was right in asking who is so unblemished that he can throw the first stone.'

Mary hated living so close to the prison. Her stepmother had chosen this part of Holborn to set up her publishing house because it was close to the city, and the house was cheap and large, with five stories. The suburb seemed likely to become an area for artisans, since many silk weavers plied their trade from the large, wide-fronted buildings, but it had never become either fashionable or a creative hub. The proximity of Newgate prison and the noise of the cattle being driven to nearby Smithfield Market in the early morning made for an unsettling existence.

That afternoon it was a relief to push past the throng and see the familiar door and huge rounded windows of her house, with the Juvenile Library on the ground floor and the stone carving over the door. It showed Aesop reading his fables to children gathered at his feet. Then, as they climbed the stairs to the drawing room, with each tread the murmurs of family dissonance grew louder. With Shelley at her heels, Mary hunched her shoulders, preparing herself for the embarrassment of becoming just another member of the Godwin household.

# 2

'There is a meaning in the eye of love,
a cadence in its voice, an irradiation in its smile.'

*The Last Man*, Mary Shelley

Shelley had often been a guest at dinner at Skinner Street in the past month, while he tried to borrow money to give to Mary's father and keep him out of debtor's prison. Shelley the acolyte, the young man who wrote admiringly to Godwin about his ideas and hung on his advice, became Shelley the saviour, as Godwin appreciated that this son of a baronet was a promising and willing source of finance.

Dinner that evening in Skinner Street took its usual course: Godwin pontificated, Mrs. Godwin simpered. The boiled fowl, roast mutton and vegetables stood on the sideboard ready to be served. The wine was poured for all but Shelley, who drank only seltzer. Tonight, with Mary's return from Scotland, there were three girls hanging on Shelley's every word.

Mary found his appearance unusual, and a little exotic, especially as she had so recently been among the brawny men of the highlands. His pale skin seemed slightly translucent and his eyes were penetratingly soft. He appeared an ethereal being who might be expected to offer insight and empathy, and when someone attracted the full beam of his attention, she saw how he could make them blossom. But Mary suspected his deep appeal was more subtle. He had told Fanny, Mary's half-sister, something that she had faithfully transcribed into her notebook and showed Mary: *that everyone should be treated as though they have the potential to be much more than they are.* That is what people saw of themselves, reflected in his gaze.

The long summer evening began to fade and the servant came in to light the candles. As the first course of trout was served, Mary glanced down the table at the other two girls. The candlelight flickered on her sisters' faces, as if reflecting their insubstantial parentage. The two years away had made her re-examine the complicated family in which she had grown up.

There was Fanny, three years older than Mary and also Mary Wollstonecraft's daughter from her mother's first, illicit love, before she married Mary's father. Fanny was listening modestly to the conversation and contributing rarely. She believed that Shelley understood her deep anxiety about her position in this household — the only child without a natural parent — which was why she was always determined to be useful and dutiful. He listened to her, she felt valued, and his eye never strayed to the pock-marked side of her face.

Next to her was their stepsister, Claire, boisterous and giggly as usual, thoughtlessly interrupting as something occurred to her. Mary could not understand how she never seemed embarrassed by her mother, the shrill and sycophantic Mrs. Godwin, Godwin's second wife–Mary Jane Clairmont as was. She still made Mary cringe whenever she spoke. Claire had not known her Swiss father but she would romanticise his fine qualities to anyone who asked. Mrs. Godwin had never married him though she had adopted his name, so Claire was known as Claire Clairmont. She saw herself as gay and carefree and was confident that Shelley appreciated her independent character and her creative soul.

Mary was conscious that, in contrast to her sisters, she was trying to seem thoughtful and assured. She was uncertain what Shelley might see as her best self — and if it was a view she would recognize.

'Of course, my situation is limited at present,' said Shelley, in answer to another anxious pitch by Godwin for financial assistance. 'While my father refuses me a decent allowance I have only my prospects of the baronetcy to fall back on. But we shall manage something, my dear sir. We will see the lawyers again tomorrow.'

This seemed to satisfy Godwin. 'You will not regret a connection with one of the most known men of the age,' he said pompously, gesturing for a refill to his wine. 'It will insure for you a great deal of respectability and recognition for your work.'

He gazed benignly around the table, barely missing Mary's disapproving and embarrassed look, which duty obliged her to disguise behind a cough and a napkin.

Since I have been away, my father seems to have become less prepossessing to look at and more dogmatic in manner, Mary thought, guiltily. Or is it that I never saw him clearly before — saw him only through the eyes of an uncritical child?

William Godwin, as the author of the renowned *Political Justice*, knew himself to be one of the great thinkers of the past decade. He was short and stout, with a large round head, high forehead and, as befitted one who lives in the mind, his dress was shabby and his beard unruly. He saw it as a sign of wisdom to be silent for long periods, then either embark on a long rant about the politics of the day or more often — and here he was most eloquent — a long complaint about how society failed to honour and support its great men, among which he counted himself.

Fortunately Shelley seemed entirely in sympathy with this point of view and agreed that men of fortune, like himself, had an obligation to support those whose only resource is their intellect. Gratified, Godwin looked at his daughter.

'Well, sir, and what do you think of my Mary, come back to us almost a woman? I have always been anxious that she should be brought up like a philosopher, even a cynic. Her desire for knowledge is great and her perseverance in everything she undertakes almost invincible. She is bold, too, my dear Shelley, and she can be imperious. Take care, that you do not run foul of her.'

Shelley replied with a soft, ironically complicit smile at Mary. 'I will, though I am glad to have met Miss Godwin at last. Do we hope for some writings from her pen that will echo her mother's? A child of yourself and Mary Wollstonecraft has a powerful inheritance.' He addressed Godwin, but his eyes were still on Mary.

'She has tried her hand at some childish stories, and we certainly hope for more mature offerings. But I fear there will never be a woman who excels in the field of literature – or at least, till the softer sex has produced a Bacon, a Hume or a Shakespeare, I will never believe it.'

'Oh, but surely …' Shelley leapt to the defence of womankind. He seemed startled at this incongruous declaration by Mary's father, who had after all married her mother — a celebrated champion of women. His challenge was cut short by an interjection from Mrs. Godwin.

'How is dear Harriet, Mr. Shelley?' she asked in an oily tone. 'We hear your wife is enjoying the company of her father and sister at Bristol. We miss seeing her here at Skinner Street. She is so lively with such good conversation, is she not, Claire?' she smiled, turning to her daughter.

Claire answered her mother's remark carelessly. Her mother's inappropriate manner upset her less than it did Mary and Fanny.

'I'm sure that Mr. Shelley knows his wife is always welcome at Skinner Street when she comes back to London, Mama. She did indeed teach me much about ways to tame my unruly curls, though I am not sure I have the perseverance to act on her advice.'

Claire was handsome rather than pretty. Her animation in conversation, so quick to contradict or confirm with a toss of her thick black curly hair, made her features seem alive and that added enormously to her attractiveness. She was one of those girls who flirt without the consciousness of it. The idea of Shelley, his intellect, his passion, so clearly appealed to her that her mouth almost hung open when he spoke. She was only eight months younger than Mary, but seemed naïve in her adoration — a puppy with a new master.

'I hear your wife keeps a carriage now, Mr. Shelley,' cooed Mrs. Godwin. 'And do tell, are the horses black, and are the fittings of brass or iron?'

'She does keep a carriage, though I can ill afford it,' replied Shelley, rather tight-lipped. 'I have no idea of the quality of the fittings.'

Mary had tried all her life to forgive her father for her stepmother, or at least to understand. Mrs. Jane Clairmont married William Godwin when Mary was three. She had brought two children of her own to the marriage, Claire and Charles. Mary had heard the tittle-tattle, that she had stalked Godwin, obsessed with achieving bohemian respectability. William Godwin's obsession had been someone to care for Mary and Fanny. To be fair, the children's' book publishing house Mrs. Godwin set up had kept the Godwin brood from being totally cast adrift amongst the sharks of London's debt collectors, but it was a close-run thing. With the birth of the Godwins' own child, William, it became a household of seven souls. Though, to his credit, Godwin took responsibility for them all, he had no financial acuity. He survived by borrowing money or calling in favours from rich patrons. They were always on the brink.

With her newly distanced perspective, Mary wondered if her father ever regretted his marital bargain. Mrs. Godwin's preferred method of getting her way was with a tantrum, her big bosom and chubby jowls wobbling with anger at a supposed slight or the lack of obedience of one of the children. Claire had her mother's temperament, and hysterics were often heard vibrating the four stories of Skinner Street. It was not a calm atmosphere for a thinker. Mrs. Godwin's venal curiosity and shallowness also repelled many of Godwin's admirers, and they came less often to drink gin and water in the Godwin drawing room.

Mrs. Godwin seemed oblivious to Shelley's cold response. 'Do you think her father will make some extra provision for your little baby girl — Ianthe, isn't it? — and Harriet, while you are temporarily impecunious? I would like to think a father would help all his daughters,' she added with emphasis, looking directly at her husband as she gestured to the maid to pass him the plate of meat. 'More mutton, Mr. Godwin? Try the new Harvey's Sauce that I ordered from Elizabeth Lazenby's warehouse in Portman Square.'

Mrs. Godwin then smiled broadly at her family and her guest and avoided Mary's eye, though her smile tightened with resentment. She felt that she had done her best with 'that girl' for thirteen years. She failed to understand why Mary should be considered the intellectual, better than her Claire. Claire's virtues, like her singing voice and her French, were never, to her mind, properly appreciated.

Fanny had been quietly attending to the needs of the company, ensuring the ham and mutton found their way to everyone's plate and the glasses were filled, and in particular that Shelley was served enough bread and vegetables to satisfy his needs. Now she sensed the underlying tension and changed the subject.

'We have been quite gay while you were away, Mary. There have been many good performances at the theatre that we have been able to attend. Do you visit the theatre, Mr. Shelley?'

'No, I am not a lover of plays. I think the acting is often not up to representing what the playwright means.'

'That's a shame, Mr. Shelley,' said Claire, with a great, pouting show of disappointment. 'I was hoping to have your advice on my play.'

'Your play, Claire?' asked Shelley, politely.

'Yes, it's called *The Ideot*,' said Claire, grandly. 'I have been working on it for months. My ambition is to have it produced at Drury Lane.'

Mary wondered if her family could possibly be more embarrassingly self-important. Perhaps she could avert what must certainly be Shelley's poor opinion by making it seem like just one of Claire's juvenile fantasies.

'I think you would prefer to be acting at Drury Lane, would you not, Claire? Fanny wrote to me that that this is your new ambition.'

Claire's jaw tensed, her black eyes flashed and she stood up and glared at her stepsister.

'So, we cannot all be budding geniuses of philosophy, can we? Because of our brilliant parents, can we? Some of us have to work hard on our own natural talent.' She turned and flounced out of the room.

'You can see, Mr. Shelley, that Claire would indeed be a good actress. She loves drama.' Mrs. Godwin laughed uncertainly. Now she was less confident of her victory in getting Mary packed off to Scotland, while Claire stayed at home and enjoyed lessons in French conversation. Mary had returned mature and self-assured and, in contrast, Claire seemed even more of a spoiled child.

Mary trembled, at this moment not feeling in the least self-assured. I should never have taken on Claire, she thought. She is so much more ruthless. Her jabs into the soft underbelly of my self-esteem are always harder and deeper than my soft scratches to her ego. Only she guesses how vulnerable and sensitive I am about my ability and how I constantly doubt whether I have any of the genius that is supposedly my heritage.

Claire's outburst dampened the mood. Shelley tried to restore Mary's composure by quizzing her about Scotland and her stay with Isabella Baxter, and drew from her descriptions of rambles among the sublime scenery and a confession of some romantic scribblings in praise of it.

'Will I be allowed to see them, Mary?' he asked.

She hesitated. 'One day, perhaps, when I know you better.' She bit her lip and fell silent. That was a coquettish remark, she thought, worthy of Claire but totally unlike herself. Claire had unsettled her. Did she, somewhere deep inside her carapace of calm, have a need to best Claire in those skills which were Claire's alone? Vivaciousness, flirtatiousness. If so, she was making a poor job of it, as Shelley seemed unaffected, merely smiling politely.

As in dining rooms throughout the country, the discussion turned to France.

'Do you think the Treaty of Peace will finally be signed in Paris, Papa?' Mary asked.

'A peace has been offered to them three times already. All of the Allies acknowledged the necessity of leaving France great and powerful, but the ambition of Napoleon made negotiations ineffectual. The Allies are not even asking for reparation, and they have offered France their 1792 borders. This time with the Allies actually holding Paris the French will have to accept, and ship the tyrant off to Elba.'

'We must hope so,' agreed Shelley. 'Though I regret the return of Louis XVIII. We've enough of bad kings here, with mad George III, and the libidinous Regent. It would have been a better world if the principles of the Revolution had not been compromised.'

'At least Louis has to accept a constitution that gives a strong parliament — votes to ninety-thousand people, freedom of religion and the press,' Mary said. Then she added with excitement, 'What is most important, they have promised us to abolish the slave trade!'

Shelley was enchanted by such political vehemence in one so young. 'True! But I am afraid there will need to be a much longer struggle to actually stop slavery in the world.'

Their accord was startling and the ectoplasm of future hours stretched across the table between them, briefly obscuring the company.

'Do you not think, Mary, it will be nice to be able to visit Paris at last, and again be free to travel through France into Switzerland?'

Mary's reply was lost as little William came tumbling in to say goodnight.

'Tell Mary about the Frost Fair,' he demanded, climbing on Fanny's lap and pulling at the ribbon on her dress.

'Ten year old boys need to be in bed,' laughed Fanny, kissing the top of his head.

'But we actually walked across the Thames,' William protested. 'I had a donkey ride and a swing on the ice and we watched a sheep being roasted, right there on solid ice, and we ate the meat on bread, and, you'll never guess, they had an elephant to walk across, from one side of the river to the other ...'

'And you ran so fast to get a good view your feet skated from under you and you got a very wet rear!' interrupted Fanny, and they all laughed.

'I wish I'd seen it,' said Mary. 'I must say though I'm not sorry that the weather turned a little milder in April. One of the things I was looking forward to, coming back to London, was my daily walk to St. Pancras. Goodnight William.' She kissed his cheek as he came around the table. 'You will have to make a little lecture on the subject of Frost Fairs for delivering to father's friends. I'll help you.'

Soon afterwards, Godwin took Shelley down to his study to drink strong gunpowder green tea and, Mary supposed, to discuss his dire financial straits. The others went to the drawing room and Claire returned to the company, sulkily, but unable to resist the opportunity to sing for them. Mary suppressed her resentment and read aloud from *Political Justice*, the chapter on *Self Love and Benevolence*, trying not to emphasise the passage that preached against rivalry.

# 3

'If her childish dreams had been full of fire, how much more vivid and overpowering was the awakening of her soul when she first loved! It seemed as if some new and wondrous spirit had descended, alive, breathing and panting, into her colder heart and gave it a new impulse.'

*Valperga*, Mary Shelley

Over the next few days Mary often found that Shelley just happened to be sitting reading in the churchyard where she walked every afternoon, and soon they were meeting by appointment. For an hour they talked of poetry, politics and science, and the means to create a better society. He held forth on the vegetable diet as a cure for sickness, and a community of poets as a cure for complacency, but he also appeared to give her opinions a value she felt they hardly deserved.

One morning, Mary was helping Fanny pack for a visit to their aunts in Ireland. They were thinking of employing her as a teacher in their school. The older girl sat Mary beside her on the bed and took her hands.

'I feel that something momentous will happen while I am away,' said Fanny, anxiously. 'Be honest with me, Mary. You are not too fond of Mr. Shelley?'

'Oh, Fanny, I'm afraid I might be. It's as if I absorb his warmth and it makes me feel so strong. You and I have been brought up to think and to speak our minds, but this is the first time there seems to be purpose to thinking!'

'Yes,' Fanny smiled, weakly. 'He has a way of making one feel one's ideas are of value.'

Mary, intoxicated by her own enthusiasm, did not catch the sadness in her sister's tone.

'Before I went away, every thought I expressed publicly had to run the gauntlet of Claire, and you know how she can be: either wild enthusiasm or spite and envy, you never know which. It was relaxing in Scotland, living with Isabella and her comfortable family, but our conversations were only young girls' fantasies. With Shelley, I have a sense of always being on the brink of something important, of a deeper level of understanding.'

'Mary, you are so young. Is it more than intellectual? Be careful while I am away.'

Mary blushed. 'I will, Fanny. I know he's married. But … When he looks so earnestly into my eyes as I'm describing some wild imagining, I have to work hard to keep my emotions locked away, boxed inside. Sometimes I am afraid they might burst through.' But the casing is becoming more flimsy every day, thought Mary. The pressure is building. And Shelley has the key. She held her breath as if an exhalation would open the way for more than a sigh. 'Don't worry about me, Fanny', she smiled a tight-lipped smile. 'I am strong.'

To his friends, Shelley now appeared wild and furtive with bloodshot eyes, and was even more unreliable at keeping appointments than usual. He stayed up late in his rooms, ostensibly working on some scientific experiments, but courting trouble from his landlady for continual pacing. His friend Hogg was waylaid by her when he went to visit.

'Can you speak to him, please, sir? He won't stop to speak to me. He rushes up those stairs and rushes down again; and those smells, like rotten eggs last night. He never seems to sleep or even sit still, all night long. It's fair wearing out my nerves.'

When Hogg dutifully relayed these concerns, Shelley took him by the shoulder, propelled him out of the front door, and almost dragged him through the back alleys to Skinner Street. It was eleven a.m. and he rushed them into the Juvenile Library, put his finger to his lips to the young man behind the desk and they scooted through the shop and up some back stairs. When they arrived at a reception room on the second floor, Shelley stood in the middle and hissed, 'Mary!'

Mary emerged from the hall with a quill in her hand, a little bewildered. Her hair was undone and falling in curls over her shoulders. Shelley was introducing her to Hogg in a conspiratorial tone, when a noise on the stairs alarmed him.

'I'll see you in the churchyard at three,' whispered Shelley, and Mary nodded keenly and tiptoed away, while Shelley reversed the process of their entry until they were safe in the street. Hogg would ever afterward tell people that Shelley had appeared like a man suffering an insurrection, like a little kingdom.

'Why the secrecy?' Hogg asked, later.

'I have not declared myself and I don't know how Godwin will react. Mrs. Godwin will certainly be horrified.'

To allay suspicion, even before the reason for suspicion was properly acknowledged by the conspirators, Claire sometimes went with Mary to the churchyard. She sat under a tree and read gothic romances while Mary and Shelley walked, talked and read poetry and politics. At home, Mrs. Godwin's antennae were vibrating. When Shelley dined with them he appeared to understand Mary's feelings too well.

Claire suspected everything and loved being part of the drama, a desire that overshadowed any jealousy. Mary needed such an enthusiastic ally and she had to trust she did not intend to betray them, though when Shelley came to see Godwin, her knowing looks made Mary nervous.

Each day the conversation in the churchyard edged away from the philosophical towards the personal. One warm, breezy afternoon they were sitting under a large willow tree, poetry books discarded on the grass, reading aloud abandoned. Mary was intently watching a sparrow fossick for tidbits, while Shelley seemed unable to keep still. His hands were in and out of pockets or running through his hair. He was first standing, then slumping, then pacing. Finally he seemed to gain courage, knelt in front of her and took a deep breath.

'Mary, I must be honest with you. You cannot fail to see how I feel about you. Though I value your intellect, it is far beyond that ...'

She interrupted him, laying a hand on his arm.

'Your situation … we should not …'

'Yes, I am married to Harriet. I have a child. They are facts. They are incontrovertible and I know I can ask nothing of you,' he said unhappily, covering her hand with his. 'I also know the duty I owe her, even though I bitterly regret our hasty marriage.'

'So why did you marry her? You must have loved her a little.'

'I was eighteen, such an impetuous boy. I had just been sent down from Oxford along with my friend Hogg for writing a pamphlet about atheism. My father all but disowned me. My sisters were sympathetic and Harriet was at their school. She helped me get messages to them and they sent me little packages of money by her. We became friends. The other girls at school persecuted her because of her friendship with a wild and irreligious man like me. She was desperate not to go back and face them, but her father insisted.

'Not much of a threat,' said Mary, sceptically. 'Did it not occur to you that your sisters must have suffered the same, or worse ostracism, but were perfectly able to cope?'

'I see that now, but at the time she begged me to take her away, even threatened self-harm. I didn't … I don't believe in marriage. I believe in the pure connection of souls. But Hogg convinced me that simply helping her to flee her parents' home would damage her reputation in society and it was too much to ask of a young woman. I trust Hogg, he is loyal.'

'My father married my mother against both their principles, and that was also to protect her from cruel critics,' replied Mary, thoughtfully.

'There is another obstacle to my happiness with Harriet. Her sister, Elizabeth, who is much older, and whom I now hate more than I can find words to express, is with her every waking minute. She intrudes in every discussion, encourages Harriet to buy carriages and clothes that I can ill afford and mocks when I encouraged her to learn Latin and read books other than romances. I believe all Elizabeth ever wanted was for her sister to be married to the son of a Baronet.'

He took both her hands and pressed them between his. Mary glanced over her shoulder to make sure they were still hidden from Claire's view.

'Harriet was an idea constructed in my own youthful mind. I thought I could mould her and teach her. She is beautiful and she is noble in her own way, and I will always be her friend and protector, but the real partner of my life must be one who can feel poetry and understand philosophy. I loved Harriet as a friend and I still love her in that way. But if that love were all the world, yet, if you will be my partner, our present and future love will be the essence of the universe.'

Mary's heart was beating hard but the pounding of the blood could not quite subdue her practical nature. 'We both have a lot to lose, you more than me,' she said. 'I have my good name, though I don't care much for that, and there is the possible disapproval of my father, but I believe that in the end he would support me. For you it would be disastrous. If we declare ourselves, it would mean social ostracism — they might not publish your work! And then there would be the utter and final disapproval of your father. He already hates you for your views on religion and politics, and your elopement with Harriet, the daughter of a merchant. You will probably lose even more access to your inheritance. I know that wealth doesn't matter much to you, but you have such plans to use it for the benefit of others!'

'My lovely Mary, I will suffer anything to be with you,' he replied, his grip on her hands tightening so much that she almost cried out. 'I am sorry if I speak too soon, but I am in agony, and can only ask for your pity. Whatever our fates from now on, I will always love you and the world will be impossible without you. But what can I offer? I have no grounds to divorce Harriet, and Hogg made me aware of the sacrifices a woman would make without the protection of matrimony.'

She looked into the blue eyes, so intense, sending out silken skeins of sincerity. A web is being woven here, she thought, but am I the spider or the fly? She decided that it didn't matter.

'I am my mother's daughter: she flouted convention. I am my father's daughter too, and you know very well that he wrote of marriage as slavery. Though by now he has had two wives, I am sure his beliefs remain unchanged. We need no legal association. I will be with you because you are the companion of my heart and always will be.'

In later years Mary would reflect on how seriously she had considered Harriet that afternoon. It seemed to her that she had. The ill uses of women in marriage was a theme of her mother's writing, and she felt obliged to plead Harriet's cause, at least begging that she should not be discarded without thought or provision.

'Don't worry, Mary,' soothed Shelley. 'I will always consider her welfare, but I'm sure in years to come Harriet will be miserable, too, if I give up this, my one chance at happiness. I fear the despair I would feel would be so great it would cause me to absent myself from hers or any world,' and his shoulders drooped to match his desolate tone.

Then suddenly, from these low spirits, he sprang up, all action and determination. He thought of a plan. Shelley always had a plan and while it was in his mind, he was fearless in its pursuit.

'We will go to Switzerland and invite Harriet to come with us! We will be a community. You will be my lover, and she will be our friend. I will write to Harriet, get her to come up to London, and explain it all to her. If she loves me truly, she will not deny me this happiness. We can leave the odious Elizabeth behind and set up home in Switzerland, away from prying gossips. You and I will be able to study and philosophise and Harriet can care for the children, and, and …'

He trailed off. It was impractical, it was improbable, and Mary tried to quieten the inevitable stab of jealousy. Shelley had an ideal of community living, and he thought that the possession of one human being by another was wrong. Does this mean, she wondered, that he sees me only as an intellectual and philosophical mate?

Then, as if sensing her anxiety, he drew her up against the trunk of the overhanging willow and kissed her with a passion and sensitivity that quelled her doubts, and whispered: 'But you, you are Penelope and I am Odysseus who has won you over all competitors. No, you are Maia, the shyest and most beautiful of the Pleiades with lively eyes, and I am Zeus who will love and care for you forever.'

Claire was alerted by their looks at each other on the way back to Skinner Street. That night, in Mary's room, she demanded to be told 'the whole truth' and, unwarily, Mary exposed her new level of happiness. Claire was not shocked, and she began by expressing happiness for her, but she was looking at her stepsister in a slightly sideways, assessing way.

It was her 'how does this affect me' look. Claire always saw things in relation to herself. The world was a cavern of delights to which she must struggle for access, before the boulder was rolled across.

This was no longer a temporary adventure in which she had a dramatic role. She understood that Shelley and Mary were truly together. She suddenly realised that she was more than half in love with Shelley herself and this was yet another instance where Mary had got the prize due to her unfair advantage of parentage.

Then Mary told her about Shelley's proposal that they should go to Switzerland, that Harriet should join them, and her reservations about it.

'Well, of course you would hate that,' Claire said. 'Shelley doesn't understand that having liberal parents doesn't really mean you'll embrace all forms of free-thinking. Before you came back from Scotland, I often discussed the idea of Communities of Philosophical people with him. These people should have free association amongst themselves, to work, to learn and discuss. They would love, but would refrain from owning another. You wouldn't understand. I would never want to be owned by a man.'

Mary worried about the effect of Shelley's ideas on Claire. She thought about the perversity of the need for confession and resolved she would learn to keep her secrets. A confidence given to a friend is never of active use, she decided. It is either to flatter one's own sense of importance or to bind another to you. Though once the words are in the world they are more permanent and destructive than Pandora's evil gifts.

# 4

'Nothing that I ever read in tale or history could present a more striking image of a sudden, violent, irresistible, uncontrollable passion, than that under which I found him labouring.'

*Peacock's Memoirs of Percy Bysshe Shelley*, Thomas Love Peacock

For the next few days, Shelley was overflowing with schemes and devices that would fulfil his design for their future lives and finally he saw the perfect opportunity.

'I will talk to Godwin tomorrow,' he said, as they snatched a moment in the hall after he had spent a long evening with her father. 'I was bursting to do so just now, but tomorrow the £2500 we have been negotiating becomes available. I will tell him that he can have half of it, which he can use to keep the Library from the marauding creditors and set it back to rights if he uses it judiciously. The other half is for us, Mary. Most of it I will leave for Harriet, to cover my obligations, but we will have just enough to see us into Switzerland. Godwin will be pleased with me because of the money, will he not? Nor can he reproach my devotion to you.'

She hesitated. 'I hope you're right, but I'm scared. He may think he should get all the money. He may be angry. And what of my stepmother? She is all respectability. She will hate us. But Fanny, good Fanny will be on our side I am sure, when she gets back from Ireland, and perhaps Claire can work on her mother for us.'

Shelley silenced her reservations, gently pressing two fingers to her lips. His eyes were glowing. 'Our freedom day, Mary,' he said, as he slipped through the door into the gas-lit street. 'Look for me at twelve.'

Mary slept very little, but stayed in her room until ten next morning. Then she went downstairs to her father, surrounded by his books and writing materials in his study, carrying her own copy of *Political Justice*. She asked him to explain a passage on the relationships between men and women, to set his mind on a path that would lead in the right direction, but he was already buoyant about the money to come from Shelley, and could barely pay attention to Mary.

'£2500, Mary! All our worries are over. It has been months of work with the lawyers, though, and mostly done by me because Shelley has been extremely inconsistent in his appearances. He can be very lazy in following through a proposition. Still, I must applaud the sentiments of those such as Shelley, who care not for the acquisitions of mammon except inasmuch as they can use them to help the deserving.'

His puffed chest proclaimed the name of the deserving and her heart sank. She went back to pace in her room.

Shelley called as promised, at twelve, and he and Godwin went to the lawyers for the signing over of the money and then, as she afterwards discovered, for a long walk in Regents Park. At about two, the door banged and her father's angry voice demanded her presence.

He was often irritable and short-tempered, but she had never seen him so furious. He seemed shrivelled and grey-skinned, and every outburst of anger seemed to diminish him further.

'Mary, how could you, what are you thinking? It is insane. He has betrayed me and seduced you. That man will never be welcome in my house again. He has a wife and a child. The man is a monster … behind my back … and to give me only half the money … the scandal.'

Mrs. Godwin was in the corner, weeping copiously and noisily into her handkerchief. Mary's sisters and William were huddled in the hall pretending to talk.

'But Papa,' Mary whispered, shocked and humiliated. 'I love him … I am promised …'

'Enough,' he hissed, turning away. He collapsed into his chair and put his head into his hands. 'Go to your room. I cannot look at you.'

She fled upstairs, the tension and anticipation of the past few weeks bubbling down her cheeks. She could not believe that her father would react so badly against Shelley, his benefactor. He needed him or he would face ruin. She could not believe that the father who had taught her to disregard the superficiality of society and to never shrink from doing what she felt was right and just, would condemn her for behaving in the same way as her mother.

Mary cried for two days, stayed in her room and refused food. William and Claire tried to talk to her but she sent them away, thinking that they would be emissaries from her father. William came and called through her door that their father was out all day, and that he had overheard him telling Mama that he would be with Shelley, trying to persuade him to abandon Mary. She told herself she was certain he would not — but how to know what pressure her father would bring? She wrote herself notes, laying out the arguments to support their cause, still hopeful that when he had calmed down and stopped being angry about the money, Godwin would see the justice of their situation, and that his admiration of Shelley and his care for her needs would win him over.

On the second evening she was called down to his study. He looked drawn, but instead of admonishing her as she had expected, he asked her to sit with him and talk 'with all the sensibility of which I know you are capable.'

He disarmed her. He had always given her praise about her discernment, her determination and her pursuit of knowledge. He had always shown that of all the children he considered her most mature, most capable of philosophical thought, his true heir in these spheres. So now he was calm and rational, and spoke to her quietly, as an equal.

He told her that he had not been able to persuade Shelley to abandon their plans, which at first gave her hope, but then he talked about Shelley's immorality in 'seducing' her when he had a wife and child to consider. She should think of them. Her own mother had been abandoned when Fanny was an infant, and had suffered much as a result. Harriet had been a good wife and did not deserve to be abandoned. It would bring disgrace on Mary and on the whole Godwin household. Fanny and Claire would be tainted. All of her father's detractors would see it as proof that his writings encouraged degeneracy. What guarantee did she have that Shelley, notoriously unreliable, would not abandon her on a whim too?

All of this was delivered with the kindly, lecturing tone that she was accustomed to hearing from her father when he was explaining some nicety of politics to her, and made her feel the pull of filial duty so much more than if he had harangued her. He shifted the ground, appealing to her head over her heart, making it into a debate. He insisted that a rational person would see how untenable her position was.

She protested of course, that they were in love, that her happiness was at stake, that he himself had taught her to shun the opinions of the world. He countered that it was the happiness of others which was the greater good.

'And your step-mother would never speak to you again or, in all probability, allow me to!' was his final word.

That almost re-formed her wavering resolution. The opinion of her step-mother was the last thing she valued.

He saw her expression. 'If you have any further doubt, read this,' he said, passing her a letter.

It was from Harriet, addressed in part to her father and in part to Mary. Shelley had apparently summoned her from Bristol to explain the situation. The letter contained all of the protests to be expected from a soon-to-be-abandoned wife. She was blameless. This was, in all probability, a passing attachment, and Shelley was prone to take up with people with great intensity and then drop them. She begged them both to send Shelley away until his ardour cooled. Her last argument was the most telling, the news that she was again pregnant, some three months, and this undid Mary.

'The remedy is with you,' her father said, gently. 'All you have to do is to write to Mr. Shelley and tell him you will have nothing more to do with him; that you think you have been hasty, that it would be too cruel to Harriet and that you owe a duty to your father.'

So she did. She wrote and sealed the letter, citing duty and filial love as reasons they could not be together. She broke two quills as the force of her unhappiness bore down on the paper. She took it down to her father to commit to the Penny Post, and then she went back to her room and cried some more, but this time with a sense of finality and helplessness. She tried to find comfort in her mother's books, especially *The Wrongs of Women*, or *Maria*. Her reading lit on a passage where Mary Wollstencraft counselled that with some feelings we should: "*not necessarily coldly ransack the understanding or memory, til the laborious efforts of judgement exclude the present sensation and damp the fire of enthusiasm.*"

Mary felt as if her mother were speaking to her directly, telling her that in this case she should trust her feelings not her reason, and it tortured her.

Claire tried to say comforting things, but her keen interest in all the details only enhanced the sense of tragedy.

'You poor thing,' she groaned theatrically. 'You must feel so desolate. Do you think Papa will relent? Has he burned his bridges with Shelley? What did he say to him? What did Harriet's note say? What had Shelley told her?'

'Harriet said that Shelley had asked her to tell me the situation was acceptable to her, because although she loved him, above all she wanted his happiness.'

'Do you think she does? Or does she just want to be Lady Shelley?'

'I think it must be difficult for Harriet to separate an advantageous marriage from the disinterested love for the man. She was only sixteen when they ran away.'

'And so are you.'

'Yes.' She considered – trying not to be wounded by the implication. 'But I don't come as a supplicant, a gothic heroine in need of rescue. I come to him as an equal.'

The next day there was a quiet tap at the door of their room. It was John the porter, looking furtive. He had a bucket of coals in one hand and in the other a small package, which he silently passed Mary. He ducked his head and, keeping his eyes down, hurried down the corridor towards the stairs.

It was a despairing, disbelieving letter from Shelley, full of declarations of love, certain that her letter had been coerced from her by Godwin. He would talk to Harriet again. He would ask his friends Peacock and Hogg to persuade her to support their cause. A foolish expectation, thought Mary. What possible benefit could there be for Harriet? She cried again for the idealistic foolishness of him – believing that by sheer effort of will he could make everyone happy.

Claire urged her to write back and said she would take the letter herself, casting herself wholeheartedly into the role of conspirator. Mary wondered, bitterly, if she just wanted to delay the end of the excitement.

Mary wrote that she could not envisage any way that the obstacles in their path could be overcome and enable them to be together; that she had to have strength for both of them, and much more in the same vein. It was trite, and as bitter as the taste of her tears.

Claire took the letter to his lodgings, uncomplaining in spite of a drizzle and streets slippery with dirt. She brought back from him a small package, which proved to be a copy of *Queen Mab* inscribed to Mary. On the flyleaf he had written *"You see, Mary, I still love you."*

Then she wrote in the back of the book:

> *I love the author of this book beyond all powers of expression and I am parted from him. Dearest and only love, by that love we have promised to each other, although I may not be yours I can never be another's. I am thine, exclusively thine — by the kiss of love.*

The next day, about midday, there was a commotion in the shop downstairs. Shouts and bangs brought the two girls and William into the drawing room, and they huddled behind the sofa in fear of their lives.

'What is it?' whispered William, wide eyed and shaking.

'It's robbers. Let us hope they don't murder us, too. Or maybe it's a disgruntled Spirit, come to terrify us,' Claire, shivered. She had been reading a gothic romance only that morning.

'It's more likely to be creditors, come for the furniture, but anyway, it would be better if we keep quiet so they don't know we're here,' Mary said, hushing them.

Just then there was the sound of footsteps clattering up the wooden stairs, and they pulled their skirts closer in and crouched lower, trembling with fear.

It was Shelley who ran in, pale, with staring eyes, his hair sticking out at odd angles, calling, 'Mary, Mary!' His coat was half dragged off his shoulders, pulled from behind, by a sobbing and desperate Mrs. Godwin, with Mr Godwin at her heels. Shelley had a bottle in his hand and waved it wildly into all the corners of the room, as if uttering an incantation, while their parents tried to herd him back down the stairs.

Mary leapt up from their hiding place, crying, 'Shelley!' Claire and William leapt up too, Claire shrieking high pitched screams at the sight of him, which added to the tumult.

Shelley dragged himself towards Mary pulling his restrainers along with him and fell to his knees, holding up the bottle to her. She saw it was laudanum.

'I cannot, will not, live without you, Mary,' he sobbed, clasping her skirts. 'Take this and I will follow you to the grave. We can be together in death if not in life!'

Her will to put duty before love dissolved at the sight of his ravaged sincerity. How could she doubt that this man loved her truly?

She tried to embrace him, to stroke his hair, to calm him, as her family continued to call for help in removing him, knowing then that she was lost, that somehow they would be together.

'Be calm, my love,' she whispered, putting her mouth close to his ear. 'I will be with you, you have my promise. There will be a way. Give us time to find it.'

He looked up, staring into her eyes, wanting to believe her, and then he went limp and unresisting. He reminded her of the beggars on street corners, who stare at passersby, hoping for a coin but expecting a kick. It shredded her heart to see him so vulnerable.

She found some strength, and said out loud, in as firm a voice as she could manage, 'I think you ought to go, Mr. Shelley. I have given you my answer in my letter.'

Shelley yielded to the hands that guided him back downstairs, and she heard her father muttering to him before the door closed behind him.

Two days later, the money drawn against his inheritance, the 'post-obit' money as the contract was called, was paid over to Shelley and, as promised, he gave half to her father. That same evening Godwin was called to Shelley's lodging by Shelley's friend Peacock. Shelley had been found almost senseless from having taken a large amount of laudanum. They walked him up and down all night and by morning he was sufficiently clear headed to sleep a drug free sleep. That next morning there was a letter delivered to Skinner Street that he had written the previous evening, saying that he could not, would not live without her. If she would not be his Partner for Life, there would be no poetry for him in this world. He enclosed some verses that made her spirit soar.

> Upon my heart thy accents sweet
> Of peace and pity felt like dew
> On flowers half dead; thy lips did meet
> Mine tremblingly; thy dark eyes throw
> Their soft persuasion on my brain,
> Charming away its dream of pain.

> We are not happy sweet! our state
> Is strange, and full of doubt and fear;
> More need of words that ills abate; —
> Reserve or censure come not near
> Our sacred friendship, lest there be
> No solace left for thee or me.

> Gentle and good and mild thou art,
> Nor can I live if thou appear
> Aught but thyself, or turn thy heart
> Away from me, or stoop to wear
> The mask of scorn, although it be
> To hide the love thou feel'st for me.

That was the day she finally decided that nothing would prevent her from running away with Shelley. In all of the censure that he had from her family as a result of his feeling for her, he had never for a second reconsidered his generosity to her father. Godwin, on the other hand, had not been prepared to uphold his own principles and his daughter's honour and refuse the gift of the man he accused of sullying that honour. To which of these men did she owe the greater debt? Which of them should command her admiration? Once it might have been her father, but his principles had clearly been completely desecrated by debt. Now the choice was absolutely clear.

Again Claire, with the help of John, transported their letters. They made their plans. This time though, she didn't tell Claire the details. As it was, Claire was hard put to keep the melodrama suppressed. When she sang for them in the evening in her strong, clear voice, she would choose love songs and throw Mary meaningful glances. Claire was such a child, Mary thought in exasperation.

It was Wednesday 27th July. She went to bed late, in her room next to Claire's, feeling like Hero waiting for Leander. In the darkness, with no thought of sleep, she tried to calm her mind by identifying the night noises of the city, the carriages with the iron shod horses on the cobblestones going north to Grays Inn and east to Clerkenwell; the police whistles following yells and pounding boots. She listened to the bells – the deep bell of St Paul's, the higher pitch of St. Bartholomew's. When the hall clock chimed three she slid out of bed, and, by the light of a small candle, put a few necessary items into a bag and pulled on a simple black silk traveling dress. It is the small things in this world that decide our fate; the too-loud creak of an old wardrobe door, the accidental knocking of a footstool in the gloom; these trivial occurrences, which, on another night would have been an unnoticed thread in the fabric of time, on that night took on the design of the universe.

Claire stirred and woke, opened her door to see Mary in the corridor and in an instant had understood what she was doing. She begged to go with them.

'My existence at Skinner Street will be a nightmare after you've gone,' she said. 'It will all come out, how I have helped you. My mother and your father will blame me for helping in your 'downfall'. There will be recriminations, histrionics; they will never trust me again.'

Mary demurred, panic struck at the thought of Claire as a companion.

'We are going to France, then Switzerland. It will be very rough and uncomfortable. We have little money,' she said, hoping that Claire's inability to face crisis calmly would be a deterrent.

'But that is perfect,' Claire cried, her voice rising. 'My French is fluent and conversational, I will be the greatest help to you. It would look as if you had a chaperone, and would smooth the way through any awkwardness or discrimination as you travelled. Oh please Mary, please.' Her voice started to take on a hysterical edge. 'I would be just there to help the two of you, I promise. I will not get in the way.'

In hindsight Mary realised she was very naïve, and not a little stupid, but she was terrified Claire would wake the household, and, if she were discovered, she was not likely to have the opportunity to leave again.

'Shhh, shh, very well,' she answered distractedly, 'I will go and meet Shelley to discuss it and come back for you.'

Claire started back into her room to get her own black silk traveling dress. Then she paused and thrust her head back out of her door to call out suspiciously to Mary's retreating back, in a loud whisper.

'You promise to come back for me?'

'Yes, yes, I promise. Sshh. Get dressed – and bring only a small bag.'

So there were two life-changing decisions for Mary that night. The first was to abandon her home and her standing in society to defy her father and trust wholeheartedly the call of passion and the echo of a like soul. The second, and, she saw later, the more significant, was to take Claire with them.

# PART TWO

Europe 1814

# 1

'After talking over and rejecting many plans,
we fixed on one eccentric enough, but which,
from its romance, was very pleasing to us.'

*History of a Six Weeks Tour*, Mary Shelley

Four am. She ran along under the dim light of the single street lamp. She saw Shelley waiting at the corner of Holborn and Hatton Garden, the chaise waiting next to him, the horses jostling restlessly, their breath steamy in the cold morning. He was peering anxiously through the gloom of the dawn, and when he saw her, ran to meet her, hugging her to him with a great sigh of relief.

'I felt that we were toying with life and hope,' he breathed. His joy turned to anxiety as she looked uncertainly back towards Skinner Street. 'What is it? You don't have second thoughts? Are we pursued already?'

'No, no, it's Claire.' She paused. 'She wants to come, too, and I fear if we don't bring her she will create a scene and wake the household.'

'Then we have no alternative. Anything, to get you safely in the chaise and away.'

Was there a hint of excitement in his voice? She was not sure.

There was no time to reflect. She rushed back to Skinner Street with the driver, and Claire was by the door, watching for her, both their boxes at her feet.

While the driver took the luggage back to the chaise, she took a note for her father from her pocket and put it on his desk. She had quoted his own philosophy and her mother's in defence of their decision, and said that she confidently hoped he would become reconciled to their actions.

Now she added hastily, 'Claire came too.'

Crowded and undignified in the two-person carriage, they rattled through a London stretching its early morning limbs, arteries energised by cattlemen driving pigs and cows towards Cow Lane and Smithfield Market. Dogs scavenged noisily. She was almost faint in Shelley's arms from exhaustion and excitement, but was sustained by the thought of leaving the grime and squalor of London and going to the mountains of Switzerland, as clean and sublime as the mountains of Scotland where she had been so happy. The sense of moving towards something purer, a more spiritual existence, seemed to sanctify their flight. There were no regrets, except perhaps for Fanny, who would take the brunt of the anger that would rise, with the dawn, over Skinner Street.

For Mary, the eleven-hour ride at top speed to Dover was an eleven-hour waking nightmare of nausea. They were terrified of being followed, but still had to stop when they changed the horses so she could rest and recover. Reaching Dover about four in the afternoon, they found they had missed the afternoon packet to Calais. They sat by the jetty, tired, dispirited, and still anxious about pursuit.

'I must go to find a boatman who will be persuaded to leave this afternoon,' said Shelley, looking anxiously at Mary's pale face. 'I have an idea. It will undoubtedly take me at least an hour. Why don't you have a sea bathe? It will help cure your sickness.'

'But it will cost a shilling, and I'm not sure I have the energy,' objected Mary. 'And what about our boxes?'

'I will get a boy to take them to the harbourmaster's office. You will be refreshed, I am sure. Claire will look after you.'

'Oh yes,' agreed Claire, eager to prove useful. 'Look it is not far down the promenade, you can see the bathing-machines from here. It's low tide. Perfect.'

Shelley dashed off to find a boat prepared to take them across the channel, and Claire and Mary found the table where they wrote their names in the book, paid their money and were conducted up the steps of a wooden bathing machine, a large box carriage on wheels. Inside, they put on the drawers and one piece flannel chemises that covered them from neck to knee, weighted with lead pieces in the hem so the skirt would not float up in the water. They heard the driver hitch the horse to the front and they sat down suddenly as the box lurched down the beach into the sea.

'These boxes don't have hoods like the ones we used at Margate,' said Mary, as the horse was unhitched and she opened the back door.

'No, but they have side flaps,' Claire laughed, as she ventured her toe into the water which was now at the same level as the back of the box. 'We know no-one here who will see us from the beach.'

A guide, a woman in a blue flannel jacket, petticoat and straw bonnet waded across from another machine to help them down into the sea. She took Mary first, and dipped her under the gentle waves. Mary came up spluttering.

'Two more at least, Mary,' called Claire. 'You know three is the prescribed minimum number of dips to restore health.'

Mary allowed herself to be dipped twice more, then the attentions of the guide turned to Claire, who gleefully dipped half a dozen times. The girls then dried themselves and got dressed in the box, while the horseman drew them back to shore.

They found Shelley arguing at the customs point. He had found a small boat but the Customs refused to examine their boxes instantly, so they had to leave them to follow on the packet the next morning.

As they left the shores of England on a beautiful, balmy evening, watching the white cliffs fade into the dusk, they felt a great relief and a sense of freedom. It should have been a two-hour crossing, but once on the English Channel, a storm came up and made it twelve hours of endurance. Mary was horribly seasick and slept fitfully, her head in Shelley's lap. Claire was quiet and determined to be strong and unhysterical, to prove that she would not be in the way. More than once they despaired of reaching France, or indeed of staying alive as the thunder burst over them and waves rushed into the boat. Claire thought herself into the role of warrior maiden and the sailor's glances were admiring. At last, there was a change in the wind and when they finally landed on the sands of Calais, it was dawn. Shelley lifted Mary's head and whispered, 'Mary, look. The sun rises over France.'

For them it seemed to symbolise a new beginning.

It was Tuesday, and there were few people there to greet the boat, but those that were there, were strange to English eyes. There were some women with woven grey jackets, tight at the waist, and one with a bright red petticoat, carrying vegetables and bread along the path by the quay. They had huge golden rings in their ears which showed beneath their caps, but they looked reassuringly clean for all that – more than they were themselves. The long night on the packet had made them feel squalid and dirty.

They were the butt of ribald and angry sounding comment from the men who were lounging about the dock. For most, some part of their dress was a remnant of military uniform — long loose great coats, jackets, caps or cocked hats. It was barely six weeks since the victory at Waterloo that finally ended Napoleon's ambitions and he had been sent to exile in St. Helena. Louis XVIII had been restored to the throne twenty days earlier.

'This is the aftermath of war,' said Shelley. 'Sitting in London we only hear the jingoistic outpourings of the press — Napoleon and the Directoire and the terrible ambitions of the French.'

'And certainly about England and its victories and superiority,' interjected Mary.

'Yes, and look, these are the poor men we have feared and who have filled our imagination. These are the poor remnants of a defeated army, with no more army pay and no more army discipline. They are the ones who really suffer. Of course they have only hate in their faces — they have no hope now. For years they have been told how to fight and how to think. They hate the peace. What is to be done for them?'

Further up the beach they had to pass a military barrier, with soldiers under arms, but they gave the three foreigners only a cursory glance and allowed them through.

As they left the sands, they stopped an exotic looking man with an earring, and Claire asked the way to the Inn of Dessein. They had read of it in a book by Laurence Sterne which was much admired in London: *Sentimental Journey through France and Italy,* and they thought this would be a fitting place to start their travels. It was only two streets to the Rue Royale and, in spite of fatigue, they felt an intense excitement at the strangeness and adventure of it all.

All around was the babble of everyday, accented, strange-sounding French. The women wore their hair piled high with none of the curls on the neck or forehead which were fashionable in England, and paraded in odd-looking dresses with short jackets and high bonnets. To their delight, the hotel appeared charming, like an old chateau, with a yellow wall, an archway, gables and lovely, long gardens. Birds sang in welcome.

Inside though, it felt more foreign, with unexpected contrasts. The breakfast room had plain and cheerless white walls on which were hung enormous looking-glasses in elaborate but faded gilt frames. The floors were of naked brick, but there was a superb marble hearth. In this same room there were wash basins on gold tables to which they were directed to refresh themselves after the journey. Smells of soup and stew were wafting from the kitchens.

Shelley and Mary were given the best bed-sitting chamber, known as 'Sterne's room' — number 31 — and they felt comfortably at one with authors and travellers through generations. That evening they started a combined journal to record their journey.

'I feel like a character in a Romance,' Mary whispered to Shelley.

'The heroine, who lives happily ever after.'

The only mar to their happiness was the guilt Mary felt about her father. Then, about eight o'clock, a messenger came to Shelley and Mary's sitting room.

'A fat Madame come who say this man run away with her jeune fille,' he said, indicating Shelley with a rolling of his eyes, and explanatory gestures. 'She is making the great noise downstairs.'

Claire flew down to quiet her mother and after about half an hour came back, flushed and angry, to tell them that she was spending the night in Mrs. Godwin's room.

'I can't think straight. She is berating me. My head hurts, but if I don't stay with her now she will fetch the police.'

She gave Shelley a letter from Mary's father, which said, amongst other things:

*"I could not have believed that you would sacrifice your own character and usefulness, the happiness of an innocent and meritorious wife, and the fair and spotless fame of my young child, to the fierce impulse of passion."*

To Mary there was no word and she felt an overwhelming sense of injustice. The pedestal on which she had placed her father, who had written that relations between men and women should not be constrained by the laws of man, was irredeemably fractured.

'How can he?' she asked, disbelievingly.

She sought for explanations. Because only her stepmother had set off in pursuit, she was inclined to put much of the blame for his conservatism on her and on his weakness in failing to resist her.

Claire's absence gave Mary and Shelley their first time alone without subterfuge. They walked freely around the edge of the town as dusk came, remarking on the lack of enclosure of the fields and peacefully watching the hay-making across a pleasant rural vista. An old shepherd in a strange cocked hat stared at them, undoubtedly wondering at this young man whose arm shamelessly encircled a young girl dressed in totally inappropriate black silk – the only dress she had brought with her.

The route followed a hill and they walked beside a dry stone wall that underlined the view. Shelley took her waist and exuberantly lifted her on top of the wall, while he climbed up and balanced on his toes like a small boy, next to her.

'We did it Mary.' He jumped down and laughed up at her on her throne, then laid his head on her lap and she laughed, too, and touched his forehead.

'We did it. We are here in France and with the war only ended a few weeks ago, we are some of the first to see the effects of it. I wrote a poem once, as a child, about a Frenchman. *Mr. Nontingpaw,*' she said inconsequentially.

'I can't wait to read your writings, Maie,' he said affectionately.

'They are in one of the boxes. I hope you're not disappointed. Besides, we have time. All the time …'

'What was it like with you and Claire as you grew up?' he asked suddenly thoughtful.

She tensed, mentally on tiptoe, adrenalin-poised for flight or fight, and paused before answering. Should she be honest? She felt, obscurely, this was a first test of her skill at grown-up relationships. Her preference was to be honest, by nature she even tended towards the blunt. Could she tell him how Claire constantly saw her ideas as self-aggrandisement or perceived them as a personal threat, worthy of retaliation with some barb? Even the most abstract became personal for Claire. Everything related to her; her feelings, her nature, her needs were the centre of any universe. Mary suspected, though, that if she unburdened her childhood resentments to him it would not show her in a good light.

'We are the same age. We were naturally together a lot. There were times when we were both excited by the grown-up conversations that went on in the drawing room in the evening over the gin and water. All those excitable men and women, all those loud discussions about politics and poetry. We always begged to be allowed to stay up and listen and sometimes we were, when Papa thought highly of a visitor, or hoped we might learn something. One night we had already gone to bed when we heard Coleridge arrive, very noisy, saying he wanted to read a new poem. We always found him a little frightening — that large head and those bulging eyes — but he was nice to us and he has such a compelling voice. So we crept down the stairs and hid behind the sofa, while he read *The Ancient Mariner*. At the end there was a pin-drop silence and so they heard our gasps. We were packed off to bed and we huddled together all night, terrified by visions of the old sailor with his shaky finger pointing at the ghost ship.

'It's my stepmother who has been at fault in moulding the worst of Claire's behaviour. She kept her close and didn't reign in her tantrums and she fuelled her jealousy of me. Perhaps by being with us, Claire thinks she will escape her clutches, though it looks as if Mama will recapture her, doesn't it? It's strange, I hadn't really suspected she would want to get away. She never seemed to mind her Mama's behaviour and she liked being her favourite. With me gone, there would have been no competition or comparison. For me it is

different. I've always thought Mama was not my father's equal and I
suppose Claire knows I don't care if I am approved in that quarter.'
That at least was a nod to candour.

'Yes, Claire is well rescued from her mother, and I can see your
father has a struggle not to have his creativity submerged by his wife. I
have sympathy for him, I know what it is like to be yoked to someone
who does not share your philosophy.'

Now it was his turn to have his demons exposed. The shadows
were moving quite quickly across the fields below and the hay wagons
clattered gently into the twilight. He put his elbows onto the wall
and stared out at the darkening panorama. The silence lengthened
with the shadows. Mary knew he was thinking of Harriet and she
felt resentment at this, the second young woman to mar their first
evening of happiness. Still, she tried to be reassuring.

'It wasn't your fault. She caught you at your lowest ebb and you
did what you felt was honourable. Harriet begged you to rescue her,
didn't she? In any case, if you had simply taken her away as she asked
instead of marrying her, you'd still feel the same guilt now at leaving
her and the same obligation, wouldn't you?'

She had not intended it to come out as a question, but she felt
the beginning of a throbbing behind the eyes and the shortness of
breath that were the physical symptoms of her doubts. Ever since she
was a child, this sense of bursting, of a head incapable of containing
such strong emotion, had accompanied her at times of stress. The
unspoken question was, how was she to be certain that for him, this
relationship with her would be different?

He put his arms around her waist and pulled her off the wall,
swinging her around twice, before landing her gently and kissing her.

'Remember, our love is sacred, Mary.'

As they walked back to the hotel, she was aware these were also
metaphorical footsteps which contained her last opportunity for
turning back. No, she was prepared to believe in his sense of justice
and of destiny, and that was the night she conceived their first child.

The next morning, Claire burst into their room about ten o'clock,
eyes rimmed red from fatigue and tears, and threw herself into a

chair. To Mary's relief, she was much too preoccupied to comment on the tossed bed clothes or notice that neither she nor Shelley were fully dressed. Nor could she see their bare feet, which had their own soft and caressing dialogue.

'It's no good, I'm exhausted. It's all pathos and pleas and hysterics and Shelley is all treachery and I will be a forsaken wretch with no future. She says she will appeal to the laws of the municipality of Calais to return me to my family. I can't take it. I will go back with her on the next packet.'

Mary's colour rose and her fists tightened as she felt her usual anger with her stepmother for her narrow-minded and controlling nature. This time though, it was heightened by jealousy that Mrs. Godwin had pursued Claire while her own father had not cared to follow her.

Shelley looked at Mary's inarticulate fury and interpreted it as opposition to Mrs. Godwin's desires.

'Take a half hour to consider if it is what you really want,' he said gently to Claire.

He used no persuasion, but Claire heard the compassion and also saw Mary's rage She recalled unbidden her own sense of adventure and her longing to be unfettered by social bounds.

Within fifteen minutes she had returned to Mrs. Godwin to tell her she was resolved to continue with the runaways, and that lady departed, tight-lipped and speechless, her arguments as dried up as her disposition.

Mary felt a base, gloating sense of victory over her stepmother. It seemed to mark her own new womanhood. Later she wished with all her heart the victory had been Mrs. Godwin's.

At the time though, they set off in high spirits at six o'clock, after their boxes had finally arrived on the packet.

'Boulogne, here we come,' said Claire.

'And on to Switzerland,' added Shelley.

'Happiness our final destiny,' rejoined Mary.

Their transport was a Diligence, a rather curious thing, to their eyes. A two-wheeled carriage, drawn by three horses yoked in front and one behind. They had to enter from the front, and their postillion, who constantly leapt on and off the horses to make repairs to the harness as they travelled, was a small man with a pigtail, who was polite, but not servile. This sense of ease with their betters, a certainty of their own worth, seemed to them to be a surprising characteristic of the lower orders they were encountering in France. It contributed to their sense of escape from the constraints of the English society that had sought to subjugate them. It offered the possibility of remoulding society in their own image.

# 2

'A traveller's existence is all sensation, and every emotion
is rendered active and penetrating by the perpetual
variation of the appearance of natural objects.'

*Lodore*, Mary Shelley

Three days of travelling brought them to Paris, and a small grubby apartment in the Hotel de Vienne, which they had found on the recommendation of the peculiar little pigtailed driver. They had to take it for a week; in Paris, it seemed, it was not possible to take anything for a few days. At least it had a good size bedroom and a small closet with a bed for Claire and another room to use as a sitting room. The window looked over the neglected architectural grandeur of the Place Vendome, with its cracked and dirty doors, window frames and shutters. In the middle was a column, one hundred and forty feet high, with a statue of Napoleon as conqueror of the Austrians. Since the conquered Austrians had recently been overrunning Paris, the irony of this was noted with a white flag superimposed at its peak.

Mary was ill from the heat and the stress of the journey. It was so hot that they lay in their rooms until noon before braving the oppressive streets. There were more soldiers than ever in Paris, often parading along the Boulevards in drunken half-formed regiments, both cavalry and infantry. Soldiers crowded the squares, many with bandaged heads, arms in slings or limping with crutches, often more than half drunk. The rest of the Parisiennes behaved as if it were a holiday, sitting on the benches on the Boulevards or in chairs in cafes, eating ices, reading newspapers and watching the spectacle with supreme detachment.

'Who would have thought that so recently there was a battle for possession of this city, and these poor creatures were trying valiantly to defend it?' said Claire as they walked down the Rue Saint Denis. 'Now they are nothing but entertainment for the masses.'

'This is the Arch of St. Denis. Napoleon's troops marched through here.' Mary pointed and looked up as they walked through. 'They must have felt glorious then. This magnificent structure.'

Claire and Mary walked either side of Shelley to prevent him giving money to every ragged and pathetic soldier they encountered. It was not that they didn't also feel sympathy, but they had to live, too, and they had precious little ready money. Both needed at least a few more clothes, they had brought so little.

Shelley had hoped to get a loan in Paris to supplement the small amount he had kept after leaving provision for Harriet. He had found a solicitor, a M. Tavernier, whom he hoped would help him to borrow against his inheritance. He also thought he might get an advance from Hookham, his publisher in London. He was angry at the difficulty of it all, when he felt his wants were so few.

They went sightseeing to kill the time, but they were as highly strung as Arabian thoroughbreds anxious for the start of the race, and inclined to be irritably dissatisfied with everything they saw. The Tuileries they hated for the boring formality of the layout of the gardens and the lack of grass. The Louvre had only one good painting.

'Oh this is intolerable,' Mary complained, as they sat in the gardens and watched the gay promenaders, meeting friends or flitting amongst the statues and urns with dogs and children. 'We've wasted a week getting passports and papers for travelling. As for this negotiation with the solicitor … Is he ever going to produce anything, Shelley? I am so anxious to be on our way, to get out of this sticky, noisy city.'

'Today I should hear from London,' said Shelley, but without conviction.

So, when they got back to the hotel, they were elated that there was a letter at last, though it was hardly what they had hoped.

'This is a despicable letter from Hookham,' Shelley said, in disgust. 'He won't send any money and he says there are complaints from creditors.' He gasped. 'Listen to this: he says they are saying in

London that your father had sold you both to me, Mary for £800 and Claire for £700.'

Mary felt a small satisfaction that she was considered to be worth more than Claire — if not by much.

'I know this is a rumour started by Harriet as revenge,' groaned Shelley, crumpling the offending paper and consigning it to the floor. 'It's typical of her small-mindedness. Hookham's taken in, so he's certainly not going to help us.'

He looked around the room, at their boxes and their few possessions. Then he patted his pocket.

'I'll sell my watch and chain, which will pay the hotel, and then maybe Tavernier will get something for us tomorrow so we can leave soon. I long for the countryside and the start of our adventure as well, Mary. This feels like marking time.'

He looked so desolate that she went behind him and kissed him on the ear while taking his arms to move them stiffly back and forth like a soldier. 'Then let's quick ... march ...,' she said, propelling him in front of her while he protested until they finally fell over a chair and collapsed in a heap, laughing.

The next day Tavernier did provide a little money and they decided to walk across France to Lake Lucerne in Switzerland rather than get a carriage. The plan was to make their limited funds last and anyway, it seemed adventurous and romantic. Their fussy hostess at the hotel was completely alarmed at the thought of two such young girls almost alone among fields and villages only recently ravaged by war. She said there were too many disenchanted soldiers roaming the countryside, but the trio had the optimism and invincibility of the young and nothing dissuaded them.

They bought a donkey to carry their small bags, while the larger boxes went on by coach to Lucerne. One of those had all the writings Mary had promised to show to Shelley — her poetry, her stories, her journal. That box never arrived and she never found out what happened to it. In some ways she was relieved. She was beginning her new life — it seemed appropriate that her imaginative life should be recreated as well. She was happy to offer a clean slate to be inscribed by Shelley's inspiration.

The donkey was a worthless beast which refused to move if loaded with more than one bag and defiantly planted its hooves if they tried to ride it as well. They pulled it and slapped its haunches and Claire was sure it had been mistreated and stroked it and sung into its ears — all to no avail. When it did walk it stubbornly stayed in the shade on the side of the road, pushing them out of the way, if necessary. They made slow progress and had to manage the other two bags themselves until they arrived, cross and tired, at the first hamlet outside Paris.

Here they traded the donkey for a mule. Shelley and Claire went to do the deal, since she had the command of French, while Mary rested.

'What exactly is the difference between a donkey and a mule?' asked Claire. 'I can see the ears aren't as long.'

'A mule has a horse as its mother and a donkey as its father,' answered Shelley. 'It is stronger than a horse and cleverer than a donkey. The ancient Greeks used them as their favourite beast of burden. They even had mule cart races in the Olympic Games.'

With the mule, traveling became much easier since it was able to carry one of them as well as their portmanteaux. Usually the rider was Mary, as she seemed more and more often to be tired or feeling sick. She felt impatient with her weakness and envied the robustness of Claire, even though, more than ever, she felt secure in Shelley's affection. On their first night together she had worried that he would find her body disappointing compared to the softer and more feminine Harriet. She had no idea what to expect or what was required of her. She had to trust him. His foreplay was to whisper that in astrology the moon rules the emotions and the heart, and she was his moon. He kept the analogy while he stroked her skin and compared it to soft moonshine. She was transported as he looked deep into her eyes and murmured about their twin souls. It felt to her like a sacrament, which bound them more tightly than any ceremony. Every night since she had relaxed her uncertainties and gained courage under his unfailing appreciation.

In spite of this new and comfortable knowledge that she could please him, there was still the challenge of Claire, tripping along, never tiring, always ready to explore some especially high rocks when Mary felt incapable of climbing, or paddle in a stream with him while Mary rested.

On one hot afternoon, when they were exhausted from walking, Shelley stopped because he had seen a swift–running steam, protected from the view of the road by overhanging rocks.

'Come, Mary, let us bathe' he said, a grin on his face, 'it will refresh you.'

'We can't, we have no bathing clothes,' Mary replied, blushing.

'We have natural bathing clothes, our skin,' he answered, looking at her sideways, and catching her arm, pulled her towards the riverbank. 'Claire will keep watch.'

'Carriages might come by.'

'They'll never see us,' laughed Shelley.

'But I have nothing to dry myself with,' Mary complained, panicking, thinking of any excuse. She wasn't certain how to react. She needed time to think, to be coaxed and reassured, but there was Claire, laughing too.

'I'll come,' she said, smiling at Shelley. 'I'm not worried people might see, and we can roll in the moss to get dry.'

Shelley looked gleeful, excited, and would, Mary thought, have said yes, but he caught a look at her stricken face.

'No, no,' he said, with resignation, 'Mary's probably wise.' He made his hands into claws, his eyes big, stretched his mouth into a grimace, and pounced towards them. 'There may be ogres lurking in the caves under the rocks.' They ran from him, Claire shrieking and giggling, and Mary feeling relieved, but as if she had failed a test which Claire had passed.

The journey was a revelation, but rarely in the way they had expected. Many of the villages they passed through had been devastated by the Cossacks as they rampaged through the countryside on their way to liberate Paris. What had once been picturesque hamlets were now an assortment of roofless hovels, with blackened beams where they had been burned and pillaged. The diminished and dispirited population seemed to have lost the will to rebuild and their efforts to re-cultivate the fields had also failed. Straggling corn was orphaned on vast stretches of ground which had been made chalky white with ash and dust. Sometimes they could not even buy milk, because the Cossacks had taken all the cows.

The only accommodation they could find was often appallingly dirty with food which was rancid, stinking and inedible and had to be shared at a table with disgustingly vulgar peasants who stared at them unceasingly. At one town, the beds at the inn were so putrid that they spent the night in chairs by the fire, disturbed by the screams of a neglected infant and the rasps and coughs of the other inmates. When there were clean beds they were no more than straw covered by a sheet, but for these they were very grateful.

For much of the time they were compensated with the most romantic countryside, with verdant hills and winding roads, which led through sweet forests laced with streams. Sometimes they led to beautiful towns, such as Provins, with its cathedral. The mountain scenery as they got closer to Switzerland was breathtaking. The summer light and the rocks covered in soft moss were a delight to their senses.

Towards the end of their first week on the road, at about nine o'clock, they reached a small village called Trois Maisons. They had been walking all day as usual, but Shelley had sprained his ankle on a pothole in the road and they had been slow, him limping and taking turns with Mary on the mule. Mary was exhausted, and starting to feel nauseous. The only place to stay was the dirtiest auberge Mary had ever seen, even worse than the hovels of the very poor in Scotland. They ate some of the stale bread and cheese they were offered, just because they were so hungry, though it nearly made them sick. A few local men leered at them and one asked Claire, in French, if she was Shelley's mistress.

'Oh no,' she replied gaily, 'I am only here to speak French,' which got sniggers from all corners of the room. One said something to her in rapid French and she blushed.

'What is it?' asked Shelley.

'He wants to know if he should come up later so I don't feel lonely,' she muttered, looking away.

Shelley, with his limited conversational French, stood up and advanced threateningly on the man, a bullish, ugly brute in a smock much stained with stuff that may not have been from the fields and trousers tied with thick cord. He managed to convey that his 'sister' should not be addressed on pain of dire retribution. In spite of his slight, rangy frame and his voice that became high pitched when excited, Shelley's intensity and air of certainty clearly impressed the natives, as did the pistol he took from the pocket of his greatcoat. They went back to their ale, muttering.

That night, Claire rushed into their room screaming that the rats had put their cold paws upon her face. She threw herself on their bed and begged to be allowed to stay with them.

'Do you think these four-footed enemies of yours will not dare invade our bed with Shelley here?' Mary asked mildly, with an ironic glance at Shelley. 'Perhaps he can threaten to blow their brains out, like he did to that dirty French boy who leered at you downstairs.'

Nevertheless Mary soothed her stepsister as if she were a much younger girl, because she knew Shelley enjoyed seeing her as the purveyor of calm benevolence, and Claire fetched her blanket and curled up in their bed while Shelley went to sleep in hers.

The next morning, early, while Claire was still sleeping, Shelley and Mary escaped by themselves for a walk along the river. Mary was quiet, exhausted from a night of wakeful fuming.

'I know you're angry with Claire for coming into our room last night. Do you think I can't tell? I resent a lost night with you too, but I can't help feeling sorry for her,' said Shelley as they strolled by the water glistening in the early sun, hand in hand. 'She is a sweet child, and she has left her security and good name behind to be with us. It is no wonder she has these nightmares, her 'horrors', as she calls them.'

'I don't think they are nightmares,' replied Mary, with a sigh. 'I think they are the same as the tantrums she used to throw in our house as we grew up, to get attention. Now, as she's supposed to be grown-up, she knows tantrums aren't appropriate and she's afraid to lose your respect, so we have the night horrors instead.'

'It is just that her character is unformed. We can mould her, teach her, between us.'

'In the same way as you were able to elevate Harriet's mind?' asked Mary, ironically.

Shelley refused to take offence.

'But with Claire we have more promising material,' he pleaded. 'She is, after all, also a product of the Godwin household and inclined to the world of ideas. Perhaps her outbursts are just the result of a sensitive temperament and we can calm her, in time.'

'And her cutting remarks to me?'

'Surely just childish pique?'

Mary couldn't explain that she resented Shelley's attention to Claire and that Claire looked at him in way that Mary feared was less than childish.

'Did you see Claire's journal yesterday, the entry she wrote after she had been reading King Lear? She wrote about Cordelia, that she was enjoined to "Love and be silent," and this was true — Real Love would not show itself to the eye of broad day, it would court the secret glades. What do you make of that?' asked Mary.

'Well, I think it's good. I'm sure she was thinking of us. After all, our journals are not hidden.'

Mary could not say she was scared Claire was avowing her secret love for Shelley. She didn't want to damage how he saw 'his Mary', as an intellectually and emotionally superior being. Though she did not feel superior, she felt base. Her instincts were those of a vengeful Hippolyta. She wanted to wreak retribution on her rival. Instead, she tried hard for a moderate tone.

'I do feel a tiny bit of sympathy for Claire, I suppose. I don't think when she came on this 'adventure' she realised how hard it would be for her to be the third to us two, when we are so wrapped up in each other. '

'Yes, and she is always cheerful and enthusiastic. She delights in each new town, always saying that this is where we should settle to live — until the next one, which she declares as more delightful still.'

Not all of the villages were delightful, nor were all of their experiences idyllic. Because of Shelley's sprained ankle, they had to hire a four-wheel voiture and Shelley was not a good invalid. He complained endlessly, unless his mind was distracted by some scenery or by their reading a book together. Mary was perversely grateful, for it did at least mean they were united in discomfort, and left Claire as the only hale member of their party.

'This forest is divine,' Mary threw down the book she had been reading aloud — her father's novel *Caleb Williams* — and lay back and closed her eyes, so she could enjoy the patterns the dappled sunlight made on her lids.

'If I read the words *deep mossy arbour* in a novel, I would think of it as fantasy, but here it is! Real!' said Claire. 'I feel as if I am in *Midsummer's Nights Dream*!'

'How long have we been here?' Mary asked Shelley, rolling over to his spreadeagled form and delving into his pockets for his watch. 'Our elegantly filthy voiturier will be very upset at being kept waiting. He will no doubt treat us to another rapid fire, unintelligible diatribe.'

'The only words that are clear are Anglais and terrible,' laughed Shelley.

'And they are spat out frequently,' agreed Mary. 'We are not supposed to want to stop and enjoy the countryside. Obviously an unfamiliar concept to him.'

'We pay him for it,' Shelley said, as they walked back to the road, only to find that the driver had disappeared.

'Now what?' wailed Claire.

'Walk,' said Shelley, grimly. He pulled off long thick branches to make them walking sticks and set off, limping. 'I suppose he has gone on to the next auberge where he can refill his grubby little wine bottle, damn him! Let's hope it's not too far.'

They had walked two miles when the rain started.

'What have we done to deserve this?' shouted Claire to the thunderous skies.

'What gods do we have to appease, Shelley?' asked Mary, wiping away dripping fronds of hair from her cheeks and trying to stop globules from sliding down inside the bust line of her dress.

'Zeus, and only human sacrifice will do.' Shelley pointed at each of them in turn. 'Eenie, meanie …'

Claire shivered and giggled nervously, but Mary said, 'oh no, it's always the weakest that has to go. Come on, Claire,' and she caught Claire's hand and they squelched after Shelley, laughing.

'Please, please,' begged Shelley, limping away off the side of the road under the shelter of the trees.

'What about a statue,' he gasped as his ankle squelched in the mud. 'Gods like statues'. They found some stones and built a pyramid under the shelter of an old oak tree. Mary made a leaf garland to crown it, and as she did so, the sun appeared through the branches.

When they finally caught up with their unrepentant guide at the next auberge, after another mile of damp trudging along the dirt road, the people at the fireside merely gawped at them and refused to move away to allow them to dry themselves. As a final straw, the innkeeper had only one room and expected them to share it with the voiturier. That night they again slept in the chairs by the fire.

After an uncomfortable few hours, they were up early and, before they set off, walked to the outskirts of the village to look at some grand gothic ruins. On their way back they encountered a man dressed in rags, who stopped them to explain that he had lost all of his cows to the Cossacks, and his cottage too. He had with him a young girl of four or five, clearly beautiful underneath the grime, but lethargic and dull with hunger. He asked them if they could help in such a humble way that they immediately took the father and daughter to their auberge to find some food. The girl had a natural grace, which no poverty could disguise, brightening as she sat on Shelley's knee and he fed her bread and cheese. They asked her name and found it was Marguerite Pascal. Shelley, through Claire, introduced himself as English nobility and offered to take the child with them. He painted a picture of the wonderful life she would have, and how she would be able to relieve her father of his burden. The others in the inn were scandalised as they overheard the suggestion, and a murmuring began that sounded hostile. Claire whispered to Mary that she was worried lest at any moment they might be physically thrown into the street. The girl's father drew her close, and let them know she was all he had and he would not part with her. So Shelley gave him all they could afford, and father and daughter went on their way. Among the general populace they were redeemed to the status of eccentric but benevolent foreigners, and the innkeeper charged them double the rate.

The desolation of the poor farmer made Mary recall the probable suffering of those they had left behind and, as they sat in the voiture on the next stage of the journey, she wondered out loud to Shelley about Harriet's wellbeing.

'I will write to Harriet directly, tonight,' he insisted. 'I will tell her that she is not forgotten and urge her to join us at Geneva. I will remind her I will always be her friend and have her best interests at heart when other friends will not be as true. I will find a sweet retreat for her close to ours and that I will care for her. She must write to us at Neufchatel to tell us of her plans, so we might know when to expect her. What do you say, Mary? Shall I add that you anticipate our reunion with pleasure?'

Mary was taken aback. She knew that in Shelley's mind he had planned for Harriet to become part of their group, but she had never really expected it to happen. As a woman, she thought there were limits to what another woman would accept.

Although Shelley's belief in Harriet's response to his invitation seemed idealistic and unrealistic to Mary, she knew it sprung from real concern, and if she did come there would be a genuine welcome from him. Shelley would have adopted the world if he could.

Mary spoke carefully. 'I think, for the moment, assurances from you alone will be sufficient. She may not be able to believe as readily in my wholehearted welcome. If she comes, she can find it out for herself. Don't forget, she will also have to forgive us.'

'Harriet is of the merchant class,' added Claire. 'She is unlikely to approve of unconventionality. Though it would be nice if she brought some of the money!'

Later that night, when they were alone in the tiny bedroom with only a single candle and the light of the full moon, Shelley recalled Mary's comment about the need for Harriet's forgiveness as he watched her gaze stray out of the small, uncurtained window and beyond the hills. He guessed she was reaching out to her own family in her imagination.

'You are thinking of Godwin,' he said.

'Yes, and Fanny.'

'Do you regret …??'

'Every part of my being desires only to be here with you,' she replied, solemnly. Then she added, mockingly lifting his shirt and sniffing, and affecting to examine his hair and his ears, 'that is, those parts of you which are not affected by the dust and the filth, and the smell of the peasants who never wash, and the fight for hot water, and the rancid bacon and the horrible …' but at this point Shelley put his hand over her mouth, and they collapsed together, laughing, onto the dirty, rickety mattress.

# 3

'The mountains of Switzerland are more majestic and strange, but there is a charm in the banks of this divine river that I never before saw equaled.'

*Frankenstein*, Mary Shelley


Mary and Shelley were trying, in frustration, to explain who they were to the postmaster at the Bureau de Postes in Neufchatel, Switzerland. A kindly Swiss, tall and courtly, observed them struggling for a while, then approached and spoke in English.

'May I be so bold as to ask if you are from England, and offer help?' They replied that they were, and thanked him.

This Swiss gentleman proved to be their saviour in translation, though there was no English saviour in the form of money from Hookham, nor was there a reply from Harriet to Shelley's invitations.

Their new friend saw their disappointment.

'May I further suggest, since you are young, with anxiety and travel-worn, that you have run away together with a Great Love.'

They looked at each other in astonishment and laughed.

By the time they had reached the long-desired and sublime scenery of Switzerland they were all exhausted, sick of travelling and inclined to quarrel. At least Claire and Mary were. Claire had no patience with Mary's constant tiredness and need for rest, loud sighs greeting every delay, although she was amazingly concerned about Shelley's sore ankle.

So that morning they had left Claire sleeping at their lodgings and gone to the Poste alone. Though they struggled with their French to make themselves understood, it was a relief not to have to use Claire as interpreter for once. She tended to use her power as their voice to dominate any situation and they were never quite sure that she had got the communication right, in spite of her supreme confidence.

They privately suspected that some of their disasters on the road might have been a result of misinterpretation.

Their new and clearly erudite protector took them through the cobbled streets and into the gardens of the magnificent Hotel Peyrou, which extended down to the Lake. It had been built, he said, by Pierre-Alexandre Peyrou who was a friend of Rousseau and had been the publisher of his *Confessions*. The Swiss was impressed by their knowledge and admiration of that philosophical work. Clearly it was not expected of two very young and very down at heel foreigners. Mary was glad they had finally been able to bathe after the two weeks of travelling during which they had only been able to wash their hands and face. She was conscious that her hair was loose and she was wearing her black silk dress which was torn in places, even though she tried to cover it with the shawl she had bought in Paris. Shelley was even more dishevelled than usual. His hair, uncut for weeks, was wild and circled his smooth, oval face like fractured sunbeams, and his shirt was grubby. However, the Swiss seemed politely oblivious and, as they sat on the summer terrace, he insisted they try some of the slightly crumbly, mould-ripened cheese for which the town had been famous since the 6th century. It came in a little heart shape and smelt like mushrooms. It tasted delicious but a little sharper than expected from its soft texture.

He helped them decide their travel plans and recommended they take a coach to Lucerne, then go around the lake by boat. Shelley leapt at the idea. Ever since he had first glimpsed the smooth expanse of the water, he had been longing to cast himself adrift on it. The Swiss gentleman then helped them get a place on a coach for the afternoon, and showed Shelley at which bank to get money.

Later he came to their lodging to see them safely off and met Claire, who managed to look childlike in her dishevelment. He was clearly astonished by her presence and asked her why she had come. Claire gaily trotted out her usual rejoinder, that she had come to practice her French, but he seemed unimpressed and was silent. Claire then gave him one of her penetratingly hostile looks, which transformed her from ingénue to Inquisitor.

'I hope, sir, that you are not one of those 'gentleman' who are so narrow minded as to judge the world by the bigoted standards of European so-called Society,' she said, glaring back as she marched towards the ramp

Mary blushed and fiddled with their luggage to hide her embarrassment. The Swiss then took Shelley aside.

'This is not good for a Great Love,' he said. 'You must go back to England where the young lady cannot make so intimate a triangular. This drains the energy of the Great Love.'

Shelley seemed taken aback by this and was thoughtful as they set off. He thought it might be possible that the strain of Claire as the constant third was telling on Mary. For the first time he confronted the fact that Claire was not just a young girl to be educated in the ways of free-thinking philosophy, but was a young woman, of a similar age to Mary, and perhaps the girls' squabbles were not just sisterly spats but had other undertones.

When they arrived at Brunnen where it was their plan to take a house, only the most dirty and ugly were to be found. Because they had to have somewhere they rented a place which seemed slightly better than the rest, but one night was enough to highlight the problems.

'This house we have taken is called a Chateau, but it is a filthy, two roomed dungeon,' Mary pointed out. 'It's freezing and it is not yet winter, and the stove doesn't work. Shelley and I sat up 'til two working on his new Romance, *Alastor*, and the ink was too cold to drip off the pen. The curtains are damp and there is a smelly case of stuffed birds. Most of our view across the lake is just of cottages. You have to try to stare through them at the peaks of the mountains to lift the spirits.'

Claire, though, was childishly delighted, praising the universally wonderful Swiss and crowing over the sack of silver louis Shelley had got from the bank.

'What a fortune!' she gloated, running her fingers through the coins. And this sublime scenery! Did you notice how, the minute we crossed the Swiss border, everything was clean and everyone looks cheerful and friendly? My mother said my father was Swiss. This is my spiritual home! What a wonderful life we will have here!'

Shelley and Mary exchanged looks.

'It looks a lot but it is only 38 francs and won't buy much, and we badly need new clothes as well as food and paying the rent and a servant,' said Shelley, taking a deep breath. 'We must seriously consider going back to London. Hookham sent no money, and clearly Harriet is coming with none. We must think. Only by my presence there can I raise money, and if we spend what we have now we won't have the means to return. As it is …' he trailed off.

Claire flared up. 'How can you even consider it? What about me? You brought me here. You made me come to help you in your wild romantic dream. I have suffered for you. I left England for good. I cannot go back with my tail between my legs! How could you not have thought about money? How did you expect us to live? Aren't you aristocracy?' Her voice had been getting shriller and she spat the last word. 'Shouldn't you know more than us commoners, even more than the wonderfully knowing daughter of the great thinkers of the age?' she sneered at Mary.

By now she was hysterical, and went to grab Mary's shoulders and shake her, as if to physically remove her doubts about Switzerland. Shelley roughly pulled away Claire's arms, face black with anger. Claire sobbed and Mary went, as always, to calm her. She got her some water and led her to her bed, and put her hand on her forehead to soothe her. Shelley touched Mary's arm.

'We must talk,' he whispered, as Claire's sobbing abated.

Sitting by the lakeside as dusk fell, they were quiet for a while.

'I must acknowledge that Claire is too volatile,' he eventually said, slowly. 'And she upsets you. When she is near you are like a watch, smooth outside but coiled inside. I see the tautness of your limbs and feel you holding in your resentment. You are afraid to be natural. I can get briefly angry and let it go, but you store it all up, a squirrel with sour nuts. I admire your calmness, Mary, but when you are dealing with her it has a different quality. Your radiance is muted, like sunbeams in the mist.'

She hoped perhaps he finally understood.

'What are we to do?' she asked. 'She is compromised in the eyes of society by coming with us. Only here, or somewhere like it, away from London gossips, can she have any respect or freedom. It is the same for me – but at least I have you.'

'I know, and I'll always support her. Like Harriet, she is my responsibility. Mary, we can help her. We have only been away for a few weeks. In time, away from her mother's influence she will be calmer, more caring. In London there are more resources for study. Perhaps there we could find her some occupation, but here she is totally dependent on our company.'

'I know,' replied Mary, bitterly.

'In any case, we can't afford to stay,' went on Shelley. 'I didn't think we could even afford to get home. Before we left Neufchatel I was talking to our Swiss friend and he gave me the idea that we could get home by river – along the Rhine. And it's cheap!'

'What a clever idea. But is it safe? Because there's another thing.' She paused, looked down shyly and slid her hand into his. 'I think I'm pregnant, that's why I've been so sick.'

'Mary, how wonderful,' he laughed. 'Just think what our progeny will be, the product of love and intellect. Yours that is,' he said, kissing her and putting his hand gently on her stomach.

'Claire will be jealous, let's not tell her yet,' Mary suggested anxiously.

'It would stop her sarcasm at your frequent illness though.'

'Yes, but direct it who knows where? I do not want to be alone here with her when my time comes. She has no womanly experience and we know no doctors here or anything of their midwifery practices. In London I could at least have Fanny with me, she would not desert me, and she is kind and practical. I wish she had come, not Claire!'

'That settles it, we leave tomorrow' Shelley made to spring up. 'Now we go back and face Claire's wrath.'

Mary put her hand on his knee and pulled his arm tighter around her shoulder. 'Let us continue to read some of Tacitus first, to calm our nerves.'

So they huddled on the lakeshore as the sun began to set, and Shelley continued to translate *The Siege of Jerusalem* from the *Histories* and they lost themselves in a world of strategy and corruption and an understanding that human nature had, sadly, improved little in nearly nineteen centuries.

They left the next day, and three days later, August 30th they were in Germany on their way back to England. It was Mary's birthday, she was seventeen. Their journey back to the English Channel on boats down the Rhine and through Germany and Holland took two weeks. It was often uncomfortable and they were bedevilled by beer drinking, smoking, lower class Germans. The boats were flimsy, and there was always real danger of tipping or falling out as they descended rapids or coped with strong winds, and none of them could swim — but Shelley loved it. He drank in the willowy islands and rugged hills, overshadowing vineyards and picturesque towns that dotted the lower banks. His eyes glittered in reflection of the river, and he had a peaceful aspect as if the nereids were his constant companions and no harm could come to them.

As they were travelling between Mannheim and Mayence they were becalmed one afternoon near a town called Gernsheum and the batelier decided it would be a few hours before they could set off again. Claire dozed in the late afternoon sun and Shelley and Mary seized the opportunity to go onshore and walk alone, tramping through the forest paths towards the hills. After about an hour they came upon a little inn, and stopped for refreshment. As they drank a glass of seltzer in the courtyard they could see a ruined castle on the hills in the distance, looking especially grim in the half light and, with gestures, they asked the innkeeper the name of it.

'Burgh Frankenstein' he said and, with a suggestive leer and a chuckle, drew his finger across his throat. Because they had no German they could get no more information, but in their return to the boat through the encroaching darkness, they imagined dark, devilish shapes among the trees, and pursuers whose footsteps crackled on the rough ground in concert with their own.

At Mayence, they were joined on the boat by a schoolmaster who spoke a little English. This part of the Rhine along which they were travelling had a multitude of ruined castles along its banks and they thought to ask the schoolmaster about Castle Frankenstein.

'Ah yes, Castle Frankenstein, an interesting story,' he said. 'The local people tell of Johan Dippel, who lived there about one hundred years ago. He was a heretic and an alchemist – he claimed to make the elixir of life! He described it as made from animals, but some of these superstitious local people believed it was made from dead bodies. In the end he was imprisoned for his beliefs and poisoned while incarcerated. No one has lived there since.'

When they arrived on the Dutch coast, at Maasluis, where they were to embark for England, the weather was impossibly rough and none of the captains would sail. It meant another costly night in lodgings before their boat left. The next day the English captain decided to brave the swell and the journey to Gravesend was another nightmare of sickness for Mary.

Claire was hearty and totally unaffected. She blithely chattered to Shelley about her novel, *The Ideot*, even while he tried to ignore her and soothe Mary. Claire set great store by her book, which she had originally started as a play. It was the tale of a girl living wildly, educated only by contact with nature, whose opinions and actions depended on her own innate and high sense of morality and for which, because they inevitably conflicted with worldly opinion, she was deemed an idiot. It was easy to see that Claire saw herself in this paragon, a free spirit whose opinions were vastly superior to those of others. Shelley was still working on his Romance, *The Assassins*, about an ideal society — always Shelley's aspiration. The next day when the wind dropped, Mary started a novel called *Hate*.

# PART THREE

London 1814 — 1816

# 1

'You know what our life in London was – obscure but happy –the scanty pittance allowed him seemed to me to amply suffice for all our wants; I only knew then of the wants of youth and health, which were love and sympathy.'

*Falkner*, Mary Shelley

The boat limped into Gravesend and relief at the prospect of dry land drove out anxiety about their uncertain future. Besides, the boatman was demanding his money and, when Shelley turned out his pockets, he found there were only pennies left over since they had stayed the extra night in Maasluis.

The boatman was an Englishman and was inclined to be impressed when Shelley assured him he was the son of an English knight, embarrassed to have inadvertently run out of funds, and that if he could get to London he could readily get ample money to pay him and reward him for his patience. Mary said a silent prayer of thanks for Shelley's peculiarly persuasive blue eyes and confident charm, which seemed to blind the weather-beaten seaman to their distinctly un-aristocratic soiled clothes and tattered boxes.

He was not, however, entirely credulous. He would go with them and wait with the girls until the coin was in his hand.

'Think of me as your personal bodyguard,' he said, with a sly, knowing grin.

He went with them on the river-boat to Dartford and on a chaise to Bloomsbury, where Shelley left Mary and Claire as less than willing hostages, to await his return with money.

It was a cold day and they waited, shivering, for two hours in the chaise, the boatman pacing outside, until finally Shelley came back breathless and angry.

'I ran to the bankers only to find that Harriet has spent every penny. I know I gave her a free hand but I didn't expect her to spend it all. I had no choice but to go to see her myself. The banker told me I should find her staying in her father's house in Chapel Street. She refused to see me at first. I had to send up three times and to throw myself on her mercy and, when she did consent to come down and see me, I had to listen to her bitter, vile reproaches. She wouldn't even let me see my daughter, Iolanthe. She gave no reason why she had ignored my letters.'

'Shh,' calmed Mary, wrapping her arms around his trembling shoulders.

'She made me promise to go again tomorrow, and for that concession she graciously gave me twenty pounds.' He sneered as he showed the notes in his hand.

They paid the boatman and the driver, which left them enough for the Stratford Hotel in Oxford Street. They ate a dinner of boiled vegetables and good English apple pie, sent the linen to the laundry, and collapsed into bed to the newly unfamiliar and intrusive sounds and smells of London life.

As they fell asleep, Mary sighed. 'Our little play of fantasy and adventure seems to be turning into melodrama.'

'Or perhaps black comedy,' replied Shelley, yawning. 'I am not looking forward to tomorrow. I resent the constant battle with my father for money and the negotiations with money-lenders and lawyers to get enough to live on. It's not as if I want to live a profligate life. I eat a vegetable diet; I drink no wine; I try to fulfil my obligations to Harriet, to you and Claire and my promises to your father. I only want to do good, lead a simple life and write poetry.'

'Oh, my father,' mumbled Mary, her eyes closing. 'We have to send to Skinner Street tomorrow for our clothes. He'll know we're back. I'm dreading that, too.'

The next morning they rose early, at nine, and read the *Times* and the *Morning Chronicle* over breakfast to see how the world had progressed in their absence.

'I see there are to be negotiations with the Americans at last, in Ghent,' said Shelley. 'Let's hope our grasping masters see fit to give them their independence.'

'Men like to keep power for themselves,' said Claire. 'If women ruled the world, there would be no wars.'

'You're wrong,' responded Mary. 'They would be wars over different things, because there would still be some women who became corrupted when they had power, but they'd be different kinds of wars. More arguments than fighting, more threat of sanction or some such.'

'There would be fewer gullible fools who would blindly fight for causes that didn't affect them and they didn't believe in,' Shelley added.

Later they walked with Shelley to see Ballachy, the lawyer, about getting money, with little success except promises for further discussions about post-obit loans, and other ways to borrow against the inheritance he expected when his grandfather, Sir Bysshe, died. He was already 82.

'I fear it's going to be a long drawn out process to negotiate any funds. I'm sorry, we will have to be patient,' said Shelley, uncharacteristically pessimistic.

Shelley had two more frustrating meetings with Harriet, who one minute played the supplicant and the next, the shrew. They were seriously alarmed by the demands of the coach-maker, Charters, for payment of £522.61.

'Harriet demanded she keep the coach and has had it refurbished while we were away. I have insisted her father pay, but she will see me arrested first, I am sure,' complained Shelley, and Mary and Claire were united in blind and devoted hatred of Harriet.

They found lodgings in Margaret Street, near Cavendish Square, two small bedrooms and a parlour. Shelley yet again charmed a credulous landlady, as the aristocrat with his wife and her sister, awaiting his allowance. Godwins sent their clothes but refused to see them. London seemed unbearably oppressive after their careless freedom of the past six weeks.

Living in Europe, life had been full of adventure and in many ways easier – they were together against physical adversity. Their new challenges were more personal and harrowing. Debt, moral approbation and animosity are harder on the soul than sore feet, dirt and cheating coachmen.

Life in London fell into a different pattern, drawn by poverty. They could not shop or pay for entertainment, so they rose late and worked or read for much of the day. They read Voltaire and Greek odes, and histories of Rome. Shelley read Cicero and Claire read the poems of Lord Byron. For light relief they read *The Monk* by Lawrence, the best gothic tale, they all agreed, and *Alexy Haimatoff,* a risqué novel by Shelley's old friend Hogg who had, so far, shunned them, though Shelley had written to him of their return. Shelley, when he was not out on business, wrote more of his Romance and Claire and Mary wrote some of their novels. They wrote in their journals. Shelley often read out loud to them, sometimes in the evening, sometimes, if the weather was bad, for a whole day — poems of Southey and Milton, and some of his own. They played chess and word games. Their meal was the supper provided by the landlady and buns Shelley bought on the street.

A few days later, about eleven in the evening, Mary was almost asleep in bed. Shelley was writing letters and Claire reading in the parlour when she heard the sounds of rattling at the window and looked out to see her older brother Charles throwing pebbles up at it. Shelley went to open the door and slip him quietly into the parlour, so the landlady would not immediately eject them for their licentious habits. Charles explained he had come back from Scotland the previous week and had crept out of Skinner Street to visit them, defying the Godwin ban on contact. Shelley woke Mary, who came back down, alert and agog for news of Skinner Street.

'They want to put Claire in a convent,' said Charles conspiratorially, looking sympathetically at his sister's horrified expression. 'Fanny has been forbidden to see or communicate with you as well.'

Mary sighed. 'Yesterday Mama and Fanny walked twice up and down the street, pausing only for the need to readjust a shoe just outside this window! Shelley rushed out to speak to them, but the shoe miraculously fixed itself in time for them to present their backs to him, and hurry off.'

'You, my dear, are considered lost to the civilised world.' Charles smiled ruefully at Mary. 'You are a betrayer, you are hard-hearted, you are in thrall to the satanic Shelley. Mama is mortified by the story put about London that father sold you and Claire to Shelley. Everyone assumes that Shelley has 'two wives', not counting Harriet, of course.'

Mary suspected she was the only one who saw Claire's slight smile before they all gasped with suitable horror.

'Your father knows I love Mary. I told him so,' Shelley protested. 'I gave him money out of respect for his genius, as he well knows, and so does most of London.'

'Father is very angry, and he is pulled along with the raging tide of Mama's disapproval,' replied Charles. 'There is nothing else she talks about, day or night.'

'I know she is the cause of his hardheartedness,' said Mary, chin quivering, poised between rage and tears. 'Here he is, the great liberal, the champion of open relationships, the man who fathered me from a woman revered as an envoy of women's right to behave according to their own feelings, and he refuses to acknowledge his only true daughter living in a loving relationship. I feel as if it's a rejection of the memory of my mother. After all, he married her when she was unmarried with an illegitimate daughter. It's so hurtful. It is a betrayal of the affection I supposed he had for me.' She was almost weeping now and Shelley put his hand over her shaking one.

'I detest her,' she continued, with quiet venom. 'She plagues the life out of him. She is only interested in the fate and reputation of Claire.'

The room was silent.

'I too worry about my little sister,' admitted Charles, sheepishly. 'Though I don't accuse Shelley or Mary. I know she is impetuous — you are all impetuous — and I know you, Shelley, will look after her ...' his voice carried the slight inflection of query, in spite of his confident manner.

'Well,' Claire interrupted them. 'If Claire may speak for herself. I have no interest in a convent. I am perfectly happy as I am. Don't worry about me, Charles. I care not a jot for the opinions of the world. I wish to live a life of philosophising. I wish for adventure. I don't want to depend on anyone, although at the moment, of course, I am another trial for poor Shelley, but not for long. I will write plays, or act. I will be the friend and equal to men. I suppose it is hard for Mama. She was always prejudiced about our respectability, having worked hard to obtain it for herself.'

'I think Godwin also worries that he will seem the instigator of this ungodly behaviour through his writing, and his creditors will be harder on him,' said Charles. Also that Shelley's ignominy will make it harder for Shelley to raise money from his father and cover the debts of the bookshop. Finances are pretty dire.'

'So, Godwin is sacrificing the company of the two people he loves best in the world – Mary and Shelley – to gain the approval of those money-hungry people he detests,' sneered Claire.

'He assumes he can cut Shelley, but Shelley will still feel obliged to support him,' Mary said, looking in wonder at Shelley, who shrugged.

'And I probably will,' he said. 'He is still your father and he is still a genius. Though at the moment I can barely feed us and certainly cannot fulfil Harriet's demands.'

'Ah, Harriet,' mused Charles. 'There is another voice that gushes poison into my mother's ear!'

Shelley was visibly shocked. 'Harriet goes to Skinner Street?'

'Oh yes,' said Charles. 'She and her father are working against you all over London. She tells her story of abandonment with tears on her pretty cheeks, and her condition is another nail in the coffin of your reputation.'

'She does not say how I promise to stand by her, to be her friend and protector? How she will not see me or let me see my child? I try to recognise she has the stronger claim and respect that, but it is the hardest part for me, not seeing Ianthe.'

This, said with real sorrow, surprised Mary, because Shelley had not admitted before how much he suffered from a sense of loss about his separation from his daughter. The men she knew did not discuss their feelings about children. With a pang of guilt, Mary realised she was so caught up in what affected her own life that she had failed to see this wound in him.

'She does not say, I suppose, that my largest debts are for her expenditures on a carriage and clothes and that I cannot meet them,' he continued. 'Nor that her attack on my reputation is prejudicing the lawyers and moneylenders against me? Bah.'

Charles was beginning to look uncomfortable, so Mary changed the subject.

'Have you seen Wordsworth's new long poem, *The Excursion*? Shelley got it for us yesterday, just as it was off the press?'

'I loved the *Story of Margaret*,' said Claire, dreamily. 'It was so beautiful.'

'You are hopelessly romantic, Claire. Mary and I were very disappointed. Wordsworth has become a slave. He is now perpetuating the idea of Christian devotion over sublime nature.'

'Well, in your poem about him last year you predicted the purity of the *'Poet of Nature'* would be sullied once he took a job and joined society, and it looks as if you were right,' said Mary. 'It's very sad.'

'Are you sorry, then, to be back in London?' asked Charles.

'There are too few good friends who have stood by us, and too many lawyers, debtors and moneylenders to make acquaintance with,' muttered Shelley.

'But Hookham has been to dine with us at last,' Mary said, trying for optimism. 'Shelley has explained how he does not want to abandon Harriet, but be her friend, and Hookham now recognises it is in Harriet's best interest as well as ours for him to help Shelley to get money, so he is nearly reconciled.'

This was a mantra that they had repeated to many people. It was a strain to constantly insist that Shelley wasn't an unfeeling monster and Mary wasn't a husband-stealing harridan. Then there was also the need to represent Claire as a sister and companion and not Shelley's mistress. They explained and repeated this over and over. It was as if with repetition it might be more true. As if they were proving it to themselves as well as others. Both Shelley and Mary suppressed pangs of guilt in their own way, and the health of both of them suffered from the nagging uncertainty of their situation. They knew they were meant to be together, but the impact on others was not part of their ideal moral world. Claire was more dismissive of other people's reactions. Mary tried not to blame her for that, supposing that because the main decisions had not been hers, she felt less responsibility.

'Peacock is also somewhat reconciled,' giggled Claire to Charles, meanwhile. 'What an unusual fellow! He is so cynical, he finds everything amusing. He teases Shelley unmercifully on his vegetarianism. He says all his pains could be cured with a large beefsteak.'

'Who is Peacock?' asked Charles.

'A capital fellow,' replied Shelley. 'An older man of twenty-nine. Hookham showed me his poems a couple of years ago and that is how we made our acquaintance – *The Genius of the Thames* and *The Philosophy of Melancholy*, a fine piece of philosophising. He likes boats and commanded a ship of the line for a while, and is fond of nature. Mainly he loves the study of Greek. He has spent years on it – taught himself in the Reading Room of the British Library and encouraged me to learn it, too, though I used to think only Latin was important.'

'As a result of Mr. Peacock's reappearance in Shelley's life, I am to start learning Greek tomorrow from a stern teacher,' Mary said, bowing to Shelley. 'My taskmaster has a high opinion of my ability to master the language, but I fear he will be disappointed.'

'Maie, your character is so far ahead of mine in dedication and application. What has taken me years, you will conquer in months.'

'Hmm.' Mary considered the debris of the table, one end of which was covered in scientific apparatus, crusts of bread and cake and half empty glasses, and on the other end manuscripts fought for a place with books and magazines, abandoned pens, half-finished letters and Shelley's abandoned collars.

'My character is definitely ahead of yours in a desire for order. I think I need to go to bed now to gain some energy for creating space in this dirty hell hole in the morning. We pity the maid.' She raised her eyebrows and kissed Charles on the top of his head, then sat briefly on Shelley's knee as she kissed him, too.

'Come again soon, Charles,' she said as she made for the stairs.

Shelley's obsession with the natural philosophy of science had been a surprise to Mary, but not as much as his practical experimentation.

'We are privileged to live in an age of great scientific innovation,' announced Shelley, rushing in to the parlour next afternoon, waving a paper, with Claire on his heels. 'Look, here it announces two shows of Mr. Garnerin and his Theatre of Grand Philosophical Recreations. We must all go.' He threw down his fawn kid gloves with the tear in the cuff, defiantly. 'Tonight. Hang the expense. Hang the new gloves.'

'Wasn't he the first person to jump from the sky in a parachute? Doesn't he still give performances defying gravity with an ounce of silk?' asked Claire, still puffing from the exertion of keeping up with the enthusiastic rush.

'He has delved much further into the scientific mysteries. I hear his shows display many wonders of modern science.'

The show was as spectacular as promised, using electricity to mimic a thunderbolt, and produce fire from water. There were phantasmagoria in which they seemed to see a lady with many heads. It finished with a wonderful display of fireworks, which produced neither smell nor smoke. Shelley was riveted.

Mary feared more wires and crucibles of liquids would appear on the parlour table alongside the solar microscope and the extremely thumbed and stained copy of *The Elements of Chemical Philosophy* by Humphrey Davy. At Eton, Shelley had a teacher, James Lind, who had instilled a fascination with scientific experimentation. Shelley longed to understand the physical world as well as that of the mind. He often talked of galvanism, how Lind had made a frog's leg jump by passing an electric current. Until they were back in London, Mary hadn't realised the depth of this passion for chemical experiments, nor the potentially lethal impact of his obsession on working papers, table tops or cushion covers, as smoke rose and glasses full of foul-coloured liquid shattered. It did not add to their acceptability as tenants, or help to unpurse the lips of landladies.

Every day, Shelley made another excursion to see money-lenders and lawyers. As time passed without any success, he became pale and anxious. When he went out he insisted that either Mary or Claire went with him and, though Mary was often too sick, there was always Claire, energetic and eager. Mary thought it was because he needed moral support and she was desolate that it was not her providing it.

'No, no, Mary, that is not it,' confided Shelley. 'I have a mortal enemy who is always after me. If he finds me alone, he will undoubtedly attack.'

'Surely you can have no enemies,' laughed Mary. 'Who on earth would want to harm you?'

'It is from my time in Ireland. I was there to try to support a repeal of the Union and emancipation for Catholics. I wanted to stir the consciousness of liberal thinkers and philanthropists. I made speeches and published pamphlets. Then, when we were back and living in Wales, there was a disagreeable, blustery sort of Englishman called Leeson in the neighbourhood, who thought he was patriotic by hating everything not English, and taking it on himself to see threats to his English pride everywhere. Someone gave him one of my pamphlets and he saw it as double treachery, me being of the nobility. He promised to run me out of the county and reported me to the Home Office. Of course, they were perfectly aware of my actions and did nothing, mostly because they knew how futile they had been. Unfortunately Leeson saw it as a matter of honour, and came in the middle of the night and tried to shoot me.'

Mary gasped, but was practical, as always.

'Surely this was more than a year ago, and you are no longer near him.'

'You do not know the mind of this scoundrel. After we tussled in the billiard room and exchanged fire, I pursued him out of the French windows. He vowed to come after me and kill me, however long it took.'

'Is this the stuff of your nightmares, when you wake screaming?'

'Yes, I see his face everywhere. In the street I always fancy he is in the crowd. Sometimes I even see him peering through the window.'

'How could having one of us with you help? We could hardly fight off an assailant!'

'I don't think he would attack if there were a witness. He would have to find me alone.'

Claire had come quietly into the room while Shelley was speaking.

'Poor, poor Shelley,' she cooed. 'We will stay by you and deter this vicious monster.'

Mary, forced to murmur agreement suppressed her instinct to quench the flames of these fancies with cool reason.

On most evenings, because Mary's pregnancy made her tired, she went to bed early, leaving Shelley, the insomniac, Claire, and sometimes Peacock, to talk far into the night. Mary had still not told Claire of her pregnancy. Shelley did not understand why not and nor, really, did Mary. Except that she had a sense of having something special that was hers and Shelley's that she didn't have to share with Claire. Something up her sleeve as a trump card – or rather something in her belly. She wore an extra petticoat under her high-waisted light muslin dress so it would not cling and reveal her changing shape. She hugged her knowledge to her as she lay, nauseous, listening to the murmur of the fireside discussions as they continued without her.

Their favourite topic was escape. They hated London's smell and dirt and longed for the country. With Peacock, they concocted a scheme to go to the west of Ireland where they would all live among nature, free from the oppressive morals and constraints of their time. They would form the Association of Philosophical People. Those who were like thinkers would come and join them. They would live simply, at one with the woods and the rivers, eating a vegetable diet, rambling and botanicising. Peacock loved the plan, except for the vegetable diet — but Shelley said he should catch fish — and they would all live in this Utopia for the rest of their days.

In the meantime, they made do with a walk up to Primrose Hill in the afternoons, to a pond they called the 'Lake of Nangin'. Mary made little paper boats and Shelley and Peacock set fire to them and watched them sail over the water, propelled by the heat of their burning sails. They experimented with different shapes and had races, involving the help of the crowd of small boys who collected to cheer.

'You know, Peacock, I should like it if we could get into one of these boats and be shipwrecked,' Mary overheard Shelley say joyfully. 'It is a death I should like better than any other.'

Mary's sudden chill was justified by the clap of thunder and a downpour. They ran home to dry their clothes, drink tea and analyze poetry and the meaning of life. They hatched plans to change the world and discussed politics: the failure of the French Revolution and the position of women in society. Shelley urged them to read *The Empire of the Nairs or The Rights of Women* by Lawrence.

'I have admired this massive romance for years. The Nairs were a cradle of an ancient civilisation in India that did not distinguish between its citizens in terms of class, race and gender, as we do.' Shelley was passionate in admiration. 'It is my ideal society, where women are not constrained by marriage but form relationships based on love alone, and those relationships end when love ends.'

'What happens to the children?' asked Mary, practical as ever.

'Women are responsible for the children, but inheritance is matrilineal, so they are also the beneficiaries of the means to raise them.'

There is something particularly attractive, thought Mary, about a man who values women as a species. Many men think that women only want them to be brutish or dominating. How little they understand us.

Claire, in particular, had an affinity with Shelley's admiration of a Nair-like society.

'I have a theory of a Subterraneous Community of Women,' she said, excitedly, eyes shining. 'They would work subtly, within the borders of society to change the thinking of politicians and to rouse the common people to a sense of their value.'

Shelley loved this idea, and continued to discuss the details with Claire at any opportunity.

One evening, after Mary had again retired early, Claire and Shelley stayed talking around the fading fire. The next thing Mary knew it was daybreak and Shelley was shaking her.

'Mary, you must see to Claire, she is hysterical!'

What is it?' she rubbed at her sleep-laden eyes, trying to make sense of his anxiety.

'We were up late, talking first about her Subterranean Community of Women, then, as it got past midnight, we talked about spirits and ghosts and forces of evil. Claire said my eyes looked sinister and powerful and she ran to her room. I was preparing to sit next to you and read when she came running back down the stairs. Her face, Maie, was one of terror, white and drawn, with wide, starting eyes. She said her pillow had moved in her room of its own accord, from the bed to a chair. I led her back to the fire to talk to her and calm her.'

He embraced her and whispered, 'Mary, she wanted me to comfort her. She tried to cling to me. I took her hand and told her of your pregnancy. I hope you pardon me for this, but it had the desired effect, at least for a while. I simply read to her to try and settle her until daylight — our candles burned very low and we feared they wouldn't last — but she seemed all the while even more distracted, trembling and fearful.'

'Where is she now?' Mary tried to force her sleepy brain to replace hatred with compassion.

'As it got light she looked at my face again and said it had the same, terrifying otherworldly look of the nighttime. She said her horrors were my fault and I did not understand her. Now she is shrieking and shaking on the floor.'

'Bring her into this bed,' Mary instructed, and he went down to get her.

Claire came in, not looking at Mary, wrapped in a blanket, and she did look a pathetic creature — tearstained face and eyes, pale from lack of sleep Mary guessed, rather than fear. She lay down on the bed and Mary laid her hand on her shoulder. She gave one convulsive shudder, then closed her eyes and slept.

Shelley crept out and then five minutes later came back in, round-eyed. He came around to Mary's side of the bed, knelt and whispered to her. 'The pillow is on the chair as she said.'

'This proves conclusively, exactly what?' Mary sneered. 'I am glad I did not have to invent gothic tales to get you into my arms.'

Shelley looked satisfyingly shocked at her callousness.

'Well, at least she now knows about the baby,' Mary muttered. 'That should give me respite from barbs about my lack of stamina. It might be too much to hope that she will see this as changing our domestic arrangements.'

'No, but I will explain to her my friendship does not mean I want to create a love triangle and that I hope one day she will find someone whose nerves vibrate in tune with hers as mine do with you.' He pulled Mary over and kissed her frown.

'Just talking is not enough,' she hissed, refusing to be mollified. 'It's talking that gives her the wrong impression. You seem to sympathise with her and you don't take my side. Just this morning, when she demanded to learn Greek as well, you could see it irritated me, but you were warm and encouraging to her.'

'Because she is such a child and I like to educate her. She will be better for understanding the philosophers.' He smiled over her shoulder at the sleeping Claire. 'Why did it upset you so?'

'I know she has no real interest. She only wants to do it to be like me and impress you.' Mary felt Shelley tense and knew he could not understand her jealousy – which it is what it was. She told herself it was irritation and anger at childish sentiments and behaviour, but all the time she feared Claire would show her up as unworthy of the pedestal on which Shelley had placed her. She knew her way to block Claire's ascendant was to be cool, composed and contemplative — the things in her that Shelley admired — and she fought for control.

'Oh, I suppose as you say, we should humour her.' She turned her back on Claire, rolled out of bed and put her arms around his neck.

'As long as you also humour me, in all things,' she purred into his ear, and he picked her up and carried her through into the parlour and shut the door on the rest of the world.

Later in the evening Shelley had a talk with Claire to explain that while he admired much about her character, Mary was the mirror of the purity and brightness of his soul. He explained this did not mean that he did not love Claire as a close friend, a sister, but she must not presume too much.

Claire had hysterics. She screamed that he misunderstood her. That she had no interest in him. That she was sorry she had ever come with them. She called his ideas biased and narrow. She refused to talk to him for days.

They sometimes saw the Godwins walking along Holborn, and their family still cut them dead. Then Fanny sent a note asking to meet Claire, without Mary, whom she was forbidden to see. Claire reported that Fanny had been deputed by Mrs. Godwin to suggest a position as a governess they had found for her or, if that did not please her, that she should go to live with a nice family in the country, to remove her from the moral corruption of the Shelley household.

'So what was your answer?' asked Mary, struggling to keep any trace of hope from peeping through her tone.

Mrs. Godwin's machinations, though, had come too late, because by then Claire was imbued with notions of freedom and a growing sense that she was a beacon, representing a new generation of free women.

She said proudly, 'I told her I would accept only if the family was guaranteed to express contempt for the laws of England and if they allowed me unfettered access to my friends, by which of course I meant you.'

Shelley laughed at this, and was impressed with her sentiments and her resolve. He told her so. The household imbalance was restored.

# 2

'How hateful it is to quarrel – to say a thousand
unkind things – meaning none – things produced
by the bitterness of disappointment'

*Journal*, Claire Clairmont

On the Saturday evening, when the debt-collectors came, there was
just enough warning for Shelley to go into hiding.

As they sat down to dinner, the servant handed Mary a letter. She
said a lady standing in the field opposite, had given a boy a farthing
to bring the note across. Claire was the first to rush to the door and
recognised Fanny, with her shawl over her head, anxiously peering
at the house and clearly poised to flee if she were seen. Shelley was
close behind Claire, and the pair of them ran across to her, dodging
a carriage, and Claire catching her heel in a rut. Shelley caught hold
of Fanny's skirt but she screamed and pulled away from him as if
he were red-hot. Shelley and Claire chased after her until they were
breathless, but saw her slip back through the door of Skinner Street
before they could catch up with her again.

While they were chasing Fanny, Mary opened the note and read,
stomach churning, a warning that their address had been given away
to the Bailiffs. Her hand shook as she showed it to the others when
they came back, Claire limping heavily. Shelley was bewildered and
angry and searched for a scapegoat. He convinced himself that it was
Hookham who had betrayed them.

'He is the only one who knows this address, apart from Peacock
and the Godwins. I thought he was a friend.'

'From what I can see, we have as much to fear from our friends as
our enemies,' sighed Mary. 'Perhaps it was accidental. The bailiffs are
cunning. Hookham is a prig, but not a real enemy. He wouldn't want
to see you in prison.'

'But he always seems to take Harriet's side,' complained Shelley.

They knew they had been living on air and expectation, avoiding the landlady as she stood waiting behind her sitting room door for them to come in, gradually running out of excuses to delay payment of the rent. Already they had moved lodgings to Margaret Street in Pancras to keep their address secret from Harriet, but there had been constant threats from her creditors. Harriet's father refused to pay any more of her debts and they devolved onto Shelley. Harriet became more shrill and demanding as it became apparent to her that Shelley's involvement with Mary was not just a passing whim, but at the same time she was more hostile to Shelley, undermining him behind his back and refusing to let him see her or his daughter.

'Anyway, we are safe for a few hours.' Mary was thinking aloud and starting to gather up essentials. 'They are not allowed to arrest you between midnight Saturday and midnight Sunday, but we must make sure we leave here tomorrow. I will go and pack,' she said, starting for the stairs. Shelley, who had been pacing, eyes glazed in thought, caught her arm and put his around her.

'No, just I will go,' he said, with determination. 'It will be better if we keep their attention on this house. If they think I am living here they will watch for me to return. I will go and stay with Peacock at his mother's house in Southampton Street. We can trust him absolutely. Tell no-one else.'

Mary went pale. 'We cannot be parted,' she whispered. 'Let us go to the country, or abroad again.'

'My only chance of getting money is in London,' Shelley replied, taking both her hands. 'I must stay and take the risk, even though to be away from you for even a single night will eclipse the moon from my sky.' He stared at her, willing her, needing her to be strong.

Claire burst into tears and Mary felt possessed of a panic, which invaded her lungs and consumed her breath. She battled to regain control and to look back at him with confidence.

'We have survived much greater hardships,' she smiled, weakly. 'I will go and put some of your things in a bag.'

'What about the landlady?' wailed Claire. 'You charm her, but if you're not here she will evict us for sure.'

'I will sell something,' said Shelley, and Mary said, at the same time, 'Can we worry about Shelley, not ourselves?'

Mary and Shelley exchanged looks, exasperated and tolerant, respectively, and Mary went to pack Shelley's bag.

The next morning they tried to find consolation in fervent activity, but they were like ducks bogged in a muddy pool. All their efforts only churned the waters and got them little closer to comfort. Peacock called, and agreed that Shelley could hide at his house. He went to prepare his mother for their guest. Claire went to Skinner Street and demanded to see Fanny, who reluctantly confirmed that Hookham was the source of Harriet's, and the bailiff's, knowledge. Harriet had worked on Hookham and wheedled the address from him.

Shelley and Peacock visited both Hookham and Harriet, in the vain hope of making the latter see reason, but both were conveniently out, so Shelley wrote to them.

'The woman is an imbecile,' he said. 'What possible benefit could it be to her to have me imprisoned, except for spite? How does she think I can do better at raising funds in prison?'

'She wants to frighten you,' said Claire. 'I suspect she thinks that by separating you from Mary you will come to your senses, see it as an infatuation, come back into the fold of society and her arms. You know, all of the cant that everyone whispers to her all the time. My mother still believes it too.'

'I suppose to them it's only been three months — certainly in the category of an aberration — while to us it seems a lifetime already,' agreed Mary. 'Though prison is a drastic means of separation.'

'In a debtor's prison, she, as my wife, could live with me, but you couldn't,' said Shelley, getting up and staring out of the window. 'Aourgh,' he almost screamed, as he batted his hands against his head. 'Why can she not understand? I have explained again and again how she will always be my close friend. I'll do everything I can for her. I would have her live with us, if she would, and share our miserable crumbs. But she cannot get it into her head that Mary is my one great love, the partner of my soul, while my love for her is as a friend, a friend.' He emphasised his words with a clenched fist slammed onto the table, so several inks came shudderingly close to splattering the carefully copied final drafts of his new poems.

'Harriet is selfish and unfeeling,' said Mary, who, however, understood more than she would ever admit to Shelley about why Harriet would not consent to live with them and, for that matter, why she would continue to fight for her marriage.

'She perverts so many of your old friends and acquaintances,' Mary continued. 'They can only think of her as a "good wife". She put up with your restlessness, your politics, and your vegetarianism — though heaven knows we all do that. She is also beautiful and has been only sweet-natured to them. They understand you have found a meeting of minds in me, but they think you should treat it as merely an *affaire* and that you were wrong to abandon the perfect Harriet.

'Anyway, thank goodness for Fanny,' she sighed, seeing his despondency.

'Yes, thank goodness for Fanny. She clearly is not so fully corrupted by that poisonous household as we feared. Though I can't see why she pulled away from me yesterday.'

Claire had been listening to this with growing anger.

'You are the blindest man that ever existed!' she spat, glaring venomously at an alarmed Shelley. 'Can you not see how much Fanny adores you? When you first came into our house, before Mary came back from Scotland, you charmed Fanny, carelessly, as you do everyone. She thought you cared for her. She was destroyed when you ran away, and with her own sister. Taking me was the final insult. I think she would have been content to have been the third and would have been a quiet and undemanding one too. Unlike me. She would have simply sat at your feet and worshipped you. It's just the same with Harriet. You think your love was based on friendship, but for her it was, still is, a great passion. You are selfish. Everyone can't tailor or shift their feelings just to accommodate your changes of heart! No, no, don't touch me.' She shook off Mary as she tried to put an arm around her, and turned on her instead, pushing her back.

'You, the supposedly all-knowing, sensitive one. How is it that you can't tell how another woman feels? You don't know how to be inclusive. You shut us all out. You won't let Shelley fulfil his dream of a free association of like-minded individuals. You would never have allowed him to include Harriet in our household, and she knows it. So does Fanny. You say the right things, but he is yours, just as if you were married,' and she bolted from the sitting room.

Two minutes later she passed the door in her street clothes. 'No, no,' she cried, shaking off Shelley's hand as he came out to restrain her. 'I need to walk by myself.' With that, she was gone out of the front door.

'That girl has no concept of friendship,' muttered Shelley, white-faced. 'Remind me, Mary, if I ever forget again, that I must not allow my sympathy to be misconstrued, to weaken the tranquility of my one great love. It is she who doesn't understand. I have thought that her character is yet unformed. That she can change and learn to subdue her angry feelings, but I begin to despair.'

In the evening, Shelley left to go with Peacock, and Mary and Claire sat in silence until bedtime. Claire had returned, red-eyed from the wind in the Kentish Town fields, where she had been walking by herself, as she made a point of telling Shelley. She drew him aside and whispered to him on the sofa, looking contrite, and pleading, while Mary pretended to read at the other end of the room. After half an hour, Claire came across to Mary and said she was sorry, that the tension and anxiety of the situation had made her say things she didn't mean, but her eyes were seeking Shelley's approval, even as Shelley came to deliberately take Mary's hand and squeeze it.

Just then Peacock called to collect Shelley and sensed the brittle atmosphere. He took one look at the trio and laughed at them.

'Come, have you no better occupation just now than to quarrel? If you were aboard ship I would put you all to work in the galley. That would make you comrades in misery!'

As he left with Shelley, Shelley whispered to Mary. 'She has promised to control her temper. Help her?'

After they left, Mary, try as she might, could not bring herself to speak to Claire. It is always me, she thought to herself, who has to compromise, who has to make the first move towards reconciliation.

Claire, she knew, could keep a feud going much longer than she could herself. The apology was false, as they both knew, and Claire was practiced at generating a haze of hostility, which pervaded every crevice of a room.

# 3

'Highho love, such is the world.'

*Letter to Percy Bysshe Shelley*, Mary Shelley

At eight o'clock, Mary had been dressed for four hours and had been sitting at the window, peering at every figure who appeared to be heading towards the house, when a porter finally arrived with a letter from Shelley.

He asked her to meet him at the shop of Adams the microscope maker, in Fleet Street, at twelve. He wrote that it was in the jurisdiction of Middlesex, not London, so they would be safe from the bailiffs. His feelings of desolation without her were worse than he had imagined.

So she waited, anxious and restless. Claire woke at nine and seemed to want to be polite to Mary, or at least to talk enough to get a share of the news. She begged Mary to read to her to pass the time, and Mary read *She Stoops to Conquer*. Though she could barely keep her mind on the comic romantic misunderstandings, the play was probably a good choice, as she could not have been diverted by anything more serious. On the stroke of eleven, Mary left and flew down Oxford Street and then along Bow Street. She felt uncomfortable and furtive as Bow Street Runners came and went into the Magistrates court, even though they were interested in criminals, not debtors. She pushed past the crowds of hawkers in Drury Lane and the queues in Fleet Street waiting for Mrs. Salmon's Waxworks Exhibition to open. She was at Adams shop by eleven forty five and walked up and down outside until twelve thirty. Shelley did not come.

Peacock's house was close by in Southampton Row, so she set off for there in hopes of finding him, almost running, praying he was not found and taken. He was not there, but Claire was.

'Why did you come?' asked Mary, more sharply than she intended.

'I couldn't sit by myself,' said Claire, defiantly. 'Peacock is not here, though,' she whispered, aggrieved. 'I have had to support the ramblings of old Mrs. P. for the past hour, who hasn't a notion what's happening. She just knows that Peacock went out two hours ago.'

'Well, wait here, I'll go back to Pancras and see if Peacock has gone there looking for me,' ordered Mary, agitatedly.

She went to Fleet Street on her way back, just in case Shelley had come, but the street offered no familiar tall, slightly stooping silhouette. So she spent a wretched hour walking back to their house in Pancras. The hated smoke, stink and endless cacophony of London oppressed all her senses. By the time she had reached the boarding house, she was desperate with worry.

At Pancras there was no Peacock and no note. The landlady was out and the house was silent. She paced for an hour in frustration, constantly watching the street. When two burly men with an air of intent came up the steps, she knew them to be bailiffs, and their insistent knock at the door sent her, shaking, into the silent shadows under the stairs. They went, eventually, and when Mary dared to peer out again, there was the warming sight of Peacock sidling up the steps, his sardonic eyes for once not full of humour, but fear.

'Did you see them, Mary?' he panted, rushing in and slamming the door behind him. 'We must not let him be taken.' Mary drew him further inside and they stared at each other in mutual terror.

'He has been at Ballachy's the moneylenders all morning and couldn't get away to meet you. I was with him 'til one, then he sent me off with this for you.'

He gave Mary a letter and a copy of *The Times*. In the letter Shelley asked her to meet at four at the London Coffee House, in Holborn, Ludgate Street. *The Times* carried an article about the horrors of the slave trade, which Shelley had marked for her. Mary was full of indignation about how there were still nightmarish and barbaric practices, especially in the Caribbean, in spite of abolition seven years ago. Mary thought of those suffering slaves as her spirits sank at the prospect of another hour's walk, and her belly rumbled from lack of food. She had only a few pennies.

'I'll go back to my mother's,' said Peacock. 'You go and meet Shelley and come to my house afterwards. Oh, and he wants me to take his microscope, to sell, I think.'

'You are a good, dear friend. We can walk together some of the way, and you can listen to me rage about the slaves. It will distract me.'

Mary found Shelley in the Coffee House, in a dark back corner. She bought them a small cake to share.

'You are so pale, Mary,' he said, anxiously, touching her cheek. 'Did you have breakfast?'

'I'll be all right. I'm just a little weak. Pancras is rather far. It was awful to wake up and turn over and not to see you there. I am so distraught that I can't be with you to cheer you. I know I am the only one who can truly lift your spirits.'

'Dear Mary, I love you so very much, and we have been so happy …'

'We will be so again, very soon,' cut in Mary, dragging up all her reserves of optimism.

Shelley brightened. 'Ballachy seemed sympathetic to my litany of misfortune. He brought in a friend who he thinks may lend me £400. He will tell me by Thursday. Thursday! How will we eat for three days? I can't live entirely by Peacock's good graces. He has little enough himself. Did he get the microscope? We must sell it. It is our last valuable. You can go to Davison's in Stone Street …'

He looked at Mary and changed the sentence. 'I mean Peacock and me. Stone Street is outside the city limits. Can you go and ask Peacock to meet me here with it? Stay at his house until he comes back with money.'

Mary was too exhausted to protest, and too exhausted to pretend she was not. They said their goodbyes, and Mary tried to walk off with an energetic spring, which failed her as soon as the door sprang shut.

When she arrived at Peacock's, he was looking out for her and Claire was all concern.

'I went back to Pancras looking for you, but you'd both left there, so I came back here. What a day of to-ing and fro-ing it's been! There were frowning men, bailiffs I think, that went to the door as I left.'

'Then that's the second time today,' Mary shuddered.

'So I must take this microscope to Shelley.' As Peacock stood up and picked up the box, Claire jumped up too, picking up her shawl.

'I'll come too. Poor man, he needs as many friendly faces as possible.'

Peacock glanced at Mary, but saw she was too tired to formulate a good objection. He was back in half an hour.

'Claire has gone with Shelley to the shop,' he said, cautiously. 'He wanted me to come back and take care of you. Claire is sufficient to ward off the Leeson threat.'

Peacock found Mary some fruit and rolls and sat her on the sofa with a blanket, though it was quite mild.

'That is so good.' She tore chunks out of the rolls and devoured them with relish. 'The devil of a landlady swears she will not send up dinner 'till we pay the rent.'

'How far into your term are you?' he asked, gently.

'How can you tell?' Mary looked at him in surprise, running her hand over her belly. She had thought her rounding shape was invisible under her high-waisted chemise and long pelise. 'It's four months.'

'It was a wild guess,' grinned Peacock. 'Our mutual friend has certainly proved himself fertile. I mean, I didn't mean ...' he blustered as he realised the reference to Harriet's pregnancy would not be tactful.

'But eat, my dear, it's wonderful news. Shelley suffers from not seeing his other child. This will give him joy.'

'We talked last night 'till late,' he continued. 'Your man is a perfect idealist and I am a perfect cynic. Perhaps because Love is my middle name I'm inclined to repudiate its power over me, but your philosopher is a true believer in love. He swears himself its slave and you the intelligence that governs him. You, he says, "each become wiser as you imitate each other's excellencies". But for myself, I fall in love so often that one young lady who rejected my marriage proposal last year — with great good humour I may say — said my inconstancy as a lover "was enough to make the Thames turn round and change its current". Though I suspect it was my penury rather than my inconstancy that caused her refusal. A thousand a year is prerequisite for an attractive suitor.'

'Will Marianne be of the same opinion?'

'Ah, the lovely, light-headed Marianne de St Croix! I am doomed to be eternally disappointed!' He threw himself melodramatically into a chair, clasped both hands across his heart and groaned. 'There is only the poisoned cup to relieve my agony,' he sobbed melodramatically, rolling his eyes back up into his head, so the pupils disappeared under the long curls that flopped across his forehead.

Mary laughed for the first time in that awful day. 'Well, can you hold off on the laudanum for another few days, otherwise Shelley will have nowhere to sleep.' When Claire came back, with good news about the sale of the microscope for five pounds, she found Mary dozing, exhausted but peaceful, in the armchair.

The next weeks were a horror of sneaked meetings in coffee houses, parks and churches. Mary often had to wait for Shelley and hated walking up and down the street alone. Always there were manoeuvres about money. The petitioners, the bailiffs, the money lenders, his uncle, Sir John Shelley, the solicitors, Harriet, and Godwin were all members of an ensemble that Shelley was trying valiantly to conduct, while the evidence of his senses told of the discordant disharmony of his efforts. There was no music to be had anywhere and he was whirling around on the podium out of time with the universe.

During those weeks he studied hardly at all and wrote nothing.

'Do you think that Wordsworth could have written such poetry if he had to deal with moneylenders?' he asked Mary.

Mary was the repetiteur, trying hard to stand in for, and support Shelley when he could not be everywhere. Hookham redeemed himself and was willing to act as intermediary where he could. Peacock talked to him and found that he was horrified that Harriet had given away Shelley's address. He certainly did not want to see Shelley in prison. Hookham had standing as a respectable publisher, so his word counted in financial circles. Shelley tried to raise money on post-obits and on the sale of Goring Castle in Sussex.

It was tedious and heartbreaking. The Penny Post that went six times a day was their lifeline, scribbled always in haste with no respect for grammar.

Mary to Shelley

*For what minute did I see you yesterday — is this the way, my beloved, we are to live ... In the morning when I turn to wake I look for you — dearest Shelley you are solitary and uncomfortable — why can I not be with you to cheer you and press you to my heart. Oh my love you have no friends why then should you be torn from the only one who has affection for you — but I shall see you tonight and that is the hope I shall live on through the day — be happy dear Shelley and think of me — I know how tenderly you love me and how you repine at this absence from me — when shall we be free of treachery?*

*I was so dreadfully tired yesterday that I was obliged to take a coach home — forgive this extravagance but I am so very weak at present and had been so agitated through the day that I was not able to stand — a rest will set me right again.*

*Heaven bless my love and take care of him.*

*Goodnight, I am woefully tired and sleepy — I shall dream of you — a naughty one.*

Shelley to Mary

*Oh my dearest love why are our pleasures so so short and so interrupted! Know you my best Mary that I feel myself in your absence almost degraded to the level of the vulgar and the impure. Oh! those redeeming eyes of Mary that might beam on me before I sleep! Praise my forbearance oh beloved one that I do not rashly fly to you — and at least secure a moments bliss!*

*I will not forget the sweet moments when I saw your eyes — the divine rapture of the few and fleeting kisses.*

*I have written a long letter to Claire though in no mood for writing.*

*Your thoughts alone can waken mine to energy. My mind without yours is dead and cold as the dark midnight river when the moon is down.*

*My own dearest love Goodnight.*

As always Claire could go on errands if Mary was too ill. As always Claire was grumpy if she was not welcome when Shelley and Mary met. No longer was she prepared to sit under a tree while Shelley and Mary talked, as she had been three months earlier. Now she saw herself as an equal partner in their affairs and wanted time with Shelley too. Shelley sometimes wrote to her personally, but she wanted Mary to read out all of his letters to her, as well. She felt she had a right to know all that was happening. Mary censored them as much as possible, leaving out the declarations of love and anguish, but Claire knew them to be there. She wrote long letters to him that she did not allow Mary to see. Two weeks after the fugitive regime had begun, there was an explosion. It was Friday. Mary had arranged to meet with Shelley in Grays Inn Gardens and Claire insisted on going too. Shelley was not pleased to see her, but tried to hide it.

'Shall we walk?' asked Claire gaily, and took Shelley's arm, as he was glancing nervously about. 'This is a good place to meet. The Walks here are so fashionable, with so many people strolling about, we are not remarked upon.'

'Could we just have a little time by ourselves first, Claire?' asked Mary with a tight smile. 'Is it too much to ask?'

'Shelley?' demanded Claire. 'I need to be part of these discussions. I am the one that talks to Charles and Fanny to get news. I run errands for you and suffer the privations of our life as much as either of you.'

'Yes, Claire, that is true,' Shelley said, disengaging his arm and turning Claire to face him. 'But Mary is my, my ...' and he turned to look at Mary, who was shivering slightly in the November chill, drawing her shawl tightly around her shoulders to ward off the wrong words. At a meaningful look from Shelley she walked on ahead and he turned again to Claire. '... my surpassing love, my redeeming love. I have explained this to you, Claire. I will always love you truly, but it is different. And see how fragile Mary is now. How much she needs me. I am so unhappy. Please do not make it more difficult for me.'

'I am very disappointed in you, Shelley. I had thought you kind and considerate but I see I was wrong. You just think of yourself too. You, unhappy?' She increased her pace so that they caught up with Mary. 'You can be 'together' tomorrow night. It is Saturday and you can come home then until Sunday. Can't you wait until then? Clearly not. My feelings count for nothing. All the loyalty I have given you both. You always play your cards well,' she spat, glaring at Mary. 'Poor sick Mary. Always poor sick Mary.' Then she took off down the long walk until she merged with the fashionably dressed afternoon strollers, women in sarsnet and silk promenade dresses and high crown bonnets, on the arms of dandies, with their cares well hidden under powder, pearls and lace ruffs.

'She has the faculty of making me more uncomfortable than any human being in the world — a faculty she never fails to exert.' Mary shook off his hand as he tried to soothe her. 'And you do not disillusion her enough. There is always something in what you say that gives her hope of a closer relationship. A veiled promise. One day it will have to be resolved. I know you believe in open, loving associations, and I would try for your sake, but I don't know if I could stand it if it were with Claire.' As her eyes grew damp, she dabbed at them angrily with the end of her shawl.

'Shh, shh. See this catalpa tree? It is 200 years old and it must be sixty feet tall. Though it has shed most of its leaves, look, there are still a few green ones clinging to its branches determined not to die. Mary, do look. They are heart-shaped. Here, let's pick one each. Take them home and press them together between the leaves of a book. In *Emile*. This is us, pressed together forever. Tonight we will go and stay at a hotel, at the Cross Keys, and will be alone. What do you say? Hmm?' He squeezed her tightly around her waist and lifted her chin so that she had to look at him. 'Hmm?'

'We can't afford it,' she muttered, trying to smile through the knowledge that he had not answered her, but they had barely an hour before Shelley's next appointment with the lawyers and she didn't want to quarrel. Shelley cast around for neutral, binding gossip.

'Let me tell you, Hogg came and dined with me last night! You remember, my conspirator from Oxford? He has been away on the circuit, it's hard work for him, I suppose, though he seems to flourish. You liked his book, didn't you? *The Memoir of Alexy Haemetoff*. It was good to see him, and he was witty but not especially warm. He is only just back from the North, he says, but I think he has been cutting us because he did admire Harriet. Very much. He wanted to get … closer to her. In truth I encouraged his approaches … I felt that two people who loved me could … Still, Harriet would not have any part of it. You will meet him soon. When we are out of this mess. He will adore you I am sure. If he doesn't he will no longer be my friend.'

So there it was. In the open. No longer abstract or tenuous. The ideal of Free Love that he had been prepared to put into practice, to share his wife with his friend, if it had not been for the small-mindedness of Harriet. So, thought Mary, I have to be different, more liberal, more inclusive, more radical ... But please, not with Claire.

# 4

Cease, cease, — for such wild lessons madmen learn
Thus to be lost , and thus to sink and die
Perchance were death indeed! Constantia turn
In thy dark eyes a power like light doth lie

*To Constantia, Singing,* Percy Bysshe Shelley

Shelley wrote in their joint journal that Hogg was 'pleased with Mary.'
'Like a new variety of cake,' she said crossly to Shelley. Nevertheless
Hogg had proved himself agreeable.

Unlike Claire.

'You go and talk to her, Mary,' pleaded Shelley. 'She has not come
out of her room in two days, since we came here.'

'She is cross with you for moving us here, to Nelson Square.
Southwark was not what she had in mind when we finally escaped
the clutches of the dragon landlady in Pancras.' Mary was trying not
to show delight that it was Shelley who was the target of Claire's
venom for once.

'You'd think the silly girl would be pleased we can finally pay the
rent and can eat, with the worst of the creditors paid off and no more
hiding. It's quite comfortable here, and it's just over the Blackfriars
Bridge from Peacock's mother's house in Southampton Row and
Hogg's lodgings near the Temple. Since these are the only two of our
friends who visit us ...'

'You asked her and that was your mistake. I know, it was meant
to be just a general discussion, but she said she wanted Pimlico, and
this is definitely not Pimlico. The wrong side of the Thames as well.'

'It is important that we are out of the jurisdiction of the city of
London, in case there are new creditors to avoid.'

'She sees that as your problem alone, my dear. Anyway, we can
just enjoy our own company for once, while she is 'sick' in her room.

Here, you finish the letter to Mr. Hooper and see if he will let us have the house in Nantgwilt to rent. How wonderful it would be to see Welsh mountains from our drawing room window instead of London fog.' Mary drew the lace curtain aside and peered into the bleak November afternoon.

'I would love to have my baby in the country,' she smiled dreamily.

'We still need to get more funds. There are your father's debts too.'

'Shelley, are you trying to be a kind of saint, worrying about him as well? He won't even speak to you.'

'He is your father. He is still a brilliant man, just one who can't manage his money. How will it help us or the relationship with him if I abandon him?'

'Why is it always my family intruding in our happiest moments? My feckless father, and Claire upstairs sulking. Let's just sit here by the fire, eat cake and read *Candide* together and ignore them all.'

Shelley's nerves were vibrating as a result of the tension in the house. He liked harmony, even when it was he who had caused controversy. Especially then. The disputes between Claire and Mary he shrugged off, unconcerned with who was at fault. When he knew himself blamed, he wanted only to be restored to favour. That evening he exerted all of his charm and persuasive powers to try to convince Claire that the arrangements were not a direct slight to her. Mary struggled not to see it as vanity.

Next morning, Claire was running up to her room in her nightwear. 'Fanny says Mama's at death's door. I must go at once.' Mary had heard the commotion of Fanny's early arrival and was halfway down the stairs when she heard Fanny saying, anxiously, 'No, no, I was allowed to come and get you on the express understanding that I didn't speak to Mary or Shelley.'

'I have nothing to wear,' Claire screamed from her room. 'My good dress is with the laundress and I cannot go to Mama in this torn rag.' She came to the doorway, shaking her second best muslin at Mary.

'I'll mend it for you, or you can wear one of mine.'

'No, no, no.' Claire rushed back into her bedroom and opened the window which looked onto the street.

'Fanny,' she yelled down to the startled girl, who was already several yards along the road. 'Bring me a dress from Skinner Street.'

'But it will take her an hour, in this freezing weather, too,' protested Mary.

'I ... need ... a ... good ... dress.' Claire said it through clenched teeth with blazing eyes. She pushed her hard, propelling her backwards out of the room as Mary tried to reason with her, and then slammed the door in her face.

Shelley slept through it all and was not up until one pm, long after Claire had left for the Godwins.

'I am in despair with my family,' she complained to Shelley, as he breakfasted on plums and rolls. 'Claire is out of control. I am so scared that one day she will really hurt me. When she lashes out, she is maniacal. She might have hurt the baby!'

'She doesn't mean it, Maie, she is just young and hasn't learnt restraint.'

'No, take this seriously, Shelley. You give in to her too much. Even I do, because I am scared of her temper. Someone needs to stand up to her and it has to be you.'

'Why me? She'll be fine; she just wants to gain affection. You know she needs a lot of affection. She needs it to be shown, all the time.'

'You are a coward, Shelley. You just don't like to be on the wrong side of her. I am young too, but I don't scream or physically lash out when I don't get my way.'

'I think she will learn, if we teach her, and you, my Pecksie, my good and wise robin from Mrs. Trimmer's tale, you have better weapons in your tongue.' Fortunately for him, this last was said with an affectionate smile.

Mary was not mollified. She hated feeling this rage at the unreasonableness of the situation, at Claire, but most of all, at Shelley's utter failure to see it from her perspective, to see it as it was. Though this could not be the thing to undo them, because that would give Claire victory. So she changed tack.

'Then there is Fanny; she is a slave. How dare she come for Claire but not speak to me. She is my real sister. I am the only one of that whole sorry brood who is her blood relative. Why can't she stand up to them? Her loyalty should be to me. I'm sure Claire loves that it appears she is more in favour.'

At four o'clock a letter came from Claire to say that she had been persuaded to stay the night at Skinner Street and, while Shelley muttered about her lack of resolution, Mary's heart soared.

'You are a fool to waste your time in the law, Alexy. The irony is that it's called the learned profession, but it keeps you from pursuing real learning.' Shelley was quietly berating Hogg, sipping his fourth cup of tea, and occasionally rolling up small pellets of his bun and aiming them at the noses of unsuspecting fellow patrons, who looked up at the ceiling for falling debris.

They were in the Holborn coffee house where they had drunk tea for two hours, and the owner suspected Shelley of mischief, but could not quite catch him at it.

'You have been a good friend. Mary is coming to like you.'

'She's a remarkable girl, Shelley. She's devoted to you. You certainly have the females of the species at your feet.'

'She is my one true love, Jefferson. Have you ever seen me so content? It's the first time in my life that I've found reason and intellectual passion combined in one person.'

'Then why do you bother with Claire? Why don't you encourage her more strongly to go back to Skinner Street. You know it would make Mary happy. Instead, again, you just persuaded Claire not to stay there.'

Shelley was quiet for an unusually long time.

'Claire can be fun; she's energetic and uninhibited. She doesn't have Mary's pedigree or understanding but she expects less of me. Sometimes Mary can be too cautious and critical and Claire brings a little balance, and I love her singing. Above all, Jeff, there is the challenge. I won't be beaten. I failed with Harriet, but with Claire, I want to make sure she is imbued with the spirit of learning and thinking. The Godwin household was so divided. Mary and Fanny were tutored by Godwin but Claire came more under the influence of her superficial mother. She deserves my best efforts.'

'Fine sentiments, Shelley, if a bit pompous, but you don't have a good record of a third woman in your entourage enhancing your relationships. The experiment hasn't worked for you in the past, in spite of your rhetoric.'

'I still believe in communities based on liberal principles. Not on base desires but on loving, rational warmth.'

'Harriet didn't feel that way about me,' muttered Hogg, ruefully. 'Even with your encouragement.'

'Harriet was not as enlightened as Mary. Mary may come to care for you more deeply, Jeff. There is no one I would more happily share Mary with than you.'

'Then Mary would share you with Claire?' asked Hogg, with irony.

November was bitterly cold. The snow in the streets quickly turned to ice and slush and, combined with the frozen horse droppings, the streets were treacherous. Mary was getting heavy, was constantly sick and was weak because food would not stay down. Shelley was anxious for her safety and her health amongst the sneezing, shivering populace.

'My little dormouse,' Shelley called Mary, affectionately. Shut up in her little nest, in the bed or on the sofa.

Shelley, though he could happily spend whole days companionably in a chair with a book and a bread roll, alternated with days of restlessness. He needed to go out, either on the endless search for the best financial negotiation or to do errands and buy food. So it was almost always Claire who went with him. When they came running in from the cold, shaking their boots, hanging their coats on the hall stand and laughing, Mary was unforgiving.

'I hope you had a nice time hopping around town.' Shelley looked at her with concern.

'We have to do these things Mary. We need food. We need books. Here, I have the taffeta you asked for.'

'It's been two hours,' complained Mary. 'Did it not occur to you that I miss you, that I am lonely here by myself? I work and I read, but it's your company I am craving.'

Claire came into the doorway, glancing at Mary, before going up to her room. She didn't smile.

'Oh, Mary, everything takes more time in the cold, you know that. Look, I've been to a new bookseller, the Minerva Library in Leadenhall Street. They've given me a whole box of books. I offered him a post-obit bond — £250 for every £100 that we spend — and he said yes! Isn't it marvellous? So we can spend our time more profitably. Look I got a Petronius — you may not like that, they say it's debauched — and Louvet's biography. I thought you may like to write his life, he was one of the key people in the Revolution, you know. I also have a lovely copy of Plato's Apology to replace the one that went missing in the move. Hogg was here for some of the time was he not?'

'Yes, yes, Hogg was here. Sometimes, I lose patience with that man. He has too much respect for the customs of the world. He doesn't necessarily think independently or at least think enough for himself.'

Even so, Hogg was growing on Mary. He was something of an enigma. Even though his predilections were the pastimes of the ruling classes — hunting and fishing — he was still prepared to sit and argue about virtue, about morality and the politics of the day. Most importantly, he was sympathetic to Mary. She felt he restored the balance in the household, that he was on her side, and she was less inclined to argue with Claire when he was there. It was ironic that when they had spent days and weeks being disgusted with the practices of lawyers, Hogg, who was a lawyer, should be so much part of their household, though Hogg at least tried to defend those who needed defending.

'So here is a tale to support your prejudices about the inhumanity of the law, Shelley,' he began, one evening after supper. Mary thought that his grin, which was slightly lopsided, always seemed to add a touch of ruefulness to his stories, while his tone carried the certainty of an advocate. Mary often felt it necessary to challenge his certainty, but he didn't seem to mind.

'It's also a story of romance and tragedy that will appeal to this company's predilection for both. I had to plead for a William Sawyer who had been forbidden to marry his love, Sarah Gasket. The young couple made a suicide pact and after William had killed Sarah, on her request, he tried to shoot himself but failed to die, then he cut his own throat and still survived. So now, in spite of my best efforts, he is to hang for both murder and attempted suicide.' They happily railed about the inhumanity of the law until past midnight.

On November 2nd, a letter from Hookham told them that Harriet had given birth to a boy some days earlier. She called him Charles. Shelley was delighted with the news.

'This is perfect,' he enthused to Mary. 'A boy! This is wonderful … for the inheritance, of course. A boy to continue the line, Mary, this is wonderful.'

'Yes, so you said. A boy. From your real wife,' replied Mary, with disdain.

'It's just because of the inheritance that I'm so pleased.'

'She didn't even tell you herself.'

He went to visit Harriet and came back fuming.

'I didn't get past the door. She threw me out. She wouldn't even let me see the baby. I don't know what I said wrong. She didn't like it when I mentioned the inheritance. I also told her that you are pregnant, which didn't seem to please her, either. Never mind, I must write and tell my father and it will sit well with some of the lawyer's negotiations, that my line is now secure. I'll write to them, too.'

'You girls are more like men in the way you philosophise. Look at Mary cutting out sleeves while she lectures me on Hume's philosophy, telling me that beauty in things exists in the mind which contemplates them,' said Hogg, fondly. Patronisingly, thought Mary.

Mary looked at Hogg, short, rotund, with a beak-like nose and a soft stillness of features, which made him seem always to be contemplating a judicious sentence. Such a contrast to Shelley's waif-like energy and other-worldly ambivalence. Could she care for him the way Shelley wanted?

As they lay in bed that night, Mary asked Shelley, 'Do you really want me to do this?' Shelley rolled over and hugged her. 'You know

I don't believe in relationships based on carnal lust, but on caring. Hogg cares for you.'

It was true Hogg cared in any way that Shelley didn't. It was as if he filled in the gaps. To Shelley she was a phenomenon, to Hogg she was a female. He noticed when she was sad or sick, he brought cushions for her back and caresses for her bruised ego when Shelley and Claire left her alone too much.

Mary forced herself, though, to voice her real fear.

'Is this so that you can bed Claire with a clear conscience?'

'No, no. You must make the first move. The decision is all yours. I do think Claire would be more settled if I could have that stronger influence over her, but she must see it as part of a wider pattern. So if you take on Hogg ...'

Mary's stomach churned, or perhaps it was a kick of her baby that catapulted her into reality.

She put her hands on her stomach and stroked it.

'I can't trust my emotions while I'm in this state, and I'm too sick to deal with a physical relationship.'

She put Shelley's hand next to hers on her stomach.

'Can you give him hope, at least?' Shelley asked.

'Yes, I think I can do that. We both love you, which is the starting point.'


1815 arrived and a new year brought new upheavals.

Three days in January. For instance.

On New Year's Day Hogg made it formal, sending to Mary a written declaration of his love. Shelley, who was clearly aware of his intentions, took Claire out as soon as the letter arrived. Mary felt manipulated, but just a little flattered. So, she wrote him a note:

*Dearest Hogg,*

    *As they have both left me and I am here all alone, I have nothing better to do than to take up my pen and say a few words to you.*

    *You love me you say — I wish I could return it with the passion you deserve — but you are very good to me and tell me that you are quite happy with the affection which from the bottom of my heart I feel for you — you are so generous and disinterested. But you know, Hogg, we have known each other for so short a time and I did not think about love — so that I think that also will come in time.*

*But you will be here this evening, though as the sun shines it would be a fine day to visit the divine statue of Theoclea, but I am not well enough. I was in great pain all night and this morning but am just getting better.*

*Affectionately yours*
*Mary*

That afternoon Hogg himself was at the door, bringing sympathy, gratitude, consolation, and the offer, kindly received, of a first kiss.

On January 2nd there was a pounding on the door. Shelley and Claire were, fortunately, out. It was Harriet's creditors demanding to see Shelley. They were demanding payment from Harriet's husband. Sent there by Harriet.

'We'll have to move again,' complained Mary to Shelley. 'What a horrible woman she is. Can't she leave you alone?'

Shelley took Claire to look for new lodgings, and Mary was completely unsurprised, but disgusted, that they found them in Pimlico. 'You are so weak, Shelley,' she said with disappointment. 'You must be loved at any cost.' Claire was unbearably smug during the upheaval.

On January 6th, there was a letter from Field Place that Shelley ripped open almost before it left the hand of the post-boy. 'He's dead. The old curmudgeon is dead.'

'Sir Timothy, your grandfather?'

'Yes. I can't be a hypocrite and shed tears. He was so judgmental about me and the main instigator of my family's disapproval, and of my lack of allowance. This is the best news.'

'I must go to Field Place for the reading of the will.'

'They have asked you to go?'

'No, but I'll go anyway. I need to know how it is to be arranged.'

'You'll go alone?'

'No, no. I'll want company,' said Shelley, with slight embarrassment. 'Let me think. You're certainly too fragile to come. I'll take Claire. You'll be all right for a few days, Mary, won't you? Hogg will look after you. I must be there.'

Shelley looked at Mary's face and saw, with an unusual moment of insight, it was not for her physical well-being that Mary was concerned.

'Don't worry, Mary. I have promised you. Nothing until you are ready.'

'What happened?' asked Mary, three days later, when Shelley returned and Claire had gone to her room with her bag.

'The old hypocrite, Mary. They wouldn't let me into Field Place to hear the will read. I'm still not welcome at home. My father is angry with me. So I sat on the porch and read *Comus*. Well, they couldn't exactly eject me from the grounds.'

'How appropriate that you should read Milton's play about virtue,' said Mary, sarcastically.

'His anger was exacerbated when his friend, Dr. Blocksome, was sent to tell me to go and saw your name in the fly-leaf as I closed the pages. Then my uncle, Shelley-Sidney, came out and told me about the contents of the will. My grandfather had a mistress! Old Sir Bysshe, who was so outraged by my morals, has four children by a Mrs. Elanor Nicholls of Canterbury Place Lambeth and, what's more, he provided for them in his will! Luckily, he's too much of a traditionalist to try to leave them anything connected with the estate, but they got money enough. There is a codicil which means I can have income now if I entail the estate. It is complicated. I will have to see the will and think what it means and negotiate with my father. Now I'm too tired to think.'

'I'm pleased it may mean income. Eventually. But that's not what I meant.' Mary was pale, and at six months pregnant, her sloping shoulders were drawn back to support her burden. Her stance and her pallor combined to give her a statuesque dignity.

Shelley took a step back to look at her properly. Then he embraced her.

'You have been worried. I am so sorry.'

'I have been even more sick than usual with worry. I don't want to rush into this thing with Hogg. It has to grow naturally. It's been barely two months. There is no volcano of passion, to erupt as ours did. It is to be a love of a different kind.' Mary's voice sunk to a whisper in his ear. 'I am more scared of the power it would give Claire. The claim she would make on you.'

He kissed her hair and held her firmly. 'She came to my room, Maie. She was clearly wrong-headed about what I had intended.'

'I told you.' Mary tried to twist free, but he still kept her close.

'She threw herself at me and when I demurred, she was persistent. I kissed her, Maie, that's all. Just a kiss. I explained to her, yet again, that your wishes had to be my first consideration. She sobbed and I comforted her. She lay on my bed till she slept, but I swear that is all.'

'Then clearly I must try harder to speed my own affections,' choked Mary, escaping to the bedroom and a night of unrelieved sickness.

Mary tried, and saw the pleasure that Shelley received from her efforts.

Mary to Hogg:

*My own Alexy, I know how much and how tenderly you love me. We look forward to joy and delight in the summer when the trees are green and I have my little baby. With what exquisite pleasure we shall pass the time. You are to teach me Italian, and how many books we will read together. But our still greater happiness will be in Shelley — I who love him so tenderly and entirely and whose life hangs on the beam of his eye and whose whole soul is entirely wrapt up in him. You have such a sincere friendship and want only to make him happy — no we need not try to do that for everything we do will make him that without exertion.*

She truly felt she would manage it. She wanted to manage it. She wanted to believe she wanted to manage it, but she felt paralysed by uncertainty. Everything seemed to wait on her embracing the new status quo. She felt that all of them, Shelley, Claire and Hogg, were watching her and only her distended belly defended her against their unspoken pressure. She blanked out the difficult decisions by constant work on learning Greek and by determined reading — embarking on six volumes of Gibbon's *History of the Decline and Fall of the Roman Empire*. But nothing could dampen the embers of anxiety. The resentment between her and Claire smouldered, often sparking into spats or, when Shelley attempted to play fireman, moderating into smoky silences.

The winter chill got into everyone's lungs and they were all ill with increasing frequency. Shelley's lungs were particularly vulnerable and he coughed the whole of those nightmarish few weeks, as he was locked up with his solicitor. He couldn't sleep at night and dozed each evening in a chair, then read or worked until three am, and Mary worried for him.

She blamed the mess of those five weeks for the labour, which came two months early.

Hogg was there and went for Dr Clarke, who came within five minutes of the birth. The baby was born alive, but was not expected to live.

'Look at her, Shelley.' Mary cradled the tiny being and held her to her breast. 'I will feed her my milk and she will not die. Look, she suckles.'

Shelley sat on the bed beside her and stroked the minute hand.

'My brave Maie.' Shelley kissed her.

Shelley sat with them all night, dozing beside her and bringing her water. In the end she sent him away because he was coughing so much she could not rest.

Next day he sent for Fanny and she came and stayed, defying the Godwins' ban. Claire's brother Charles also visited, having raided Mr. Godwin's linen cupboard to bring them fresh sheets for the beds and to cut up for the baby, and Mary felt herself the vortex of the universe's benevolence.

'Just twelve days, Jefferson. My baby lived twelve days.' Mary threw herself at him, wailing wretchedly, as he came rushing in.

'What happened?' asked Hogg, leading her to the sofa and wiping her face with his handkerchief. 'She was doing so well. You were nursing her all day, everyday. She was sleeping well ...'

'I don't know. I don't know. I awoke in the night to give her suck and in the candlelight she appeared to be sleeping quietly so I didn't wake her, but in the daylight we saw that she was dead.'

'Oh my poor Mary.'

'You are such a calm person, Jefferson. Can you stay today? I need you. Shelley is gone for Dr. Clarke. He is terrified I will die of milk-fever. He is already exhausted from sleepless nights and endless coughing, and he believes he will die too, after his visit to Dr. Pemberton.'

'Do you think Dr. Pemberton is right about his consumption?'

'I don't know.' Mary's sobbing grew louder. 'Oh, Alexy, I am not a mother anymore. This past week has been a revelation. In spite of my love for Shelley, I hadn't thought I could feel such a passion for another human creature. That baby owned me, and now I am cast adrift.'

'No, no, you are here with those who love you. There will be lots more babies.'

'Before you came I drifted into a doze from exhaustion and I dreamed we warmed the baby by the fire and she came to life again. This anguish is worse than all the fires of Hell I ever imagined. It burns every nerve and leaves an unfeeling void.'

'Where is Claire?'

'Gone with Shelley, of course. She is much more concerned about him than me. That's all she's done, is be with Shelley. When we had to move, three days ago, she organised it with him. She goes to the doctor with him and sympathises with him so much that he believes himself the worse, and so he has little time for me.

'This is her fault,' continued Mary, bitterly. 'If she did not plague our lives I would not have had a seven month baby.'

'That's probably a little unfair,' soothed Hogg, stroking her hair.

'Is it? I hear that worry can induce an early labour. In any case. It has to stop. She has to go. Shelley has to choose. It's her or me.'

# INTERMISSION

Shelley and Byron
Lake Geneva 1816

'The rest of the world, and she among them,
judged of her actions, by their consequences.'

*The Last Man*, Mary Shelley

'I don't know why you love the water so much, when you can't swim, Shelley,' said Byron, pulling gently on the jib as the boat bobbed in the calm lake. 'We nearly drowned yesterday in that squall. And you, you idiot, sitting there on the locker holding on to the rings, shouting at me to go, insisting I wasn't going to be allowed to save you.'

'It's simple,' answered Shelley, smiling ironically. 'I can never rival you as a poet. Poetry must be preserved at all costs. I won't imperil your valuable life by letting you cast it away to save me.'

'You're either an idiot, or the least selfish man I ever knew.' Byron was mildly exasperated.

'I am selfish in enjoying these past three days exploring the lakeside villages. The wild magnificence of the scenery. The mountains, so bright with snow, coming down those broken slopes to the lake. The air so blue and the groves of walnuts and chestnuts. The peace and good conversation between us.'

'You make me believe that life could be near perfect right here and now, Shilo. I'm even beginning to be imbued with your damned philosophy – and your dosing of me with Wordsworth. I seem to be writing poems about Deep Love and Thought. You've got a lot to answer for. The only little fiendish blight on the horizon is Claire, and the bastard you tell me she is about to produce. I don't know how this happened, Shilo. Where were you back in May when the young lady stalked me?'

'Mary had given me an ultimatum about her. It was her or Mary. Mary couldn't stand having her in the house anymore after she lost the first baby. I finally came to an arrangement with my father about an income and I sent her down to Lynmouth to stay with an elderly lady. To have a 'holiday'. She was supposed to come back to stay with us when we moved to Bishopsgate, but she disappeared to London. In any case 'stalked' is a harsh, expression.'

'She stalked me. The consequences of not being in love are perhaps as disagreeable as anything except being so, but I'm certainly not in love with her. Be fair, Shelley. If a girl of 18 comes prancing to you at all hours there is but one way.'

'She was that brazen?'

'Look.' Byron took some papers from his inside pocket. 'I brought these to prove it to you, just a couple. You know I keep all letters. Look at this one.' He passed it to Shelley.

*An utter stranger takes the liberty of addressing you. It is earnestly requested that for one moment you pardon the intrusion and laying aside every remembrance of who and what you are, listen with a friendly ears. A moment of passion, or an impulsive pride often destroys our own happiness and that of others. If in this case your refusal shall not affect yourself, yet you are not aware how much it means to another. It is not charity I demand, for of that I stand in no need: I implied by that you should think kindly and gently at this letter, that if I seemed impertinent, you should pardon it for a while, and that you should wait patiently for I am emboldened by you to disclose myself.*

*I tremble with fear at the fate of this letter. I cannot blame if it should be received by you as an impudent imposture. There are cases where that you may stoop to assume the garb of folly; for it is the piercing eye of genius to discover her disguise, do you then give me credit for something better that this letter may seem to portend. Mine is a delicate case; my feet are on the edge of a precipice; Hope flying on forward wings beckons me to follow her and rather than resign this cherished creature, I jumped through at the peril of my Life.*

*If a woman, whose reputation has yet remain unstained, if without yet a guardian or husband to control, she should throw herself upon your mercy, if with a beating heart she should confess the love she has born you many years, if she should secure to you secrecy and safety, if she should return your kindness with fond affection and unbounded devotion, could you betray her, or would you be silent as the grave?*

*I am not given to many words. Either you will or you will not.*

'She said she wanted my advice on her play. I'm on the Board at Drury Lane, as you know. Then it was her novel. I was honest about both. She has some small talent but not enough to survive among the London literati. Then it was on how to be an actress. I recommended her to Kinnaird, but she didn't take it up. She wrote or called on me every second day. She told me your story, yours and Mary's; she certainly has a flair for drama. She described you as the man she had loved and for whom she had suffered. She swears that she is not jealous of Mary, but now accepts that Mary will be first for you. Wise man. I half fell in love with Mary myself when Claire brought her to meet me. That was one reason I agreed to meet in Geneva – and of course to meet the author of *Queen Mab*,' he smiled and inclined his head to Shelley.

Shelley laughed ruefully. 'Mary's theory is that it has been a ploy for Claire to best her. You are a major celebrity; I am a little known and not much loved, poet. You are Baron, I am a mere Baronet.'

'Can you really assure me that the brat is mine? She was certainly *intactus* at our first encounter. But then?'

'I can,' replied Shelley. 'I have to confess I visited her at Lynmouth once unbeknownst to Mary. I felt sad for her and thought she was lonely, but it only served to make her more angry, to find that Mary remained my main concern. Then when she learned Mary was pregnant again with William … well.

'After that I paid for her to accompany her brother Charles on a business venture to Ireland. She came to Bishopsgate when William was born, but Mary was very anxious about his health, and Claire was not tolerant. That's when she fled to London. She stayed with the Godwins. She is single minded and determined. And she wanted you, I'm afraid.'

Byron sighed, 'I was even more vulnerable than usual to female incursions after my separation from Belle, and Claire was more interesting than the usual run of my carnal connections, quoting Dante in Italian, and talking of free love. Her mania for secrecy suited me, as well. London society had enough of "kiss and tell" about me. So what now?'

Shelley played with the rudder as a light breeze threatened to take them too close to shore. 'I will provide for them both, Claire and the baby, in my will, but we must keep it a secret from the Godwins, from my father and from London society. There would be gossip that the baby was mine and Mary and I would be even more unwelcome in that desolate island than we already are. We think we should go to Bath and take separate lodgings there for Claire and us until the baby is born. But will you acknowledge it, Albe?'

'I may consent to raise it, when it is fit to leave its mother, but I will have sole control and I will not have any contact with Claire, Shiloh. She is a vixen. She plagues me constantly for signs of affection which I have never promised. Her tongue is so vicious when she is angry. I fear that she will prove to be another Caroline Lamb.' He shuddered.

'Yes, you do seem to generate obsessions in women. I fear that Caroline's epithet for you, "mad, bad and dangerous to know" will outlive you. You know that she has written a novel about you, *Glenarvon*? Have you seen it?'

'Not yet. It's being sent. God damn the woman!'

'We will reach the Castle of Chillon soon,' said Shelley, anxious to change the subject now that some concession had be made about Claire's baby, to change the subject. 'Remember Rousseau mentions François Bonnivard who was chained to a pillar in the cellar for six years after fighting the Duke of Savoy? They say you can see the wearing away in the floor of his pacing.'

'A subject for verse, perhaps?' replied Byron, staring at the battlements of Chillon as they came into view, impressively rising out of the lake, the morning sun reflecting off its turrets and the snow-capped mountains behind.

He turned back to Shelley. 'Nurture your Mary. I respect her, she commands sincere admiration and she is worth a thousand Claires. Don't risk her for Claire. Don't let your blessed philanthropy blind you to Mary's needs. And have her finish that story about the monster.'

# PART FOUR

England
Bath and Marlow 1816 — 1819

# 1

'My intellect could master all except my fate.'

*Journal*, Mary Shelley

*Write my book.*

Later, when Mary looked back over her journal entries that started from the time they had arrived in Bath in September, she realised how often she had included this phrase. Writing her book was her escape from the assault of the real world.

It was not that her alternate fantasy world was a carefree creation, but it was always in her head as a dark passion consuming much of her thought. By contemplating the anguish of her creatures, she was able to temporarily forget her own.

Shelley was too preoccupied to write much, so reading, correcting and discussing Mary's work generated the creative energy in the household. He really believed in her project and she loved how unselfish he was about it. When she asked him to edit her pages, he tried hard to remember that his own writing was different to hers, more literary and abstract, and to suggest changes in keeping with her style. No offence was taken if she ignored them. He mainly contented himself with directing her to read Humphrey Davy for the latest scientific revelations, especially about electricity, and passages in Milton's *Paradise Lost* for thoughts on creation and Hell.

For a few weeks after they got back from Geneva, it appeared that their careful planning would work. Mary went straight down to Bath and found an attractive apartment for herself, Shelley, William and the stray kitten they had adopted in Geneva. They had also brought the young nursemaid, Elise Duvillard, back with them. Although not quite a stray, they had adopted her too, and were all rather fond of the diminutive blonde seamstress. She adored William and, having six siblings herself, was a caring and capable nursemaid. Because of her past trade, she was also useful in making baby clothes and in helping Mary and Claire to remake or repair their dresses, as the fashion changed and Claire's shape expanded.

The apartment was in the Abbey Churchyard, two doors away from the entrance to the fashionable Pump Room of the Spa. Opposite, in the cobbled yard, was the entrance to the fifteenth century gothic masterpiece that was the Cathedral. Mary knew Shelley would love the architecture if not the habitués. She took the rooms in the morning and by the afternoon she found their disadvantage was the coach traffic coming in from Cheap Street, crowding the churchyard and setting down hordes of fashionable visitors intent on drinking the spa waters, known to guarantee good health or new acquaintance.

For Claire she found rooms very close, in New Bond Street, with a motherly landlady. Claire, who was disgustingly blooming in pregnancy, was introduced as Mrs. Clairmont, whose husband was detained on business in Europe.

Shelley went first to London to deal with his financial affairs, and then to Marlow in Buckinghamshire. Peacock and his mother had moved there, to a rambling old villa called the Hermitage, and Shelley stayed with them while he went looking for a house to lease, where they could move after Claire had the baby. Their fantasy was a big house in the country, with a garden for their little Willmouse, preferably near the river. They wanted one place they could settle into and call home, now that there was an agreement with his father and the terms of the inheritance would soon be settled.

The only benefit for Mary of their exile in Bath was that she had an excuse to go and meet Shelley in Marlow, without Claire. She got on the coach, deaf to Claire's protestations that it was all too much excitement for Shelley's health, that William was getting a chill, and that she hadn't enough money to pay the washerwoman. A week without Claire! Her head was already lighter. A week without Claire, even if it meant staying with the Peacocks, felt to Mary like a little parcel of life wrapped in tissue and tied with curling ribbons. Anyhow, Peacock, previously Harriet's champion, was quite accepting of her now. She had felt his attitude towards her change from cynical to polite, to pleasant, and latterly, even to warm. She could tell because, in his new book, *Melincourt,* he had directed some of his sardonic wit, that spared no-one he liked, towards her. Its heroine, he said, was a young girl whose mother had died in childbirth and whose father: "*a man of great acquirements, and of a retired disposition, devoted himself in solitude to the cultivation of his daughter's understanding; for he was one of those who maintained the heretical notion that women are, or at least may be, rational beings; though, from the great pains usually taken in what is called education to make them otherwise, there are unfortunately very few examples to warrant the truth of the theory.*" Mary was not sure if it was flattering to be portrayed as the exception that proves the rule.

There proved no perfect house to be found as yet, and a week was long enough away from Itty Babe, even at the expense of returning to Claire. Shelley went on for two days in London and Mary returned to Bath. They agreed that Shelley would see Mary's half-sister, Fanny, if she could escape the Godwins temporarily, and get the family news.

'How was Fanny?' Mary asked Shelley on his return, as they walked along the streets of Bath, down the elegant length of the Grand Parade towards Pulteney Bridge.

'She was so pleased to see me and it was good she agreed to meet. Godwin, of course, was ignorant of it. She wanted news of you, of Claire, of Willmouse. Details. Of what we were writing, reading. From your letter she had an idealised view of our life here. Still, she couldn't understand why we had come to Bath.'

'What did you say?'

'As we agreed, I said we came so that I could take the waters for my consumption. It rings true, because she knows the doctor diagnosed my illness before we went to Geneva. That was our avowed reason for leaving Bishopsgate in the spring, for the clean air of Switzerland. Of course she doesn't know of Claire's persuasion, or of her ulterior motive to be near Byron. It was true, in a way. In spite of the foul weather we had there, I do think the mountains helped. I feel a lot better.'

'I am very glad of it,' smiled Mary, as they reached the bridge lined with shops, and passed the seller of warm Sally Lunn Bath buns.

Shelley stopped to buy them one each and continued talking, though indistinctly through a mouthful of lemon-scented soft pastry spread with clotted cream.

'I pointed out that this city has long literary associations to inspire us. I diverted her with the lovely legend about the city having been founded eight centuries before Christ by King Lear's father, Prince Bladud. How he was driven from the Court because he got leprosy, and became a swineherd and passed the disease onto his pigs.'

'Of course' interrupted Mary, impatiently, 'it's an entertaining story, but not much of a reason to be here. In any case, I think it's an unlikely legend, to believe he just stumbled on hot mud that cured the pigs when they wallowed in it and it cured him too, and hey presto, we have a grand spa town!.'

'You are such a cynic!' Shelley laughed. 'Why do I love a cynic?' He shook his head in mock despair, and Mary raised her eyebrows and lowered her lashes in a confused and doomed attempt to look wide-eyed and demurely innocent. 'Well, in any case I also mentioned, let me see, Addison, Pope, Smollett, Goldsmith, and Sheridan who have lived here. Was that all right? Mary, if they have left only a little of their collective genius germinating in the stones of these walls, we should be able to nourish the flower of your imagination for your book while we're here!' He squeezed her hand where it rested on his arm, and beamed,

'Hmm. Do you think to sweeten me with metaphor? At least you didn't mention blossoming. If you'd said blossom I might have become violent. I resent blossoming.' Mary narrowed her eyes at him. 'We won't be here for long enough to absorb much, I hope. Anyway, Fanny would most probably have believed that you wanted the waters for your health. She's very worried about your health. Do you think she did believe you?'

'Yes, I think so, but she was clearly looking for an invitation to visit.' Shelley bit his bottom lip, guiltily. 'I felt a little sad to ignore her hints.'

'She wasn't at all suspicious? It would be awful if she gave any cause to Papa or Mama to suspect Claire's condition.'

'No. She thinks that we don't want her because we see her as Mrs. Godwin's ally against us. She tried to say others poison people against us, not your stepmother. According to her, Mama Godwin just relates gossip about us, which she 'happened to hear' from a cottager in Bracknell, where she 'happened' to stop for a rest when she was walking, on a visit to a friend. Of course Bracknell is where I lived for a time with Harriet and her credibility is high there. Mrs. Godwin clearly chooses to pass on any calumny about us and Fanny does not want to think the worst of her.'

They came to Sidney Place, walked through the Hotel and paid their sixpence to walk into the broad acres of Sidney Gardens. A small band was playing on the balcony overlooking the grounds and they set off along the main walk through luxuriant overhanging trees, past pretty arbours and small waterfalls. It was a chilly autumn evening so there were relatively few promenaders on the path. They avoided the Labyrinth, with the sounds of lost revellers shrieking and laughing from inside, and made straight for the canal path, which ran below the pretty iron bridges and out of sight of the rest of the gardens. Shelley always felt soothed by water.

As the sounds of the music faded, Mary asked, 'What's become of the plan for Fanny to go and teach in Ireland, at the school of Everina Wollstonecraft, our mother's cousin?'

'Everina was in London, but she's gone back to Ireland and Fanny has evidently not gone with her. She would not be drawn to explain, and Everina does have financial woes, but ...'

'You think it is her association with the seducer and the whore that blights her prospects?'

'In all probability.'

'Fanny feels Godwin's financial disasters most strongly. She takes responsibility. She wants not to be a burden and she feels helpless to contribute. Remember how she told us to write small in our letters because she has no money of her own and can't pay the postage for the weight of too many pages, when she receives them? I can understand it, but I still can't forgive her for being so abject. She should stand up to them.'

'Poor Fanny. I would like to help her.'

'We could not abduct another member of the household, and only abduction would do. It's our side or theirs.'

They walked silently for a while along the rough pebbled towpath by the canal, both resentful of the way they were forced to account for the reactions of others. Mary longed for nothing more than to be left alone with Shelley. She picked up some pebbles and hurled them angrily into the water, punishing it for the actions of the world. The narrowboatmen, hearing the splashes, turned to look, but seeing that it was only some eccentric gentry and not a drowning, continued to drink and punt their wares down the canal.

Shelley's contemplation of their difficulties resulted in a coughing spasm, as it often did. Although they had decided not to fully believe the diagnosis of consumption, made before they went to Switzerland, it had scared them both. There was no doubt that Shelley was not strong. Although she did not understand how the mind could affect the health, Mary felt sure that Shelley tolerated mental anguish by routing it into his chest or his side, his weakest points. She was close to insisting that he eat meat as a strengthening measure, though it wasn't a battle she wanted to fight. When they found a place to live at Marlow, near Peacock, she would co-opt his wonderful cynicism and they could assault Shelley's sensibilities together.

They went back up some steps by a bridge into the main part of the Gardens and sat in a little pavilion. Mary had a boy bring them seltzer water. From here the man on the Merlin Swing swayed occasionally into their view, suspended above the Labrynth as if in flight, calling out directions to those lost inside.

'We should go back after we've drunk this. We've done enough walking for you today,' she said, firmly.

As they started back, they took to discussing the troubles of Victor Frankenstein, instead of their own.

'Any more ideas on how the story will unfold?' asked Shelley.

'Well, he creates a man-like creature of course. From dead body parts. It will be huge, I think. Seven or eight feet, to allow him to build all of the complex bits inside more easily. Because it has to be fully functioning. That also makes it more scary and dangerous.

Victor will be horrified with the inhuman look of it and will reject it, and then the creature will take revenge on him and those he loves. So first of all I have to start by describing who those people are and also why he has such a passion for natural philosophy and the urge to unravel the mysteries of creation. Then I want to give the creature a voice. So often the monstrous is left without any motivation except evil. I think evil comes from a more human cause, don't you?'

Shelley smiled, fondly. 'Does Victor grow up in Geneva?'

'Yes. Rather aristocratic, of course. Now, what do you think? I have him with an older, philanthropic father, who had married the daughter of a ruined business friend, who died. The mother is a paragon of virtue, of course. Mothers have to be in tales, whatever they are in real life. Victor has two brothers — I can't deal with sisters. Both are much younger. One is twelve years younger, whom I have called William, because he has lively blue eyes and dimpled cheeks, like our William. Then there is a best friend, Henry something, and an adopted cousin, Elizabeth, with whom he is to be in love and is promised to. Are they enough earthly ties, do you think?'

'It seems ample. Do they all die?'

'I'm not yet sure. The mother certainly will, from natural causes, because he needs to be free from her steadying influence. Probably all the others are killed by the creature. I'm not as far as that, yet.'

'What about his education. How does he develop his passion?'

'A chance encounter with the works of the alchemist Cornelius Agrippa will start him spending his youth looking for the Philosophers' Stone and the Elixir of Life, and trying to raise ghosts. Then he goes to university and encounters real, modern science such as chemistry and biology, but the lust for solving the mysteries remains. The science, though, gives him new tools.'

'So what he achieves will be through science, not magic.'

'Exactly. So it will be his human decision to play God. There is no Devil involved. Now I am just up to where he goes away to Ingolstadt, to university, a restless boy, really. Unhappy with the teaching he is getting. Arguing. Wanting more. You must read through the first three chapters for me. Well, two, and the beginning of three.'

Shelley snapped his fingers. 'Yes, yes. There's something I meant to tell you …' He kicked some pebbles while he thought. 'Oh, that's it. In London, I was looking through the books we had left stored at Marchmont Street, and started reading Fontanelle's *Life of Newton* again. Listen, Mary, Newton was supposed to have said: *"I was like a boy playing on the sea-shore, and diverting myself now and then finding a smoother pebble or a prettier shell than ordinary, whilst the great ocean of truth lay all undiscovered before me."* That would be how Victor felt I think, don't you?'

'Yes, undoubtedly. He reminds me of you. Always certain that there is a great truth if only it can be grasped.'

'You understand me too well, Maie,' Shelley sounded grateful. 'I will go to my grave searching for it.'

They left the Gardens and walked through the dusk back towards Abbey Churchyard, past the lamplighters, and past the taverns which were starting to fill with shop-keepers and street-hawkers coming in for their supper and ale and a little congenial company.

Shelley's breathing was still quite laboured and his hand unconsciously moved inside his coat to clutch his chest as he walked. In contrast to his weak health, for once Mary felt strong. She had just finished breast-feeding eight-month-old William and her body, for the first time in a year and a half, was her own.

When she looked at her baby and his attempts to communicate and to crawl, she felt she was watching the formation of letters on a beautiful blank parchment. There was a creative delight in motherhood that she had not expected. She had suppressed memories of her difficult pregnancy, and was already thinking of the likelihood of a sibling for William, now she was no longer breast feeding. Shelley might not be overjoyed. He saw himself as a loving father and he had his own father's example to counter. Shelley envisaged parenting as having a mind to mould and a partner to sail paper boats, and this model had yet to spring fully functioning into their lives. Their apartment was too small for William to have a separate nursery and the chaos of Elise chasing a crawling, bare bottomed, bawling baby around the parlour to get his arms into his nightgown was not conducive to poetic inspiration. It was a topic to be broached carefully, gradually. Maybe starting with some discussion about 'Itty Babe's' new ability to say something approximating cat.

Shelley pre-empted her intentions by suddenly asking, anxiously, 'Did you hire a piano for Claire?'

'Oh, Claire, Claire. Yes, I did. It arrives tomorrow.'

'Is she comfortable and well?'

'Comfortable, yes, and physically well, but she has written long letters to Albe, and every day when there is no reply she is more frantic. She comes every afternoon and plays sometimes with William — now of course she is an expert on children — and we walk in the town, even though she is poor company. She talks of nothing but Byron. Speculates on what he's doing. Makes excuses as to why he has not written. Praises and curses him by turns. It is so frustrating. She is so blind to the real situation. She cannot see that she has any fault in his rejecting her.' Mary shook her head irritably.

'On the one hand she writes things like '*I would die to please and serve you*,' and then she can't help herself from making pointed remarks about his half-sister, Augusta Leigh, bound to infuriate him. I mean, I don't know if it's true about Byron's illicit relationship with her, but what good does Claire think it's going to do to mention it?'

Shelley sighed. 'Apparently he told her that the gossip was true about him and Mrs. Leigh, but I am sure that was to make Claire leave. He was quite desperate to disentangle himself.'

'Now she thinks she has the ultimate hold. A baby.' Mary's tone was cynical. 'She really has no idea about relationships.'

She was thinking about Claire's last letter to Byron. The table and sideboard were usually scattered with half-finished notes, novels and poems, their journals, and letters in progress — none of them covered or hidden. Claire had been unusually close about her most recent one to Byron. Mary suspected that in it, Claire had been rude about her, and she couldn't resist trying to see. So she asked Claire to open up the letter so that she could send her remembrances at the bottom, and was rewarded with a glimpse of her name and a few words: *Your favourite, Mary, is impertinent enough and nauseous enough …* How did Claire possibly think that displaying her jealousy of Mary would help her cause with Byron? It was unfathomable. And if she did think that Mary was his favourite, how did criticising her help, either?

'I will write to Albe and ask him to send her a line, or at least a message via me,' said Shelley, thoughtfully. 'Do you think we are right to encourage her in wanting to give her child to him to bring up?'

'Yes.' Mary was definite. 'If he keeps his promise to do so.'

'He gave me his word. He is a gentleman,' Shelley replied, a little stiffly.

'Ah, a gentleman,' muttered Mary.

It took her by surprise sometimes to remember that her Shelley, her own Elfin Knight, was heir to a real title. The values of fair play from the playing fields of Eton had moulded him, even though he always pointed out that he had avoided sports at all cost. Byron, a Harrow man, and he shared the instinctive code of the English Public School, however much they wanted to flout or reform the conventions of society. Mary's father was middle class, the son of a dissenting minister. Her mother was the daughter of failed farmers. Although Shelley and Mary travelled as equals on intellectual aspiration, their baggage was vastly different. Shelley seemed not to notice, but Mary understood the influences. It was why he felt so comfortable in Byron's company. It was an intrinsic familiarity, unusual amongst their bohemian literary peers.

When they got back to The Abbey Churchyard, Claire was there, arranged to advantage on the floor with Elise, cutting out nightdresses for William. She bounded up at the sight of them, loose curls flying, scattering scissors and pins, and rushed to embrace Shelley.

'There you are!' she cried, pulling back to examine him critically. 'I don't know what Mary can be thinking, taking you off after you'd spent sixteen hours on the mail coach, and with your poor, painful head.

'Now, I have got the cook to send up bread, cheese and fruit, since I had no idea when you'd return.' She paused to glare at Mary. 'So eat something and tell me all about London.'

Shelley took off his coat, further undid his collar, took a peach from the sideboard and threw himself into an armchair.

'Thanks, sweet girl,' he smiled at Claire. 'Forgive me, I am rather tired. What can I tell you? I signed the settlement with my father; I made a will; my debts are paid; I have an income but no capital. I have taken Albe's third canto of *Childe Harold*, and his other poem, *The Prisoner of Chillon*, to the publisher, as he asked. The capital is reeling from the trial of two policemen, Bow Street Runners. They induced men to commit crimes so that they could then capture them and gain the reward. Human ingenuity and greed, eh! And I saw Fanny. She's well. Are you feeling well? No sickness?'

'Only of the heart,' replied Claire, looking to be about to burst into tears.

'I know, poor Claire. Let me talk to you more tomorrow, when I can think clearly.' He picked up her shawl and draped it around her shoulders and guided her to the door. 'Elise will walk back home with you.' He took Mary's hand and they went into the bedroom.

If things had stayed as they were, Mary might have thought that their life was no worse than it might be. It was just five months until Claire's term. Freedom. They could go to Marlow, make up a story about the child, maybe his 'Aunt Claire' looking after him or her. Claire would have a new obsession to take her focus off Mary and Shelley. The two of them would roam the woods and rivers, Shelley would write and the world could go hang. They could get some control back over their lives. Control was what she most desired. Not control over others, but a sense that she had a chance of making things happen to her design. Shelley was different, all dash and rush to get things done and then happy or frustrated at the outcome.

For the moment, control seemed to be becoming even more elusive. In their isolated situation the letters that were usually their life-blood, now seemed more like vampires that were draining it.

Shelley wrote to Byron, full of praise, encouraging, engaging, hoping for a spring visit, reporting on Claire's health. Asking, but not asking, for him to give her and them some word of reassurance. *I do not know how great an intellectual compass you are destined to fulfil. I only know that your powers are astonishingly great. Shall we see you in the spring? You will destroy all our rural arrangements if you fail in this promise. You will do more. You will strike a link out of the chain of life, which, esteeming you, and cherishing your society as we do, we cannot easily spare.*

Claire wrote a sentimental, sycophantic letter to Byron, complaining of his cruelty and bemoaning her suffering. *If you will write me a little letter to say how you are, and above all if you will say you think sometimes of me without anger and that you will take care of the Child, I will be as happy as possible. I love you my dearest friend and you shall, even if it makes me miserable, do as you like.*

Fanny wrote to them, with a touch of hysteria and perhaps, with hindsight, desperation. She blamed their servants for spreading the gossip about them. Anyone but Mama. Mainly it was her tone about Godwin that incensed Mary. Fanny pleaded for Shelley to take over Godwin's debts. Worry about money was stopping him from writing and the new novel was essential to his health and to alleviating his financial woes. *Is it not your and Shelley's duty to prevent, as far as it lies in your power, giving him unnecessary pain and anxiety?* Shelley had promised £300 to Godwin when he thought there might be some left over after the settlement with his father. However, one of his father's conditions was that he did not enter into any more debt, and Shelley had told Godwin that he couldn't shoulder this obligation after all and sent him a cheque for £200, all he could afford.

Godwin wrote an angry letter to Shelley on the same day. *I return your cheque because no consideration can induce me to utter a cheque drawn by you and containing my name. You may make it payable to Joseph Hume. I will negotiate myself out of the danger of prison if I can.*

Fathers. Sisters. Mary was despairing. Her respect for her father was deep-seated, but he had cut them for more than a year now. She wanted to beat her fists against his chest and whine that he was being unfair. From Claire she only ever expected difficulties, but if there was any other member of her disparate family that Mary had been close to, it was Fanny, and now she felt betrayed. Of course she felt a duty to her father, but he was her father, not Fanny's, so who was Fanny to accuse her and Shelley of not doing enough?

# 2

'Of what materials was I made that I could thus
resist so many shocks, which, like the turning of
the wheel, continually renewed the torture?'

*Frankenstein or The Modern Prometheus,* Mary Shelley

Just two days after the last letters from Fanny and Godwin, came
another from Fanny. Mary would always clearly remember the
moment of its arrival. It was a fine, crisp autumn Tuesday morning
and she was sitting at breakfast with Willmouse on her knee, feeding
him some bread and laughing at his attempts to stuff more into his
mouth. She was temporarily distracted by the play of morning sun
on the Abbey wall carvings opposite, which animated the angels
climbing Jacob's ladder to heaven, so, when William reached up to
pull her hair for attention he managed to poke her in the eye instead.
She squealed in pain and dumped him on the floor to wipe her
streaming eye with the hem of her petticoat and the baby squalled
at the unfathomable change in the mood of the morning. The maid
rushed in to help, clutching a note marked *urgent*.

Fanny wrote that she was in Bath. Now. This morning. She had
arrived on the overnight mail, on her way to Bristol, then Ireland, she
said. She had an hour at the Greyhound Inn coach stop. Could she
see them?

Mary woke Shelley. They were seriously alarmed.

'We must see her, but she must not see Claire. She might expect
to see her too,' puffed Shelley, as he pulled on his trousers.

'It is interesting that she addresses this to all of us. So why is she
going to Ireland?' wondered Mary as they got coats and gloves and set
off to the Inn. 'She said the aunts didn't want her. I hope she is not
going to harangue us about paying Godwin's debts.'

Their meeting with Fanny was strange. They had only half an
hour with her by the time they got to the inn. Fanny was waiting

patiently sitting on a bench outside. She was alone in the bustle of steaming horses at trough, postboys running with laden bags, impatient passengers stamping their feet on the footpath in the chill or drinking warm possetts as they waited for the coaches to be loaded for the next stage of the journey. She looked fresh enough after her overnight trip from London. The small French locket watch that they had sent her from Geneva was prominently pinned to her brown pelisse, which was trimmed with fur and pulled tight against the nip in the air. It covered her best dress — a striped blue skirt with a white bodice — not her traveling clothes. Mary had not seen her for six months and her main thought was how much smaller she was than she remembered. Surely her memory could not be so flawed. The sense of her sister as diminished, persisted as she hugged her.

They walked together, slowly, part of the way down North Parade. Their conversation was horribly stilted, constrained by things unsaid and unsayable without painful bluntness. No-one wanted to create tension that couldn't be resolved in so short a time, to leave accusations or recriminations hovering like unswatted flies. So Mary asked cheerfully after her father, his health and his progress with his book, as if they had just called round for tea to some mild acquaintance, where the only possible answer to such an enquiry is one of cheerful optimism. Fanny duly replied with platitudes about Godwin, clearly having decided not to be accused of being on a mission to extract promises. When Shelley asked about her journey and why she was going to Ireland, her eyes darted and sunk. She merely said there were opportunities for work and quickly turned the conversation to the beauty of Bath and the lovely Bath stone on the terraces they were passing. Shelley obligingly talked about the famous people who had lived in them, Wordsworth, Oliver Goldsmith, Edmund Burke. She asked about Mary's book and was told about the plot and the progress. She asked what Shelley had written lately, and did not remind him of his promise to send her his descriptions of his tour around Lake Geneva. Her voice quivered as they returned to the coach yard and she kissed Mary, telling her that she loved her and was jealous of her independence. She also said that their mother would have been proud of her, a comment which surprised and unsettled Mary. She hung back while Shelley shepherded Fanny the rest of the way through the small crowd and saw her to the coach. She watched him take her hands in his and saw her sister look at him with what seemed some deep sadness, start to speak, then turn and climb into her seat.

'She was going to ask me something, I'm sure,' said Shelley, as they walked back.

Mary burst into tears.

'She seemed so … absent,' she sobbed, snuffling into Shelley's handkerchief and trying to avoid the curious glances of passers-by by pretending a hay-feverish sneeze.

'It is all so strange, only telling us she was here at the last minute and not giving a proper answer about where she is going.'

They walked on in tensioned silence until Shelley said the thing that hung over them, unspoken because of the ramifications that complicated simple guilt.

'Did she want us to invite her to stay, do you think?'

It had all been so sudden. They had no time to discuss how they should respond, to think through what it would mean, to weigh up how much Fanny needed it against the wrath of the Godwins and the weight of further responsibility and social opprobrium, after the lesson of Claire. Neither had been prepared to speak without consulting the other, or without having had time to find out from Fanny what she really meant.

They kept themselves busy for the rest of the day. Mary had started drawing lessons and her lesson that day should have been a soothing retreat, but she sat in Mr. West's studio with her pencil unsteady, ruining sheet after sheet of his best paper as she stared at the curves of the fruit and flowers in the still life. The lines would not come right. It was like the insides of other people's heads. They seemed smooth and balanced, but the arrangement was really infinitely complex. Why had she not understood Fanny? What should she have done? She picked over and over the events of the morning, looking for shapes and patterns. Fanny must have decided to come at the last minute or she would have written sooner. Had something happened at Skinner Street to prompt her flight? A fuss with Mrs. Godwin?

Too much pressure from Papa? She had seemed so detached, as if she were absenting herself from an unkind reality. The time had been so short at the coach station. All the questions had formed afterwards. Mary regretted her last, angry letter to Fanny, accusing her of being Mama's apologist. That woman had much to answer for. She remembered suddenly that, when they were in Geneva, Fanny had written that Mrs. Godwin accused the three of them of making fun of Fanny. It was unkind and untrue, but Fanny had so easily believed her. She must have felt really friendless. Poor sweet, plain, Fanny. Did she also love Shelley, as Claire had implied, and feel jealous and rejected? Mary interrogated her own feelings to see if that thought, once planted, had, subliminally made her less sympathetic to Fanny. Fanny's last remark to her this morning, about their mother, bothered her. She recalled that Fanny had she would not live to be a disgrace to such a mother. The chair clattered as Mary stood up suddenly and begged Mr. West to forgive her for cutting her lesson short.

Claire came in the afternoon and was told of the visit and her narrow escape from detection.

'Thank goodness. She would have taken the news straight back to Skinner Street, and Mama would have believed it your child,' she grinned at Shelley. 'Then she would have been distraught thinking herself the only rejected sister.'

'I'm not so sure,' said Mary sharply. 'I think we might have trusted her. I wish we had. I wish I had, and made her stay. What if she does love Shelley? I think she,' and her emphasis was on the last word, 'would have been happy to be with us as our friend and see the possibilities of a home where she did not feel a supplicant. She is the only one of us who doesn't have a parent in Skinner Street.'

Claire blushed with fury at Mary's implication. 'So, you would welcome her, I suppose, as a tranquil influence and Shelley could have more Wollstencraft genes to mould. Clearly you chose the wrong sister to take away.' She glared defiantly at them both.

'Now, we should not worry,' Shelley interposed to defuse the impending storm and to reassure them all, including himself. 'Perhaps there really was a last minute call from the Irish aunts and we will hear soon that she is safe and settled. That's what we all want.'

Shelley had been reading Don Quixote to them and continued after dinner. Mary knew straightaway it was a an unfortunate choice. Even though comic, Quixote's desire to chivalrously rescue maidens, was, on this evening, too close to Shelley's natural inclination. He felt that he had failed Fanny who was clearly in need of rescue. He frequently paused, his attention wandering, eyes rolling across the words as if they were too slippery to make sense. All he asked of the world was the means to set it right, but he felt frustrated at every turn. He always seemed to be losing the battle with narrow-minded, prejudiced people, who failed to see beyond convention, who missed the possibility of beauty and harmony, who persecuted the innocent, like Fanny.

The following day, Wednesday, there was another letter from Fanny, saying she hoped never to return and bother them again, since she would be dead by the time they received it. It arrived at seven pm, and Shelley immediately rode off to Bristol to chase after her. He returned at two next morning and found Claire and Mary sitting up, huddled around the dying fire, waiting for news. He had none. Claire slept in the chair.

He dozed for a few hours then set off at eight to catch the morning coach and again travel the thirteen miles to Bristol. He came back at eleven that evening, drawn and weary.

'I went to every inn and interrogated every coachman in Bristol,' he said, struggling through exhaustion to tell them. 'Finally, about seven, I found a driver who remembered her. She had taken the Cambrian Coach to Swansea, in South Wales. She took it early yesterday morning and he had just come back with it on the return journey. He said that when he dropped her off she looked tired but appeared calm and she went to the Mackworth Arms, the coaching inn, to rest. I'll go to Swansea tomorrow and we must hope for good news.'

The next morning, Friday, he tried to reassure Mary as he again set off early heading for Swansea.

'I may not be back tonight. If I take the fastest route it is a difficult journey. It's eighty miles and the Severn crossing is difficult. I'll hire post horses again, and ride — it's faster than the coach — and hope for good tides for the ferry. Then it's another few hours to Swansea. But I will be back tomorrow, I hope with Fanny. She must have been in great distress, but we must pray the journey has calmed her. Get some sleep tonight. I'll be back before the mail could reach you. Work, Mary to keep your mind occupied. Write a scene where Victor is anxious about the fate of someone he loves.'

Mary wrote and read all day. Claire stayed, also reading and staring out of the window at the heedless throng in the Abbey Churchyard. They were both so full of things to say, that they barely spoke, for fear of the power of the words in the world.

The following morning, Saturday, Shelley returned and his eyes were as dead as the tone of his voice as he told them what had happened.

He had got to Swansea and gone to the Mackworth Arms. He found them in uproar as a young female had been found dead in her room the previous day. An overdose of laudanum.

'I questioned the servants and they said that she had long brown hair, was about 23, and was wearing a blue-striped skirt with a white body, a brown pelice with a fur trim and lined with white silk, just what we saw her wearing on Tuesday. They also mentioned a small watch. There can be no doubt because the police, trying to identify such a respectable looking girl, had told them that her stockings were marked with a G and there was M.W. on her stays.'

'My mother's stays,' Mary gasped and her legs gave way.

Shelley helped her to the sofa as Claire started sobbing and sat down too. Mary encircled Claire's shoulders and Claire grasped her hand tightly.

'The body had been taken off for a preliminary inquest, and the newspaper reporter had taken all the details for the next day's edition,' continued Shelley.

'The worst thing was, they said there had been a suicide note. The reporter had taken it to copy before he gave it back to the coroner.' He paced the room and pulled at his hair as he spoke. 'They found the remains of a torn-off piece which had been burnt, apparently. It seemed to have been torn off from the place in the note where the signature was. I think that, as she lay dying, she worried at the last about Godwin's reputation, maybe mine too, tore off her signature and burnt the torn piece in the candle so no trace of the letters would remain.'

'I had to wait 'til this morning to see *The Cumbrian* and read it. He produced the paper from inside his coat and threw it on the little sofa table in front of them, where it lay, curled and venomous. The young women shrunk back and stared at it in paralyzed silence.

'What did it say,' asked Mary, her voice barely a whisper. 'No,' as Shelley offered her the paper, 'read it to me.'

Shelley cleared his throat to release his shaky voice, and read.

*I have long determined that the best thing I could do was to put an end to the existence of a being whose birth was unfortunate, and whose life has only been a series of pain to those persons who have hurt their health in endeavouring to promote her welfare. Perhaps to hear of my death will give you pain, but you will soon have the blessing of forgetting that such a creature ever existed as …*

'Unfortunate,' whispered Mary. 'We have some lessons our mother wrote for Fanny, when she was two, and she addressed them to "*my unfortunate girl*".

'Who has hurt their health for her? Papa?' sobbed Claire. 'She is, was, so misguided. Papa's problems are his own doing. She was the least of his worries. She makes it sound as if they accused her at Skinner Street of causing their problems.'

'Fanny was one of those people who was inclined to interpret others' pain as a reproach to themselves,' replied Shelley.

'What did you do? Will she be taken as a suicide?' asked Claire, horror in her voice. She knew that suicide's bodies were often buried in unconsecrated ground, and were prey to "resurrection men" who sold them to dissecting rooms, and for who knows what else.

'I went to the coroner and asked that she be declared "dead" not a suicide. He can influence the jury. It was a good bribe. I didn't give my name. I just said I was concerned it might affect people I knew. I also paid him for his silence. Fortunate for me the aristocracy has a reputation for paying well to cover its mistakes,' he said bitterly. 'I'm sure he took her for my cast-off mistress.'

'Mary, did I do right?' he asked, anxiously. 'I can still go back and claim the body. I don't know anymore. I am bone tired and my brain has stopped functioning.'

Mary's eyes were muddy pools in a storm-ravaged field. 'Try to rest now, we have a day to decide,' she replied, attempting to steady her voice and sound solicitous. 'Papa must be told. I will write now.'

'Yes, do, but I think he may know. As I came through Bristol this morning they told me that yesterday another, older, gentleman had been making the same enquiries as me. It sounded like Godwin. If he is still there he would see today's newspaper.'

As if in response to this conjecture, almost immediately there came two letters from Godwin to Shelley and one to Claire. The first of the two to Shelley had been written the previous evening and explained that Godwin had received a letter from Fanny and presumed they had too, because when he got to Bristol he had heard that someone that sounded like Shelley had gone to Swansea looking for a young woman of Fanny's description. He had returned to Bath, not wanting to make too much of a fuss, and assumed Shelley would inform him when he had found her. The second letter to Shelley, written from a hotel in Bath, said he was about to depart immediately for London. He had seen *The Cumbrian* that morning, and understood its dreadful meaning. He expressed sadness, but Mary thought his note showed more panic than sorrow.

As Shelley was reading it aloud, she snatched it from him angrily.

'Look, all he's concerned about is that we don't tell anyone it's her, don't make a fuss. There are some of his cronies waiting for the coaches and he can't let them know why he's here! What does yours say, Claire. Let me see.' She snatched that too, from an astonished Claire. 'Oh, yes, here we are again, don't tell your mother. Where's the letter, the comfort, for me? '

'Anyway, it's a relief he didn't try to see us,' said Claire, stroking her swelling belly.

'Is it?' replied Mary, angrily. 'He's a man, he probably wouldn't have noticed your condition. He's my father, for goodness sake. There is no excuse, there is no Mrs. Godwin here. Why would he not rush to my side? It's my half-sister. He was father to that girl since she was three. His wife's blood. Should we not comfort each other? Even you, Claire, you grew up with her too. He is so full and puffed up with principles and pretensions he has no space left for his heart.'

'Or perhaps it's guilt, and he can't face us,' suggested Claire. 'He must feel dreadful that he failed to notice how unhappy she was. Shall I call for tea? I need something.' She looked inquiringly at Mary as she pulled the bell. 'It was your mother's disease, wasn't it?'

'What do you mean?' asked Mary sharply.

'She tried to commit suicide twice, didn't she?'

Mary stared at Claire. The insensitivity always came like a punch in the stomach. She could go for days, lulled into unguardedness, with Claire being bright and friendly or sympathetic. Then, out of the clear sky it came. A comment you would only expect from someone who hated you. Always Mary cursed herself for letting down her guard.

'Once with laudanum, too,' continued Claire, with satisfaction at her perspicacity. 'You don't know how much that sort of thing influences a young child. Gets into their brain. Of course your mother was rescued at the last minute by her lover, wasn't she? Perhaps Fanny expected that too, deep down.' Claire was moving books to make space for the tea. She didn't look at Shelley, but her past accusations at Shelley's unheeded effect on Fanny were circling in the air, like vultures. Shelley was very pale and very silent.

'You weren't fond of her,' Mary stated baldly to Claire, through tight lips. 'It's easy for you to judge her ... and us.'

'It's true we weren't close, but I lived with her for the first fourteen years of my life. Of course I'm upset, too,' protested Claire. 'She adored Shelley, and you know she felt that you and Shelley misunderstood and abandoned her.'

'Don't you see, you stupid girl, that if it wasn't for you we wouldn't have had to be here to keep out of her way!' Mary screamed, rushing out of the room, nearly colliding with the maid carrying a tea tray.

Shelley looked at Claire, shook his head in frustration, and followed Mary. In their bedroom he put his hands on her shaking shoulders.

'Ignore her, Mary. Grief is always difficult. People say what they don't mean.'

'It's so ironic, that she has what Fanny wanted but she is neither grateful nor gracious. What's more it was Fanny who has had to put up with her mother.'

'So maybe that is something that makes her want to blame us. Mary, we must think what I am to do about Fanny's body. I feel terrible not claiming it and about her not getting a proper burial. I know the danger of the scandal. What is right, Mary? I must write to Godwin. I think I should go to Swansea and not identify the body but, as an anonymous stranger, or through a third party, give her a good burial. That is a plan, no?' Mary nodded, slowly. 'Yes, I will write now.'

The return letter from Godwin was immediate and unequivocal. *"I cannot but thank you for your strong expressions of sympathy. I do not see, however, that sympathy can be of any service to me. My advice and my earnest prayer is that you would avoid doing anything that leads to publicity. Go not to Swansea, disturb not the silent dead; do nothing to disturb the obscurity she so much desired. It was her last wish. It was the motive that led her from London to Bristol and from Bristol to Swansea. I said that your sympathy could be of no service to me, but I retract that assertion; by observing what I have just recommended to you, it may be of infinite service. Think what is the situation of my wife & myself, now deprived of all our children but the youngest & do not expose us to those idle questions, which to a mind in anguish is one of the severest trials. We are at this moment in doubt whether during the first shock we shall not say she is gone to Ireland to her aunts, a thing that had been in contemplation … What I have most of all in horror is the public papers; & I thank you for your caution."*

Shelley, against his conscience, in the interests of not upsetting Godwin further for Mary's sake, concurred. It cost him sleepless nights and anguish that he found it difficult to bury in verse. Mary came across a scribbled page that Shelley left by the bed. There were

several scraps of poems, clearly about Fanny. The longest, brought
back the tears.

> *Her voice did quiver as we parted,*
> *Yet knew I not that heart was broken*
> *From which it came, and I departed*
> *Heeding not the words then spoken.*
> *Misery—O Misery,*
> *This world is all too wide for thee*

Mary had not encountered the death of an adult close to her before.
When she was writing the scene in *Frankenstein* where his mother
dies, the sentiments came easily.

> *I need not describe the feelings of those whose dearest ties are rent by*
> *that most irreparable evil. It is so long before the mind can persuade itself*
> *that she whom we saw every day and whose very existence appeared a part*
> *of our own can have departed forever—that the brightness of a beloved eye*
> *can have been extinguished and the sound of a voice so familiar and dear*
> *to the ear can be hushed, never more to be heard. These are the reflections*
> *of the first days; but when the lapse of time proves the reality of the evil,*
> *then the actual bitterness of grief commences.*

# 3

Why fear and dream and death and birth
Cast on the daylight of this earth
Such gloom,—why man has such a scope
For love and hate, despondency and hope?

*Hymn to Intellectual Beauty*, Percy Bysshe Shelley

'Enough, enough! I think you would marry him if he were a woman!'
laughed Mary. 'I think I should be jealous!'

Shelley had just returned to Bath from Marlow by way of
Hampstead, north of London, where he had been visiting Leigh
Hunt. He could barely eat his supper for excitement. He leaned
across the table, took both her hands in his and looked at her with
intensely bright eyes.

'Pecksie, it is the first time I have felt so alive since that terrible
day in October when we lost Fanny. To meet such a man! He is so
delightfully in sympathy with all my thoughts. He likes my poetry.
He called me a "striking and original thinker" in his magazine, *The
Examiner*. Did you finally get the copy I sent? I don't know how we
failed to get that issue before. You know I sent *Hymn to Intellectual
Beauty* to be published under the name of Elfin Knight, but he insisted
I should use my own name. I warned him that I am an outcast and
that it would do him and his magazine no good, but he still insisted.'

'How wonderful to find someone in the world who appreciates
you. Wasn't Byron a good friend to Hunt too, after he was imprisoned
for libel against the Regent?'

'Yes, Byron visited him in prison and gave him money. He had
many supporters. I sent a little too, though I was living in Wales.
They say he played Battledore in prison and the walls of his rooms
were decorated with flowers. He charmed even the guards. He is such
an optimistic fellow without being insincere, or unmoved. He sees

evil and abhors it, but is tolerant of those who perpetrate it. I am so glad I decided to accept his invitation to visit, though I'm sorry it kept me from you for two more days.'

'It sounds well worth the detour. Besides I made great progress with my book. Chapter Five now. I'll show you later. Frankenstein has made the Creature and rejected him. He is now ill from shock and strain and is attended by his friend Henry Cherval. But tell me of your new friend, Hunt. How does he live?'

'He is in a lovely cottage in the village of Hampstead, close by the Heath, where there are walks and ponds and the air is fresh. His wife, Marianne is just his equal in good nature. She is a sculptress and a devoted mother, too. You will love her. Their oldest boy is six. Thornton. A delightful child, and there are two others. They seem to churn them out every two years!

'Oh,' he rummaged in his portmanteaux and produced, with a conjuror's smile, a large book bound in red leather. 'I bought you a Livy, as you asked. It is quite a good one. Not very worn. Here is the first of the seven volumes. The rest are being sent.'

'Thank you, dearest,' smiled Mary, running her finger over the title in gilt, *Historarium.* 'I've shamefully neglected my Latin. I must work harder.'

Shelley suddenly grinned, as excited as a child, 'I've found a house!'

'You leave this 'til last?' Mary almost choked on her green tea. 'Tell me immediately!'

'It has, let me see ...' He counted off on his fingers. 'A drawing room, a dining room, a library — a huge library, though all the rooms are very large — a study, five best bedrooms, two large nurseries — isn't that perfect — a water closet, and, oh, six or seven attics!'

'Does it have a garden? When do we take it on?' asked Mary eagerly.

'Yes, there is a garden, a big one. It is number one West Street, and Peacock is number 47! It has just come available. It's in some disrepair and there are no furnishings. I'll be able to sign the lease next week. I've taken twenty-one years, but we can't move in, of course, until after Claire has her baby, so that will give us time to organize painting and furnishing.'

'Oh I see. The main street,' said Mary, trying not to show disappointment. 'Well, I knew there wouldn't be mountains. On a river or a lake would have been nice, but heigh ho, the river is quite close. I have my garden and we will have our mouse-hole for this weary Doormouse to retire into. I will be content. Well, almost content. If you could magic one other favour ...'

'Now, Maie, there are two nurseries you know. Where else would Claire go?'

'Perhaps we will need two ourselves,' muttered Mary as she got up, turned away and started to leave the room.

'What?' Shelley leapt from the table and caught her arm as she went. She turned and gave a small, knowing smile.

'Too early to be sure.'

Shelley, fresh from the family warmth and harmony of the Hunts, hugged her with what seemed to be real satisfaction.

Timing is everything, thought Mary.

Would that the universe felt the same.

The gods that they didn't believe in gave them ten hours of remission, before unleashing a salvo in the shape of a single sheet, twenty line letter.

It arrived next day as they breakfasted.

The fire was lit and they were cosy as the winds whipped outside. In the churchyard the morning frost still silvered the cobbles and a coal porter, hurrying to finish his morning rounds, skidded, his heavy boots unable to grip and the counterweight of his sack upending him.

Mary was watching him and trying not to laugh. 'It may snow before the end of December even in this supposedly milder south-east. What a year of bad weather!'

'It's been such a disaster for the poor this year,' agreed Shelley. 'The failed crops, the high price of bread. The Spa Fields riots show how desperate people are. Never before has London seen twenty-thousand rise up in protest. So admirable, to gather without violence. Still it has made little difference so far. The streets of London, when one passes through, are still filled with vagrants.'

'I hope you don't go there too often. You find it hard enough in Bath. What has become of that young family you picked off the streets last week. Poor children, all three crying for hunger.'

'Oh yes, I forgot to say. They are getting along better after we sent them to London. I have paid for two more weeks lodgings and the husband, John, has found work with a candlemaker. His employer was kind enough to send a note on his behalf.'

Elise had kept Claire company the previous night, and was not due to return until ten. It was just the two of them with William on the floor between their feet, trying to catch the patient cat's tail, and make it stay still long enough so that he could bang it with his blocks.

Shelley picked him up, took him to the sofa and sat him on his raised knees. He started to recite *Ode on the Death of a Favourite Cat Drowned in a Tub of Goldfish*, by Thomas Gray. He mimed it all with great exaggeration, the *velvet paws*, the *purred applause, a whisker first and then a claw*, and then the bit about *tumbled headlong in*, and the desperate mewing of Selima, the tabby. He made his eyes huge and pawed the air pitifully.

'You'll terrify the poor boy,' laughed Mary, watching little Will, who was staring at his father with an open mouth and serious concentration.

'Nonsense,' said Shelley, miming the death throes of the drowning cat with horrid gurgles. 'There's a valuable lesson to be learned from this poem. All that glisters is not gold. It was the first poem I learnt as a boy.'

'He's not yet one!' expostulated Mary.

'Never underestimate the power of poetry,' smiled Shelley, as Will finally made up his mind that his father was just crazy, and giggled, too.

Ever since Fanny died, Shelley's routine had changed. Instead of getting up at midday, and going to bed late into the night or in the early hours of the next day, he now was up by eight or nine, and went to bed before midnight. He could not explain this even to himself. Partly, Mary thought, it was because Claire was not living in the same house. She had always been prepared to keep him company, long after Mary had retired. Partly, though, it was as if he needed to recast himself in a more sober mould, to be a different person than the one who might, if he were prepared to consider the thought, have failed Fanny.

Milly, the maid, came in to collect the breakfast plates and stoke the fire.

'Leave that dish of raisins for William, please, Milly,' smiled Mary.

Milly bobbed her head and produced a letter, which she held out to Shelley.

'It's from Hookham,' said Shelley, eagerly, putting the child off his lap and getting up to take it. 'Some news, I hope, of where Harriet is hiding.' He opened and scanned the letter.

All colour drained from him. The letter fluttered from his hand to the floor and he stared at it as if watching a spider crawling down the skein of a web.

Mary picked it up. There were the sparse lines in Hookham's business-like hand.

Harriet's body had been taken out of the Serpentine river in Hyde Park four days ago. A pregnant Harriet had, as Hookham put it, destroyed herself.

'Oh my love.' Mary went to him, but he was inarticulate, inanimate, moulded in ice.

'Claire and Elise will be here soon,' Mary was thinking rapidly. 'We must get you out of the house; we must walk and talk. Quietly. Alone.'

She got his coat and his gloves and put them on him, like dressing a child. He was unresistant, his eyes focused inward. She got her own coat, bonnet and shawl and stood with him, watching the door. As soon as her stepsister and the nurse came in, Mary hurried Shelley past them.

'I'm sorry, Shelley is feeling the want of air, a little suffocated. We must walk for a while. William has breakfasted.'

They closed the door on the astonished girls and went down into the street. Shelley moved stiffly, like one in pain, following the pressure of Mary's arm but taking no lead. They walked through the comparative quiet of Union Street, towards Milsom Street, where Mary judged that the bustle of the shops and the shopkeepers setting up would energise him. Eventually he started to show signs of returning to the unwelcome present, muttering to himself and shaking his head.

'Is it me, Mary? Am I cursed to curse others?'

He started to shake and Mary took them into Milsom's Tea House. They sat in a corner, as private as possible among the rising buzz of chatter, as the place started to fill with adventurous early shoppers, their cold breath steaming as they came in, stamping their feet to restore circulation. She ordered strong gunpowder green tea, gently rubbed his cold hands and spoke with quiet intensity.

'Of course not, my dearest, dearest, love. You have done no wrong. You had made a good income provision for Harriet and the children and you tried to be her friend, but she would have none of it. We don't know yet what happened, what drove her to it.'

'I asked Hookham last month to find out her whereabouts. She had never replied after I wrote to her explaining my will. I thought it might be the ogre-sister Eliza, directing her as usual or not telling me she had gone away. Were the children with her? I knew nothing. Know nothing. She has never let me see them. And pregnant? What degradation had she come to?' His eyes were damp with emotion. His voice, which was normally high and child-like, but strong, was weak and quavery as if, in the last hour, he had passed through the seven ages of man.

'I've missed the morning coaches. I'll get on an overnight stage to London this evening. The Monarch or the Regulator from Bristol stop here around six. There is also the five o'clock mail coach. I will take a seat on one, even if I have to be outside.'

'No, no!' Mary was horrified. 'You would not survive a night in this freezing weather on top of a coach. Do you have a death wish too? We will stop immediately at the Westgate coaching inn and see what can be done.'

As they left the tea room and walked to the coaching inn, Mary felt there was so much to say, to question, but she was scared of inciting too strong a reaction. How could she tell what he really felt? How could she ask? Should she assume he felt guilt and try to ameliorate that? Or would he blame Harriet for lack of sympathy to his and Mary's situation, and should she try to temper his anger? Would he mourn Harriet for herself or for her motherhood ... The children ...

'What about the children?' It came out before she could think.

He turned to look at her, a little beseechingly. 'Mary, you will love them, won't you? For my sake?'

'Of course, sweetest Knight! Those darling treasures shall be much loved companions for our little William! They are only, what, one and four years old? They're too young to know much of this.' Mary tried to sound confident, but could not suppress the memory of Claire's barb about the effect of her own mother's suicide attempt on Fanny.

'I hope that the Westbrooks, Harriet's father and Eliza, don't make difficulties,' muttered Shelley, as anxiety crumpled him, his normal stoop exaggerated, his frown lines deepened.

Money changed hands at the coaching inn. A large bribe got Shelley an inside seat on the six o'clock stage.

'You will have to marry, I suppose,' said Claire coldly, when they got back to Abbey Churchyard and told her what they knew. 'The Westbrooks will not let the children go into your household otherwise.'

Mary and Shelley looked at her in astonishment. 'Marry?' they said, almost simultaneously. Then looked at each other. Had there been an interrogation, both could honestly say the fact of Harriet's suicide leaving them free to marry had not crossed their minds.

'I am their father!' protested Shelley, angrily. 'I have the right to them. Just because I did not assert my right, to spare Harriet's feelings ... They would not dare.'

'Oh, they would dare,' said Claire, mildly. 'Even if they didn't hate you as much as they do, the thought of Mary, the great seductress, getting her hands on them will spur them on. Get advice, Shelley. I am right.'

Shelley paced the floor of Hookham's plush office on the first floor of his bookshop and circulating library in Old Bond Street, where the smell of leather bindings and parchment for once failed to sooth him. He was angry, hysterical, befuddled, depressed and anxious. Those emotions appeared to be massive chains that circumscribed his movements, jerking him as he reached the limit of one, only to set off again and be pulled back by another. The older man watched, sitting at the double sided walnut partners desk, reading aloud the report of the inquest, not on Harriet Shelley, but on Harriet Smith. This unfortunate had lived in lodgings in Elizabeth Street, Hans Place, near Hyde Park and behind the Chelsea Barracks. Her landlady and the maid had told the coroner that this Harriet, this pregnant Harriet, had mostly stayed in her room for two months before she disappeared in early November. She had been taken to the lodging by a plumber and the same plumber had identified the body.

'It is definitely her?' asked Shelley, turning again, abruptly, to return the mild and concerned gaze of the small, dapper bookseller.

'No doubt at all. Harriet was a friend of the Landlord's daughter at the Fox and Lion, where the body was taken. The fiction of Smith is kept to avoid scandal. There has been strong influence, though, from the Westbrooks to avoid a suicide verdict.'

Both Hookham and Hunt had spent the past two days and much of the night talking to friends and acquaintances of the Westbrooks, and listening to coffee house gossip to piece together the facts, or at least the most credible rumours. They reported that a week after she disappeared from her lodgings, her father or Eliza had asked the plumber to drag the Serpentine and local ponds.

'What made them do that?' asked Shelley. 'Did they suspect self-harm?

'Perhaps,' answered Hunt, sitting at the table, his head periodically drooping with exhaustion. 'Sit for a minute, Shelley, do.'

'Why was she called Smith?' demanded Shelley, continuing his restless perambulation, 'and who was this plumber?'

'Perhaps a friend of her father?' answered Hookham, anxious to cast the best light. He had always been fond of Harriet. 'He went with her to take the lodgings in the beginning. Also, friends of Eliza say that Harriet was lately staying with a groom called Smith, an older man, perhaps married.

'Those who are acquainted with the Westbrooks whisper that Eliza mentions a lover called Captain Maxwell, who was sent overseas with his regiment,' added Hunt, dispassionately. He had never known Harriet. 'Servants at her father's house in Chapel Street say that about a month ago, when she came to see her father, who is ill, perhaps dying, she was refused entry by Eliza who said he would not see her.'

'The plumber, the groom, the captain! My God, to what depths had the poor woman descended? Her father clearly disowning her. Sending her from his house. How had her so-called precious sister abandoned her to this fate? All condemned her. It is all but murder! I see it! That evil, conniving Eliza, since she no longer had Harriet's connection with me secure, wanted all of her father's money and encouraged poor Harriet in her desire for self-harm. Now she will want the children.'

His voice had become shrill and ranting. Then he stopped abruptly and stood still.

'Where are the children?'

'No-one knows. Apparently they have not been seen in the house for three months. It sounds as if they were sent away at the same time as Harriet, but where is a mystery. I would think Eliza has to tell you now.' Hookham's voice was gentle, calling on the skills he used in reassuring fretful customers about the delivery of rare books.

'Longdill, my solicitor, thinks as long as I marry Mary they will have no cause to keep them.'

'Mary will be soothed by that, I think,' said Hunt, sincerely, as if it were his duty to nudge his friend into the world of current obligations.

'Really?' said Shelley, looking startled. 'Why?'

'Because she will see that this is the sincerest way she can support you and show her love,' replied Hunt, with the authority and wisdom of ten years of marriage.

'Yes,' said Shelley, thoughtfully.

Just then a clerk knocked on the door bearing a letter for Shelley. He unfolded it and glanced first at a note and then slowly read a longer page underneath. He gasped.

'That woman!'

He was shaking, but from within, so it seemed as if he would erupt with passion, and his eyes were moist and shining.

'See this.' He passed the note and letter to the others and banged the desk so hard, with his clenched fists, groaning loudly, that servants ran in and were shooed away by Hookham.

'She sends me this letter. She says it is a copy of Harriet's suicide letter. She says it was Harriet's last wish that she should have Ianthe. Oh, my head will explode. What does it mean? This is a foretaste of damnation! Mary, where are you? Clasp me! Save me!'

He fell backwards into a deep, soft, high backed armchair, arms outstretched, as if he was being dragged unwillingly into the depths of Hell.

Hunt went around the desk and looked over Hookham's shoulder as they read. Shelley watched them through lowered lids.

'Is it real?' he asked, deflated. 'That beastly viper is capable of the worst calumny. She could have forged this.'

'Does it sound like Harriet?' asked Hunt.

'Perhaps,' said Shelley, reluctantly. 'But Miss Eliza Westbrook lived with her all her life. It would be easy for her to reproduce like Harriet.'

'This is a supposed copy,' agreed Hunt, thoughtfully. 'There must have been some sort of note or else why would they have dragged the ponds? Anything could have been added, though.'

'She had threatened to end her life before. It was used to encourage me to marry her. Why just Ianthe, do you think?'

'Perhaps it is an implied bargain. You get Charles, she keeps Ianthe?' Hunt was uncertain, troubled, his usual equanimity challenged by the unfolding drama.

'She will not get her! I am her only surviving parent. I want to look after her and I certainly don't want that monster to have her. As it is she'll be poisoning her about me. We have to get her out, now.' Shelley was a man in a maelstrom, face distended, body twisting. 'What grounds could she have for keeping them? I have acted as a gentleman. Harriet had £200 a year from me, when I could not afford it, and she had £200 from her father. They are all well provided for in my will. I would have been a proper father to them had she not prevented me and if I had not acquiesced to her wishes. I would have been her friend too. How is she come so low? How did she abandon the children, too?' He subsided and dropped his head to his knees, so that his voice was muffled. 'It is my fault. If I had never allowed her to persuade me to rescue her and marry her. If I had not tried to open her mind and her sensibilities. If I had left her among her own class. Her father would have married her off to a respectable shopkeeper and she would have been unenlightened and happy. Poor Harriet. If she had never met me ...'

Hookham and Hunt glanced at each other and hastened to assure him that this fault was not his, and the kindness of friends muffled the accusatory voices in the shadows.

Mary, who always had dismissed marriage, found she could think of nothing else. Shelley wrote that he had told Longdill he was under contract of marriage to her. It was to ensure there was no barrier to their having the children, but Shelley was gracious in presenting it to her as a benefit that she would confer on him. Even though they knew it was a mere form. Mrs. Godwin wrote to her urging it and claimed Godwin would not survive if the precious ceremony failed to eventuate. Godwin wrote to them both hysterically demanding it as the price for reconciliation. Reconciliation with her father would certainly ease her mind and remove nagging guilt and frustration. Marriage would make life easier, more straightforward. They would not always be at a moral disadvantage. Sadly, she thought that if they had been married when Fanny came for their protection, there would have been no barrier to their offering it.

She interrogated her own feelings. She had got so used to thinking of their relationship as outside of normal boundaries. If she had met Shelley before Harriet, would they have married? Would she, like Harriet, have demanded it? It would make a difference to other people, but would it make a difference to them? Would she feel more secure? Not in his love, but there was something. Honesty forced her to tease at it, to winkle it out from underneath the carapace of denial. It was that it would be clear to everyone it was she who was chosen. Clear to everyone, including Claire. No more speculation about Shelley's two women. No more hope for Claire.

In the meantime, she desperately wanted to be with Shelley to soften his sorrow, but Claire, at the beginning of her ninth month, was nervous and demanding. So for the next few days Mary could only await the post and new developments and shop, optimistically, in Bond Street for clothes and toys to welcome Ianthe and Charles.

Claire, who was mountainous and finally admitting to exhaustion, spent most of her time lying on the sofa. It was wet and treacherous outside and so that Claire could stay safely inside, Mary spent much of her time in Claire's apartments in Bond Street. They were warm and comfortable, with two fires in the parlour. Fashionable shops lined the street below and the lights of the street lamps and the shop windows made flickering patterns in the puddles. She had made all the preparations for Claire's lying-in; the linen, the bowls, the towels, were all organised. Claire watched Mary, hawk-eyed for signs of satisfaction about the impending nuptials, calling her Lady Mary until Mary exploded.

'It is not funny, Claire. It really is not amusing. You know I didn't look for this.'

'All those lovely principles sacrificed to necessity. Or maybe necessity. I think the Westbrooks will try to keep the children on the grounds of Shelley being an atheist, anyway. Morally unfit. Harriet always threatened that, probably under pressure from Eliza.'

'It's not a risk we can take, to stay unmarried. Then there's the Godwins. It will be better for you if your condition ever came out, if Shelley is married to me. They will be less inclined to be suspicious about the father.'

'Hmmm.' Claire did not seem impressed by this argument. 'Little spoilt blue-eyes will have to learn to be third in the pecking order of infants, and wait his turn at table,' she said, smiling sweetly at William, who was sitting on his mother's lap, being fed sweetmeats. There'll be money to burn, now, no longer having to support Harriet. We can get some new linen and some good paper and some more music! I am sick of playing the same old pieces. She sighed. 'Don't give me your disapproving eyes. I only say what we all think.'

'Some of us make an effort to be sensitive to the fact that there has been the death of a young woman, the mother of Shelley's children,' Mary muttered, feeling an unwanted solidarity with Harriet. 'Don't forget there will a queue, including your brother Charles who wants £80 a year from Shelley to enable him to get married in France, and Godwin who always is in want, and Peacock who is sometimes in want, and who knows who else Shelley takes under his wing.'

'You know, it's not surprising that these women who admire Shelley think kindly of death. Here, look, I've been reading Queen Mab.' She dangled the bound pages in the air, then found her place. Listen to this:

> *Mild is the slow necessity of death:*
> *The tranquil spirit fails beneath its grasp,*
> *Without a groan, almost without a fear,*
> *Resigned in peace to the necessity,*
> *Calm as a voyager to some distant land,*
> *And full of wonder, full of hope as he.'*

When Shelley wrote it was imperative that Mary come to London as he was getting a marriage licence in the next few days, she was abjectly grateful. It was not so much with the expectation of the magical ceremony, but for the excuse for a brief escape.

'Suppose my condition comes to term while you're away,' wailed Claire. 'I have no-one to help me! Shelley doesn't care or think about me.'

'Shelley constantly thinks about you, and he is greatly concerned for your well-being, as you well know,' soothed Mary suppressing a liberating selfishness. 'But this must be done.'

# 4

Now has descended a serener hour,
And with inconstant fortune, friends return;
Though suffering leaves the knowledge and the power
Which says:—Let scorn be not repaid with scorn.
And from thy side two gentle babes are born
To fill our home with smiles, and thus are we
Most fortunate beneath life's beaming morn;
And these delights, and thou, have been to me
The parents of the Song I consecrate to thee.

Dedication to Mary Shelley *To Mary* in *The Revolt of Islam*,
Percy Bysshe Shelley

It was a scene English mythology is built on, but which, like all myths, has only a tenuous hold on reality. For a whisper in time, it might have been captured by an artist thus: an unseasonably warm late April day, an acre of cashmere lawn reaching to the enclosing high hedges of fir and cypress trees; apple trees which are just beginning to blossom are dotted around, their pretty pink-tinged white flowers ruffled occasionally by a light breeze; flower beds crowded with spring colour, golden roses, red snapdragons and purple pansies; sheep grazing in the fields beyond. Children run and tumble happily in this idyll, and centred in the foreground on white cane chairs, with a table half set for tea, sit two young women dressed in white muslin. They are both advanced in pregnancy and their body language shows them to be in intimate conversation.

'You're the first female friend I've had since Isabella in Scotland.' Mary smiled at Marianne Hunt. 'You're so much older than me and I feel you know more about friendship.'

'An old lady of twenty-nine,' laughed Marianne, not at all offended. She was a small, fair-haired woman with an open smile and sympathetic eyes.

'Anyway, old enough to feel like an older sister, because …' Her voice faltered.

'I know about Fanny,' said Marianne gently. 'She must have been a great loss to you.'

'She annoyed me sometimes. She fussed and was pedantic.' Mary's jaw tightened. 'But she was more like a mother to me than Mary Jane Godwin ever was. Is.'

'We have so much in common, do we not?' Marianne tactfully diverted the conversation. 'Both six months pregnant. Both married to men who are passionate about politics and poetry and who want to change the world!'

'And both burdened with annoying sisters who are in love with our husbands and who live in the same household,' joined in Mary, lifting her chin and half closing her eyes as she regarded Marianne.

'How do you bear it? Betsy Kent with you all the time? You've had years more than me to learn to manage it.' Mary was earnest. She really wanted to know if there was an elixir to douse her continual smouldering feelings of antagonism towards Claire. In her waking dreams she saw her life as a love letter thrown into a dying fire, very slowly being blackened and consumed at the edges.

'I don't, very well,' grimaced Marianne, honestly. 'We often clash. She's the intellectual one. I know Henry is fond of her and talks easily to her and values her opinion in literary and political matters. Sometimes it hurts, but she is my sister. What can I do? Send her off to be a governess? What else is there for a respectable single woman? No, I just have to hang on to the fact that he loves me.'

'Which you know very well. He is clearly devoted to you. My dear, he can rarely keep his hands off you. And he is devoted to the children. Children are such a bond, aren't they? It's an extra layer to a relationship. It's a way of looking into the future together.'

'It's true,' said Marianne, looking fondly at some of her brood — Thornton, John and Mary — playing a game on the grass, with Alice, the Hunts' nurse. At three, four and five, they were beautiful little children. Shelley was particularly close to Thornton, the oldest one. When they had been staying in Hampstead with the Hunts, before they moved there to Marlow, he would take him for long walks on Hampstead Heath. Little Thornton preferred to walk with him rather than his father because he walked more quickly and didn't stop continually to gaze abstractedly as did Hunt. Shelley loved to play with all of the Hunt children, making scary faces and covering his face with hair and pretending to be a monster with horns.

Marianne was an unexpected delight for Mary. As Hunt's wife, she was almost invisible to most of the literary and artistic elite who were at her fireside daily: Keats, Wordsworth, Haydon the painter, Hazlitt the essayist. While Hunt encouraged and critiqued them with endless enthusiasm and good humour, she quietly presided over the chaos of the household with equal warmth and practicality. Staying at the Hunt's, Mary had again felt a little like a child in her father's house, when he was a locus for the thinkers of the day. The buzz of ideas and argument, of sonnet writing competitions and storytelling, was so unlike the isolation of the past two years with Shelley. She wanted to create some of that excitement here, in Marlow. The house was big enough to have guests and not too far from London. Now Hunt and his wife were staying while Hunt looked for a new and cheaper house for his family in London.

Mary always participated in the discussions. Quietly but firmly, she made sure her opinions were acknowledged. Though she did not have an enthusiastically domestic bone in her body, still, intellectually, she felt she could learn from Marianne and could copy some of her hospitable ways. Observing Marianne, she tried to learn the art of tolerance and to be more open. She was aware that people saw her as acerbic and quietly disdainful, and some found it hard to take in a woman. Marianne's sweet manner had to just be a trick she could learn to reproduce. Or maybe just on this picture-perfect day she felt that changing one's personality was perfectly possible.

'How is Shelley taking the judgment of the Lord Chancellor about his and Harriet's children?'

'Not well.' Mary became grave. 'He pretends to be resigned to it but it affects his health. The other day he collapsed screaming with a pain in his side. Have you seen the poem he wrote *To the Lord Chancellor?* It lets out all his frustrations. This is the verse I remember:

> *Oh, let a father's curse be on thy soul,*
> *And let a daughter's hope be on thy tomb;*
> *Be both, on thy gray head, a leaden cowl*
> *To weigh thee down to thine approaching doom*

'I hope that Hunt publishes it in *The Examiner*. Nothing could make things worse. Well, no, I suppose it could.'

'What did the judgment say, exactly? Just a moment.'

Marianne opened the writing desk on the table beside her and took out some paper and small scissors.

'While we're talking I will take the opportunity to make a shade. Just a first try at capturing you. I think it will be difficult to indicate your lovely superior mind! Just turn your head slightly so I have you in full profile. I must get that lovely long neck and smooth shoulders. Please carry on talking. About the judgment. I am going to make your mouth smile, even if it isn't.'

Mary obediently turned her head to show Marianne her profile, and pushed her soft hair, that she was wearing loose, away from her shoulders so that her friend could cut out her likeness. She spoke quietly, trying not to move her mouth too much.

'Lord Eldon said the charges that he had "blasphemously derided the truth of the Christian revelation and denied the existence of God as the creator of the universe" and that he had deserted his wife to co-habit unlawfully with me, and had expressed a disdain for the institution of marriage and the customs of society, were true, and the probability was that Shelley would feel obliged to convey his beliefs to his children. Thus he was unfit to be in sole charge of their upbringing. Shelley pointed out that this was based on his poem Queen Mab, which he wrote five years ago, when he was nineteen and that he married me as soon as he was free. The problem was he didn't actually deny his views, just said he was prepared to compromise for the sake of conforming to society's beliefs.'

'Yet to deny a father the right to his children!' Marianne tutted and shook her head as she worked. 'It's unheard of! If antisocial beliefs were a reason, half the fathers in Christendom would be denied their parental rights. It's usually the mothers I feel sorry for. Almost always they lose the right to see their children at all and that's barbaric too. How are those Westbrooks fit to raise them? An invalid and a grasping witch woman.'

'Well, he hasn't given them custody as yet, thank goodness. Now they and Shelley have to submit a proposition for a third party to care for the children. In the meantime, Shelley still can't see them.'

From the Sir William Borlase's School, which occupied several acres next door, came the sounds of boys voices raised in excitement as they were allowed a half hour to play. Even before the Hunts came to stay, there was no escaping reminders of a world populated by other people's children. Mary saw young Polly come out of the back door, carrying cakes for the young ones. She put them on a seat and joined in the game. She was a village girl whose mother lay dying as Shelley was on one of his visits to the local cottages. He promised to take her in and care for her, and here she was, a delightful nine year old. Another soul for Shelley to rescue. Changing the world one person at a time, thought Mary. They were teaching her to read, and she was a grateful pupil.

'Who does Shelley propose as your choice?'

'Longdill, his solicitor, we are thinking.'

Just then, little William came unsteadily out of the house, clinging onto Elise's hand. He could just totter independently, though his only pace seemed to be running, and he set off at a charge immediately he saw his mother, wobbly forays alternating with collapsing knees, almost tripping on his flannel skirt, not yet fully programmed to the demands of being a non-feathered biped, as Shelley was fond of putting it, quoting Plato.

Swinburne, Marianne's youngest, only seven months, was in Elise's other arm. When William came within a few paces of Mary, she opened her arms to him, encouraging him to lurch into her lap. Laughing, she caught him, swung him up onto her knees and kissed him. She stroked his fair curls.

'The trouble is, Shelley is terrified that since he has been publicly labelled a bad parent, they will also take little William from us as well as this one.' She gently rubbed her swelling belly. 'He thinks of us going to Italy.' She sighed. 'We've just taken a twenty-five year lease on this place, this delightful Albion House. I was hoping to settle.'

'Do you think he will really want to move soon?'

'Not yet, it's so ideal here. We have that room the size of a ballroom for a library and he seems to be managing to shut out the horrors of the world in Bisham Woods. He goes there most days to write, *Laon and Cynthia*, mainly, and walks along the riverbank to local villages. He has found a boat to go on the river and he is always happiest by water. There is Peacock, too, living just a few hundred yards away, who eats here most evenings. I want to like Peacock, because he was loyal to us when we came back to England, but I think I like him best a bit farther removed. He is beginning to get on my nerves. He is just too cynical, even for me.'

She leant towards Marianne, confidentially. 'I suspect he comes partly because he is more and more drawn to Claire. He might ask her to marry him. Shelley doesn't believe me, but I see how he looks at her when she is playing on that hideously expensive grand piano we ordered for her, through your friend Vincent Novello. The best, as Shelley told Claire.' A long pause. 'So she is reassured that she is loved.'

Mary said the last words with such bitter agitation that Marianne despaired of her remaining still any longer and, glancing towards the house, put away her artwork and suggested they take a stroll about the gardens. Mary called Elise and gave William back to her. The nursemaid took the little boys down to the far end of the lawn to where Millie was supervising a game of catch. William promptly fell on the ball that Thornton had dropped and clutched the prize to his chest, running off with it, giggling and refusing to return it.

The garden had a rough stony path around the perimeter, just wide enough to walk arm in arm. It wound through clumps of delphiniums and borders of roses, and around grassy mounds sheltered by trees. The smells were of approaching summer, a mixture of blossom and birdsong. Most of her life Mary had lived in cities. An English garden was almost too comfortable. She wondered if, over time, it would blunt the darker side of her creativity. Her novel needed her blackest thoughts and it was still her refuge. Would Victor Frankenstein make a mate for his creature? This moral dilemma occupied her thoughts. She had been writing non-stop for the six weeks they had been alone here before the Hunts came. Five pages a day. Nearly finished. Shelley had been reading the *Book of Job* and *Paradise Lost* out loud every night. Punishment. Retribution. Moral certainties. Victor would be punished for trying to bring scientific advance to mankind. To make man independent of a Creator. Like Prometheus, his punishment would be continuous. Doomed to see his family and friends killed. Doomed to chase the monster forever. She worried, and Shelley argued, that this would pander to religious certainty and imply that man should not aspire to scientific knowledge. Though she wanted the story to sell. So Victor must suffer for his presumption. She argued back to Shelley that at least the creature's voice represented the oppressed and the sufferers of prejudice, even though the public might not see it. They had enjoyed the stupefaction of Hayden, the painter, sitting at Hunt's fireside when Mary read the chapter where the creature berates his creator. Hayden, the supremacist, 'knew' the negroes were the missing link between humans and apes.

Mary dragged her thoughts back to the simple observation of the breeze in the leaves. Perhaps even their gentle rustling seemed like conflict if you lived among the branches, thought Mary.

'Is it so bad with Claire?' asked Marianne, tentatively, still concerned at Mary's recent vehemence.

'Marianne, you've only known Claire since she has had Alba. She was different before. This is the first time since we've left Godwin's home, three years ago — I can't believe it was only three years ago — that I don't feel so oppressed by her. The baby absorbs all her energy. She has less time to focus on criticising me to Shelley, and that was one of her most treasured occupations. She wants to prove she is the best mother and about that I don't feel threatened. I think Shelley believes because she is now marked off to Byron, I'll be less jealous, but he's not sure. He adores her singing and I know he is writing a poem about it and thinks I won't like that, so he tries to keep it from me. Men are like babies. They think if they cover their eyes you can't see them. He's called it *To Constantia, Singing*. That's the heroine of a book about a strong independent woman who doesn't believe in marriage, which is of course how Claire sees herself.'

'And Byron? Have you heard from him?'

'Not a thing. He hasn't acknowledged our letters. We don't know if he even knows about the baby. The rumours have him in Greece or Albania and it worries Claire enormously. She still deludes herself that Byron will take her on again with the child. Shelley also hopes he'll ultimately feel obliged to take responsibility for her. In the meantime we are on tenterhooks lest she be discovered to be the mother.'

'What do they think in the village?'

'They are told that she is the daughter of some friends of ours in London, sent down to the country for her health. This is the story we tell everyone, especially my father of course, even Peacock and Hogg. Having your brood here is good too. Who can tell with this … What is the collective noun? Cacophony of children?' She smiled as one of the children accidentally fell on another, and there was an outburst of sobbing protests. 'Shelley told Becks, the upholsters from Bath who came to make this house ready for us, to say to curious villagers that the new owners would associate with no-one, would not go to church and cared nothing for local opinion. Shelley thought this would make everybody stay away from us. Of course it has had the opposite effect. We are now an object of intense local curiosity.'

Marianne giggled. She looked towards the house, and saw Claire coming down the garden steps with Alba in her arms, followed by the maids with tea trays.

'Here comes the tea,' said Mary. 'With accompaniments,' as she took Marianne's hand to join her stepsister at the table.

Claire's baby was a delicate-looking little girl with large, solemn, blue eyes. Claire supported her on her lap, nuzzling the warm creases of her neck, luxuriating in the warmth of her undemanding, uncomplicated little body. She gently curled the wispy, dark hair on the back of the child's neck around her finger and touched the tiny cleft in her chin, which always reminded her of the poor baby's father.

She refused Elise's offer to take the baby away to where the other children were having their tea.

'They are lovely at three months, aren't they?' smiled Marianne, screwing her nose at the baby, who rewarded her with a wide smile.

'Yes,' murmured Claire. 'I have just been lying in bed with her while she slept. Watching her. I don't know how often I'll see her, if Albe takes her, but he can give her so many advantages. A good education. Financial security. Recognition as his daughter. I can't even acknowledge her as mine. Even with a pretended foreign marriage. Everyone would suspect her to be Shelley's.' She looked at the older woman piteously, avoiding Mary's eye.

'Why won't Albe acknowledge her or me? I would be happy with the crumbs from his table. I don't expect him to marry me. Marriage is a trap for women as well as men. But not even a letter.' She turned to Mary, her eyes fierce. 'I do think you should write again. You are his favourite. He would not ignore your wishes.'

Mary pursed her lips and started to speak, then saw Marianne's down turned, embarrassed eyes, paused, and took a deep breath that turned into a cough. The eruption of smouldering conflict was forestalled by two disheveled, noisy figures, who burst into the garden and flung themselves onto the lawn.

'Why is it that men seem to take up so very much space?' asked Mary of no-one in particular. 'The world would be three quarters less crowded if there were no men!'

'What sort of a welcome is that for two weary travellers?' Shelley grinned up at Mary. 'Especially those who have just walked thirty miles from London to lay at your feet?' He found his hat which had half fallen off onto the grass and did a cavalier sweep across his chest, comical in a prone position.

'Your husband,' said Hunt to Mary, who flinched at the appellation, 'is like an automaton. He keeps on going and going and going ...'

'I am Veritas, I walk with measured steps,' acknowledged Shelley, with satisfaction.

'Then I am Mendacium, stuck in my tracks, half the time,' replied Hunt with a rueful smile.

'Stuck in the mud, more often,' pointed out Shelley, gazing meaningfully at Hunt's spattered trousers. 'Where are your shoes?' Mary suddenly noticed Shelley's stockinged feet. 'Where are his shoes?' She repeated to Hunt, who raised his eyebrows. 'No, don't tell me. There was a beggar on the road …' She knelt and lovingly inspected his feet for damage, tutted at him, then stroked his cheek and kissed the top of his head. 'Elfin Knight.'

Shelley looked up at her. 'Not a beggar. A poor labourer who had to choose between spending his last few coins on bread for his starving family, or shoes so that he could work and provide for them. These Corn Laws have made bread barely affordable. I would make Lord Liverpool give all of his own shoes to the poor. Anyway, now one family has a chance. I told him to come on Saturday with the others, and we would help him.'

'We will do what we can,' agreed Mary.

'And thinking of bread, my kingdom for some bread and cheese,' he pleaded with her, with large eyes.

'Not much bartering power there,' replied Mary, as she got up to ask the cook for some supper for them.

'And some spruce beer, Marina,' called Hunt after her, standing up to go and sit next to Marianne and put his arm around her.

Shelley got up as well, threw his jacket on a chair, and went over to Claire, tickling the baby under the chin.

'How is little Alba coming on? Any change in two days?'

'She changes every day. Every second. We have finally settled her with the asses' milk. I did so hate weaning her.' She looked at Shelley pitifully, and he nodded sympathetically.

Mary came back out of the house and heard the comment.

'You know to be feeding her yourself would have completely given it away, especially when Papa stayed last week.'

'Did he suspect?' asked Marianne.

'Suspect that she is Claire's? I don't think so, but he was puzzled. Having so recently reconciled with us, though, I think he was reluctant to probe.'

'Thank goodness Mama was away,' shuddered Claire. 'She would have sniffed me out!'

'Someone had told Godwin I gave ... lent you money.' Shelley looked quickly at Hunt, who gestured dismissively. 'He's anxious that it should not eat into the available monies I can give him.'

'Hah!' Hunt made a snorting, cynical laugh, which was such a good imitation of Godwin, that everyone collapsed into laughter. Claire was giggling so much that she decided to relinquish her baby to Elise after all.

'He is still a great writer, though,' said Shelley, trying to be serious. 'His new novel, *Mandeville*, is almost done.'

'What did he think of your novel, Mary?'

Should she admit that he had shown little interest? Her relationship with her father felt more complicated than before, even though her marriage had supposedly mended it. Godwin had been persuasive in recommending the ceremony. Mrs. Godwin had hysterically implied he would hurt himself if it did not take place, though Mary suspected she was mainly relieved because a marriage would regularise Claire's position too. Though the gossip wheel that was London society hadn't seemed to grind any more slowly as a result. Mary's old friend from Scotland, Isabella, was still banned from meeting her, lest the Shelleys' views corrupt her household. She wrote secretly to Mary that her husband had told her that when Shelley visited London, Mary and Claire took it in turns to live with him. Rumour was such a difficult monster to slay. It was fed in corners of drawing rooms and salons and slept under the skirts of salacious matrons. While Godwin now boasted of his daughter's good marriage and felt able to hold his head up and stay under the same roof as them, Mary and Shelley felt defensive that their principles had been compromised. Mary, especially, felt forced to decry the principle of marriage, especially in front of Claire, whose subtle sneer, whenever Mary was referred to as Mary Shelley, implied her certainty that Mary really welcomed it. And her disdain.

'I think my father is a little bemused by my novel, and finds it rather frivolous. He expected me to write more like my mother, I suppose,' said Mary, sadly.

'So, let us take stock of the company.' Hunt leapt up and stood in the middle of the grass like a ringmaster, twirling and gesticulating at each of them like prize performers.

'We have Marina writing a novel about a dark and magical creation of a crazed inventor wherein man can challenge the limits of the accepted world.' He made a pirouette and bowed low to Mary.

'We have Couchion, alias Monsieur Shelley, writing a long, long poem to awaken hope in mankind that love can triumph over oppression, especially religious oppression.' He spun around to Shelley and bent low, arms wide.

'We have me, the Hunt, alias Caccia, writing a not quite so long poem, about the nymphs of wood and field and sky, to encourage the love of pleasure and to ban bigotry and prejudice.' He joined his hands above his head and whirled crazily.

'Somewhere in the wilds of Margate we have Keats, alias Junkets, who may yet join us. He, being the third recipient of our challenge to write a long, long poem of myth and Cynthia, is, I am sure, incubating unsurpassed meditations on beauty.' He pressed his fingers to his lips, kissed them, and flung the imaginary kisses to the winds, accompanied by high leaps.

He stopped breathlessly and looked at Claire. 'We have our songbird, Miss Clairmont, writing something amazing ...' He looked inquiringly at Claire.

'Oh, a small thing about human passions, and the way that people are misjudged and falsely vilified,' said Claire, and Hunt tipped an imaginary hat to her and held it out to an imaginary audience.

Hunt did a small dance around the circle and they all clapped.

'So here we have the world put completely to rights, and the sun is shining in agreement, and those wispy white clouds are the beards of Plato and Aristotle, who are smiling down at us. Now, the only question is ...' and he bent and tiptoed quietly from one to the other wagging his finger. Then, after a long pause, he leapt up with a shout. 'Who will be published first?'

They all laughed cheered loudly until he shushed them and went over to Marianne.

'And of course, there is the beautiful Marianne, who already embodies all the fine qualities we aspire to, and only has to show by example!' He kissed her loudly as she blushed and they all cheered again.

# 5

'Poor Mary's book came back with a refusal, which put me in rather ill spirits. Does any kind friend of yours Marianne know any bookseller or has any influence with one?'

*Letter to Marianne Hunt*, Percy Bysshe Shelley

Three weeks later, Mary sat at a small desk in the vast library, her tired eyes falsely glittering in the pool of candlelight. She placed a final sheet on the top of a pile of manuscript paper in front of her and put her pen away in her green writing case. Five inches of neatly stacked paper. Five inches of endless work day and night spent making a fair copy, ready to go out into the world.

Her thoughts were nervously anticipating the next day when they were going to London.

Shelley will take it to Murray, the publisher. Shelley thinks Byron will honour the promise he made on the lake at Geneva, when he said that my work will be published with his – even though he didn't finish his ghost story. I am not so sure. He plans to tell Murray privately that it is mine and refer him to Byron, even though to the world it will be anonymous. Shelley will present it as being from a friend of his. He has written a preface to say as much, even though this is a risk. To many people, an association with Shelley is not necessarily a good recommendation.

She had thought long and hard and decided that she would not put her name to the book, though Shelley had wanted her to. She could not properly explain to herself why.

Because … Because I have to face the possibility that I am a coward … that I am scared of criticism? Because I am scared I will be compared with my mother? My mother would never have hidden her name from the world. I am letting her down. Shelley thinks me too modest. It is not modesty. I will be veiled like a harem woman, but not oppressed. Frankenstein has been liberating. At last I have a voice that is uniquely mine, not Shelley's, not my father's, not my mother's. It is like my child, though, that I have nurtured this past year, and moulded and groomed to be fit for the world. I want to give it its best chance. I want it to stand on its own feet, not be judged by the prejudices and expectations that cling to its parent.

Mary looked at the plaster statues of Venus and Apollo, scraped for them by Marianne, which they had set either side of the window in the library. Inspiration. Light and love. She pushed the stray hair back from her high forehead, tied the bundle of paper with a blue ribbon and gave it a gentle pat of reassurance and encouragement, snuffed the candles, then went to bed.

An author is hatched with feathers ripe for ruffling. Mary preened when Murray liked the novel and squawked loudly when his reader, Gifford, said that it did not fit with the style of the Publishing House.

'He is prejudiced against us, because of all the attacks on Hunt, Keats and me in the *Edinburgh Review*,' grumbled Shelley.

'No. He doesn't think it's an appropriate book for a woman.' Mary slapped the table in anger. 'He is old fashioned. He thinks women should write books like *Pride and Prejudice* and *Mansfield Park*, that Murray's had such success with. By 'A Lady'. I am clearly not a lady!'

It proved difficult to get Frankenstein accepted by a publisher. After Murray, Shelley sent it to his own publisher, Ollier, who found the story too alarming for his taste. Then Hunt had the brainwave of trying Lackington, a publisher whose list included many works on alchemy, ghosts and magic, and, ironically, *Phantamasgoria*, one of the books of ghost stories they had read out loud to scare themselves, in that dark summer in Geneva.

'They are not a serious house,' worried Mary. 'I will not be taken seriously. They advertise the cheapest prices in England at their bookshop.'

'What is good though, is they never accept credit, so at least we will get paid,' Shelley replied. 'I have negotiated forty percent after expenses. You are still only nineteen. It is your first effort. To be published anywhere is a grand achievement. The bookstore in Finsbury Square is the largest in London. They say a coach and six can be driven inside!'

'Horses don't buy books,' rejoined Mary.

They were sitting in the drawing room of Albion House. It was August, four in the afternoon, and the fire was lit. As the idyllic summer had trickled away, the summer of boat trips on the Thames, of a house bustling with visitors, of picnics, composition and creation, harsher realities filled their lives. It became colder and wetter and the house absorbed the rain and stayed damp. It felt as if mildew grew in the pores of their skin, and with every shiver of the leaves, Shelley felt a corresponding pain in his side. There was a synchronicity, Mary sometimes thought, heretically, between Shelley's worst complaints and her confinements. The baby was due very soon. Was there an unacknowledged battle in Shelley's body between the joy of parenthood and the loss of her attention? She tried, with all her strength not to allow the pregnancy to remove Shelley from centre stage in the household. The confinement was only weeks away, and Sir William Lawrence, supposedly the best doctor in London, spoke gravely of Shelley's health, implying a disease of the lungs, and suggesting a change of air, perhaps Italy. Mary was not sure she could contend with the difficulties of such a major move, assuming all was well with the baby's delivery. She did not even have a good nursemaid ready to help with the birth and the baby. Marianne was supposed to send one down from London, but dear Marianne, though well intentioned, was not always reliable.

The nurse from London arrived a week late, but Mary's baby was also late and Shelley, who knew Mary wanted him there, was like a tethered, wounded animal, unable to concentrate on writing, wandering among the poor lacemakers in the village, distributing blankets and sheets he had had sent from London, and gaining an eye infection that had probably come from a villager, and that caused the nurse to banish him from Mary's room.

'If it is a girl we will name her Clara, after her aunt,' said Mary kindly to Claire as the pregnancy hung on. The imminence of a new life made her mellow and warm towards family in all its flawed forms. Claire was pleased. Claire was the name she had chosen for herself. Her mother had christened her Jane. Mary's choice of a name made her feel that Mary at least approved of one of her decisions, and there was household harmony in Mary's last two weeks of confinement.

Clara Everina finally made her entrance on the evening of 2nd September, giving Mary surprisingly little trouble. She was healthy and looked the image of Shelley. Shelley was delighted to have a girl, but his health deteriorated more rapidly, and he sent for the Hunts for comfort and distraction. As soon as he saw that Mary and Clara were safe, he left for London for another consultation with the medical experts and to spend time juggling their business affairs. He took Claire with him.

'I am relieved Claire's gone, she's never much help,' Mary told Marianne, who happily coddled her and little Clara, though nearly eight months pregnant herself. 'I feel she's critical every time Clara cries. I hate that she will be sympathising with Shelley, dramatising his illness, yet not doing anything practical, like making sure he wears a scarf against the wind. I swear that her sympathy makes him worse. Then she pesters him about Byron and Italy, and he feels torn because he has promised Byron not to show her his letters. She doesn't think how difficult it will be for us to move and particularly to sell the lease on this house. The money we've spent on it. Of course she has an ulterior motive. Byron has finally said he will take Alba. He wants to call her Allegra, by the way, so that's a sign of ownership. So be it. Now we have to get her to Venice and it's difficult since he won't see Claire. I don't want to go, especially so soon, with Clara such a baby, but it is getting impossible to conceal Alba. Allegra. Then there's expense of course. Shelley has not even paid for the wretched piano yet and his cousin Captain Pifold is threatening to have him jailed because of a loan he has failed to repay.'

'When you go back next week, will you get Shelley to bring down a sealskin hat for William? And a new pelisse. You choose it if you can, but not too expensive, dear Marianne. It's so cold and damp here, I can't even go for a walk with him without warmer clothes. I need to spend more time with him so that he is not jealous of Clara. Please don't forget!'

'I won't,' promised Marianne.

'I shall write it on your traveling bag,' said Mary, with a laugh. 'You and Hunt are like babes. Neither of you can keep a thing in your head for a minute.'

Mary and Shelley sat on a low ottoman huddled around a late night fire. Sitting close, fused together, her head on his shoulder. A blanket was draped across both their shoulders. Only a few candles remained alight in the drawing room and the only sound was a drip from the ceiling, a reminder of the heavy rain in the afternoon. She was relieved to have him back here at Marlow for a short weekend, because he was in town for longer and longer periods. Letters were such an agonising way of discussing the things that would change their future. There were delays, they crossed on their journeys and, once hurriedly written and sent, the thoughts in them could not be amended for days. Her frustration made her tense and she gripped his hand tightly. There was so much to do and to decide. She wanted him to make some firm plans about their future. He was, as usual, either wildly impulsive or catastrophically given to procrastination. When they were together normally, she had learnt to deal with him, understanding how his mind worked. She would introduce things gradually, just enough to water a seed without inducing an immediate, possibly bad, harvest. Shelley listened to her and valued what she thought and he usually enjoyed making decisions together; it was another intellectual game. Lately, though, she felt on the cusp of becoming a harridan. She had threatened to wean Clara and go to London if he did not come down this weekend. If she were certain of their choices she would not doubt that her persuasion towards the right one would prevail. This time there were so many unknowns that she doubted her own wisdom, so her powers felt dulled. She now craved any sort of certainty.

Shelley was numb with anxiety. Mary's presence calmed him, but he knew this was temporary and he had to face their problems. His constant pains and lethargy were a never-ending reminder of 'dark and cold mortality'. There might be so little time to gain acceptance for his notions in the world; so little time to care properly for all those who needed him. Mary was right. He was making decisions without sufficient consideration, or putting off making any decision at all. Worst of all, after the summer interlude of creativity writing *Laon and Cynthia*, his intellect was utterly imprisoned by the tediousness of everyday business. Only the horrors of society roused him again to try to make a difference. The disproportionate mourning for the young Queen Charlotte, compared with the callous attitude to the hanging and beheading of the three protestors of the Pentrich Rising who were ignorant peasants incited to rebellion by an agent provocateur for the government. At least Ollier published his protest pamphlet which pointed out that, though poor and insignificant, they were human beings deserving of sympathy, and it found some sort of audience.

'We know we must leave this house,' Mary said finally, trying to sound decisive. 'It is cold and miserable and not good for your health. I need to be with you in London, to look after you. The lease has only been advertised for a week or two, but if someone buys it, I can come as soon as I can pack up our things. We must pack them properly this time. Every time we move we lose half our possessions. We buy the same books three times over because they have been lost in a move. But London is only for now. For your health we must go somewhere where the sunshine will drive out the pain.'

'I know you think the coast of Kent is the best idea,' replied Shelley, biting his lip. 'Only think what we could do and see in Italy; imbibe not only sunshine but breathe the same air as Plato.'

'I would love Italy, but the cost of getting there … And we would be abandoning Godwin. Well, he would feel abandoned.'

'Yes, he would. He now has another moneymaking scheme for me to invest in: buying some property. Supposedly it would make income for him and a long term profit for me. It's very complicated, but I don't think we can allow Godwin's feelings to determine this. The reality is that we will have very little to spare for him, whatever we do. Even the lawyer's fees for the Chancery case have still not been paid.'

'Not another post-obit loan.' Mary turned his face to her. 'Promise me. The negotiations will take so long. We will not be free to make any decisions about our future.'

'I know.' Shelley kissed her in reassurance which stopped short of a promise. 'It is important we get Alba, I mean Allegra, to Italy, to her father, before he loses interest.'

'That is a consideration in favour of Italy,' Mary nodded vigorously in agreement, relieved Shelley had brought it up first. 'It would cost us such a lot to send her there with a nurse, anyway, we might as well take her ourselves. At least it would mean that the cost is not wasted. It should be soon, before everyone finds out about her. It's getting harder to keep her a secret.'

'I know, but the post is so slow. Claire wants reassurance about her right to visit the child and Byron will give no quarter. He will not promise anything except to take and acknowledge the child. He still makes me promise that Claire shall not see his letters and won't write to her himself. He wants the child sent with a nurse, and Claire will not hear of it. She must take her herself. She doesn't help by writing to him long tirades about how he misjudges her and how worried she is that he will neglect and be cold towards the child, together with some bitter character analysis about how cruel he can be to those over whom he does not have power – such as she sees herself. Her outspokenness can be charming, but she can sound so bitter.'

'She returned from London last week in a foul temper and I think that your latest letter from Byron was mainly the cause. It didn't help that your letter to me arrived late so I didn't arrange for Joseph to go to Maidenhead to pick her up and she had to get a coach. Somehow of course, the Allegra situation is all my fault. When she is scared about giving her up, it is me that is pushing for it, to spite her.'

'She is deeply fond of the child and she is worried in case Byron will not love her enough.'

'Well, of course, but I think the truth is that if we didn't push her, in a year or two she would be angry with us because we hadn't organised it. I think we have to just trust that Byron will behave well. At worst, if he is not fond of her, she will have the name and advantages.'

'He is at Venice now. I will talk to Claire tomorrow and write to him again. If only the wretched man would offer her a grain of comfort.'

'And the books?'

'Your book, my dormouse, is with the printer. I made those few corrections, as you asked me to do, and I think that all is well.' Mary snuggled closer. He hadn't used that particular pet name in a while.

'Our *History of a Six Weeks Tour*, as it is to be known, is with Hookham. It was encouraging of him to suggest we publish our diaries and letters from our first trip together. It is good that we have something published from us both.

'And, I have a surprise for you,' he continued, smiling. He went over to his traveling bag in the corner and produced a sheet with a flourish. Ollier is going to publish my poem *Laon and Cynthia*, and this is going to be the *Dedication*.' He took her hand and pulled her over to the table, sat her down, rearranging the blanket over her shoulders and gently pulling back her loose curls, and fetched two candles for her to read by. 'It is called *To Mary*.' Then he sat back and watched her face as she read the fourteen stanzas which, he felt, perfectly expressed his feelings for her.

Mary read and wept. The lovely lyrical description of their life together was the most seductive, warming declaration of love that any man could offer. Whatever came, it was worth it.

Of all the verses, those she secretly treasured most were those that spoke of the optimism of the past months:

> *So now my summer-task is ended, Mary,*
> *And I return to thee, mine own heart's home;*
> *As to his Queen some victor Knight of Faery,*
> *Earning bright spoils for her enchanted dome;*
> *Nor thou disdain, that ere my fame become*
> *A star among the stars of mortal night,*
> *If it indeed may cleave its natal gloom,*
> *Its doubtful promise thus I would unite*

*With thy beloved name, thou Child of love and light.*

*The toil which stole from thee so many an hour,*
*Is ended,—and the fruit is at thy feet!*
*No longer where the woods to frame a bower*
*With interlaced branches mix and meet,*
*Or where with sound like many voices sweet,*
*Waterfalls leap among wild islands green,*
*Which framed for my lone boat a lone retreat*
*Of moss-grown trees and weeds, shall I be seen;*
*But beside thee, where still my heart has ever been.*

… and those that seemed to hold out most promise for the years to come.

*And what art thou? I know, but dare not speak:*
*Time may interpret to his silent years.*
*Yet in the paleness of thy thoughtful cheek,*
*And in the light thine ample forehead wears,*
*And in thy sweetest smiles, and in thy tears,*
*And in thy gentle speech, a prophecy*
*Is whispered, to subdue my fondest fears:*
*And through thine eyes, even in thy soul I see*
*A lamp of vestal fire burning internally.*

# REFLECTION

Paris 1842

Who, when he makes a choice, says, Thus I choose, because I am necessitated? Does he not on the contrary feel a freedom of will within him, which, though you may call it fallacious, still actuates him as he decides?'

*The Last Man,* Mary Shelley

'I was thinking, today, that this was almost the beginning, here in Paris, twenty-six years ago. We were tired and dirty and had no idea what we had done or where it would lead us.'

'So much easier that way, to be young and unheeding, than when we understand more about the likely consequences of our choices,' replied Claire. Her tone was bitter.

Mary was sitting in Claire's apartment in the Rue Clichy. It had the feel of being half-furnished. Claire had delighted in pointing out the lack of sufficient sofas and complaining of the costs of furnishings and repairs. It was the first time they had been face to face in years. The tea things sat ready to be arbiters of more than taste.

Mary realised just too late the disaster of raising a topic involving consequences, and tried to steer the conversation into more neutral, philosophical areas.

'I believe there are some points, vortices in time of which we are unaware, when small choices will radiate into all the subsequent patterns of existence.'

'The end of 1818 was like that.' Claire was not to be diverted. 'The beginning of the end of everything. If our choices had been different, then ...'

'We may think we make the choices and that it is free will, but we are blown inevitably along by the gentle winds that attend our birth and then gather strength through custom and obligation. Really we have only illusional power to resist.' Again Mary tried to depersonalise the discussion, to calm Claire's rising hysteria.

'We were having such a good time in London those last few months, living near to the Hunts. The theatre, the dinners, the conversation, the music. Allegra was unnoticed among the Hunt children. Hunt even persuaded Shelley to love Mozart.' Claire's eyes blazed into Mary, and her description of pleasure sounded much more like accusation.

'It was not all plain sailing, remember? There was all the fuss when the publisher made Shelley revise *Laon and Cynthia* and change it to *The Revolt of Islam*, and take out reference to what was considered incest and blasphemous libel. He hated doing it, but he was finally recognising that he needed to engage the sympathies of an audience.'

'Listen to you. It's all about Shelley's work and Shelley's reputation. It was then and still is now. What about me? Do you recall at all how much I didn't want to let Allegra go? I still remember, a visceral memory, the warmth of her undemanding, uncomplicated little body. How many nights was I allowed to enjoy that? I nearly died to let her go.'

'You had to …'

'For Shelley's reputation? Why did I care about that? Why did I care about his reputation?'

'I was going to say for Allegra's own sake. To do the best for her. But yes, for Shelley's health and his reputation too. You cared because you loved him.'

'I loved Albe too. Those few months of passion. What is the point of having bedded the most desirable man in the world if no-one knows? Why wouldn't he acknowledge me? I would have been happy to be just his friend, but not even a letter. Not a line for me in one of his to Shelley. He asked after you, not me.'

'Byron didn't care for me like that.'

'Shelley was fond of me, at least, but I was sweet girl, and you were dearest love. Still, why couldn't we have been three? Three is the perfect number. Indivisible. Two can easily be broken.' Claire went to sit at her piano and play a crashing chord, then got up again.

'You are a strong and talented woman. Everyone says so. An ornament to the female race. I wanted your book to succeed. I really did, for that reason. I never believed that Shelley tried as hard to sell mine to a publisher. It was all, always, about you and Shelley. You weren't going to rest until Allegra was gone. You had your two babes. Why did I have to give up Allegra? Why should I have married Peacock just because he asked me, as you wanted me to? I didn't love the man. He didn't take me seriously. I didn't want to marry.'

'We didn't want to force you. It just seemed an easy alternative.'

'Not we. You. Shelley always understood me. Oh, why did I ever give up my darling girl? How could I ever have trusted that Byron would take care of her? What choice did I really have? Even at the last minute I remember sitting on the beach at Dover and saying, screaming, no, I would not take her. Why did you persuade me? You give up everything to the depraved condition of society. Why did we ever go to Italy? Just leave. Go.' And the door slammed.

'Why did we ever go to Italy?' echoed Mary, to the empty room.

# PART FIVE

Italy 1819 — 1821

# 1

'There were no degrees which could break my
fall from happiness to misery; it was as the
stroke of lightning — sudden and entire.'

*Mathilda*, Mary Shelley.

Mary tensed, shifting her reclining position on the sofa slightly as she heard Shelley's footsteps clattering down the uncarpeted stone stairs of the Tuscan villa which was their new home. She stared around the room with its frescoes of country life with a sense of unreality, distanced suddenly, as if looking down into the room from above. The disheveled, grown-up, childless child lying in the centre, whose pallor reflected the whitewashed, vaulted ceilings, was a self she could not recognise. She shuddered and leant down to pick up one of the books abandoned on the floor beside her — a little pile of works concerned with the sufferings of the righteous, *Carissa Harlowe* and the *Book of Job* among the most recent, to look as if she had been profitably occupied. Did it help her to immerse herself in other's sufferings? She was not sure. Perhaps it only served to intensify her sense of the world as a subtly orchestrated hell, of practice or imagination. Perhaps it was better to read Dante's *Inferno*, with representations of Hell that were at least poetic, or Livy on the Roman wars. War was always honest hell, however much it was romanticised.

Shelley had spent all day in his little glassed-in eyrie, with it's perfect view of the sea, working on *The Cenci*. Burying himself in *The Cenci*.

She wished she did not see his expression of fading hope as he slowed at the door and came in, coatless, shirt untucked. She wished she could help him, even more than she wished she could help herself.

She untucked her legs from the sofa so that he could sit beside her and noticed a tea stain across the front of her white shift. She was becoming slovenly.

'Will you come to Mrs. Gisbourne's for dinner tonight?' Shelley asked, and though he tried to sound matter-of-fact, she heard the undertone of desperation. For her to say yes. To see just a spark of the old Mary.

'I'm sorry. I feel a little unwell.' Her hands circled her stomach, where there was a very slight swelling that needed to be protected at any cost. At any cost? Did that include her relationship with her husband?

'Take Claire.' Nothing could be worse than to be alone with Claire. 'I'll have an early night.'

'Maria Gisbourne will be worried about you.'

'You know I can't risk this baby.'

Mary felt as if every limb was a weight beyond her strength to move. Nor was there any longer a connection from her brain that had any authority over them. With brief determination, she went to the window where blue shutters had been closed against the afternoon heat, and pushed them open, letting in the languid light which bathed the Tuscan hills to the east, and glistened on fishing boats returning to the port in the West. Just beyond their garden, the peasants were singing as they used a water wheel which would draw water to irrigate the fields overnight. The pastoral scenes of the frescoes on the walls of the room seemed to synchronise seamlessly.

'How was the afternoon's writing?' She smiled, trying to find, in their work, the neutral ground that bound them when all else failed.

He smiled, gratefully.

'I'm up to writing the murder of Cenci. In the standard accounts of it he is bludgeoned to death at her bidding, some say by his daughter, Beatrice, and some say by her servant. I'm thinking that in my play, Beatrice will induce two servants to murder her father, but not have a direct hand in it. What do you think? Will the audience have enough sympathy for her? Should I remind them here how he has violated her? Or is it too shocking to harp upon? I think strangling, too, rather than bludgeoning. Do you agree? I need you to read this, Maie, and tell me what you think. You are so much better at storytelling than me. I can't always get the organisation of the story right. I can only put the feelings into words.'

'But such glorious words.' She turned to smile at him and held out her hand for the pages he was clutching. He came across to give them to her, put his hand on her arm and looked to the horizon. He had ink smeared across his forehead where he had pushed away his hair as he wrote in the sticky heat of afternoon. She reached up and rubbed at it.

'The evidence of honest toil,' she smiled.

'It's easy to work. It's so beautifully quiet here.'

'It is quiet because there are no children,' Mary choked, the tears, never far away, defying her best efforts at suppression.

'Mary, I can't ...' and he pulled away and literally ran through the door.

Giving in to the despair, she found her way, sobbing, to her room. She lay down and looked longingly at the bottle of laudanum on the dressing table. Because of her pregnancy she could not even wash her mind clean of memories with drugs. Shelley at least had that privilege. For a month, sleep had been almost unattainable. Sometimes she wondered if her current state, permanently nauseous, almost catatonic with grief, was not worse for her unborn child than the possible effects of a drug. Sleep may help her to get healthier, but she couldn't risk it. Though what were the prospects in the world for the poor thing growing unawares inside her. She and Shelley were undoubtedly cursed. To have had three children who had not survived. Was it retribution for their flouting of the rules, for their responsibility in Harriet's death, Fanny's death. Had these sins been so bad, and should she now believe in a personal, vengeful God, or a universally balancing karma?

She looked at the miniature of William by her bed and fingered the lock of his hair in the small case. She remembered Shelley's despair in Rome after a thirty-six hour vigil, when the malaria finally won the battle for her child's small, beautiful body.

Stop. I must stop thinking. I must stop the images. Thinking is unendurable. A life sentence. I must escape. I need oblivion. Like Fanny. Like Harriet. Who we thought so selfish. Now I see that only a mother or a lover isn't selfish. And I'm not either of those, now. Half a mother, half a lover, or less. Can I hope that I will be either again? She lifted her shift and stroked the slightly shiny, distended skin of her stomach. It is showing more quickly, my fourth pregnancy. In a month I will be twenty-two. I must put my hope in this baby, who has not had a chance to live. A heavy responsibility for an unborn child.

All I can do is run away inside. Hide inside. My elfin knight can't rescue me here. It is lonely. And still not safe.

Later that evening, before supper in Casa Ricci, Shelley sat with Maria Gisbourne in her extensive library, with large casement windows that opened across fields of vine trellises interspersed with fig and olive trees, towards the distant sea.

'You look as if you've had a bad day, my dear.' Mrs. Gisbourne touched Shelley's arm and looked into his face, sympathetically. 'I can always tell. Your eyes look as if they have drawn the mist from the mountains.'

Maria Gisbourne was a handsome, if not beautiful woman, dressed conservatively in grey, her dark hair, silver threaded through, tucked authoritatively under her white cap. She exuded the certainty and calm that had encouraged Mary and Shelley to choose the port town of Livorno as a place of escape as they fled from the memories of Rome. She had found them their villa, close to where she lived with her husband and son, Henry. The families saw each other almost every day and Henry, an aspiring engineer of thirty-two, was showing signs of being drawn to Claire.

They walked out through the glass doors and strolled up and down in the gathering dusk, breathing in the lingering spicy-sweet smell of myrtle. They would have presented an asymmetrical profile to anyone happening to glance out from the villa: his tall, rangy aesthetic silhouette against her small, rounder motherly one.

'How is Mary today?' she asked, quietly.

Shelley stopped and looked down at her, his jaw clenched so tight it was an effort to speak.

'Mrs Gisbourne, I just want her back. I want Mary back. With me, in spirit as well as body.'

'It has been barely a month since William died, and less than a year before that it was Clara. It's more than anyone should have to bear. The grief can't be dismissed and it's so hard to share. You're both battling to survive in your own way and don't have enough strength to support each other. Give it time, my dear. Be patient.' She looked thoughtfully at the peasants setting off back to their villages in ragged lines along the pathways between the rows of vines and olive trees and glossy myrtle hedges, some hand in hand. Sounds of their laughter drifted up and from a distance there seemed nothing but carefree happiness. Happiness was always better imagined from a distance, she thought.

'Try to see your love for each other as a small island of rock to which you are both clinging, to survive the storm. The wind is still howling and the seas are still raging and you are clinging to opposite sides of the rock and can't yet manoevre yourselves around to be closer together. Just know that one day the seas will be calm again, and the sun will emerge to dry the slippery surface, and you will reach out and find each other.'

Shelley inclined his head to her in wry deference. 'A wise and poetic image, Mrs. Gisbourne, but I still can't even grasp any sort of reality. I can't believe William has gone. I suppose I want a little normality with Mary to feel connected to the world. These dramas of Calderon you have me read ... I do find consolation in them, and inspiration. A Spanish Shakespeare, indeed. *"All who live but dream they act here,"* he says. Is that right, Mrs. Gisbourne, do you think? Are we dreaming this whole horror of personal tragedy and public ignorance and misery? Do we only think we act or invent? Will we wake up to a glorious society of courage and virtue? '

'Even if it is a dream, we have to behave as if it is real, don't we? I think it is more likely we are just actors in plays of our own devising, *"strutting and fretting our hours upon the stage"* as Shakespeare says. Still, we must hope we still have some hold on authorship.

'Now come back inside to eat. There are custards and tarts enough to suit your vegetable-eating taste. You must get strong. And talk to Henry about the steamboat. He is so excited that you are going to provide the funds to build it. When you brought me the letter of introduction from Godwin, I was completely taken aback. I had not spoken to him since I refused his marriage proposal when my first husband, Mr. Reveley, died. I think poor Godwin was very hurt, but I saw him as a friend, not a husband. He guessed rightly that I would enjoy meeting Mary, all grown up. I nursed her as a baby after Mary Wollstencraft died. My little Henry was only ten, but he remembers it all so well. He loved that little girl. Your Mary.' She smiled at him and squeezed his arm as she took him indoors.

'And what of your other children, Mr. Shelley?' asked Mr. Gisbourne, at supper. 'Has there been a resolution in the case?' He was a gruff man, with heavy whiskers and a bureaucratic temperament, given to brief temper tantrums if feeling slighted. Shelley had seen him throw a dish across the room when Henry crossed him. It was to be wondered whether Mrs. Gibourne had done better than Godwin in her choice, but she seemed to be quite sanguine about his temper and her glance alone seemed to calm and direct him.

'There has, Mr. Gisbourne,' replied Shelley. 'The Chancellor has lodged them with our choice of guardians, though we had to search for an excessively god-fearing rural couple. I, of course, contribute to their maintenance. Even so, and this is what rankles, I am only allowed to visit the children under their supervision. Harriet's sister and father, however, and my parents too, can visit them completely unsupervised! I am such a monster that I would corrupt my children of five and three with notions of godlessness and teach them to abhor proper social behaviour! I would do this while I made them paper boats and played fairy tales, as I did with William.'

He had become heated, but tailed off and looked around as the table went quiet. At once the Gisbournes and Claire entered loud protests about the unjustness of it all, and his blameless character.

Reaching for the loaf in the middle of the table, he ripped off a chunk with unnecessary force, put it on his plate and speared an apple with his knife. 'It came too late anyway. I certainly can't go back this year to see them. I can't leave Mary now, especially with a new baby expected.'

He forced a smile. 'So encourage me, Henry, about our profitable venture. What was your progress in getting the pistons we need? And what is your latest estimate of the time to reach Marseille from here? Will people pay to take passage on her do you think, or will they be wary of steam? How will we convince them?'

Across the fields, in the Villa Valsovano, Mary tried to write to Marianne Hunt. She asked her, in tones of desperation, to send clothes for the new baby. What a bad decision not to have brought her baby clothes to Italy. She couldn't even remember where she had stored them. Until she knew if they would come she felt incapable of making the decision to buy more. It was asking a lot of Marianne to find and send them, but who else would? She tried to find other trivial things to write about but the image of Marianne's warm smile was too much. If only she were here, and if Hunt's never-ending optimism were here for Shelley to draw on.

In the end, she wrote what she could not avoid: *I feel that I am not fit for anything and therefore not fit to live, but how must that heart be moulded which would not be broken by what I have suffered — William was so good and beautiful and so totally attached to me. To the last moment almost he was in such abounding health and spirits. His malady appeared of so slight a nature that the blow was as sudden as it was terrible. We had the most excellent English surgeon to attend him and he acknowledged that these were the fruits of this hateful Italy. But all this is nothing to anyone but myself and I wish that I were incapable of feeling this or any other sorrow. But ...*

She threw down her pen and put the unfinished letter under her pillow in case Shelley or Claire should see it on her table. Unable to rest, she picked up Shelley's poem and wandered up to his study, sat listlessly at his desk, turning over the manuscript pages he had given her to critique. She looked at clutter: an old paint box, some hooks, a cup, an inkwell, a scattering of bills and half finished poems, many sketched over with drawings of trees or boats, books of chemistry and old metal nails, new volumes of Calderon and a wooden bowl filled with quicksilver, in which floated two cogs attached to a long screw, to represent a boat of sorts.

Mary remembered how Shelley had done this to show William the wonder of the heavy screws not sinking into the liquid silver.

He had felt the loss of William more than the death of Clara. Clara had only just had her first birthday and was not yet a fully formed individual to him. He had not nursed her for six months as she had. And he did not feel the huge bitterness about her death that she felt.

It was Claire's fault. Shelley's fault too for being so ready to meet Claire's demands. However much she had resented Claire before, now there was a hard sliver of pure hatred lodged like a splinter in her soul.

If, if, if, if when they were staying at the Baths of Lucca last September, Claire had not been so dramatically insistent in wanting to see Allegra so soon after she had been delivered to Byron in Venice. If she had not bullied Shelley into taking her there. If he had not had to hide her presence from Byron and imply that the whole family just happened to be close by, at Padua. If Byron had not conceded that Allegra could visit them for a week, and offered them all his villa in Este. If Shelley had not had to justify his lie by summoning Mary and baby Clara so that they left the Baths of Lucca and travelled three hundred miles to Este, via Florence to get passports, even though Clara was really too sick with a fever to travel.

Claire had never once acknowledged Mary's sacrifice. Never apologized. As far as she was concerned she had lost her child, too. It was true that they had not had any word from Byron about Allegra for the past nine months. But she was still alive, at least.

She forced herself to concentrate on his writing. It was the only way she could be with him. She saw that the verse he had left for her included lines that Beatrice speaks to Cardinal Camille:

*'that fair blue-eyed child*
*Who was the lodestar of your life:'—and say—*
*All see, since his most swift and piteous death,*
*That day and night, and heaven and earth, and time,*
*And all the things hoped for or done therein*
*Are changed to you, through your exceeding grief.'*

When he came home tonight, she would have blown her candle out, maintaining the fiction that she was asleep. And he would creep in and touch her hair on the pillow and kiss her forehead, an invitation and a reproach, neither of which she could accept.

# 2

And here like some weird Archimage sit I,
Plotting dark spells and devilish enginery,
The self-impelling steam-wheels of the mind
Which pump up oaths from clergymen, and grind
The gentle spirit of our meek reviews
into a powdery form of salt abuse,
Ruffling the ocean of their self-content;

*Letter to Maria Gisborne,* Percy Bysshe Shelley

The heat continued through August. As Mary said to Maria
Gisbourne one evening, after supper in the Villa Valsovono, 'In
England the summer heat is reluctant and apologetic, but in this
pestilential country, it is aggressive and demanding.'

A daily ritual had developed and the soothing sameness of it gave
a continuity to their lives, smoothing the ragged edges. Shelley and
Mary wrote in the morning, while Claire had an early bathe in the
Palmieri baths on the sea, a half hour walk across the fields, returning
invigorated and virtuous to her singing lessons. Mary had started
on a new novel, which she called *The Fields of Fancy.* It went slowly
and she knew she sometimes rambled across the dark, bitter story
of the incestuous love of a father for a daughter, but it was another
world to inhabit and one in which she could describe the loss of love
and life, and in which she planned no redemption for her characters.
In the late morning, Mary read Latin, at the moment Lucan's epic
poem, *Pharsalia.* Her Latin was becoming fluent and she found she
could become absorbed in the story of the glories and tragedies of
the Roman wars. She thought of Lucan in 65 AD, forced to commit
suicide at twenty-five as a punishment for conspiring against Nero.
Shelley would be twenty-seven next week. What would be his legacy

should he die now? His poems were sublime, but none had caught the public imagination like Byron's. Unlike Byron, he had no vanity, but he thought that poets could and should be the legislators of the world. He wanted a voice that would be heard. Mary had been trying to persuade him to write something likely to be popular with a wider public, and this play, *The Cenci*, was his answer. Although it was a tragedy, he had written it for 'the multitude' as he said; a tragedy like *King Lear*.

His hopes were another load of guilt for her. After Frankenstein had been published in three volumes, the notices had been mixed, but most praised the power of the writing and some saw the subtleties in the story. Walter Scott had been one of the most favourable, saying that *"upon the whole, the work impresses us with a high idea of the author's original genius and happy power of expression"* and *"descriptions of landscape have in them the choice requisites of truth, freshness, precision, and beauty"*. He had thought it was written by Shelley, though Mary had quickly disabused him. Some reviewers had been prejudiced by the dedication to the radical, Godwin, and thought it subversive and *"diseased"*. One had got wind of the author being a woman and thought it unsuitable to her sex. Even the less favourable reviews, though, were tantalising enough about the story for it to become quite popular. The first five hundred print run had nearly sold out. Shelley had been completely unselfish in promoting it, sending it to eminent people and supervising the advertisements. Shelley, as Byron had said to Mary, did not have any envious impulse.

It seemed so unfair that her generous husband, with all of his talent and enthusiasm, should be ignored or vilified, while she had such comparative success with her first effort, of much lesser quality. She needed him to shine.

They all dined at two, and in the afternoon, with the shutters drawn against the heat, Mary and Shelley rested and read books together. Sometimes, as her pregnancy advanced, she dozed as she listened to his smooth and expressive voice, with her head on his lap. In the coolness of the late afternoon, they strolled among the vines and then in the evenings they would take supper with the Gisbournes at either of their villas. Shelley seemed a little better. The pains in his side, which had returned with crippling and frequent intensity after they left Rome, seemed to have abated, but there was still an array of potions on his table and the local doctors, he had seen three, recommended they seek the warmth again for the winter.

One evening, the Gisbournes were at Villa Valsovono as usual and they sat in the drawing room, Shelley and Henry poring over drawings and sketches, Mrs Gisbourne and Mary playing chess.

Claire sighed loudly. 'I would like to sing my new song for you but those cicadas are too much competition. They will drive me to distraction.'

Shelley looked up. 'In 500 BC Anacreon wrote a poem about them and described them as 'harmonious".

'Well, they don't harmonise with my notes.'

'How do you find your singing master, Claire?' asked Henry, gazing adoringly at Claire, oblivious of his mother's close and disapproving watch. 'He is supposed to be the best in Leghorn.'

'He is much the classical Italian.' Claire stroked her throat, tenderly. 'He divides the voice into chest register and head register with the passagio between. I can do the chest register but I have to improve my head register, for resonance. Tra la laaaa!'

'To best the cicadas,' laughed Mary.

'And how are you now, Claire, after the adventure of this afternoon?' asked Henry, hoarse with concern.

'Yes, what exactly happened?' asked Mary. 'I slept through it all. The afternoon heat makes me doze.'

Henry stood up and spread his arms, with the air of one enjoying centre stage.

'About three o'clock, I was in my study and I looked out and saw Claire running down the hill towards our villa, hair loose and streaming, tripping over stones, and screaming "Henry, Henry, help, murder!"' He looked at Claire's darkening brow. 'But looking magnificent in her distress.' He smiled at her, nervously.

'Anyway, I ran down to meet her and she said, "Come quickly, murder, you must do something, save Shelley," and of course I ran back here with her straightway.' He looked around at his enthralled audience, though Shelley had gone to stand with his back to them and stare out of the window.

'When I arrived, there was Shelley, pistols drawn, threatening two coachmen who were trying to get around him to hold back the coach horses, and Shelley was forcing them to move away so that John could drive off. They had large clubs with them and I'm not sure whose nerve would have held longest.'

'Mine,' came a retort from Shelley.

'They spoke a local dialect which I know, so I tried to soothe them,' continued Henry. 'It transpired that they thought you were all escaping without paying the rent. Shelley is late with payment and the landlord had set these men to watch the house!'

'Damned impertinence!' snapped Shelley. 'In any case, the coach was only going to be repaired.'

'Yes, but if I hadn't been able to persuade them of the truth of it, you would have encountered some real difficulties. Not least with the police. I had to remind them that we were your friends and guarantors, and that they knew us from some years of local residence. You are always too quick with those pistols, Shelley. It was very tense for a while, before they allowed the coach to go.'

'They went off muttering to each other and swearing loudly back at us, with lots of raised fists,' added Claire. 'Shelley, you should be gracious enough to thank Henry for his intervention, at no small risk to himself.'

'Thank you indeed, Henry. Now back to more serious matters,' and he moved a protractor across to him, tapping the drawings in one of the scattered notebooks. 'Show me again how this low pressure engine will work. You say a forty inch cylinder?'

'Is this thing actually going to work?' asked Claire, wandering to the table and turning one of the sketches to face her, screwing up her eyes to try to fathom it. 'An iron steamboat? I still find it hard to believe, though I'll be the first on board, of course,' and she gave them both an impish grin.

'Don't you remember last year? The Savannah went from Georgia in America to Liverpool using partly steam, in just thirty days. And they are using steamboats everywhere now, even on the Thames and on Scottish Lakes. In the New World they are using them everywhere on rivers as commercial enterprises. Some ply to Ireland too and they have crossed the Channel. I know people are nervous about them — they'll catch fire, they're not safe — but it's the way of the future, Claire. Not to be dependent on sail. Never becalmed. Not to worry about the direction of the wind. Think of it.'

'Ours will be better,' said Henry eagerly. 'We will have two inline wrought-iron paddle-wheels, 16 feet in diameter, and eight radial spokes. And no sail at all!'

'It's two hundred and fifty miles from here to Marseilles by sea.' Shelley was no less enthusiastic. 'Robert Fulton in America made five miles per hour and some steamboats have made seven. If the ship leaves in the morning, it will mean one night on board, and arriving the next afternoon at the latest. Compare that to three days journey by coach, and staying overnight at uncomfortable coaching inns. Our steamboat will have cabins and staterooms with carpets and mirrors.'

Claire had been getting impatient since she was no longer the centre of attention, even though Henry clearly turned to her for approval most of all. Mary and John Gisbourne were setting up a game of chess. Mrs. Gisbourne was embroidering a sleeve.

'I wish you would use your engineering skills to make a balloon that could be guided to fly between cities, Henry. Then I could get in and fly to Venice or Ravenna, wherever my darling is, and see her.'

Mrs. Gisbourne pursed her lips. Although she was a woman of liberal political views, she was enough of an Englishwoman to disapprove of Claire's bastard, Allegra, of the child's father, and of the reports of his licentious behavior that trickled along the underground canals of gossip in Italy. As she told her husband, she valued Shelley and Mary highly and Claire was pretty, and could be entertaining, in a brittle, tactless sort of way, but that was different to being a candidate for their son's hand. The Shelleys had told them the truth about Allegra, which was a secret scandal known to very few, and they would certainly not pass it on. But they knew. And Claire was critical and picky about potential husbands. Mary had told Mrs Gisbourne, bitterly, how she had refused Peacock, someone she actually admired. She professed to abhor marriage, a very selfish opinion in Mrs.

Gisbourne's eyes, creating as it did an extra burden on poor Shelley. Anyway, she didn't want her lovely, sensitive boy rejected by this difficult girl. Thank goodness there was talk of the Shelley household going to Florence, for Dr. Bell, for Mary's pregnancy. She would miss them, though. Mr. Gisbourne agreed with his wife, as he always did.

'I will go and see my baby,' continued Claire. 'I must take charge of her. It is coming on to winter. I am so full of anxiety for her health I feel I must burst. The summer in Venice I fear has done her no good, it is full of dysentery.' She did not notice Mary's sharp intake of breath. 'The selfish brute, I am sure he cares nothing about her diet. I hope he dies of indigestion. Shelley must take me.'

'But we don't even know where he is.' Mary looked up, holding her knight. 'Last we heard was six months ago and she was safe with the British Consul General's family in Venice, the Hoppners, which seems best if he is cavorting and debauching around the country as we occasionally hear. The last rumour was that he was in love with an Italian Countess at Ravenna. He doesn't answer our letters, so we don't know. In any case, Shelley is not well enough to chase around the country, nor can we afford it. And he has no passport to go from here to Ravenna.'

'But he can manage to take you to Florence in winter, which everyone says will be ruinous to his health, so you can have the best medical attention from Dr. Bell for your confinement? Selfish, selfish, selfish.' Claire, outraged, stormed over to Mary and threw up the chess board so the edge of it barely missed Mary's face. 'I wish you were dead, too.'

She stormed out and Shelley caught at her arm as she passed, saying, 'Claire we are all concerned ...' but she threw him off, shaking her head so hard that her dark curls came loose from their clips and fell across her face, and ran on. They could hear the sound of her thumping on the iron banisters as she ran up the stone stairs. A servant came hastily from the kitchen, but seeing it was Claire, threw up her arms and retreated, muttering and tutting.

Mary sat with her head in her hands, while John Gisbourne quietly picked up the scattered chess pieces. Shelley went to Mary, belatedly to her mind, and gently moved her hands to check that she wasn't hurt. He looked around at the others and smiled weakly.

'I'm sorry, it is hard on her, with no news. We do all worry.'

But Mary made no move to ameliorate the atmosphere, and the Gisbournes were already standing to leave.

In their room, later that evening, Mary was lying in bed, in tears of frustration, while Shelley pressed a cold towel on her forehead. 'How can you be such a hypocrite? Was it not a gentleman of my near acquaintance who couldn't bear the living situation with his first wife's sister always there, influencing his wife, interfering? The constant third. Why can't you understand what a toll it takes on me having Claire with us all the time? She is so full of vitriol, and she doesn't care what she says. She doesn't for a second consider its effect on other people. Life is always scenes when she's around.'

'I'm not capable of sending her away, Mary. I can't do it. I'm responsible for her.'

'And she's useful to you. Someone to walk with when I'm pregnant or nursing.'

'It's true I like that. I need to get out for my health and do not like walking alone, as you know, although lately she hasn't come much. She's been slow to get out of bed and slow to get dressed. I think she is suffering very badly from anxiety about Allegra. It's crippling her.

'In any case, her brother Charles will be here soon, for a visit. That will redress the balance a little, won't it?' His eyes were pools of warmth and concern but she stayed resolutely on their banks.

'Apart from her animosity to me, there's the continual damage to your reputation. What happens in a few weeks time, when we go to Florence for my confinement? Another round of suspicions, explanations.'

'Why worry what others think?'

'You don't. The rumours and nudges and accusations and pointing and whispering every time we are near anyone from English society, they don't touch you. It's as if you had a gossip-proof umbrella. But it doesn't cover me. I get soaked in the slimy downpour.'

'Hopefully Charles will come with us.'

'Hopefully when he leaves, he can take her with him. Why don't you use your powers of persuasion to that end?'

Charles was a happy addition in the last weeks of September. He had recently been in Spain for more than a year and was proficient in Spanish. Shelley tried to monopolise him to learn the language better so that he could read Calderon, but Claire claimed proprietorship, as he was her real brother. Though it didn't drive out anxiety about Allegra, having him there gave her some genuine family warmth. They were fond of each other. Mary had some moments of guilty clarity about the lack of undemanding love in Claire's life. Her lack of the right to be cared for. Then those moments were always blown away by the hot breath of Claire's next jibe.

When Mary was having a siesta, and Claire was discussing dinner with the cook, Charles interrupted his translation of *The Cross* to asked Shelley of news of Skinner Street.

'None of you have mentioned Godwin. It has been an unnatural silence, so I didn't like to ask.'

'Godwin is beyond my understanding,' said Shelley. 'He writes to Mary that continued grief is an indulgence. That she has a good life and that she should be strong and get over it. He has complete lack of sympathy. It distresses her, and I don't know whether I should keep his letters from her.' His look was anguished as he went to a drawer in the credenza and took out two unopened ones, running his finger over the seals, and shaking his head.

'He also says the worst things about me; that I promised him money that I haven't paid, that I am morally reprehensible, that I am aristocratically arrogant. Me! Huh. Of course Mary does not believe any of this. She knows I have given him over forty-thousand pounds. She knows my character. She knows how little we can now afford. It still hurts her, Charles. It is the last thing she can stand, and I have to protect her.'

Charles looked nothing like Claire. He was of medium height and well built, but was lighter complexioned than Claire and his hair was curly but finer than hers, so that his short whiskers gave him a softer appearance, and his smile was quick and open, with none of the underlying sarcasm of Claire. In France and Spain he had to a large extent been living on his wits, employing his boyishness and charm to find families and friends to take him in and encourage his desire to learn their languages. Shelley had given some occasional help — the world's banker, as he sometimes, bitterly called himself. Only Charles' eyes, which were hazel and a little too pale, showed a hint of the weakness which had led to his restless wanderings and propensity to fall hopelessly and unsuitably in love.

'The court case about the back rent on Skinner Street is what is causing him to be particularly desperate now, is it not? When is it settled?'

'In the next few months. He will indeed be desperate if it goes against him. He will owe seven thousand pounds. But Charles, I have done all I could to rescue him over and over. I must recognise that it is good money after bad.'

'I don't blame you, Shelley. I know you have done what you could. Look at me, I had to get away from there at any cost. I couldn't stand my overwhelming mother or my judgmental stepfather.'

'And you plan to go to Vienna?' asked Shelley, standing up and lifting his voice as the maid came in with the tea, followed by Claire and Mary.

'Yes,' replied Charles, taking his cue and smiling at the girls as they came in, Claire rushing and flopping on the sofa next to him, Mary moving slowly, carrying her six-month load with dignity and care. She lowered herself gently into a chair near Shelley and he leapt up to help her down, the maid with the tea tray crossed his path and the plate of grapes and figs, piled high on the plate, toppled to the floor. The Italian maid turned on Shelley and screamed abuse at him, arms flying and imprecating the heavens as to the stupidity of this clumsy foreigner, as he tried to apologise and pick up the fruit. As she left, she pulled off her apron and flung into onto the stones.

'There goes another one,' sighed Mary. 'Honestly, these Italian servants are ridiculous. They get hysterical at the slightest mishap. Oh that we still had Elise.'

'Yes well, she's made her own bed as it were, with the disreputable Paolo Foggi.' Claire said with a knowing smile.

Shelley turned to Charles to explain. 'Elise was our servant and nursemaid for three years, after Geneva. Then in Naples we hired a manservant who abused her and cheated us into the bargain. All Italian servants are rogues, but he was a master. We felt a responsibility for Elise, so Mary insisted that Paolo marry her, under threat of prosecution.'

'A black-hearted fellow,' said Mary. 'I just hope Elise can influence his behaviour rather than the other way around.'

'Anyway, as you were saying, Charles, Vienna? Why Vienna?' said Shelley.

'I have friends there who say they can get me teaching work,' smiled Charles. He patted Claire's hand. 'They could find you work as a governess, too Claire. I hear it is a civilised city. Better than any city in woebegone England. And the music, Claire. The same streets as Mozart, Beethoven, Schubert, Haydn.' Claire turned her head away and stared out of the window.

'Never while my darling is here,' she said, very quietly.

Shelley said, quickly, 'You're right about England Charles. We have just recently had news of that abominable massacre in Manchester. Peterloo they call it. My blood is still boiling. The murderous oppression of the weak and the poor who only seek some measure of relief and just representation.' He sunk back in his chair with an air of infinite sadness. 'Five hundred injured, fifteen killed, with the militia slashing at unarmed men.'

'What an amazing sight it must have been, though, when it started,' said Mary. 'Eighty-thousand men in peaceful protest. The idea of it is overwhelming.'

'Those brave men are the only hope for the country,' said Shelley. 'There is no hope from its unprincipled rulers.'

'Read him the poem, Shelley,' said Mary.

'You read it, Maie. It was a lot to do with you. Some stanzas are yours. The popular tone was your idea.'

'There are ninety-one stanzas, Charles,' said Claire, in a neutral tone. 'So let me pour you some more tea, first.' She went to the tea table. 'Though I especially like the bit about the Chancellor, Lord

Eldon's tears knocking out the brains of the children. A nice way to get back at him for taking yours, Shelley.'

Shelley found the copy of the poem and brought it to Mary. He lifted her feet onto a footstool. 'Your ankles are swollen,' he said, examining them and putting a cushion underneath.

Mary smiled gratefully, and read, in strident tones, the poem called *The Masque of Anarchy*. She was proud of it. She did think it came out of their joint anger at the news, though she was happy for it to be deemed all his. She especially thought the last five stanzas were a wonderful call to action to all English patriots.

*Stand ye calm and resolute,*
*Like a forest close and mute,*
*With folded arms and looks which are*
*Weapons of unvanquished war.*

*And if then the tyrants dare,*
*Let them ride among you there,*
*Slash, and stab, and maim and hew,*
*What they like, that let them do.*

*With folded arms and steady eyes,*
*And little fear, and less surprise*
*Look upon them as they slay*
*Till their rage has died away*

*Then they will return with shame*
*To the place from which they came,*
*And the blood thus shed will speak*
*In hot blushes on their cheek.*

*Rise like Lions after slumber*
*In unvanquishable number,*
*Shake your chains to earth like dew*
*Which in sleep had fallen on you —*
*Ye are many — they are few.*

Charles was impressed. 'Lucky for them, and you, probably, that you are exiled in Italy. What about you, Mary? Are you working on, anything?'

'I've just finished a short novel, *Fields of Fancy*. It's about suffering, which you might think is unsurprising. I'm not sure you'll like it. The heroine is a girl whose life is blighted by the inappropriate feelings of her father.' Mary looked at him steadily and Charles' eyebrows rose, but he said nothing. Surely Mary was not implying that Godwin harboured such feelings towards her? He looked at his sister, Claire, for a clue, but her eyes were downcast. He scoured his memory of their time in Skinner Street. Mary had certainly been Godwin's favourite. Did it explain some of his anger towards Shelley? Charles couldn't think of any comment and the silence became complicated. Mary chose to relieve his present suffering, but not his doubts.

'Don't worry my dear, My main production will be in about three month's time, around November, in Florence.' She stroked her stomach with a determined smile. 'You will be there for the fourth performance of its kind, and hopefully a successful one!'

# 3

We might be otherwise, we might be all
We dream of happy, high, majestical.
Where is the love, beauty and truth we seek,
But in our mind? and if we were not weak,
Should we be less in deed than in desire?

*Julian and Maddolo*, Percy Bysshe Shelley

Mary had been woken early to feed little Percy Florence. He was a delightful child, small but sturdy, with a thoughtful smile like his father's, and he fell agreeably back to sleep afterwards, with no fuss. She had decided to take an early morning walk along the L'ung Arno, a broad carriage way that bordered the banks of the Arno River that snaked through Pisa. She took Caterina, the new Italian nursemaid with her, assigning the cook to listen for Percy, though she knew he would sleep for at least an hour. They were well wrapped in woollen shawls and full bonnets, and though there was still a winter chill in the air, the wind had not come up, and the little passeri were chirping happily as they foraged the quiet cobblestones for yesterday's crumbs.

The light on the Arno was beautiful as the sun rose. Behind them, the porter closed the heavy wooden doors of their lodgings, Casa Tre Donzelle. Rows of three or four-storied Palazzi and Casa fronted the river, tightly pressed together, two-dimensional like a child's canvas, painted in shades of yellow and ochre, with occasional blue. With their green shutters and the brick or painted arches around the windows, it became a fairy-tale stage glowing in the spotlight of the dawn. Mary found the Arno wonderful. Such a surprisingly dominant presence. She hadn't expected it to be so wide and such a busy thoroughfare. Even at this early hour, the reflections of the palazzi in the water we were disturbed by the first navicelli, bringing their goods from the docks at Leghorn. Some were drawn along the towpath by weary-looking horses, some by camels. She had been surprised by the camels and Mrs. Mason had explained how they had been brought to Pisa in the time of the crusades and how the Grand Duke now farmed them at the San Rossore estate for use in the fields and in the draught.

As Mary said to Shelley, Mrs. Mason was the fount of all knowledge.

She had lived here in Pisa for five years and had adopted the Shelleys because of her ties to Mary's family. Mary's mother, Mary Wollstonecraft, had spent a year in Ireland as governess to Mrs. Mason, who was then fourteen-years old, and was the Honourable Margaret King. Mrs. Mason said that Mary Wollstonecraft "had freed her mind from all superstitions", taught her to think independently and to shun social frippery. The thought was in both their minds that this was how Mary Wollstonecraft might have cared for and taught her own daughter.

Now, as fortune had thrown them together, Mrs. Mason had decided to repay her debt to Mary Wollstonecraft in a small way, by being a force for good in Mary Shelley's life. Though if Fortune were a dramatist, thought Mary, her plots would be thrown out by Covent Garden as too improbable.

At nineteen, Margaret King had obediently married her neighbour, Lord Mountcashell, and they quickly had seven children. In her late twenties they travelled for two years on the continent. Mrs. Mason eventually grew tired of the shallow society of the English abroad, as well as endlessly fighting against her husband's hostility towards enemies such as books and girl's education. And so, in Naples she fell in love with George Tighe, an ex officer, a lawyer and an agriculturalist. Lady Mountcashell did not fit the image of a Romantic heroine, more that of a head matron or headmistress. She was a large confident woman, very tall and big-boned, with solid flesh and a clear calm, no-nonsense expression. Mr. Tighe, though, was a grand passion that she failed to shake off. When her husband returned to Ireland she stayed behind in Italy with her lover, which meant leaving all her children, too. Lord Mountcashell kept them, as was his right under law.

The unwed couple lived as man and wife, adopting the name
Mason. Mary had been touched when she realised that this was a
way of paying homage to her mother, as Mrs. Mason had been the
name Mary Wollstonecraft gave to her governess-heroine in her
book of cautionary tales for children, *Original Stories from Real Life*.
The Masons roamed the Continent. Mrs. Mason studied medicine
disguised as a man in Jena and wrote children's stories that were
published in the Godwin publishing house in London. She had
expected sympathy from Godwin, as Mary Wollstonecraft's husband,
but though Godwin liked Mrs. Mason's acquaintance, he could not
bring himself to properly acknowledge the couple. To him she was
always the Countess Mountcashell.

Now, in Pisa, she was a focus of their little 'paradise of exiles', as
Shelley called their new situation here. She knew the Gisbournes,
still living just a few miles away at Leghorn. The Masons had settled
in Pisa to be close to Vacca, a doctor renowned throughout Italy and
a professor at the university, when Mrs. Mason showed some early
signs of consumption. It was because of Vacca, as well as the milder
climate, that the Masons had recommended the Shelleys come there
too, and found them lodgings. Shelley's health had suffered badly in
the frosts at Florence. The pain in his side had become excruciating.
Sometimes he would roll around on the floor clutching a cushion.
His spasms were more frequent, and his headaches were worse.

Yesterday, they had gone to the Faculty of Medicine of the
University of Pisa in the Via Roma to have Shelley's first consultation
with the famous Professor Andrea Vacca. He had welcomed them
with extreme courtesy and impeccable English. He took Shelley into
his rooms while Mary waited anxiously in the ornate outer chamber.
After half an hour Shelley emerged with Vacca's arm around his
shoulder. The doctor was of late middle age, quite small but well built,
formally dressed and not showy like most Italians. No flamboyant
neckerchiefs or ribbons in the lapels. He had a soft face with a serious
straight nose, large warm eyes and gently curling hair, but cut to
gentlemanly length. Next to him, Shelley looked almost skeletal, his
tall frame more bowed than usual, Mary thought. Looking closely at

him, to try to gauge his mood after the consultation, she thought she saw a few more slivers of grey amongst his curls.

'Do not worry, Mrs. Shelley,' smiled Vacca, soft and reassuring, perceiving her anxiety. 'We will make the great poet better, you will see.' His English was really very good. It was said he had studied under the famous surgeons in London for many years, in his youth. 'I am a strong admirer of your husband's work. To be fit to write, this is the great thing, no?

'And you, Mrs. Shelley, you are planning another book, one about our poor Prince Castruccio of Lucca, your husband tells me. On your way back to Tre Donzelle, stop at the Biblioteca. You will find here, I am sure, all the books you need for your research. The library here at Pisa is much richer, much fuller than any in Italy, even Florence.' His pride in the university was appealing, and he bowed low over her hand. 'Tonight I think I will see you at Mrs. Mason's. You must tell me all about how you will tell the story, then.' He retreated back into his consulting rooms, smiling all the time.

'Would you like to go to the library now?' asked Shelley, as they walked out into the mild, crisp morning.

'Tomorrow,' said Mary. 'Though it's very encouraging that I can finally work properly on the book here. And you,' she nudged him in the ribs 'promoting my slight talents too much. Oh what will I do with you?' She smiled, shaking her head in mock despair. 'So tell me. I need to hear all about his diagnosis.'

'Vacca is of the opinion I must give up all my medicines!' he said in wonderment, laughing uncertainly. 'Amazing man, you know. He was at the fall of the Bastille, a true republican.'

'Which I'm sure makes his diagnosis all the better,' sighed Mary. 'But what does he think is wrong with you? How does he propose to cure you? You're in such pain.'

'Well, just like Dr. Roskilly in Naples and Dr. Bell in Rome, he doesn't know for sure. So that's no different, but he is inclined to think it is nephrotic. I like it that he doesn't rush to hasty judgements.'

'Your kidneys, not your liver, then. So not hepatitis?'

'He says that the side effects from taking so much medicine can be worse for my body than any possible benefit. Until the effects are all washed away and I am cleansed of them, he won't know for sure. He says my body has lots of natural defences against illness that can't work with all the mercury and resins I'm taking. Leave it to nature, he says. Horse riding, drinking pure water, the sulphur baths at San Guiliano as soon as the weather is milder. And I must try to sleep more. These are to be my cure.'

'Do you believe him?'

'He believes my nervous condition results from extreme sensitivity. It is what makes me a poet, but this can also come out in physical affliction. I must avoid strain.'

'Perhaps if he could have given us his prescription earlier, we could have missed the past two years,' said Mary, her voice heavy with irony. 'Then we would have avoided strain.'

'We have conquered and endured, Mary, like the kings of old philosophy. And at least I can stop applying these caustic patches on my side. If it's not hepatitis I don't have to purge any poison from the hepatic region. It is such a painful treatment. Vacca was definite that this should stop. I'm encouraged, Mary. He is the best in Italy. You will meet him properly tonight at Mrs. Mason's. He is so cultivated and so warm. I begin to feel we can be part of this community. He has mentioned some other scholars that we should meet. You know Galileo was a professor here?'

'It would be nice to expand our acquaintance with local people. The judgemental English in Italy do not want us any more than we do them!'

'By the way, where is Claire, today?' asked Shelley, casually.

'At Mrs. Mason's perhaps, or still walking in the Argine with Laurette.'

The Masons lived in the Casa Silva, on the west bank of the Arno, supported by George Tighe's income from some estates in Ireland and her allowance from Lord Mountcashell. They had two children of their own, Laurette who was ten and Nerita two years younger. Mrs. Mason never talked about the loss of her first children, even though Mary was passionately curious and noticed that she could not allow Laurette to sleep anywhere except in her room or an adjoining one. She was such an advocate for good parenting and so knowledgeable about raising children that she was writing a book, *Advice from a Grandmother*, even though she had never seen her own grandchildren. She was the perfect friend, the perfect mentor in every apparent way, but there was something, some reluctance in Mary that kept her from stripping her soul to her as she would to Mrs. Gisbourne or Marianne Hunt. Her main pleasure in Mrs. Mason was that in her she found someone who truly understood the deep feelings of motherhood. The pleasure she found now when feeding little Percy almost obliterated, at least temporarily, the past two horrible years. Pleasure, thought Mary, was a word too devalued by crass usage to express the sensation of feeding her baby. Every ounce he sucked strengthened the boundaries to their small, secure fiefdom, where the warring demands of outside allegiances were muffled by the peace inside.

Mary was savouring this thought as she walked with Caterina beside the river and then crossed the Ponte Della Fortezza as the city woke up. On the other side of the river they encountered some criminals condemned to hard labour, chained in pairs, each pair guarded by a policeman with a gun. The wretched, pale creatures were repairing part of the river wall and their chains made a heaving clanking noise that beat against the quiet of the early morning. She was not sure yet how she felt about Pisa. It did not have the beauty of Rome and it seemed half populated compared to the bustle of those cities. The inhabitants all seemed scruffy — bargees and beggars — and those who weren't were students who looked just as bad. The tower that leaned, the baptistry and the cathedral were fine, and there was the mild climate, the library, Vacca, and Mrs. Mason to make amends for its shortcomings in refinement.

If Mary could not quite find the perfect soul mate in Mrs. Mason, Claire seemed to have no such reservations. Did she sense Mary holding back and did that make Mrs. Mason seem the perfect confidante, Mary wondered. She knew it was an uncharitable thought and that Claire had as much right ... maybe need. Already Claire spent much of her time at Casa Silva. The girls treated her like a big sister, romping and climbing all over her. Claire loved it, and it suited her well — a child at heart — as Shelley remarked to Mary, watching her fondly. Or not prepared to grow up, as Mary muttered in reply.

'She is my mother's greatest friend, you know,' said Claire, as she, Mary and Shelley walked through the iron gates into the courtyard of Casa Silva that evening, with its vines and the bare chestnut tree. 'She showed me all the letters Mama wrote to her after we left. Poor Mama. She poured her heart out to Mrs. Mason. And now Mama is publishing her latest children's book.'

Mary bit her lip, hoping that Mrs Mason was alert to Mrs. Godwin's manipulations.

Vacca was already there, and seemed happy to meet them again.

'There are very few English families in Pisa, ten at most,' he said. 'It is a pleasure to make the acquaintance of others equally as refined as Mrs. Mason and Mr. Tighe. Mrs. Mason has been studying with me. If she were a man, she would be a great asset to the world of medicine.'

'I always seem to find uses for my small knowledge,' smiled Mrs. Mason.

She made sure that everyone was comfortable in the sitting room. It had several large gilt mirrors, two fireplaces and many framed prints of the region, but surprisingly few ornaments; as unadorned and no-nonsense as Mrs. Mason herself. The large casement windows rattled in the biting wind that had whipped up in the afternoon.

She turned to Claire, offering some green tea. 'Have you heard from your brother Charles, my dear, since he left you in Florence?'

Claire took the cup, looking dark. 'We have had one letter from Vienna.'

Mary tried hard to conceal a smirk. 'It is almost totally concerned with Louisa and THE INCIDENT OF THE CHIROPLAST,' she intoned theatrically.

'It's not funny,' scowled Claire. 'The way Madame du Plantis speaks, anyone would think it a classical icon instead of something to help one position the hands on the piano.'

'When we were lodging in Madame du Plantis' house in Florence, she lent Claire a chiroplast for her music lessons. When we left, Claire, uh,' she paused, 'inadvertently brought it here with our things.'

222

'Then I thought, quite reasonably, since I have it I may as well get it copied before I return it,' pouted Claire. 'So I sent it to Leghorn, to Henry Revely, Mrs. Gisbourne's son who's an engineer, to ask him to make drawings, but the stupid messenger left it at the consul's house and Henry hasn't got it yet!'

'In the meantime,' continued Mary, 'Madame du Plantis is in a rage, and accuses Claire of stealing it. Case and all, as she says. She has written a horrible letter to Charles and forced Louisa, her daughter, to break off with him; you knew he was in love with her? A "capricious, heartless scrawl" is how Charles describes her letter. Of course that is not of too much concern. Charles' passions are scarcely limpets. It is all a little embarrassing, though.'

'Embarrassing, huh! Charles thinks she has dark secrets hidden in a compartment in the case. I hope she is a Christian so that she can go to a place where her sins are punished,' said Claire, stamping twice on the floor, looking down expectantly and cupping her hand to her ear. 'Are you expecting her?'

The gentlemen laughed.

'Anyway, I wrote to Louisa to give her a piece of my mind,' Claire added and suddenly Mary's heart sank as she realised what Charles had meant when he had reported that Claire had seriously offended Louisa. This was a letter she had not known about.

All at once, a newcomer was announced, and at the same time, Elizabeth Parker, the governess, brought Laurette and Nerida in to say goodnight. The girls curtsied prettily to everyone, then looked at each other conspiratorially and ran to Claire, each grabbing one of her hands, and pulled her to the piano.

'Play now, Claire, please, before we have to go to bed!' they entreated.

They looked imploringly at their mother. 'Please, Mama!'

'Very well,' Mrs. Mason smiled. 'Just two songs now, if Claire is willing. Then off you go.'

Claire played two songs for the girls, then was carried off by them to say goodnight. The newcomer, who so far had not had time to say a word, was introduced by Vacca as Il Signore Professore Pacchiani, a professor of natural philosophy. He looked more like a theatrical villain than a professor, tall, with long black hair, dark brows that dominated his face and a smile that seemed less than open, even sly, but in the political discussion that started up, his republican credentials proved impeccable.

After they had jointly reformed the major political systems of Europe, Pacchiani smiled, sadly. 'If you want examples of the tyranny, sometimes it is not necessary to look as far as the State. Often the family is a ... what is the word ... a small example of the big one?' 'Microcosm?' offered Shelley. 'Yes, a microcosm of the State, where ministers happily dispatch enemies of the status quo. Or perhaps the State is a reflection of the family,' he said, thoughtfully.

'Do you have a specific instance in mind?' asked Mary, with interest.

'Yes, as a matter of fact. There is a young girl, just sixteen, confined in a convent very close by. Her parents have put her there until they can find a suitable husband. Or should I say her stepmother has insisted on her confinement. She is a jealous woman, I think. This poor girl is languishing for want of the company that is cultivated. She has a beautiful mind, full of the most abstract thoughts. She is herself beautiful, a young goddess. Each day she can only walk in the courtyard of the convent. She has no friends here.'

Shelley leapt to his feet. 'We must go and see her at once,' he cried. 'Mary, we must, mustn't we?' He looked appealingly at Mary, who nodded. 'You must take us there, Pacchiani. We will provide warmth and companionship to her.'

'We will, of course,' agreed Mary, but she had the peculiar sensation of a sudden flood of tears, gushing and swirling behind her eyes, building up pressure but finding no outlet. She realised that it was many months, years, since she had called him her Elfin Knight. His rescuing of her had become desperate and unromantic. Now he had been offered another damsel in distress, in mythological distress, not Mary's corporeal distress of loss and tears and grief and sleeplessness.

# 4

'To express it delicately — I think Madame
Claire is a damned bitch — what think you?'

*Letter to Mr. Hoppner,* Lord Byron

Our lives are tormented by absent children, thought Mary as she pulled on her stockings and fussed with the pinning of her hair.

'This comb you bought is useless, Shelley. It tears my hair. I must send to Mrs. Gisbourne to change it for a smaller one.' She smiled up at the maid who was trying, unsuccessfully, to help her. 'Thank you Serena, I'll do for an outing to the famously fashionable Teatro Rossi,' she said, sarcastically. 'You can go now.'

As Serena shut the door to the bedroom behind her, Mary sat at the dresser and stared at herself in the mirror, looking past her own reflection at Shelley, who was supposedly dressed but had wandered in, buttoning his shirt with unnecessary concentration.

'For goodness sake, go to Leghorn, my love, and consult the lawyer, Rossi.' Her tone was exasperated. 'He'll know what to do; how to see off that scoundrel Paolo. How dare he think he can blackmail us? Have you been sending enough money for the girl's upkeep?'

'Yes. Rossi has helped to transfer it. But do you really want to discuss this? You haven't wanted to know anything about the child.'

'These rooms are too cramped,' said Mary, irrelevantly, fiddling with the buckles on her shoes. 'We must get Mrs Mason to help us find a new house. You need a study. Things are cheap enough here. For once we are living within our budget, even if we still have our massive debts.'

'And when our boxes finally come from England with more of our books and clothes, we will need space,' agreed Shelley, not looking at her, accepting the digression. 'Although we should wait. If we go to the Baths of Pisa this summer as we should, there is no point in doing anything about it until we come back.'

'Poor Percy is still in flannel,' said Mary. 'Our own clothes will be too unfashionable by the time they arrive. I will look ridiculous, like the surly Pisans with their pointy pink silk caps. Mrs. Gisbourne promised to send striped gingham for a dress, but she was so slow, and next week they go to England. I must write and scold her for it, and for not visiting before she goes. I miss her. Wretched Claire. She's why she won't come. I have no female company except for Mrs. Mason and her girls.'

'But you have me. And your Castruccio.'

'Ah yes, him. My other man, my Prince of Lucca. He does take up a lot of my time and my energy, it's true, but it's the Princess Euthanasia and the prophetess Beatrice who are my real heroes, as you well know.'

'I think it will be a better novel than Frankenstein,' said Shelley, looking across at her thoughtfully. 'The republican and the despot. The clash of cultures. Ollier wants to publish it, you know.'

'No. The old rascal can keep his mercenary hide in its stable. He didn't want Frankenstein, and now he's not galloping off with this one. Besides, I think he cheats you; or at least fails to uphold you. He could have done more for *The Cenci*, and for *Rosamund and Helen*.'

'It is a problem for another day,' sighed Shelley, coming over and putting his hands on her shoulders. 'Mary, Mary, we must talk about the child in Naples, if you will.' He turned her round and sat on the edge of the bed facing her so that their knees were touching, and ran his finger down the line of her jaw and kissed her gently.

'Give her her name. Elena Adelaide. Elena Adelaide Shelley,' said Mary quietly, trying not to let resentment force her to pull away.

'Yes. I'm sorry.'

Claire's head appeared. She looked at them sitting, apparently in earnest conversation, paused, then pushed the door open anyway, and came in. 'I'm ready,' she said, brightly. 'How do I look? I could hardly lift my arms to put the comb in my hair. They are so sore from that long ride yesterday. I must have been really gripping the reins as we went up those hills near the sea.'

'I feel it in my calves,' said Mary, sympathetically, moving her knees away and rubbing her legs. 'I suppose we all cling on differently.

A metaphor for life. We shouldn't have let the crazy Mr. Taafe come with us. He set a stupid pace.'

Claire smiled. 'He'll be there tonight, along with the usual raft of Italian professorri.'

'Hmm, yes. The stupid, the agreeable, the learned, the bigoted and the profound,' said Shelley, getting up and drawing the shutters. The mosquitos were starting their evening assault.

'Add the polite, the avaricious and the genius, and we have seven. The sacred number of Apollo,' intoned Mary, with a gesture towards heaven. 'The Oracles in philosophy or mathematics, or anatomy or cant.' They laughed. It was one thing they could agree on. The Italian academics made up most of their society as there were so few English in the town and even fewer who cared to associate with them. In one way they were grateful for the Pisan intelligentsia, but they found them a mixed bag at best, with an eclectic share of human foibles, living proof that the intellect alone was not enough to guarantee the attainment of wisdom or virtue.

'Apart from them, the theatre will be empty. Pisans don't seem to care about any fine arts, especially opera. And they talk all through it anyway. Is Mrs. Mason going?' asked Shelley. The room was becoming dim in the filtered light and he lit a candle on Mary's dressing table and one on the writing desk in the corner.

'Yes,' answered Claire. 'She and I were having a long talk this afternoon about my situation. What is the great lord thinking, Shelley? You know him best. Mrs Mason thinks we should go to Ravenna anyway, even though he says not to. And how do you still respect him when he says that in our house she will be exposed to Atheism and green fruit, as an excuse not to send my child here for a visit? I send my letters to Mrs. Hoppner to forward. Since she looked after Allegra in Venice, she has her best interest at heart, I believe. And mine as a mother. I think it won't annoy him so much if I don't write directly, and she is the Consul's wife.'

'We can do little if he won't let her go,' said Shelley, riffling through some loose sheets of Mary's writing and keeping only half turned to Claire. He spoke thoughtfully, but was turning the pages obsessively, as if there might be answers there. 'I do wish you'd show me your letters to him, dear, before you send them. I fear you're not the most moderate of correspondents.' He and Mary exchanged a look which Claire did not fail to intercept.

'How can you say that?' Claire was instantly sharp and suspicious. 'I am the mildest, sweetest, most grovelling person to him. And why should I grovel? He promised me I should see her whenever I wanted, otherwise I would not have sent her. Should I not remind him of a promise? He says we are not near enough. We are at least in the same country. It is all excuses. And he says he will put her in a convent. That is to punish me and to say that she will be no atheist, like you.'

'Is it so bad, Claire? Here, in Italy, a convent is like a boarding school,' replied Shelley, gently. 'And really, any faith or no faith, she will think for herself when she is ready. She is your daughter. We love her too, Claire, but criticising and provoking Albe will not make him feel warmer towards you.'

'So bad? To make her a Catholic slave to ritual and bigotry? It will spoil her life. It will make her unfit to live among the English. Separate her from me more than ever.' Claire's eyes filled with tears. 'I cannot sleep for worry. I feel sick every day. Every day.'

She looked at them both with something close to contempt. She knew that, in spite of Shelley's special relationship with Byron, they were powerless to influence him about Allegra. Her nagging doubt was that they agreed with his plans. She shrugged her shoulders and turned to leave, almost colliding with Vittorio who was bringing in more candles. 'I will wait in the parlour until you are ready.'

As the door closed, Mary looked at Shelley, and saw, in the tightness around his eyes and the way his hand went involuntarily to the pain in his side, that he was in danger of collapsing under a weight of guilt and frustration. She resolved to be kinder to him than she had planned to be, over the Neapolitan child. The subject would have to be raised, but not just yet. Shelley was still struggling with the problem of Claire and Allegra.

'Claire is right to be concerned about the atmosphere at Byron's. If it wasn't that I felt he is essentially good hearted, I would despair more myself,' said Shelley, lowering his voice and glancing at the door. 'At Venice the rumours about his licentious behaviour were rife.'

'I feel sorry for him,' replied Mary, sounding unforgiving. 'His *Don Juan* has flashes of divine beauty, but there is so much disillusion and despair. And guilt. His imagination seems to lead him to the depths, whereas you, my love, thank goodness, yours leads you towards hope, a higher reality.' She smiled at him and went over to make some sense of his neckerchief and do up the buttons he'd missed. 'The practical outcome of which is that you don't know how to dress. Though I do like this yellow waistcoat.'

She smoothed its satin and kissed his neck. For all his weaknesses, she knew Shelley was the most generous being in the world and the least inclined to envy of anyone she had ever known. His admiration of Byron was wholehearted and he didn't stop believing he could help him. In the poem he had written after he had spent time with Byron in Venice, *Julian and Maddolo,* he imagined that if he *'could by patience find / An entrance to the caverns of his mind, / I might reclaim him from this dark estate.'* Even in his letters he was tender with him, as if he were a fragile patient, and put on his best bedside manner, even when goaded by Byron's careless little cruelties. Sometimes Byron seemed to need to believe that Shelley was not as idealistic as he seemed.

'Claire didn't see all the letters to me, thank goodness. Just those where he complains about the diet and the atheism. Not the one where he implies my creed is to despoil virgins, even though I have assured him I believe chastity is good for young women. That accusation is full of irony, given his behaviour, but he is a true Catholic at heart. In his mind he separates domestic life from venal pleasures.'

'Do you think he has wind of Paulo Foggi's threat about the child, Elena?'

'Perhaps. He may have heard a rumour, no more.'

'I will never know what possessed you to register it as our child. I am still so angry with you. If you hadn't done that we could still have looked after it, but Foggi couldn't have blackmailed us.' She was not sure there was any point now, in maintaining her rage, but it was a failure of trust she found hard to repair.

'I panicked. That day we left, I was not in my right mind.'

'You didn't dare tell me until we were fifty miles from Pisa.'

'You didn't want her with us.' Shelley sounded resigned rather than resentful.

'No, I didn't. A year ago in Naples, so soon after Clara died, I couldn't accept another child, especially one that wasn't my own, even to satisfy your knight errant longings. And as what? We couldn't go through the 'child of a friend' pantomime again, as we did with Allegra. The English in Italy, the gossip mill, the rumours that would get back to England. What did the *Quarterly Review* say about you, when it reviewed *The Revolt of Islam*? I remember it by heart: "*His business is to enjoy himself, to abstain from no gratification, hate no crime, but be wise, happy and free, with plenty of 'lawless love'.*" The English won't look at us when we go out, or get too close. They think you might infect them with immorality!'

Shelley spoke falteringly. 'That's why I thought if you were registered as her mother, and me her father, that if it came out we were supporting her, there couldn't be any more allegations. I don't want to be denied access to my children in England. You know it's what I fear most. I must see them one day soon, when I am well again and fit to travel. And we want to be able to take Percy with us, without worrying that the Lord Chancellor will take him away. That December was such a mess. I was so ill. I couldn't work. We had parted with Allegra, lost Clara, and then there was Elise. We had a duty to her. I couldn't let her be unprotected. I couldn't let the child be abandoned.'

Mary remembered. Shelley, in so much pain from his side, unable to write or barely think on some days. Hugely frustrated and deeply dejected. Feeling as if he were the locus of disaster, isolated, unheard, unloved by the world. Suicidal. Sensitive to even minor crises. She had been cocooned in her second shroud of grief, too focussed on not falling apart for William's sake to really notice what was happening to Shelley. The beautiful apartment looking over the Bay of Naples. The intense blue of the sea so sublime that it should have been healing, but wasn't — for her or him.

Claire had been an unnaturally quiet, untuned instrument. Depressed, as the distance from Allegra and silence from Byron seem to be more permanent, and as Allegra's third birthday approached.

There were no singing or dancing lessons to upgrade her spirits, and no local company for distraction.

Elise, their nursemaid, had apparently been equally distraught about Clara and was often tearful. She had been with them since the Frankenstein summer in Geneva and had become part of their family. Mary felt a choking even now, remembering little William chattering away to her in French. She had helped them through the birth of Clara and Allegra. Her family of clockmakers had accommodated them in Switzerland, on their way to Italy. She was the one they had trusted to take Allegra to Byron in Venice. She was a tiny, dumpy blond Swiss girl, with ruddy cheeks and small mouth, not an obvious candidate for a grand passion.

This had apparently not deterred the opportunistic Paulo Foggi, whom they had hired soon after reaching Italy and who had cheated them continually. They knew it, but their blind eye had kept the household running smoothly, while he managed their horses, hired local servants, arranged their journeys, and sometimes cooked for them. Paulo, who was supposedly helping Elise learn Italian, but had evidently taught her another language altogether.

In December Elise had confessed through her tears that she wanted to marry Paulo. She knew they would not approve. Paulo had smiled and shrugged and said of course he would take care of little Elise. Mary and Shelley, with less than perfect Italian themselves, could nevertheless smell his insincerity as strongly as they smelt the oils on his hair.

So Paulo had been sent packing. He was a rascal and a thief, and although they had put up with it for the convenience, he was certainly not a suitable husband for their sweet, naive Elise. Yes, said Elise, she understood. Yes, they were right. They swallowed their nagging sense of hypocrisy.

When, after Paulo had been gone a week, Elise had collapsed and Dr. Manzini was sent for, the reason for her excessive tears became clear. There was a narrowly avoided miscarriage. Paulo had to be made to marry Elise. He was found with his cousins, in a poor part of Naples, and he had not been happy about the baby. He had been

231

about to leave for a job in Florence and a baby was not part of his grand scheme. His family would not approve of a fallen woman. She was not Catholic. She was not pretty. He could not afford to marry. Mary had hidden Shelley's pistols and persuaded him to use a more practical weapon. So Shelley had undertaken to be responsible for the care of the baby, bribing Paulo to go through a civil ceremony with Elise at the British embassy, and made him promise to marry her in a Catholic church after she had converted, in Florence. Elise had given up the baby to their care for the time being. She trusted them and they found a good wet-nurse in a respectable family. When they left Naples for Rome they had planned to go back to visit the little girl the next autumn, when Mary could cope, but then William had died and they had fled to Leghorn, to the comfort of the Gisbournes. The Gisbournes knew the whole story and helped Shelley convert pauls to ducats and send them for the child's upkeep. They had found the lawyer, Rossi, to help. They were grateful to the Gisbournes. More than grateful.

Mary brought her thoughts back to the present.

'That rogue Paulo now has the effrontery to say he will expose you for an illegal registration?'

'Yes. That's it. He wants more money. You know, I don't believe Elise knows what he's doing.'

'Last time we heard from her, they were in Florence. I worry that she is not happy. That he leaves her alone often. I hope he is at least a little kind to her.'

Mary looked at Shelley who was staring blankly at the door which Claire had so recently closed behind her.

'There's something else,' he muttered.

The drumbeats in Mary's head fan-fared trouble, and she wanted, more than anything, not to ask. Still, he went on.

'Rossi says he is dropping hints of a larger, more infamous claim.'

She stayed silent. She could not help him. He took a very deep breath and his voice when it came, was higher than usual.

'It is worse, far worse. He implies that it is Claire's baby.' The silence seemed to stretch like a taut elastic, getting thinner and thinner, and more dangerous.

'By me.'

Mary clutched her stomach to contain the rising tide of nausea. Her legs gave way and she sank onto the bed.

Shelley came and sat by her, drew her to him, and pulled her head to his chest, feeling the dampness of her face on his shirt. His other arm was around her shoulders and his fingers were gripping so tight that she groaned and pulled away.

'How can he say that when he knows it's not true?' she cried, beating her hands on the bedclothes. 'Why would he think anyone would believe it? We can both deny it. Claire was never pregnant. Surely Elise would confess?'

'Not if he put too much pressure on her. In any case, it only needs the suggestion that it could be true. Everyone would believe it. They are looking always for something with which to accuse us. Our mail is read. I suspect a rumour has got to Byron, and it has hardened his resolve towards Claire even more.'

'Byron? Would he believe this calumny?'

'Yes, he would believe it of Claire readily, and of me because he would do such a thing himself. He would not hate me for it, but just see it as part of my wrong, idealistic thinking. He doesn't, never has, understood the difference between ideals and prudence. As if I would stain my own household.'

For a relationship to last, a good memory is unacceptable and Mary tried hard not to recall the weeks in London when Shelley encouraged Hogg to pay court to her, with the ulterior motive of drawing Claire in, of gratifying her sexual ambition towards him, of creating the perfect, harmonious free loving household. She could not meet his eye, and he understood why she closely examined her fingernails.

'Mary, you know how I am changed,' he said, reproachfully.

It was true, she knew. Fanny, Harriet, the absence of his older two children, Claire, Byron and Allegra, the loss of Clara and William: life had conspired to modify his ideals. He now knew that he could not live in a bubble of his own devising; there were too many outside with needles, poised to prick. Mary was not sure how much this pleased her. In some ways it was more secure for her, but the price was his loss of otherness, of challenge, of a little of the excitement he had for her.

'I know.'

'For the outside world, it will be true without any evidence, and that's what Foggi counts on.'

'We must put paid to this evil. Go to Leghorn. I will follow. If I stand true to the registration, he can't prove otherwise.' She looked thoughtful and nodded quietly. 'Maybe soon Elena should join us, now Percy is thriving.'

There was a noise in the hall, and they heard Claire calling up that they would be late. Mary quickly dried her eyes and took Shelley's hands in hers. She squeezed.

'There must be no hint to Claire.'

# 5

'Yet I would forget all that; and for many days I have
been as calm as a bird that broods, rocked on her tree
by a gentle wind; full of a quiet, sleepy life ...'

*Valperga; or the Life and Adventures of Castruccio, Prince of Lucca,*
Mary Shelley

At the Baths of San Guilliano, Mary at last felt like a mother
again; and like a wife again. When they had finally farewelled the
Gisbournes in Livorno, dealt with their business there, and arrived,
in early August, they were still in time for the end of the summer
season. Baby Percy was thriving. He had survived the measles and a
fever that scared them all with memories of William and Clara. He
even survived their extreme anxiety. The waters, as Dr. Vacca had
predicted, calmed Shelley's nervous exhaustion and raised his spirits.
And Claire was mostly absent.

The Baths were only six miles from Pisa. A beautiful and
fashionable little resort town, cupped in the Pisan hills with a view
to the ocean, it seemed a light and airy world away from the Pisan
summer torpor or the mercantile backdrop of Livorno. There were
inspiring walks for Shelley in the mountains, and their roomy house,
on which they had splurged forty sequins for three months, was
almost opposite the high gates which led into the ornate pink marble
of the thermal baths.

Being close to Pisa meant that some of the Pisan professori took
rooms for the summer, and their wives stayed while they commuted
back to the town, so even though it was late in the season, there were
acquaintances for occasional companionship. Not that they sought it
much. The Masons visited regularly and Mary was eternally grateful
to them, since Mrs. Mason was largely responsible for the absence of
Claire.

That woman is truly wonderful, Mary decided. Mrs. Mason, strong in stature and strong minded, assessed the dynamics of the Shelley household and took them firmly in hand. She saw how to handle Claire. She adopted a sympathetic and slightly bossy tone towards her that implied she knew best and was on Claire's side. What she 'recommended' was always for Claire's own good. She never made the mistake of implying that it would be good for Mary or Shelley too. At first Mary had resented it, but then she realised the subtlety of Mrs. Mason's help. The older lady missed nothing. She saw how Mary got impatient with Claire's continual ranting about Byron, her demands for action, her attempts to manipulate Shelley to ride off to Ravenna and rescue Allegra, and that none of it could be discussed without hysterics. She saw how Claire resented Mary's way of dealing with her own grief — suppressing it, obsessively writing, reading, learning Greek — and resented Shelley's encouragement, and his admiration for her. She had been there when Mary disastrously failed to remember the name of Claire's discarded novel and when she contradicted Claire about some facts of Byron's behaviour and Claire had screamed at her that she was cold-hearted. Mrs. Mason could tell this was the barb that dug deepest. Yes, the woman was wonderful. Unsettlingly wonderful.

Just that morning, sipping green tea with Mary while Shelley was at the Baths, she had been reporting how happily Claire was settled at Leghorn.

'She will come to visit us at Pisa next week,' she said, her upright back subduing the soft sofa. 'I have something to discuss with her. I think I may have found a place for her as a governess at Florence. The Botjis, who are a respectable family. He is a professor and they have one daughter. They want her to learn music. Claire is perfect.' Her eyes found Mary's briefly then rested thoughtfully on the sugar bowl.

'And Claire is happy with this?' asked Mary, carefully, quietly, also regarding the sugar bowl as if the delicate china might crack under stress.

'She approves the general principle. She doesn't yet know of this particular opportunity. She sees how important it is for her to be an independent young woman. It fits with her principles.'

'And what of the plan for her and Miss Field, your governess, to set up a school?'

'I think that we must take our opportunities as they come.'

Mary hesitated. She appeared to find a loose thread in her blue muslin skirt, and worried at it. 'Shelley may not like it.'

Mrs Mason set her cup down very decisively but carefully, as if her large hands had the potential to crush it.

'Dear Shelley will see how it will relieve his situation. It is all very well for him to want to embrace his responsibilities,' — Mrs. Mason seemed unconscious of the irony of her phrase ' — but he must learn to encourage Claire to break free. Think how my Taffy had to rescue him when he was assaulted in the Post Office at Pisa. These bigots will never stop while his household is as it is. And you must think of little Percy.'

'That was an unfortunate business,' frowned Mary.

'It was typical of the bigoted Englishman and the lies that are told of you all. I know Shelley thinks 'Damned Atheist' is a mild epithet. But the man had a strong right fist.'

'And a fast horse,' conceded Mary. 'Your husband and Shelley couldn't catch him.'

'Just as well, probably. Shelley is too handy with his pistols. Now, my dear Mary, to happier things. Laurette is so thrilled with the story you wrote for her birthday. *Maurice, or The Fisher's Cot*. It's so original.'

Mary felt ridiculously pleased with the older woman's clearly sincere admiration. Her shoulders softened. She smiled, and Mrs. Mason thought it was one of the rare occasions when Mary's smile was not enigmatic or ironical. It was pure pleasure.

'I enjoyed it. It was a rest from writing *Castruccio*. Sometimes I think I'm cursed by my father because he made me believe that one should not read a book without three others by its side for reference. *Maurice* was pure enjoyment, not having to check my sources or think about classical meanings 'til my head hurts!'

'You must do more,' said Mrs. Mason warmly. She felt as if her daughter, and by extension herself, had given Mary the gift of giving. It was a rare sensation for one who always cast herself as the giver and the facilitator.

'I was thinking of making some simple classical dramas on some of the Greek myths. Something light and easy to understand for a young person. Perhaps the story of Prosperpine? What do you think? A mother's love, the bringing of spring, courage, all good themes for young people. I thought I might get Shelley to insert some verses. It'd be something we could do together.'

'You are both indefatigable. Taffy and I are full of admiration. I would like to see whether Shelley really does a drama with pigs as a Greek chorus!'

'I don't think I had laughed so much for ages as I did last evening, with Shelley trying to read you his *Ode to Liberty* and being drowned out by all the pigs going to the fair of St. Bartholemew. They did indeed seem just like a chorus. A very noisy one.'

A servant knocked to announce that Mrs. Mason's carriage was at the door.

'Well, it's been a pleasure as usual, my dear,' she said, getting up and gathering up her reticule and her restrained grey bonnet. 'We look forward to seeing you back in Pisa in a few weeks.'

Mary got up too, smiling hesitantly, and then went across to catch her arm before she reached the door.

'Can you wait a moment?'

'Of course my dear, what is it?' Mrs. Mason looked gently concerned.

Mary let go of her arm and went to the window to look down into the square below. It was market day, and the colour and bustle of animals, market women with baskets on their backs, a cart with chickens, squawking and scattering feathers, colourful stands of fruit and vegetables, household ironware laid out neatly on the pavement, singing birds in cages, a dwarf fiddler playing and some young women, hair loose in bright dresses, dancing around him so that he was invisible and the music seemed to come from the dancers themselves. She watched a girl of about her own age, sitting on an upturned basket with a swathed baby in her arms, laughing and tapping her feet. An old woman, brown and wrinkled, came and took the baby from her and she jumped up to twirl with the others. It seemed so carefree.

'Will you be honest with me? '

'Of course.'

'Do you think I am unfeeling about Claire and Allegra?'

Mrs. Mason hesitated and Mary knew she was being unfair. It was if she was asking her to take sides, but she needed a perspective from an outsider who had seen inside their domestic circle. Or perhaps she was asking her to take sides. Did Mrs. Mason's support of Claire mean she felt critical of Mary's own behaviour? She needed to press the sore to see if there was pus.

'I think it's hard for both of you,' Mrs. Mason said at last, with a small frown. 'You have to remember that you at least have a child with you. Claire doesn't.'

'The only time she was really sympathetic to me was after William died. For a short while I was suffering more than her, but even then I didn't rant out loud enough for her. She thinks that if you don't cry and get angry you are not feeling. Not feeling.' She closed her eyes and breathed deeply, scared that too much emotion would alienate the older woman, always a pragmatist. She wanted to be thought of as the strong, analytical one.

Mrs. Mason looked at her sympathetically. She did not, thank goodness, come and hug her, it would have suited neither of them. She carefully pulled off her kid gloves and sat down again, nodding slowly.

'Claire finds it difficult to put herself in someone else's shoes. And it doesn't help that you are more tense with her than with anyone else. She sees it as criticism. She is insecure, you know. She needs to be constantly reassured of your love.'

'Why can't I be like Shelley? He just treats her like a child that's fun to have around, and she responds like a child. She feels he's spoiling her. He ignores her tantrums. They mostly roll off him like a summer shower. I can't do that. I get hurt. I just long to have a conversation when I don't have to worry about how to put it so that she won't be offended. And when I forget and get lulled into thinking she is my friend, it upsets me all the more that she's so vindictive. And then I hate myself for being gullible. It's a circle.' Mary's voice had risen and she just avoided a whine. There was a silence during which her stomach clenched. Had she gone too far? She was conscious of Mrs. Mason's embarrassment, but she felt impelled to continue to plead her case in Mrs. Mason's court. She was not sure why it was so important to her that she be acquitted.

'And there is no accumulation of goodwill, you see. I can make an effort for days, and we are best friends, then one small incident and we are back to mortal enemies. It is so wearing.'

'Yes, she is judgmental, but perhaps you should think how to help her.' The older lady's serious expression suddenly became a little mischievous. 'You know, I tell her to see a prejudiced person as someone labouring under a serious illness.'

Mary laughed and the tension broke. Suddenly they had the complicity of two grown-ups discussing how to handle a difficult child.

'I shall notice her looking at me with pity, now, and understand that I am imagined covered in Job's boils.'

'Of course, it is her own definition of a prejudiced person.'

'And you are a saint. Can you help her see Byron that way?'

'That's a lost cause, I'm afraid. But I do feel the great poet should be kinder to her, however much she baits him. A mother's separation from her child is a hard thing to bear. One would think there was some sensibility in his soul.'

'Albe is a child of his class. He tries to fight it with his poetry and his politics but struggles when it comes to women who won't be tamed. Women of strong opinions lead to hen-pecked husbands, an opinion he makes quite clear in *Don Juan*. Claire is his worst nightmare.'

'Yes.' Mrs. Mason agreed. 'But the important thing here is that Claire should be independent. It relieves her and Shelley of suspicion and gives you time, perhaps, to benefit from the healing power of his full attention.' She lifted her bushy eyebrows slightly.

Mary glanced at her sharply. How did she know about the rawness, there still? You can tell each other you are joined in grief, but the edges of the seam are never properly aligned again.

Her visitor made anxious noises about waiting servants and sent her regards to Shelley. Mary rang for the nursemaid, who brought Percy in to say goodbye. Mrs. Mason kissed him affectionately and took her leave, as a servant came in with the morning post.

An hour or so later, when Shelley came back to Casa Prini from the soaking in the hot springs, ruddy faced and smelling faintly of sulphur, he found Mary cradling Percy who had fallen asleep at her breast, and in tears over a letter she held in her other hand. The tears ran quietly, as she tried not to disturb the peaceful child.

'It's Godwin again, isn't it?' he said angrily, snatching it from her.

'But he is my father,' wept Mary. 'Can I see him bankrupt?'

'Look at you, Mary. You are distraught, the babe is now sick and it's probably because these letters upset you that you make him so, through your milk.'

Mary threw her head back onto the cushion and closed her eyes, but she didn't argue with him.

'My dear love, I must be firm.' Shelley took his advantage. 'He cannot write these demanding letters to you, accusing me of abandoning him and accusing you of not making me live up to my obligations to him. My obligations! I have given him almost. £5000 over the past few years. If I had kept it in trust for him, the interest alone would have done him more good. He just fritters it away. What has he done with the £100 I sent last month? He even denies I sent it! And you having to beg the Gisbournes to stand surety for £400 to get rid of some of the debt he owed for the back rent on his house.'

'Which they didn't do,' sniffed Mary.

'And do you blame them? Since they've got to London they've seen the miserable state of his affairs. I'm sure he is slandering me to them. I hope they know us well enough to block their ears. In any case, he could get money as advance from a publisher if he exerted himself. I have been too easy with him in the past and all that happens is we suffer approbation and penury ourselves because of it. How am I to pay our creditors? We owe for the piano and for the Marlow furniture still. I must have your permission, Mary, to intercept letters of this kind. They upset you too much. And we are otherwise so happy here, are we not?'

'So the principle is, if I don't know of his distress, it won't exist? Will I feel better for not knowing?'

'You must trust me, Mary. He must stop thinking of us as his only resource. Surely such a genius as he can write to his daughter on subjects that are more elevating? I shall remind him that you have no disposal of the money. Perhaps he can then think to write on other topics. I'm glad you don't have the purse strings. You'd give it all to him and then where would we be?'

Mary knew he was right. She had to put the well being of her own, precious little family before her father, even though she would like to make it right for him too, difficult as he had been. The habit of respect for her father was hard to shed.

'Very well, very well,' she said, pulling a pillow over her head. 'But I am not good at not knowing.'

'No, you're not,' laughed Shelley. 'It is your best and your worst trait.' Mary acknowledged the truth of this by pouting up at him from under her frown.

'I know, after supper let's do the Sortes Virgiliae,' said Shelley. 'Then you can see if our fortunes are changing.'

Their fortunes, as always, were very muddled. As they sat in the courtyard that looked over the canal at the back of the house, nibbling on figs, they opened the book of Virgil's *Aeneid*, closed their eyes and randomly pointed to a passage. Shelley got *'wander from place to place'* which Mary found a little depressing. Had they not earned the right to settle for at least a while? She would like to go back to Rome someday, when the painful memories had softened, and in a few years, perhaps, to go to England, so that Shelley could sort his affairs. Naples, perhaps, but since the little Naples child, Elena, had died so suddenly from fever, there was no pressing need. Mary had felt sadness about the death, but it was a mild sorrow — this was a child she had not known, or suckled — and it was overlaid with relief that Paulo Foggi could be sent packing with impunity. Shelley went into a period of self-recrimination, moaning that he attracted death to him, but the move to the Baths had served as a distraction. Perhaps the Sortes were right. Wandering from place to place had seemed to be the balm they chose, whenever crisis occurred.

Her finger jabbed '*strangers in your palace entertain*', which was pretty accurate, since Shelley's cousin, Captain Medwin, was arriving the next day, a man he hadn't seen for years. They had grown up a few miles from each other in Sussex and played together and partied together as young men. He had supported Shelley when he eloped with Harriet, so Shelley's gratitude and warmth were guaranteed.

Mary did one for Claire in Book V, and got '*the fierce virago fought, /Sustain'd the toils of arms, the danger sought*'. Mary was delighted with this one, especially the virago. Claire had got more and more anxious and tense when they first came to Casa Prini and they had fought for two weeks about everything from sewing needles to broken pens. Shelley had spent long hours in the Baths, and Mary worked hard on her book, but Claire had craved activity and company, so the sojourn in Leghorn was a fine solution. Shelley, who missed Claire, especially in the evenings, said Mary was biased, and when he did one for Claire, he got '*Longing they look, and, gaping at the sight, /Devour her o'er and o'er with vast delight;*' which did not please Mary at all, but made Shelley smile.

'Have you heard from Claire?' asked Mary.

'Only the note to us both saying she arrived safely. I'm sure going back to Leghorn for a while will be good for her nerves,' he said, diplomatically. 'She loves the sea bathing and she can have music lessons there. There are no music masters here in the mountains.'

For Godwin in Book X Mary got '*This urges me to fight, and fires my mind /To leave a memorable name behind.*' She hoped Shelley's strong words, in his letter, would have that effect on him.

They did one for the Hunts and got '*When, parted hence, the wind, that ready waits /For Sicily, shall bear you to the straits*'. Not quite the right direction, as Shelley pointed out, but it would be wonderful if they did, at last, set out for Italy. Both Mary and Shelley missed them, and by all reports, Marianne was not well. Italy would cure her and cure Hunt of his debts, they agreed.

They both thought about the Gisbournes. Book II gave them: *All gird themselves for the work; under the feet they place gliding wheels, and about the neck stretch hemp bands. The fateful engine climbs our walls, big with arms.* Did this say Henry would stay committed to the steamboat now that they were in London, or not? This was Shelley's main concern. Mary just wanted to hear from her friend and be reassured that Mrs. Godwin was not damaging their friendship.

The last one they did together, joining their hands and making their fingers point in unison. In Book I they got *'Earth, air, and seas thro' empty space would roll, /And heav'n would fly before the driving soul.'*

'What are we to make of that?' asked Mary. 'It sounds lonely.'

When Captain Medwin arrived the next day, he admired the spacious apartments opposite the Baths and seemed genuinely pleased to be reunited with his boyhood friend.

He looked more serious than Mary expected. From Shelley's description of their carousing as boys, she expected a more rakish type, but there was only a striped cravat with velvet collar and turned back cuffs on his jacket to contradict his long serious face and thinning temples. His eyes suggested a penetrating intelligence. Later Mary would think they overstated the case. His smile was wry and came a second after it was expected, which could be unsettling.

'How do you find Shelley after all this time?' asked Mary, after they had been introduced.

'As youthful as ever, in spite of that touch of grey at the temple, and perhaps a little more bent.' He patted Shelley's stooped shoulders affectionately. 'I'm sure it's because you spend even more time peering over your books these days, Percy, though to good advantage!' He turned to Mary. 'Ever since I found a copy of *The Revolt of Islam* on a bookstall in Bombay a couple of years ago, and I was astonished at the genius of this fellow, he has focused my mind on philosophy and the classics.'

Shelley flushed with pleasure. 'Oh, this man is no slouch either, Mary. He can speak seven languages and draws beautifully. Tom, come and peep at little Percy sleeping before we sit down for supper.

I hope you can cope with our limited diet,' he grinned. 'Then we can sit up all night and I can read you my latest scribblings.'

He almost bounded out of the room with Tom Medwin in tow. Mary thought she would reserve judgment on Medwin, but for the time being was delighted that he made Shelley so happy. In spite of often protesting that he hated society and would happily live on a desert island with Mary and Percy, he came alive when surrounded by a small and sympathetic circle. Medwin would fill in the gap left by Claire. At least Mary hoped he would.

The rain started in the early hours, when they finally got to bed, and they were lulled to sleep by its constant drumming. By morning the River Serchio which led into the canal behind their house had burst its banks. The canal flooded the square and cut off the road to Pisa. All afternoon and into the evening the waters rose and the rain seemed eternal. They watched as the drivers herded the cattle to higher ground, their shouts encouraging the frightened animals. Families who lived along the canal started heading up towards their relatives in the hills, woman carrying children and men with flaming torches. They were silhouetted against the dark mountains in a spectacular and eerie montage.

'For goodness sake, get out your sketchbook, Medwin, and capture that scene, we can manage this,' urged Shelley, as he and Mary gathered up the books and papers scattered around the parlour on the ground floor. Water was already seeping through the cracks under the doors. They ate their supper that night in Shelley's study on the first floor and put down mattresses for the maid and the cook to sleep there, as by midnight the water was still rising.

'It won't get up to the first floor by morning, 'said Medwin, reassuringly to Mary, but he got up three times before morning to check the rising water levels. At dawn, the water was almost up to the first floor. Shelley and Medwin leaned out of the upstairs windows and tried to get the attention of a boatman as several had come to rescue those who were trapped.

'The rain is settling down,' observed Mary. 'Should we wait?'

'No, no,' said Shelley emphatically. 'Think of the state of the rooms downstairs. At least the house is only rented. And there may be disease.' Cholera was the unmentioned demon. 'We were returning to Pisa next week anyway. I have already got our apartments there.'

'I'll get the servants and make sure all of the clothes and linen are packed,' said Mary. 'You pack up all of our books and writing into chests. They will be the essentials. Get two boats, we will need them. If a boat capsized with our things it would be a disaster. We will leave our small items of furniture. We can send for them later. Poor Medwin, you have barely unpacked.' She gave him a sympathetic smile. 'But we wouldn't want you to think our life is without adventure, now would we?'

'Mary is wonderfully calm,' said Medwin admiringly to Shelley, as they negotiated a price with the boatmen, Medwin's Italian more fluent even than Shelley's.

'She is wonderfully strong minded and rational,' agreed Shelley, as they started to carry bags to the window. 'She has been my rock, though the last two years have tested us both. I have never regretted a minute spent with her. I might say it is the one enduring success of my life.' He smiled at Medwin. 'Now is not the moment to be contemplative, dear fellow. Help me lift this one over the sill. If we can get along the canal to where the carriages are waiting, early, we can get ahead of other stranded visitors and make Pisa by lunchtime.'

As she went to take Percy from his nurse, Mary had a moment of quiet relief that this crisis could be dealt with without hysteria. Claire could shriek when told of it, later.

# 6

See where she stands a mortal shape imbued
With love and life and light and deity,
And motion which may change but cannot die;
An image of some bright Eternity;

*Epipsychidion,* Percy Bysshe Shelley

The winter in Pisa was not too cold, so it seemed they had more than their fair share of sickness. Medwin had a recurrence of his stomach infection from his time in India and Shelley was kind to him, nursing him and even applying leeches himself in between visits from Dr. Vacca. Privately, though, Shelley and Mary agreed that his confinement to bed was something of a relief because they were becoming tired of the Captain. Shelley began to call him the *seccatura,* the bore. The novelty of his company had worn off and his anecdotes of India became tiresome. He was the sort of man that should stay only three days, suggested Mary, otherwise he went off, like fish. Friendship is the most delicate relationship to manage. Lovers have a bond that is welded so tightly that it survives much, but a genuine break is difficult to repair. The bond with friends is looser, but there can be much more irritation when the joints are wearing, with no strong reason to either bear it or scrap it and start again.

The best thing Medwin did for them was to bring his friends Edward and Jane Williams to Pisa. He knew Edward through his Indian Service, and had previously been staying with them in Geneva. They melted softly into the shelter of the 'paradise of exiles', since Jane had escaped from an abusive husband and she and Edward were only husband and wife in name. The Shelleys found them delightful, especially Edward, who shared Shelley's obsession with boats. Jane was pretty, with dark eyes and dark thick hair. She could have been Mary's sister except that they found her ornamental rather than intellectual, and she was as soft and easy-going as Mary was strong and determined. She was also seven months pregnant with their second child. Her singing and playing of the piano, the harp and the guitar was especially delightful to Shelley, since in the absence of Claire, they could once more have music in the evening. To have a congenial English couple of their own age was energising. It made them feel more connected to society than they had been since they left Hunt and Marianne in England. Mary had someone to talk to and pay visits with, and since Claire was in Florence, she could relax and be herself. It was reassuring to be reminded that she could be admired for her looks and her conversation. Edward Williams proudly took on the job of making fair copies of Shelley's work, which since Claire left had fallen more on Mary, so she suddenly had the time and inclination to entertain and be entertained.

Shelley, as usual, was fighting illness most of the time. His eye infection plagued him, because it prevented him reading or working, but he nevertheless gave it as an unwelcome gift to Mary. Then there were his boils, which sometimes kept him housebound and miserable. Only little Percy was healthy and robust and for that, at least, they were grateful. He didn't seem to feel the cold, and at fifteen months Mary decided to put him in short coats so that he could exercise his chubby limbs all the better.

None of the illness, though, kept them from enjoying their most social period of the past few years. The 'paradise of exiles' made up for Mary's dislike of the Pisan townspeople, whom she still found coarse and dirty. Pacchiani, to whom they had been introduced last May by Mrs Mason, dined most evenings. He was known as Il signore professore, though he had lost his university chair one drunken evening when he had quipped to the police that 'I am a public man in a public street with a public woman.' Others called him the devil of Pisa. His wit was fast and amusing and he was always quoting from his own poems that no-one had ever seen published. He was a devotee of the Belle Inglese in Pisa and cultivated, charmed and cajoled them at every opportunity, while being cutting behind their backs. He also made a living from them by acting as an agent in the letting of palazzi and getting a monthly 'doceur' from the landlords, and by brokering some of his students to give lessons and taking a percentage of their earnings. He was an educated rogue and he was especially fond of Mary, la bella Maria, as he called her, leaning his bony frame over her to extravagantly kiss her hand. In spite of his immoderate behaviour he was well connected in the upper echelons of Italian society and introduced the Shelleys to some of the most entertaining and interesting local people.

Mary was walking for exercise with Jane Williams along the Lung Arno. They were taking advantage of a cloudless day and one on which the sirocco was not blowing strongly enough to bowl the mid-heavy Jane off her feet. They walked slowly because of Jane's condition, and with her arm resting on Mary's, Jane asked if she were to visit Emilia Viviani with Shelley that afternoon. In spite of the lack of wind, Mary's reaction was almost enough to unsteady her.

'Emilia Viviani this, Emilia Viviani that! I have been sick to death of hearing about Emilia Viviani from Shelley! I told him for goodness sake, go and write some verses about her. And now I regret that.'

Mary started to walk faster, angrily, until she remembered Jane's condition.

'You're not jealous of her are you, Mary?' Jane looked anxious and put her small gloved hand on Mary's arm, already linked to hers.

Jealous? Jealous? Mary considered. What did jealousy mean? People always thought of it as a passion, but passions give you strength and jealousy in love is a weakness. I cannot be jealous of Emilia in that way. She considered. At least not in a physical way. It's just that she's replaced Claire as someone for him to worry about and care for, and once again I am not enough for him.

'No. I'm tired of her. I think she is not all that she seems. Or rather, let me not be unjust, she is not all that we set her up to be.'

She tried not to let her emotions show but she was silent and breathing rapidly, suppressing what she knew to be true. She has youth and beauty and she is a damsel in distress. Shelley needs his platonics for inspiration. He needs someone to idealise and Emilia is the perfect candidate.

Emilia's was a fairy story, locked away in a convent by her young, jealous stepmother, who was no match for her beauty. She had become the cause célèbre of the Pisan expatriates. No one came to Pisa without visiting Emilia. The Shelleys, though, took up her cause with vigour. Mary or Shelley or both were there almost every day. On Claire's visits to Pisa, she went too. They met the prisoner in the confines of the convent courtyard, a large quadrangle framed by echoing stone walkways. There were dilapidated statues, a well, hard iron seats and a beautiful old olive tree, with an intricately twisted trunk. The convent offered benign detention, but Emilia was certainly to be pitied because she was in limbo, waiting for her stepmother to find a suitable husband for her and her father, the Count, to negotiate a dowry, which he was attempting to make as low as possible. While a convent was not unusual for the education of young girls, at seventeen, Emilia's should have been finished, and there were no companions there of her own age.

She looked like a live statue from antiquity; masses of black hair tied simply, white skin, high brow and straight Grecian nose. She had the bearing of dignified suffering and quoted the classic Roman authors in a deep melodious voice. She was a sponge for sympathy and the English visitors could tut-tut righteously about the barbaric practices of the continentals. Shelley was trying to send petitions to the Grand Duchess Princess Rospigliai in Florence, though Pacchiani warned him that because Emilia's father was in a position of some authority in the Pisan State, it would jeopardise their security as residents and so he had trouble getting signatures. Indeed, her father was not being unusually cruel by Italian standards. So they visited and took books and writing materials. They exchanged letters. On two occasions Emilia was allowed to visit Mary accompanied by the Mother Abbess. Emilia impressed Shelley by writing a long discourse on the beauty of love, which Mary secretly thought a little too flowery and overdone. Pacchiani said Emilia was 'made for love'. Mary thought she could be more loving by, for instance, not telling Shelley that Mary sometimes appeared cold. That Shelley had defended her from Emilia's accusation did not bring the comfort it should.

'I expect she will marry soon and you will hear no more of her,' smiled Jane, gently. Mary breathed more slowly. There was no doubt that Jane had a calming presence.

Jane narrowed her eyes and gave Mary an ironic grin, squeezing her arm. 'In any case I would have thought you were too caught up with your Prince to pay much attention.'

Mary gasped, then laughed. She had no idea that Jane had such wit. 'You're right I do have my real-life Prince — as opposed to my fictional one.' She looked down into her eyes, for she was a head shorter, and decided to test their intimacy. 'Do you not think that the Prince Macrocordato is everything a man should be? He is charming and witty and considerate. My Greek is coming on wonderfully with his tutelage. Homer has come alive for me and I hope his English fares as well. It is a good bargain.'

'I'm sure that it does.' Jane was smilingly complicit. Then her smooth brow wrinkled. 'Will he ever be able to return to Greece from his exile here?'

'I have no doubt that when the liberation movement in Greece finally rises up against the Turks he will be there without a second's hesitation. He is something of a hero, perhaps will even be their leader.'

Mary remembered the morning's lessons in her room. If she were to be perfectly honest with herself, and she liked to be honest, it was his physical presence that gave her as much pleasure as his insight and ideas. His romantic black flowing hair, side-whiskers and heavy black moustache. His dark, penetrating eyes and the way he held his shoulders back which gave the illusion of strength and uprightness, and made one forget that he was somewhat below normal height. He looked as if he would any moment leap onto a table, draw his sword, and rouse the multitudes. His small, round gold spectacles were a startling contrast to this impression. He was an alluring mix of scholarship and strength, and Mary looked forward to having his full attention almost every day.

'Does Shelley like the Prince?' asked Jane, as Mary steered her between some beggars and a mess of rotting vegetables that had fallen off a cart on the way to the market.

'He approves of the Prince's politics,' replied Mary, dissimulating. Another penetrating question from Jane. She would need to reassess her first opinion of her. The reality, which she did not yet know her well enough to say, was that Shelley made little attempt to engage the Prince, and made a point of being out when he came in the day to give Mary lessons.

In the late afternoon, Shelley knocked on the door of Mary's work room, and came in slowly, peering around the door. Mary was sitting in her armchair, reading, a letter half-finished on her desk.

She smiled at him and held out her hand.

'I can't get up. I'm too comfortable.' He came over, bent down and kissed her.

'How was your Greek lesson?'

'Marvellous. Homer comes alive when you read it in the original. The colours, the smells seem to be there, which are absent in translation. Have you and Edward decided on a boat?'

'I think so. We will need Henry Reveley to help, while he is back here, but ...' He wandered distractedly about the room, glancing at her work, looking for an opening to raise what was on his mind.

'Mary, there was a letter for me from Claire this morning.' He took it out of his pocket, waved it uncertainly in the air, and re-pocketed it.

'Claire has to decide whether to pledge for another three months at Florence, but she is freezing and lonely and her glands are up. Mrs Mason wants her to stay and promises to give her a letter to the Princess Montemellitto to extend her circle. Mrs M has dangerous colic so I can't discuss it with her at the moment. What shall we do?'

Mary was exasperated. 'You deal with it. She writes to you, not me. Will you tell her to throw away this opportunity with the Botjis? Will you tell Mrs. Mason that you're encouraging Claire to discard her efforts!'

'She writes to me because she knows I will have sympathy and you will have none. How can you be so cold-hearted?' Again, Mary thought. Again.

'Don't you dare call me cold hearted. Would you rather have warm-hearted Claire? Her warm heart constantly erupting into hysteria?' Tactless manipulative Claire, who adores you? Most of the time. When she's not angry with you. Get her back then, or better still go to Florence to be close to her and listen to her moping.'

He recoiled, then looking at her carefully, at the slight trembling and the clenched jaw, went to take her hands and pull her up towards him. She let herself be pulled, but kept her face turned towards the fire. 'Mary come here. My own Maie. You know that's not how I feel. Claire has grown up with us. I love her like a sister. I worry about her health.'

'You like having a harem. You haven't got over having four little sisters to worship you when you were growing up.'

'I don't need to be worshipped. Goodness knows I wouldn't stay if I did.' She gave him a sharp look. 'But, yes, I do like having sympathetic people around me. And if they like my ideas so much the better. There are barely enough people who do — I can count them on one hand.'

'We are comfortable now. We have the Williams and Mrs Mason and Medwin, seccatura or not. We have Pacchiani and the Italian crowd.'

'We have the Prince,' said Shelley. 'Or you do.'

'So what if I take comfort from someone who appreciates me? I have to smile when you expound the wonders of Emilia to anyone who will listen! I will have to be sanguine when everyone reads a poem that they will interpret as an expression of your love for her!'

'I do love her, Mary, you know that. It is the pure expression of love as the most beautiful thing in the universe. It is what we always agreed on – the ability to love more than one person is what we aspire to. It is so rare to connect with the soul of another. It is what we live for, is it not? The poem uses her as an expression of a soul upon a soul — the perfection when two halves unite. That is why I have made it the *Epipsychidion*. That's what it means. This is what happened to us, is it not?'

'You have her as the sun and me as the cold moon. This is wonderful. It sounds as if I have been superseded by the warmer, the brighter.'

'I have Claire as a comet as well.'

'You think that makes it better? Claire, the fiery, the blazing, spectacular one? If this poem is distributed it will be interpreted in the crudest way. And you dedicate it to Emilia.'

'I will make sure it only goes to a few who will understand it, and I have written it in Italian. It was meant to express our warmth and regard for Emilia. To give her comfort. To show that I, we, understand her sensibilities.'

Mary's head was beginning to throb. The arguments for the beauty of universal love were ones she had adopted in that July of 1814 when she ran away with Shelley, and could not now deny. She took her hands from his and scraped them through her hair, trying to make her fingers draw out the escalating pain.

'Yes, yes,' she muttered.

'Mary, think.' He pulled her back towards him so that her head was on his shoulder. He spoke into her hair, murmuring gently. 'It is what we do, Mary, isn't it? We use our experience to create the images in our writing. You are doing it now, in *Castruccio*. Isn't your prophetess, Beatrice, an image of Claire? Flashing black eyes ...'

She interrupted him, speaking into his shoulder. '... manipulative, deluded with self-importance ...' and a smile crept into her voice.

He smiled too and added, 'And isn't Castruccio, your hero, a man full of principle when young, who is corrupted? I wonder whether there is any element of me? Though I hope not. These experiences we use as base notes in our composition. Sometimes they are taken from elements of someone's character and sometimes form a single, perhaps uncharacteristic, incident. You know this.' He pulled up her face and kissed her forehead. She smiled back and they moved to the comfort of the chaise. 'My beautiful Maie.' He buried his head in her hair. 'I can't believe we used to call you Doormouse. I am lucky to have such a powerful soulmate as you. Always there.' He looked deeply into her eyes. 'Suns and comets blaze and die. The moon lightens the darkness. I would not want it any other way.'

She drew him to her. She believed him, but mostly she believed he believed it. The past seven years had been tumultuous. Many couples would have crumbled, but they had clung to their belief in each other, even while they both treasured their independence of mind.

After Shelley left her, Mary spent the afternoon lying down, and by the evening she was ready to receive their visitors. It was the usual crowd, Pacchiani, the Williams and of course, Medwin, as well the Prince Macrovordato's sister, the Princess, and Dr. Vacca. The Prince had promised to call in later.

Shelley was discussing the pain in his side with Vacca, when Medwin asked if they had ever heard of Animal Magnetism and asserted that he, and even Jane had used it themselves to heal pain.

He paused, and looked across at Dr. Vacca. 'If it's not stepping on your medical toes, sir. I'm sure it is not viewed well by scientific men.'

Vacca smiled eloquently. 'I am aware, of course, of the claims of Dr. Franz Mesmer. He was the one who called it Animal Magnetism I believe.'

'Yes, he believes there are magnetic fluids, a life force if you will, that flow through the body and need to be in balance. Man is linked by this life force to the universe. A responsive force exists between the universe, the heavenly bodies, the earth and animated bodies. If we can recover the natural balance in man it follows that illness will be cured naturally.'

Shelley leapt up, excited. 'A life force, in tune with the universe! This is wonderful! This is all that I believe!'

Vacca laughed at his enthusiasm, his own self-confidence and his confidence in his profession not for a moment challenged.

'I must point out, my dear Shelley, that the good Dr. Mesmer required flashing lights and sweeping gowns, indeed a whole theatre to perform his tricks. Then forty years ago the French government performed an experiment which found the effects of his methods were a result of the imagination of the subject.'

Medwin leaned forward. 'That is exactly the point, my dear sir! An Indian priest has been continuing Mesmer's work in Paris, based on just that — that it is really the mind of the subject that is directing the healing. The magnetiser puts him into something like a deep sleep. A waking sleep, Shelley. It happens in seconds. And he doesn't need the theatrical effects.'

'I would like to be open-minded,' said Vacca, 'but I have seen no proof.'

'What actually happens?' asked Mary.

'A person who has been magnetised seems to be in a sort of trance. I believe it because I've seen things like it in India. The faqirs are able to fascinate with their eyes. The person doing the magnetising asks them to feel where the pain is and to make it better. They've often come out of the trance with their pains amazingly relieved.'

'Does it last?' asked Mary skeptically.

Almost simultaneously Shelley asked, breathless, 'Really? 'Can *you* do it?'

'Not very successfully,' answered Medwin, choosing to answer Shelley. 'I tried. In Geneva we had a visitor from Paris who had closely observed the Abbe Fare's methods, and he showed us. But I've only managed it a little with one person. A friend in Geneva, and I'm not sure if they were just being kind to me.'

'Oh.' Shelley was deflated.

Medwin turned to Jane who had been sitting quietly listening to the exchange with a small smile.

'We have someone here who can do it though.' Medwin gestured to her with a bow. 'When she first tried, on me, it was amazing. I had no particular ills, but I felt an enormous sense of well being afterwards. In Geneva, a friend of ours who had bad colic was cured to the point where he could stop taking medicine.'

Jane blushed modestly, putting down the needlework on which she had been carefully concentrating. 'It seemed to come naturally to me. I also think it is important that the subject wants to feel it.'

'Jane!' Shelley took Jane's hand and pulled her to her feet. 'Can you please try it on me? What do you need? More candle? Less? Hard chairs? Tell me.'

Jane shook her head in embarrassment. 'It probably won't work, you know.'

Vacca finally looked worried. 'The problem, my dear fellow, with this type of 'cure' is that you can get a false sense that everything has become right and you mask the symptoms, then it it is hard for me to treat the root cause. Thirty years of medical training and research cannot easily be dismissed, you know.'

ALMOST INVINCIBLE

'Oh come, Vacca. I will not stop needing your attentions any time soon, I'm sure of that.' Shelley was dismissive. He was like a little boy whose mother had tried to make him choose cheese over a sweetmeat. Vacca threw up his hands.

'I think, nevertheless, that it is time I went home to my bed. I have many patients tomorrow.' His demeanour was at its most formal as he bowed to the gentleman and kissed the hands of the ladies.

To Mary he said, 'I leave your husband to your sensible care, signora,' and smiled, ruefully. 'Do not let him get carried away!'

After the door closed behind him, Shelley said, 'Let's do it now! Please, Jane.'

Jane looked for approval to her husband, who nodded, with nothing but fondness.

Mary suddenly realised how much Jane deferred to Edward. She felt a little guilt and a shock at the contrast as she thought how far Jane's marital behaviour differed from her own. She returned to her thoughts of the afternoon. She knew herself to be independently minded and even though supplicant, clingy women had transient attraction for Shelley, he would have long since tired of a woman who did not challenge him, as he did of Harriet.

'Very well, but I have to warn you that I've also seen people be surprisingly honest if they are asked questions under the effect. Have you any secrets, Shelley?' She smiled coyly at him.

'Oh you must promise not to ask any questions that are not about my health!' Shelley looked alarmed. 'Mary, will you be my watchdog?'

'It wouldn't be the first time I've kept you from trouble,' replied Mary, raising her eyebrows, and Edward laughed his big, open laugh.

Jane made Shelley stand in front of her in an area of the salon away from the window, the fire and the grouped armchairs. She begged for quiet. The candles glittered silently in the crystal. Shelley's long bony frame was a full head above hers. She looked up at him intently. It made Mary feel uncomfortable. She passed her hands around his head and down his body. Not touching, but still intimate. Never shifting her eyes. A pin dropping would have been a thunderclap at that moment. Shelley's breathing was loud, abandoned. His eyelids drooped.

'Where is the pain?' asked Jane in almost a murmur. Never ceasing the flowing movement of her hands.

'In my side.' Shelley's voice was soft, almost dreamy.

'Think of the flow of energies in your body. Send the positive energy to your side. Feel it heal. Feel it heal.' Shelley sighed. An eerie sigh, like the wind through an open window at dusk.

Jane continued to pass her hands down and murmur, and then suddenly she clapped them. It was startling. All in the room had been lulled into breathless complicity with the softness of her voice and the sultry atmosphere of illicit communion.

Shelley almost stumbled and leaned reflexively on Jane. Then he came to himself and apologised.

'Jane, you are amazing,' he said in wonder. 'I felt outside my body!'

'And your pain?' asked Mary, going over to the still shaky Shelley and guiding him to a chair.

'Hmm?' Shelley looked vague for a moment. He ran his hand down his side, trying to assess any difference. 'Yes,' he said with wonder. 'Yes, it feels duller. The pain is softer, not so sharp.' He leapt up and spun around. 'And it hurts less to move!'

Medwin grinned in satisfaction.

'Will it last?' Mary asked Jane, who had returned with composure to the sofa next to her husband as if nothing unusual had occurred.

'It may need more sessions,' said Jane.

'As often as we can,' enthused Shelley. He turned to Mary. 'What harm can it do?' Mary shrugged. 'It is almost proof of the separation of the spirit from the body,' he said in wonder.

The next day Shelley's pain was still a little better than normal. He was ecstatic. 'Jane is full of hidden talents,' said Shelley, thoughtfully, and Mary agreed, smiling with resignation, and wondering with some satisfaction how long Emilia Viviani had to reign as queen of spiritual fulfilment.

The month brought cold winds and bitter news. Byron wrote that he had found a convent with good air for Allegra in Bagnacavello, twenty miles from Ravenna. The decision to send Allegra to a convent was not unexpected to Mary and Shelley. Byron had written to them that he was uncomfortable with her being so much in the company of servants, that he wanted her to have a good religious upbringing as well as a proper education, and that above all, he was nervous about her safety. Byron had become very committed to the cause of the rebels in Naples. He was tamed, as Shelley put it, by his new love, the Countess Guiccioli and his thoughts turned from debauchery to rebellion. He had hinted to Shelley that he was helping to arm the rebels and he feared the authorities would raid his house, in spite of his privileged status. He would pay double the normal pension at the convent to ensure she got the very best of attention.

Mary and Shelley were torn between admiration for his political conviction and despair at his foolhardiness. They discussed and marveled at his contradictions late into the night, such as his generosity to the poor and his disdain for his equals. They knew their own hypocrisy. They had to write and tell Claire and to her they would be disparaging of him and his actions, but to Byron they would reply with sympathy and understanding. They felt like tightrope artistes with competing loyalties at either end of their balance pole.

To be precise, Mary had to write and tell Claire. Shelley was too much of a coward. 'You know it will be unpopular news,' she said, scathingly. 'You just want to be loved.'

When Claire's reply came, full of invective and pain, it was Mary who had to soothe. Claire ranted that if Mary were any sort of a sister or friend she would go to Florence to care for her in her misery, and Shelley should go with her to Bagnacavello to rescue her darling girl from the convent, by force if necessary. Anything so that she shouldn't suffer the horrors of the convent system. All Italian women who had been subject to a convent education were ignorant and licentious. She had looked at convents in Florence. The children were miserable. She had trusted Byron to do the right thing by her child. She should have the education of a daughter of an English nobleman. Shelley would make him send Allegra to England to boarding school for a proper education. She would pay. ('*I* would be paying,' said Shelley). She had written to Byron. ('A disaster,' said Mary).

Mary's letter in reply pointed out the impracticality of a kidnap scheme from a closed convent with high walls. She mentioned that Byron had money and contacts who would recover Allegra immediately. She said the air at Bagnacello was some of the best in Italy. She said they could not afford to mount a rescue expedition and even if they were successful and Byron confronted Shelley he would have to admit it or lie. That meant Byron would challenge Shelley and there would be the horror of a duel. And where would she and Allegra go? America? They couldn't afford that either. To be sympathetic, she said she understood what a disgusting person Byron was. She felt anxiety too, but it would be better to wait. Things would change. Byron would most probably have to go back to England to settle his mother's estate and would most likely take Allegra. She must try to be patient.

Shelley added some warm and loving platitudes to the effect that he would do anything in his power to help her if he thought it would do any good, but that anything he said to Byron only made him more angry.

Claire refused to write to Mary for three months. She wrote only to Shelley, who was warm and affectionate and refused to allocate blame for the rift with Mary.

Mary felt sickened by Shelley's emotional cowardice, but Claire's absence meant she could put it out of her thoughts. Jane was not yet a sufficiently good friend for confidences, but when she hinted at her frustration with him, Jane hinted back that men often were emotional cowards, and that they reserved their energy for physical bravery. In any case, Claire had been made Shelley's problem by Mary, really, and wasn't he generous in supporting her?

This shift in perspective dulled the irritation and truly, in the absence of Claire, Mary felt liberated and prepared to forgive anything. She blossomed in so many small ways. Her energy returned and she might even have been called gay in her embracing of their social life. She smiled more readily, and her hard edges seemed softened. Shelley was afraid it was due to the attentions of Prince Mavrocordato who could not seem to keep away. He came for lessons in the afternoon, and in the evenings to socialise, often bringing friends from the Greek community. His frank admiration was only part of it, though. She felt as if she had suddenly stepped onto a roundabout of light and that the more she absorbed the beams, the brighter and faster it went.

The Gisbournes were back at Leghorn, and Henry Reveley came up to Pisa often. The steamboat project had stalled with Henry's absence and Shelley doubted it would be revived, especially as there was talk of the Gisbournes returning to Europe. Shelley had a love-hate feeling towards Henry. He was quietly angry that he had invested so much energy and money in the project, but he had good reason to be grateful to the Gisbournes for their help with the Naples child, and Henry and he still shared their love of boats. Now Edward Williams made a triumvirate of boat addicts, who fuelled each other's enthusiasm.

Jane's words about physical bravery were made flesh a few weeks later when Shelley, Henry Revely and Williams, disheveled, in ill-fitting clothes, the three of them laughing and groaning alternately, were disgorged from a carriage at dawn shivering onto the steps of the house.

Mary and Jane sat them down close to the fire, called for tea and cakes and ordered them to tell the meaning of the message of last evening. 'Boat capsized, all well.'

'So, now please explain yourselves,' Mary mock-scolded them.

They looked at each other like naughty schoolboys and giggled.

Williams cleared his throat and tired to look serious. 'Well, you know how Shelley had asked Henry to find us a small boat ...'

'Vacca recommended exercise, you know, and it's more fun than a horse. It was only a few pauls. Ten feet long.' Shelley interrupted earnestly.

'Hmm,' said Mary. 'Carry on, Edward.'

'When Shelley and I went to Leghorn yesterday to see it, we found that the mast and sail had already been fitted, so we decided then and there to sail it to Pisa,' he said proudly, looking to Jane for approval. Jane, well accustomed to massaging a male ego, smiled encouragingly.

'Never mind that it was evening and there was a southwest wind getting up,' said Mary, disparagingly.

'There was a good moonlight,' pleaded Edward. 'Anyway, Mrs Gisbourne thought we ought to bring Henry because he knew the country and is a very strong swimmer.'

'Sounds as if that was wise,' said Mary.

'Yes, it was all my fault,' said Edward. 'The mast was very large, a bit too top heavy in hindsight. I got my coat caught in the rowlocks and stood up to free myself. When I unbalanced I grabbed onto the mast and the whole thing rolled over and in we pitched. I am not a strong swimmer as you know, but I could just make it to the edge of the canal. I must have been a sight, flailing and flapping!' He laughed ruefully. 'Poor old Shelley, who can't swim at all, was grabbed hold of by Henry in quite an heroic manner.'

'The man is a saint or a fool,' added Henry. 'I grabbed his head and told him not to worry I'd get him to shore. He said "I'm all right, never more comfortable in my life; do what you will with me," and went completely limp in my grasp!'

'When Henry dragged him onto the bank, he murmured, "it's an omen", and promptly fainted.'

'Just a short rest, old boy,' grinned Shelley.

'Then Henry went back to rescue the boat!'

'In the moonlight I saw a casale in the distance, so I dragged the others along to it and explained to the country folk there that we were shipwrecked mariners.'

'We were sopping wet so it was utterly believable!'

'They were marvellous – woke up their family to get us hot soup and bread and lit big fires to dry us off. Even lent us their clothes.' Henry gestured to his coarse breeches.

'In the morning we sent for a carriage, and here we are!' Edward looked satisfied with the outcome of the adventure, as did all three.

'Well, I hope that this is not a bad omen,' said Mary.

'It is a good omen, said Shelley ecstatically, his eyes shining. 'If something starts badly it means it will end in good!'

# 7

Do you not hear the Aziola cry?
Methinks she must be nigh,"
Said Mary, as we sate
In dusk, ere stars were lit, or candles brought;
And I, who thought
This Aziola was some tedious woman,
Asked, "Who is Aziola?" How elate
I felt to know that it was nothing human,
No mockery of myself to fear or hate:
And Mary saw my soul,
And laughed, and said, "Disquiet yourself not;
'Tis nothing but a little downy owl."

*The Aziola,* Percy Bysshe Shelley


'This is bliss.' Mary dreamily dangled her hand over the edge of the boat and trailed her index finger in the water. 'I know that one day boats will be the death of you, Shelley, but in the meantime, there are definite pleasures. Who could have a better spring afternoon than this?' She closed her book, threw her head back and shut her eyes, lowering her parasol so that the sun warmed her face. 'Fine weather, fine friends and fine fresh fruit.' She leaned down to a basket at her feet and took out a pear.

She passed one to Jane who was sitting next to her in the bow, and she smiled her thanks to Mary and beamed at the world in general.

'We were lucky to find our villa Marchese Poschi in Pugnano for the summer. It's such a pretty village and so close to the Serchio, and so close to you at San Guiliano. That lovely garden is perfect for Edward to toddle in, and there is such wonderful clean air for tiny

Rosalind, who will be needing me soon I'm afraid,' she said, folding her arms across her breasts and discreetly feeling them.

Mary looked at Edward, rowing gently, the oars making a hypnotic splish splosh that temporarily marred the tranquil surface of the river. 'A pear, Ned?' she asked.

'Hm, what?' Edward was startled out of a deep reverie.

'And where were you, Ned?' asked Mary. 'Contemplating a speech for your play?'

'You have me. I was thinking of a revision to some scenes in *The Promise*,' he confessed.

'I can't wait 'til your play is finished, my love,' said Jane tenderly. 'You must send it to Covent Garden as soon as it is.'

Edward blushed and looked sheepishly over his shoulder at Shelley, in the opposite end of the boat, scribbling furiously in a notebook in between long periods of staring across the fields with their clumps of wild lavender. Edward was in awe of Shelley's work. Even being close to genius was like getting sweet crumbs from the table.

'And you, Shelley?' Mary called across to him. 'Can I pass you any fruit? How goes Adonais?'

'Ah, I love to think in the open air, even on such a morbid subject,' breathed Shelley. 'I want this poem to honour Keats, to be a tribute to his transcendent genius. Those miserable men who scattered their insults and their slander on his work, they were the ones who pierced his heart, his fragile genius. They caused the rupture of a blood-vessel in his lungs. I have sympathy with how it feels to be on the receiving end of those barbs, but at least I am made of stronger stuff.'

'You had better be,' said Mary. 'It's your turn to row the boat back!'

'So tell me what you think of this stanzas, everyone,' said Shelley. 'My open air inspiration.' He read with great intensity:

*He lives, he wakes—'tis Death is dead, not he;*
*Mourn not for Adonais.—Thou young Dawn,*
*Turn all thy dew to splendour, for from thee*
*The spirit thou lamentest is not gone;*
*Ye caverns and ye forests, cease to moan!*

*Cease, ye faint flowers and fountains, and thou Air,*
*Which like a mourning veil thy scarf hadst thrown*
*O'er the abandoned Earth, now leave it bare*
*Even to the joyous stars which smile on its despair!*

'What do you think, Mary?'

'They are good. I think this poem is one of your best. I like the lyricism of it. The Spencerian stanzas. The critics won't like your earlier verses, though, where you blame them.'

'What more harm can they do?'

'I think it's beautiful,' said Jane.

'Well done,' agreed Edward. 'It comes so naturally to you. You really do have genius.' He stood up and gestured to Shelley to take his place at the oars. 'Now it's your turn to work the body as well as the brain. Home in time for tea, please!'

After tea at the Williams', Mary and Shelley went back to their own house at San Guilliano and played with Percy when he woke from his afternoon sleep. Then they gave him back to Caterina to have his own tea.

As they watched his sturdy little figure toddle out of the room, little feet making fast and erratic slaps on the terrazzo floor, Mary felt the release of tension that she felt at the end of every day to know that he had got safely through another twenty-four hours. She wondered if she would ever be able to relax and accept his presence in the world as a fixed element, not one likely to evaporate on a whim of the gods.

They took a walk along the road to Asciano as the sun glowed behind the hills.

'So, do you feel happy to be back at the Baths for the summer? Or do you miss Pisa?' asked Shelley

'It was a wonderful winter there. We have done so much work and we have had such congenial company.' She did not add — and we did not have Claire. 'I have been my happiest since Rome. Don't you feel the same?'

'You like the society more than I do.' He made the accusation, mildly.

She was defensive. 'It is not the social life, it's the stimulation.' Then she paused. She wanted to deny a love of society because it seemed trivial, but she realised it was true. She did crave company. She thought carefully. 'No, that's not it. You know, I think it is because we have had such catastrophes, and I was so completely withdrawn through all that time. So the bustle and energy of even a small social whirl is an affirmation that I am well. That I have survived. Yes, I think that's it. Does that sound right to you? You know me. Better than anyone.' Mary looked enquiringly, and a little anxiously, at Shelley.

'Better than Prince Macrovortado?'

'Yes definitively better than him. Even as we speak, he has taken his charms and his manliness to bestow on the oppressed of Greece. I'm sure I barely cross his mind. The Morea is in revolt. He sacrifices everything that Greece may be free. You surely must wish him well.'

'I do, I do, my love, and I will write something to glorify his struggle to prove it. I am a selfish being, though, and I am pleased to have all your attention back on me, and more of your time and your thoughts, Mary. Your thoughts above all. You see my soul.'

'So, do you agree with my self-analysis?'

'I think I do. By contrast, I only need a few people. I cling to the company of those who inspire me. Like you.'

'And Emilia.

Shelley kicked at some loose stones on the dirt road. He picked one up and threw it into the bushes, causing a squawking departure of some poor unsuspecting rondini. They both laughed, and then looked at each other sheepishly. Shelley knew the soft centre of Mary. That unlike other women an appeal to her vanity was not enough. It had been her first attraction. In some ways she had been his greatest achievement. He was proud that he had nurtured her fine mind without damping her spirit. Other things, especially fate, had tried to do that. But she had come through. They had come through.

Serious again, he replied: 'Others may have beauty and pure souls — and it's so rare I must treasure it — but only you have beauty, a pure soul *and* a remarkable mind.' He looked at her sideways and saw her reluctant smile. He put a finger thoughtfully to his lips. 'And a soaring imagination.' Another pause. 'And a sharp wit.'

Mary laughed. 'You mean a sharp tongue. Well, be careful, because a sharp tongue is usually in a mouth with sharp teeth!' And she pretended to sink her teeth into his arm.

'You know, my dearest one, the countryside here is glorious. I'd like to buy a farm with acres of chestnut groves. We could build a high fence and it could be our island, Mary, just you and me and Percy. Escaped from the bitter world. We would need few resources. Nourishing our minds with the great writers and philosophers. Our beauty and inspiration would be derived solely from nature.' They had left the town, and he slipped his arm around her waist and gestured at the pastures, the sweep of the setting sun making angled patterns through the valleys and filtering through the trees, tipping the leaves of the violets in the hedgerow.

He believed it at this moment, Mary knew. A new dream. And if she said yes? He would immediately take up the challenge, be immersed for a while and be disappointed when the dream became tarnished with reality. This was not the time. One day, perhaps.

'Sounds like an idyll, but maybe one that has to wait a while. We have taken this house for six months and our resources do not run to another lease or purchase now, do they? And what about our plans to winter in Florence if you get your way, or Rome if I get mine? You wanted to be near Claire, and the museums and the sculptures you also find so sublime. Or if we were to settle, you may prefer the sea. Then there is the issue of Allegra and Byron to consider. Oh, I am heartily sick of being practical!'

'Thank goodness you are. There are many practical plans to be made. Lord Byron wants me to visit him in Ravenna. He persists. It would certainly be a good chance to see Allegra in her convent and put Claire's mind at rest. The Gisbournes come next week for a few days before they leave for England again. With Henry.'

'Speaking of Henry, what do you make of the anonymous love letter that Claire received? Why did she send it to me if she clearly thought it was from you? Can you think of any explanation other than to hurt me? She said it must be yours because of the trees.'

'As I've already said, it had to be from Henry.' Shelley was irritated. Why did there have to be such ill-feeling? He was blameless of everything except trying to keep everyone happy. 'After all Henry did propose to her last week. He was just trying again to get her to change her mind, though I'm not sure why it was anonymous. I have told Claire emphatically they were not mine.'

'I don't know why she would not accept Henry. If she did not have your allowance she would not have the luxury of seeing herself as so independent. Poor Henry was so brave. He knew his parents would be devastated.'

'I think his timing was bad, even though he had to do it before he left for England. Claire is ill with worry about Allegra. She can't think about anything else. She needs to leave Florence for a time and go to somewhere with good air, for her health.' Mary pulled away from him, angrily.

'Don't look so alarmed,' he said, reassuringly. 'I think she could stay with the Masons in Pisa for a few days, then I will find her a hotel in Leghorn. It is close enough that she can come here for a few days from time to time.'

# INTERMISSION

Shelley and Byron
Ravenna 1821

# 'P.S. Could not you and I contrive to meet this summer? Could not you take a run here *alone?*'

*Letter to Percy Bysshe Shelley,* Lord Byron

*My dearest love,*

*We ride out in the evening, through the pine forests which divide this city from the sea. Our way of life is this: L. B. gets up at two, breakfasts; we talk, read etc, until six; then we ride, and dine at eight; and after dinner sit talking til four or five in the morning. I get up at twelve and am now devoting the interval between my rising and his, to you.*

*L.B. is greatly improved in every respect. In genius, in temper, in moral views, in health, in happiness. He has a permanent sort of liaison with Countess Guiccioli. The connection with La Guiccioli has been an inestimable benefit to him. He lives in considerable splendor, but within his income, which is now about £400 a year, £100 of which he devotes to purposes of charity. He has had mischievous passions, but these he seems to have subdued, and he is becoming what he should be, a virtuous man.*

'Good shot.'

Byron acknowledged Shelley's hit on the bottle and raised his own pistol to fire again.

Shelley gave up his pistol to Tita, the Venetian valet assigned him by Byron — a genial giant with a full black beard and a reputation as an assassin. Tita refilled the powder, handed back the pistol and took some small pumpkins from the saddlebags of the horses grazing under the pine trees. After Byron had taken his shot at the last bottle, Tita strung his stock of pumpkins in the trees, and Byron and Shelley lined up to massacre the innocent vegetables.

'For a visionary with his head in the clouds, your eye has a very earthly focus!' observed Byron. 'You are almost as good as me!'

The pumpkins all being shattered, they remounted and rode for an hour as the sun delicately relinquished its heat. They galloped through the trees and by the shore, back to the grand apartments which occupied the whole of the second floor in the Villa Guiccioli. Here Byron was housed with, his servants and ten horses, eight enormous dogs, five peacocks, three monkeys, five cats, an eagle, a crow a crane and a falcon. All of them, except the horses, squawked or clattered and barked through the corridors as the shooting party came in.

'It's good to have you here, Shiloh,' Byron threw over his shoulder as he strode off to change for dinner. 'Last time we were together was when you nearly drowned on Lake Geneva.'

After dinner they sat on the terrace. It was still mild and the air was clear. There were blankets piled for the hours after midnight. The five years since they were in Geneva seemed to have expanded Byron and shrivelled Shelley, so that the contrast between them was even more marked than it had been then. Shelley later told Mary that Byron had given up his diet of raw eggs, tea and dry biscuit and had stopped purging, so the chubbiness he had always fought had won the victory over his waistline and his cheeks. His whiskers were luxurious with a touch of grey that matched his hair. He looked older than his thirty-three years, but there was still the lazy energy and the edge of danger in his eyes. Byron, on the other hand, thought that Shelley looked frailer than ever, and he noted with satisfaction that, although his friend was four years younger, he was just as grey. He wrote to Theresa that Shelley's knobbly bones seemed all the more protruding. He was all knuckles and elbows, and even more stooped than before. The Italian sun had freckled his fair skin, but his hair was as wild as ever, he thought, rather fondly.

'Lucky you didn't have the beef, Shelley,' said Byron, taking a glass of wine from the tray brought out by Fletcher, his manservant. 'Damned tough. There is no beef in Italy worth a curse. The plum pudding was excellent though.' Byron lit his cigar, and inhaled deeply. 'So what do you think about these Neapolitans? The Carbonari have failed to hold off the Huns and Ferdinand is back in power. The fight for democracy has to begin again. The Austrian army of occupation is suspicious of me. They open my letters. My association with the Gambas, who are known Carbonari, is suspect, even though they have forced my Theresa and her father and brother into exile in Florence. I armed them, you know, the revolutionaries. Fortunately, I am just too much of a prominent figure for them to arrest me, or to come and raid my basement where the weapons are stored. But I have heard I am on a list for assassination.'

Shelley could see how the situation had dispelled Byron's usual indifference. Clearly the excitement of revolution had absorbed the energy he used to devote to licentious dabbling.

'Theresa's father and her brother Pietro are brave,' observed Shelley.

'They are. Pietro is a very good, manly fellow. Only twenty. Big eyes and long legs. Full of dreams of a free Italy. It is the poetry of politics! I am indoctrinated into the Carbonari — I bore the stupid initiation ceremonies — but it means greater danger for me, and it was one of the factors in my sending Allegra to the convent. I wanted to keep her safe. Theresa is fond of her too, little strong-willed thing. I do appreciate the support from you and Mary about Allegra. It was the best thing to do. I spared neither care, kindness, nor expense for the child. With the nuns she will have a good education, a good moral education, too. Theresa was brought up in a convent and she is a perfect example of womanhood. Innocent and ignorant of moral evil. Allegra's convent is in a country town with good air, with many children placed in it, some of considerable rank. I want Allegra to marry and live outside of the corrupt high society of England. We get regular and favourable accounts of her from the school.'

'I know that you are fond of her and mean to do the best for her, but it is hard for us, for me. With my responsibility to Claire.'

'What exactly is that responsibility, Shiloh?' Byron looked at him keenly. 'We are men of the world. What you do in your household is your own affair – except where it is concerned with that woman's claims to Allegra. Her damned moralising to me.' He rose and called his man for more candles and wine before continuing.

'Listen here. I'm not a man to keep a secret, especially of this kind. You and I suffer too much from the slanders of the world to keep its counsel close. The Hoppners in Venice wrote and told me that Elise had accused you of being Claire's lover and of her having had your child. They also said that you and Claire insulted and beat Mary. I allow for exaggeration, because I know how much you esteem Mary, but as to the other – your word will bring suspicion to an end.'

Shelley was out of his chair, knocking a table in his haste, spilling his drink over his cuff and shaking the moisture off more easily than the despair.

'This again! That the Hoppners should cause such mischief! Already Paolo, Elise's husband, has tried to blackmail us with this tale when we had shown Elise nothing but the utmost kindness.' So Shelley related the whole story of Elise and her baby to Byron.

'As if I would have fallen into the error of having Claire as my mistress, and what's more, as if I would abandon a baby! It is not to be borne. I will write to Mary at once to send to the Hoppners and refute this horrible calumny, even though it will distress her. They will only be persuaded by her certain knowledge of the truth.'

'Calm down, calm down,' soothed Byron. 'Mary is known to be unfailingly honest. That will settle the matter, I'm sure.' He hesitated. 'But you do see how it is easy to believe. The common gossip is that Claire is your mistress. I know from personal experience that Claire's morals are loose. You tell me she refuses all respectable offers of marriage. How would she be a good influence on Allegra? I am determined that the child shall grow up to have a proper position in society and a good marriage.'

Shelley was still agitated. 'This is why you don't let Claire see her?'

'I don't want Claire near me, and I don't want her berating me about Allegra. Let's change the subject.'

Shelley waved his hand in a gesture of resignation. 'Will you join Theresa in Florence?'

'We have been considering where to go. The Gambas are exiled from Florence, and by the Papal dispensation for her separation from her husband, she has to live under her father's roof. They favour Switzerland. I have already asked the Hoppners to look for suitable places for Allegra there.'

'You would hate Switzerland,' laughed Shelley, secretly horrified for Claire at the possible removal of Allegra to an even further distance.

'Don't you remember when we were there before? The gossips and the cabals of the English? They would torment and exasperate you!'

'I know. It's true. I favour Tuscany. There are fewer English in Tuscany — except for Florence — and the climate is good. What about Lucca, or Pisa, to be near you? Are there any large houses? Could you guarantee the absence of Claire?'

'Yes, either Pisa or Lucca would be suitable, but I think in Pisa we could find the best Palazzo for you. We were considering Florence for the winter, but ... we could be persuaded to stay in Pisa. Claire has a position in Florence. You don't give her enough credit for seeking to be independent.' Byron snorted.

Shelley's brain was racing. Keeping Byron in Italy would please Claire – even more so if he brought Allegra somewhere closer to her. It would then offset her anger when he and Mary didn't stand by their commitment to keep her company in Florence next winter. He was sure Mary would be delighted with an excuse to stay well away from Claire. They had promised the Williams they could winter with them in Florence, but they could probably be persuaded to stay in Pisa. Byron would like the Williams. The influence of Byron was substantial, and if such rumours as those perpetrated by the Hoppners became more widespread, Byron's power, his contacts and his purse offered them some protection.

'So, will you find a palace for me, and stay yourself?' asked Byron. 'I would like to see that clever wife of yours again. You have a rare find there, Shelley. A woman who is clever but is not a virago. Theresa will like her.'

'Her judgment will be decisive in this. We had good reasons for Florence, but I think she will see that the scales tip the way of Pisa.'

'Now I only have to persuade Theresa.' Byron thoughtfully stroked the large black hound that had slumped by his chair. 'I know, you write to her!'

'What?' Shelley was startled. 'We have never even met!'

'Just put down the reasons against Switzerland, and the benefits of Tuscany. She knows how much I esteem you.'

'I suppose my fee will be your proximity at Pisa.'

Byron smiled, lazily.

'Read me again the unpublished cantos of Don Juan,' said Shelley.
'I cannot hear them enough. They are astonishingly fine. They set
you far above all poets of the day. The whole is so new, and so much
of our age, but still beautiful. I think I may say I encouraged you
to produce something wholly new and different, but this is beyond
expectations. I despair of coming close to you in achievement.'

'You are generous, Shiloh. You must stay longer. Without Theresa
here, if you go, I cannot answer for myself, that I will not fall back
into my old habits.'

'We have discussed this, Albe. Those degenerate habits are only
a consequence of despair. You now have so much to look forward to,
and to achieve.'

'You are good for me. Tell me, what happened to your friend in the
convent? I liked the poem, by the way, *Episichidion*, but you do shoot
yourself in the foot with these love poems. They feed the scandal.'

'It was only sent to those who would understand the principle of
classical love. Anyway, she is now safely married and we are banned
all further contact. Just as you wish me to intercede with Theresa,
Emilia had me soothing one of her suitors. Is it my role to be made to
meddle in everyone's affairs? I can't deliver peace in my own. Emilia
asked for money, and I gave it. More than Mary knows. You must
never tell her.'

'We do what seems best. Last week when I was riding through
the pine forest we came upon this old crone in rags gathering sticks.
Ninety-five, with deep wrinkles and a grey beard. She has a dozen
children, and is still active. She hears and sees and talks incessantly,
but gathering wood and pine nuts is no work for such a great age,
methinks. I ordered her new clothes and gave her a pension. The
country is full of peasants equally in need.'

'Some of our supposedly better favoured friends, too. Have you
given more thought to the proposal about Hunt?' Shelley tried not to
sound too desperately anxious. 'His debts and the threat of prosecution
have caused his health to deteriorate sadly, not to mention his worry
about Marianne, who is sick.'

'Yes, I think we should proceed with our plan. Get Hunt and his
brood to come out to Italy. I will provide apartments for him and

we shall start a new periodical. You, he and I will publish all of our original works in it. We will share the profits equally. Hunt has the publishing experience to set it up. We won't have to worry about the damned censorship or approbation of those who currently oversee our every line. I like the idea. Write to him at once.'

'I will.' Shelley felt an enormous sense of relief. He changed the subject quickly so that Byron could not reflect on his decision. 'I am looking forward to meeting Theresa.'

'She is a real woman, Shiloh. She is nineteen, modest and beautiful and my destiny rests with her. She was married off almost as soon as she left the convent. The Count Guiccioli is some forty years her senior. She had thought this the way of the world until we were introduced. I did not persuade her, Shelley. Our passion was mutual. She loves me in an unconditional way that I find hard to resist. She wants me to write no more of Don Juan. She finds it offends the passions of women, and I obey her.' He shrugged helplessly. 'I can't convince her that it is just bawdy fun.'

Shelley did not dare comment on the idea of Byron influenced by a woman. Instead, he said, 'It was remarkable that her husband gave you an apartment in his palace.'

'I am her 'Cavaliere Servante', the acknowledged equivalent of a mistress. Why do we have no male word for it in English, I wonder? A very respectable position in Italian society, although English society would see it as somewhat demeaning for an English Lord. The Count was also very happy with the extortionate rent I pay for this floor in his villa. Like most Italian noblemen, he lives beyond his means. It has worked well — the staircase between here and their floor is broad … The Gambas like me, we are compadres, so they were happy for Theresa to apply to Rome for the separation. Only now she can't live with me, though at least we can be more open in her father's house. Probably just as well not having her actually on the premises. We row like the devil. She is very fiery, but we reconcile pleasantly.' He smiled at Shelley, meaningfully. 'Speaking of fiery ladies, pray tell me, how is Mary?'

Shelley laughed. 'Fiery again, I think I would say. The death of Clara and William took the spark from her for many months. Work has restored it, that and little Percy. She has a fine mind and I am overjoyed with her new novel, which is almost finished. An entirely different subject than Frankenstein. An historical novel about a Prince of Lucca.'

'Frankenstein was original, and the public seems to have taken to it, I hear, in spite of some of the prejudices of the critical magazines — but who gives a hang about those.'

'Mary will be distressed, though, about the gossip started by Elise about me and Claire. She will write to Mrs. Hoppner to deny it, from her own experience. I will ask her to direct the letter here first.'

Byron's shoulders tensed. 'Let's go inside,' he said abruptly. 'It's getting cold.'

He snapped his fingers at the curled-up dogs to follow as they walked through the double doors. 'You will guarantee I will have no trouble from Miss Clairmont if I come to Pisa?' He caught Shelley's arm, and looked at him squarely. 'I have your word?'

Shelley nodded, briefly.

Byron sighed. 'I don't know how Mary and Claire could be sisters.'

'Only step-sisters,' muttered Shelley.


*It is decided. Lord Byron is coming to Pisa. La Guiccioli has asked me to promise not to leave Ravenna without him. I have told her that if he is reluctant to come after I have returned to Pisa and found a place for him to settle, I would come back and get him. But nothing will interfere with my quick returning, and long remaining, with you, dear girl.*

*Thank you for getting your picture made for my birthday present. I wish you would get it prettily framed.*

*Kiss little babe for me. Accept one for yourself from me. And pray, dearest Mary, have some of your novel prepared for my return. Be severe in your corrections and expect severity from me, your sincere admirer. You have composed something unequalled of its kind. Yours ever, your faithful and affectionate, S.*

# PART SIX

Italy 1821 — 1823

# 1

'Claire always harps on my desertion of her — as if I could desert one I never clung to — we were never friends — I would not go to Paradise with her for a companion — she poisoned my life when young ... She still has the faculty of making me more uncomfortable than any human being ...'

*Letter to Edward John Trelawney*, Mary Shelley

'You only invited me here because Shelley said you had to! Why should we pretend?'

Claire stood in her nightgown, black hair still loose, glaring at Mary with no pretense at goodwill, no crack of warmth that would allow admittance of reconciliation.

Mary felt a soul-searing weariness.

'You're right, Claire, why should we pretend?'

It was true that with Shelley at Ravenna visiting Byron, Mary had promised him to invite Claire to visit her at the Baths. Claire was staying at Leghorn as Shelley had promised — a necessary sea change to cure a skin infection brought on by her anxiety about Allegra. After he left to visit Byron, Shelley had thought that both girls might be lonely. He also secretly wondered if, without his presence, they would have nothing to strain their relationship and might build some bridges. The sad truth was, that without his presence, there was no relationship to rebuild.

I will be twenty-four in two weeks, thought Mary. I have been a mother four times, I have a husband who loves me, I have written one published novel with another waiting on my desk. Why should I still be intimidated by this girl? This girl who has clung onto the coat tails of others' achievements all her life. She caught a glimpse of herself in the gilt mirror over the fireplace. Claire stood away from and behind her, and they could both be seen in the full length mirror on the opposite wall. The two images reflected themselves over and over, to infinity. Permanently linked. Raven, fair. Raven, fair. Shapely, slim, shapely, slim. Ying and yang.

The news, in Shelley's letters from Ravenna, seemed designed to generate friction. Firstly, Claire had not realised he had gone to Ravenna to see Byron, even though Shelley had visited her at Leghorn on his way there. Mary discovered, to her horror that he had not mentioned exactly where he was going or who he was seeing, which caused the first outburst.

Then there had been that letter about Byron's knowledge of Elise's accusations. Although Mary had refuted the charges and although both she and Shelley continually told themselves they were inured to bad public opinion, Mary felt exposed. She felt as if she were in a nightmare, undressed and undefended in a public square, while Claire watched and laughed. It was not rational, she knew. Claire clearly suffered from the scandal too. The letter, though, had come two days before Claire's visit and it made her less tolerant of her stepsister's attitude to her, that peculiar combination of shrill bonhomie and subtle, relentless criticism.

This morning, Claire had been explaining in a faux tolerant tone that the way to teach Percy to use a spoon was to mash his food and let him attempt to get it to his mouth himself. 'If he's hungry, he will do it,' she had said, airily, as the sloppy food landed everywhere, until Mary intervened to reassure the intimidated nursemaid and help Percy herself.

As soon as Caterina had taken Percy off to get dressed, Claire had again turned on Mary, and this time Mary did not feel like pretending that Claire was welcome.

Before the over-heated feelings got completely out of hand, a servant brought in the post, a letter each for Claire and Mary, from Shelley.

He had been to see Allegra in her convent. Claire clearly did not know whether to have hysterics or laugh for happiness.

'He says she is well and happy,' smiled Mary, grateful for the good news. 'He says she made him run with her all round the convent. She teases the nuns. She has friends. Claire, this is all good!'

'Yes, yes,' said Claire, bursting into tears. 'I want nothing more than for my darling to be happy.' She continued reading and her tears became angry sniffs. 'But he also says that Byron is intending to come to Pisa. So of course I won't be allowed to stay, and you and he will stay there, too, and not come to Florence. Is this your idea? Another ruse to keep me away?'

Mary was exasperated. 'Of course, it has to be all about you. You are supposed to be so desperate about Allegra, why isn't it your first thought, like mine, that Byron will bring Allegra somewhere near here? Shelley asks me to see if there a good convent school nearby, not the one that Emilia was in, of course.' She flapped her letter in Claire's face. 'You'll have a much better chance of seeing her, is that not what you want?' She stared at Claire and her tone became harsh. 'But it's not is it? At least not all you want.' She could not quite bring herself to say: you want to be with Shelley. Once it was said it would become real. Where did all the unspoken truths in the world go? Perhaps that was Hell. The first of Dante's circles.

'As if you ever cared what I want. Byron is all about mischief and cruelty. Shelley is the only one who ever cared for what I want.'

'Well, aren't you lucky I married him, so that he feels obliged,' — she put cruel emphasis on the last word — 'to be responsible for you. Otherwise, anyone might have thought that you would have felt it necessary to accept one of your offers of marriage from good men who were prepared to put up with you.' Mary hated herself for that last phrase.

'You can't stand it that I have principles. That I will not compromise my feelings to satisfy some inferior male ego. Shelley understands.'

'So what was Byron? Was chasing him upholding your principles? Let's not dissemble. It's about getting what you want.'

'Yes. I will not die a virgin at least. The act that produced Allegra was sublime. That I will allow his Lordship. I don't need to try to repeat it with another man. I don't ever want to lose control again.' It was the first time that Claire had spoken of her physical relationship with Byron. In that, at least, she had been discreet. But Mary was in no mood to give credit.

'Or perhaps in him you have found that not every man will be manipulated and fooled into doing your bidding … Or perhaps you are just not as good at it as your mother!' Yes, a very low blow, but, thought Mary, to quote Dante: *to be rude to such a one was courtesy.*

'Not everyone is as cruel and heartless as him. Or you.' Claire drew up her shoulders and dramatically wiped her eyes with a corner of her night shawl.

'I can't stay here.'

'Fine.'

'My apartment in Leghorn,' — 'that Shelley pays for,' interrupted Mary. 'My apartment at Leghorn,' Claire repeated, ignoring her, 'is not free for another three days.'

'Go to Mrs. Mason at Pisa,' said Mary, tiredly. 'And complain to her about me.'

'No, I will ride over to the Williams in the morning. They are closer. They said last night at supper that I would be welcome there if I ever wanted to visit. I shall send a note now.' She sat down at the table and pulled some paper towards her with an aggressive flourish.

Mary stared at her, trying not to let her dismay show. What can I say? she thought, with nausea rising in her throat and her head starting to throb. Another Claire victory. To go to my closest friends. To have them exposed to Claire's subtle malice towards me.

'Don't worry,' said Claire, looking up from her writing with a sweet smile, 'I will only tell them that I am longing to see their children and their sweet cottage.'

And they will be fooled? thought Mary, hoping her legs at least would be kind enough to take her as far as the door. Whatever you do or do not say to them, my imagination will surely draft a worse version of that particular play.

# 2

'So you see, Pisa has become a little nest of singing birds.'

*Letter to Maria Gisborne,* Mary Shelley

'What's the commotion?' The two girls looked alarmed and leaned out of the window to see what was happening.

Mary and Theresa Guiccioli were together in Byron's carriage, following their men who were riding back from their shooting party outside the Pisan city walls. They were discussing Edward Trelawney, the adventurer and ex sea captain who, being a friend of Williams, had chosen to join them for the Pisan winter, for the "exercise of his mind", as he put it. It was a clear Sunday afternoon in a mild winter. Fires had rarely been needed and open windows and gentle breezes made it feel like early spring. Mary found Theresa's company pleasantly uncomplicated. She was a small, curvaceous young girl of nineteen, pretty in a slightly vulnerable way that belied her confidence. She dressed in high fashion, but was not showy like many of her country-women. Mary admired her devotion to Byron and her confidence in his affection. Theresa did not hold him in the awe of the acolyte but in the clear-sighted admiration and acceptance of his faults that could only mean her love had taken permanent root. This was a nurturing that Byron had never before been offered, or had accepted in such strong measure, Mary suspected.

'Signor Trelawney is so huge,' Theresa giggled, 'like a Moor with that raven hair and those huge thick eyebrows hanging over such deep grey eyes! Do you find him handsome, Mary?'

'More ... interesting, I think — and stimulating.' Glancing at Theresa's expression, she had laughed. 'Not like that. I can't yet make him out. His wide smile proclaims him to be good-natured and kind-hearted, even as he reminisces with tales of blood and horror. He can be amusing too. He keeps me entertained and sets my imagination bubbling. I like ...'

As she had been preparing to elaborate, the carriage had come to a jolting halt, almost throwing Mary and Theresa off their seats. Now they peered out at their men up ahead. The others riding with Shelley and Byron were Trelawney, Captain Hay, Count Gamba — Theresa's brother — and the Irish poet, Taafe.

They were approaching the gate to the city, the Porta della Piazza, and a soldier had clearly disrupted the group of men in his haste to get past them through the gate. Taafe was shouting that he had been jostled and that the insolence was not to be endured. Lord Byron loudly called to the soldier to apologise.

'What's happening?' gasped Theresa.

Mary, who was leaning out more towards the fracas, replied, 'Byron is chasing that soldier, and Shelley is going with him. Oh, Shelley! His blood always boils at an insolent soldier! They've got him. They are giving their cards. Taafe is cowering at the back.'

'The soldier is hurling such curses at them. Is he drunk?'

'It looks like it. What is he saying? My Italian is not good enough for that ranting.' Mary drew her head back so that Theresa could get the best view.

'He is saying that he would have the right to draw his sabre and cut them to pieces, but he is going to have them arrested instead! They are all ignoring him and spurring the horses on through.' Then she screamed. 'He has already got through and is calling on the guard to stop them. He is swinging his sabre at them. What are we to do?'

Mary tried to pull her back so that she could see properly, too, and Theresa tried to make way and they bumped heads in their anxiety.

'Oh, Ow! They have no swords to defend themselves,' gasped Mary, clutching her forehead.

'Ah, they have all attacked him ... I think they have him ... No, Captain Hay has blood on his nose.'

'And Shelley is on the ground. I must go to him.' Mary yanked open the door of the carriage, but the coachman restrained her.

'Ayee ... Byron loves your Shelley. That man is dead if he hurt him!' Theresa was also on the path by now. The coachman spoke to her in rapid Italian.

'He says that the soldier has ridden off and Shelley is sitting up. He will go to him if we promise to stay here.' Theresa caught hold of Mary's hand and held it tight.

The coachman and the others brought Shelley and Captain Hay back to the coach and sat them inside with the distraught ladies. Theresa used her handkerchief on Captain Hay's cuts and Mary examined Shelley carefully to check he was whole.

'Trust you to be in the thick of it,' she said, clucking at him and examining the tears in his long, dingy grey and shapeless coat. Luckily this horrible garment will hardly show the damage. Captain Hay, you have dripped blood on your green velvet!' The Captain seemed faint with loss of blood.

'Damnable fellow!' muttered Shelley. 'These soldiers think they can do as they like. I don't even think he was an officer and entitled to give satisfaction. Byron has ridden back to his house for a sword. I don't like the scoundrel's chances.'

As the carriage passed through the gates to the city on their road home, they saw Byron galloping furiously back from the town towards the soldier, who was still trotting complacently, thinking the incident finished. They heard Byron shouting that he wanted satisfaction. Byron's servant tried to restrain the soldier's horse, so that the soldier would pay attention, but it reared and he got free and galloped off.

When, soon afterwards, Mary and Theresa's carriage arrived at Byron's palazzo, Casa Lanfranchi, they found turmoil, with a crowd gathering and shouting outside. They unloaded their wounded heroes, who were helped inside by the servants, and met chaos and consternation within the house, too.

Theresa, in an enormous fright, demanded of the servants what had happened. They replied in a confused gabble, and she pulled aside the least hysterical of the maids to speak to her by herself.

'One of my lord's servants has thrown a pitchfork at the soldier as he passed by calling out oaths to the house,' she reported, clutching Mary, collapsing onto a chair and looking pale. 'The servant thought the soldier had killed their master. Such loyalty!'

The incident was the talk of Pisan society, with rumours ricocheting from Florence to Rome and back again, gaining momentum. The English had led an insurrection on the guards; Byron was mortally wounded; Byron had assassinated a Tuscan colonel in a duel; the sergeant-major, whose name was Masi, was not expected to live and the English gentlemen would suffer vengeance from the Pisans. Shelley, Hay and Gamba went immediately to the Governor to put their version of events. In Italian society it was best to accuse first. Byron called in favours from Florence. Taafe boasted of his courage but refused to take responsibility for precipitating the fracas, to the disgust of those involved. Mary and Theresa were interviewed for six hours in their homes by polite policemen, who found fifteen witnesses in all to interrogate. No-one would point a finger, and by the time they had arrested two of Byron's servants, Masi was out of danger. Living in Pisa, though, became prickly for Byron and a summer out of town became imperative.

This was the good and the bad of being in the ambit of Lord Byron. He seemed to attract scandal, but it bounced off him like hail on cobblestones. Everyone else got battered and wet. There was an addictive energy, like an electrical storm, that illuminated his surroundings. Shelley was flattered by Byron's constant demands for his company, but he was also beginning to feel the need to escape. Byron's genius paralysed his creative flow. He was not jealous, or even resentful, but he felt a sense of inferiority and sadness. Then there was the heavy drinking at Byron's men's evenings and, when drunk, Byron was not above taking swipes at Shelley's past and present domestic arrangements. Byron liked men's men who would ride and shoot and get drunk. There was no natural slot for Shelley in Byron's world. The relationship with Claire made him uncomfortable. Shelley did not drink, so never lost control, and you could only judge a man in his cups. At least he could ride and shoot well. For Byron, Shelley was uncomfortably like a worthy lover, the high-minded one who understood you, who you couldn't quite make up your mind to fully embrace, and who often made you see yourself too clearly; the one whom you hurt casually because you knew they admired you unselfishly; the one you should be satisfied with while ignoring the unsuitable, shallow, profligate, exciting others.

Mary knew that the gloss of Byron was wearing off for Shelley. If I were writing my life as a fiction, she thought, this chapter would either be the apogee or the lull before the storm. For this short time we are surrounded by more friends — or at least those who are in sympathy with us — than enemies. For the first time in years, Mary felt herself to be calm and serene. She felt in control of her life, if not of fate. The scales of the universe, with all the dark memories and bitterness that balanced one side, the shadowy side as she thought of it, was outweighed by the other side, by light and imagination. Without Claire in their company, to provoke whispered asides, Mary found she could relax and enjoy society. There were concerts and balls, entertaining and visiting. Without Claire in the house noting every slight caress, she and Shelley had found their passion again, their blood heated by a slow burn of banter and allusion and a slow, sensual game of chess by the fire. Without Claire's prying eyes always happening to glance at the pages, she was able to write freely in her journal, and candidly to her friends.

*My dear Mrs. Gisborne*

*Here we are in Pisa, having furnished very nice apartments for ourselves, and what is more, paid for the furniture out of the fruits of two years' economy. We are at the top of the Tre Palazzi di Chiesa. ... on the north side of Lung' Arno; but the rooms we inhabit are south, and look over the whole country towards the sea, so that we are entirely out of the bustle and disagreeable puzzi, etc., of the town, and hardly know that we are so enveloped until we descend into the street. So here we live, Lord Byron just opposite to us in Casa Lanfranchi. So Pisa, you see, has become a little nest of singing birds. You will be both surprised and delighted at the work just about to be published by him: his Cain, which is in the highest style of imaginative poetry. It made a great impression upon me, and appears almost a revelation, from its power and beauty. Shelley rides with him; I, of course, see little of him. The lady whom he serves is a nice pretty girl without pretensions — good hearted and amiable; her relations were banished for Carbonarism.*

*What do you know of Hunt? About two months ago he wrote to say that on 21st October he should quit England, and we have heard nothing more of him in any way; I expect some day he and six children will drop in from the clouds, trusting that God will temper the wind to the shorn lamb. Pray when you write, tell us everything you know concerning him. Do you get any intelligence of the Greeks? Our worthy countrymen take part against them in every possible way, yet such is the spirit of freedom, and such the hatred of these poor people for their oppressors, that I have the warmest hopes. Mavrocordato is there, justly revered for the sacrifice he has made of his whole fortune to the cause, and besides for his firmness and talents. If Greece be free, Shelley and I have vowed to go, perhaps to settle there, in one of those beautiful islands where earth, ocean, and sky form the paradise. You will, I hope, tell us all the news of our friends when you write. I see no one that you know. We live in our usual retired way, with few friends and no acquaintances. Claire is returned to her usual residence, and our tranquillity is unbroken in upon, except by those winds, sirocco or tramontana, which now and then will sweep over the ocean of one's mind and disturb or cloud its surface.*

*Shelley has been much better in health this winter than any other since I have known him. Pisa certainly agrees with him exceedingly well. Percy is quite well; he begins to talk, Italian only now, and to call things bello and buono, but the droll thing is, that he is right about the genders. A silk vestito is bello, but a new frusta is bella. He is a fine boy, full of life, and very pretty.*

Shelley interrupted her writing. 'Don't forget to ask Mrs Gisbourne to send half a dozen Brookman and Langdon pencils.'

'No of course not,' replied Mary, looking up, impatiently. 'I'm also asking for needles in a case, pins, sealing wax, scissors, white netting silk for purses, a spy glass in a gold rim for short sight–for you of course. If you hold that book any closer you will blacken your nose. A dozen pair of stockings for Percy, a cake of Carmine from Smith and Warner's and some of the best vellum drawing paper for miniatures. Another thing, I want a cornelian seal with your coat of arms. Cornelian is the birthstone for both you and me, so that's good. Anything else?' she looked at him inquiringly.

'A coat-of-arms seal?' Shelley smiled, raising his eyebrow. 'Having Lord Byron nearby has influenced you! Just a penknife, please, with several blades.'

'Of course, all this is dependent on the Gisbournes getting some money from Ollier to pay for this. He refuses them a single sixpence! He treats us abominably. We have heard nothing from him about your drama, *Hellas*. John Gisbourne says that he suspects *Prometheus* has sold better than he, Ollier, is telling us, while he tells Gisbourne that there is no money left in our account! Yet he still wants my *Castruccio*, or *Valperga* as my father wants to call it, being miffed to have missed out on *Frankenste*in, yet he won't give me an advance. Well, he's not getting the book before we see some money.'

'Mr Gisbourne and Hogg both think we should stick with Ollier for the present though, don't they? Because of the difficulty in dealing with a new publisher from this distance.'

'I suppose so.' Mary paused, and asked, 'It is Wednesday. Will you go to Lord Byron's tonight?'

'I will. I suppose. These Wednesday night men-only dinner parties have become a feature of our Pisan society, and he always seems to want to make sure that I'll attend. Williams is going.'

'Byron sent his servant this morning to remind you,' agreed Mary. 'It's flattering.'

'It is, but sometimes I would prefer to admire my lord the writer from a distance. Byron the man is harder to admire, even now. They all sit around making vats of claret of themselves til three in the morning, talking nonsense, and since I am the only one sober, my nerves are shredded.'

'Poor love.' Mary left her desk to go and kiss and stroke his brow. 'I think that one of the reasons Byron values you is that you are clear-sighted about him. You ascribe goodness, kindness and talent in fair measure, where others are eager to see in him imaginary attributes that are romantic and false.'

'Hmmm.' He turned to embrace her, and the pile of open books that had been balancing precariously on his knees toppled to the floor with a clatter that brought the maid scurrying, Mary and Shelley pulled apart, and then exchanged a quick kiss as the books were gathered up and returned to the sofa at Shelley's side.

'Thank you, Maria,' said Shelley to the maid, trying to put on a serious face, but when he turned back to Mary, it had become genuinely solemn.

'The hardest thing is that he is so difficult to deal with and so, so insensitive. He stands on high ground and doesn't give a second thought to the feelings of the invisible masses below. And then ... his instinct is always to think the worst of people's motives and mine tends ridiculously the other way, but still ... it's wearing to second-guess how he will react. I have to try to mollify him for Hunt's sake. The new magazine must go ahead, and I must make sure the Hunts are welcomed. We have sent every penny we can scrape up to Hunt for the travel costs, haven't we? I sent £150 yesterday, plus there's the cost of furnishing the floor in Byron's palace for them. Byron thinks he is generous in accommodating them and even more so in providing curtains and carpets. He has no real concept of how financially constrained we are, and he is always suspicious because he is so used to people trying to get money from him for their own purses.' He looked dejected.

'But the worse thing is to do with Claire. He is intractable on the subject of Allegra. I know I can't persuade him to do what Claire wants. Either to let her go and visit, or to bring her daughter closer. He won't listen to me, and every time I ask, I feel as if he is sneering at me, as if he is giving credence to the idea that Claire has been my mistress. Then he threatens to send her to a secret convent. I daren't speak. Then Claire thinks I am not doing enough.' He gave a deep sigh, lay back on the arm of the sofa, and closed his eyes. 'She is behaving hysterically, writing again about kidnapping Allegra. Using force. She is becoming unstable.'

Mary stood up and walked back to her writing desk. 'I refuse to let Claire ruin this peacefulness.'

'I think we have to ask her to join us this summer, at least for a while, to calm her down.'

'No.'

'She may do something irrational if we don't have her. When she has come here secretly and stayed with Mrs. Mason, she encourages her – though probably not about the force.'

'I thought she was planning to go to Vienna to stay with Charles? You told me that Mrs. Mason was encouraging that, too.'

'Yes, and she apparently wrote to Lord Byron on that score, entreating one last visit with Allegra, but she was probably wild and intemperate in her language. She is in no fit state to go at the moment. Have some compassion. The Williams will be with us, to moderate her influence. You know how calming Jane is.' He came and stood behind her, stroking her neck, soothingly.

Mary was still for a long time. Then she turned to face him and stared very hard into his eyes. 'For a very few weeks. Until she is calm. You may invite her to join us by the sea, but you must promise to ensure she leaves after that time. Promise me?' She gripped his clean-shaven cheeks tightly, until he nodded, painfully.

'The spring always sees a visitation of ill-fate for us. It was the time of the death of the first baby, and of Paolo Foggi's blackmail, and I don't want another incident with Claire to continue the pattern. I had hoped that the affair with the soldier was this season's drama.'

She let go of him and half smiled. 'Besides, I am pregnant.' She laughed at his astonishment and accepted his delighted hug. 'You know that I am not at my best when I am pregnant. I am likely to be ill and even less tolerant of Claire. Be warned. At least you are not in so much pain, so hopefully your temper will do for us both!'

'I am now writing to Marianne.' Mary sat at her desk again, with purpose. 'Do you want to add anything to Hunt?'

'I have just written,' said Shelley. 'I can't wait for them to arrive. The medicine of his friendship will cure my every ailment.'

*My dearest Marianne,*

*I hope that this letter will find you quite well, recovering from your severe attack, and looking towards your haven Italy with best hopes. I do indeed believe that you will find a relief here from your many English cares, and that the winds which waft you will sing the requiem to all your ills. It was indeed unfortunate that you encountered such weather on the very threshold of your journey, and as the wind howled through the long night, how often did I think of you! At length it seemed as if we should never, never meet; but I will not give way to such a presentiment. We enjoy here divine weather. The sun hot, too hot, with a freshness and clearness in the breeze that bears with it all the delights of spring. The hedges are budding, and you should see me and my friend Mrs. Williams poking about for violets by the sides of dry ditches; she being herself—'A violet by a mossy stone, Half hidden from the eye.'*

*Yesterday a countryman seeing our dilemma, since the ditch was not quite dry, insisted on gathering them for us, and when we resisted, saying that we had no quattrini (i.e. farthings, being the generic name for all money), he indignantly exclaimed, Oh! se lo faccio per interesse! How I wish you were with us in our rambles! Our good cavaliers flock together, and as they do not like fetching a walk with the absurd womankind, Jane (i.e. Mrs. Williams) and I are off together, and talk morality and pluck violets by the way. I look forward to many duets with this lady and Hunt. She has a very pretty voice, and a taste and ear for music which is almost miraculous. The harp is her favourite instrument; but we have none, and a very bad piano; however, as it is, we pass very pleasant evenings, though I can hardly bear to hear her sing "Donne l'amore"; it transports me so entirely back to your little parlour at Hampstead—and I see the piano, the bookcase, the prints, the casts—and hear the far-ha-ha-a!*

*We are in great uncertainty as to where we shall spend the summer. There is a beautiful bay about fifty miles off, and as we have resolved on the sea, Shelley bought a boat. We wished very much to go there; perhaps we shall still, but as yet we can find but one house; but as we are a colony "which moves altogether or not at all," we have not yet made up our minds. The apartments which we have prepared for you in Lord Byron's house will be very warm for the summer; and indeed for the two hottest months I should think that you had better go into the country. Villas about here are tolerably cheap, and they are perfect paradises. Perhaps, as it was with me, Italy will not strike you as so divine at first; but each day it becomes dearer and more delightful; the sun, the flowers, the air, all is more sweet and more balmy than in the land that you inhabit.*

*M. W. S.*

As the spring progressed, their plans for moving to the Bay of Spezia for the summer became firmer. Mary was optimistic. The thought of relaxing by the sea was delightful. It would, she hoped, give her an easy pregnancy this time. She was working on some more children's stories as her mind turned to motherhood. Even the projected arrival of Claire did not dispel or dampen her optimism.

*My dear Mrs. Gisbourne,*

*Shelley is now gone to Spezzia to get houses for us and the Williams for the summer.*

*Our colony will be a large one, too large, I am afraid, for unity; yet I hope not. There will be Lord Byron, who will have a large and beautiful boat built on purpose by some English navy officers at Genoa.*

*There will be the Countess Guiccioli and her brother; the Williams, whom you know; Trelawney, a kind of half-Arab Englishman, whose life has been as changeful as that of Anastasius, and who recounts the adventures as eloquently and as well as the imagined Greek. There will be, besides, a Captain Roberts, whom I do not know, a very rough subject, I fancy,—a famous angler. We are to have a small boat, and now that those first divine spring days are come (you know them well), the sky clear, the sun hot, the hedges budding, we sitting without a fire and the windows open, I begin to long for the sparkling waves, the olive-coloured hills and vine-shaded pergolas of Spezzia.*

*If April prove fine, we shall fly with the swallows. The Opera here has been detestable. The English Sinclair is the primo tenore, and acquits himself excellently, but the Italians, have enviously selected such operas as give him little or nothing to do ... We have English here, and some English balls and parties, to which I go sometimes ... I have sent my novel to Papa. I long to hear some news of it, as, with an author's vanity, I want to see it in print, and hear the praises of my friends. What does Henry do? How many times has he been in love?*

*Ever yours,*
*M. W. S.*

It proved difficult to find houses, especially two close by each other for their large party. They took turns to look, and in late April, Claire had come from Florence to go with the Williams for another search.

While they were away, Mary's apprehension about the ill fate that spring always brought them was brutally realised.

'It's a letter sent over from Byron. Addressed to you.' Mary was puzzled as she took the folded paper with Byron's seal in to Shelley, who was sitting cross-legged on the floor of his study, bouncing Percy on his lap. 'You only left his house an hour ago! What could he want?'

She watched while Shelley opened and read the short note. His horrified gasp seared the air.

'What? What is it?'

Shelley looked up at her with glazed eyes. He seemed struck dumb. She snatched the letter and Percy wailed in response to his father's sudden distraction and the change in atmosphere. The nurse came in to see what was wrong. Mary read the letter and sank into a chair.

'It can't be.' She was white.

Shelley's eyes were full and his voice was barely audible. 'I just saw her a few months ago. She was lively and happy in the convent. Such a beautiful little girl. Such a beautiful little girl.'

The nurse took the crying baby out of the room, and Mary and Shelley stared at each other.

'Not Allegra. I didn't even know she was ill!' whispered Mary. They spoke as if the softness of their voices could soothe the spirit of the dead child.

'Byron mentioned yesterday that she had suffered a fever, but said that the latest news from the nuns was good.'

'Poor Claire. Poor, poor Claire!' Mary cried for the trauma that awaited Claire, with tears brewed in the memories of her own three losses. Shelley, still cross-legged on the floor, had the heels of his hands pressed into his forehead. He got up and came with his handkerchief to wipe her eyes. He knew she was feeling and remembering, their own dead children, but he had also seen more of Allegra in Venice and Ravenna, so she was more real in his imagination.

'How will I ever tell Claire?' said Shelley. They looked at each other in horror and fear, the practicalities of the situation overtaking grief.

'She is due back here tomorrow. If Byron is so close, just across the Arno, she will try to kill him.' Shelley looked seriously alarmed. 'There will be no fury like hers. She will blame him utterly. You must hide your pistols and your sword.' Mary looked anxiously about the room for other potential weapons. 'No, we can't tell her that Allegra has died while she remains here, in Pisa. We must get her away to the coast before we tell her. It's the only possible solution!'

'Yes, that's sensible, Mary, but how? We haven't found houses for us and the Williams yet. Where can we go?'

'Perhaps Claire and the Williams will have found something when they come back tomorrow?'

'And if they haven't?'

'I don't know.'

Underneath the blackness and the panic they both felt, there was a guilty pleasure in being able to agree, for once, on the right thing to do about Claire.

In the end they decided that whatever villas the others had seen, they would be enthusiastic, and agree to take them, and that Mary and Claire would set off the next day as the advance party. If they had found nothing, Mary and Claire would still be sent to the coast but as the next search party. Shelley would stay behind to supervise the packing of their furniture and to try to get more details out of Byron. They would not tell Claire about Allegra until she was safely on the coast, a good distance from Pisa and they were all together, a joint force to contain and console her. They would say the landlord had another tenant waiting for their apartments here, hence the speed. Shelley would take Edward Williams aside and explain the urgency and the deception, and Mary would do the same to Jane.

'Casa Magni might do for you,' said Edward tiredly, when they came back the next day. They were reporting, gathered around the table in the Shelleys' apartment with a late breakfast of tea and buns, shutters open to allow in the spring breezes and the sun which slanted across the room with the promise of a hot summer. 'It is a bit run down and a long way from anywhere, but it is unfurnished, the only unfurnished one we could find. The thing about Magni is that the position is spectacular. It is literally right on the sea. The Gulf of Spezia is laid out before you! It's not too expensive for you, I think. They might negotiate, and will take a six month lease. Nothing at all for us though, that we can afford, but that shouldn't stop you. We will keep looking.' Even though he had been met by Shelley with the news about Allegra and understood their need, he found it hard to keep disappointment from his voice.

'Could we all fit in there?' asked Shelley, quick to pick up on his friend's tone.

Jane, Edward and Claire looked at each other, surprised

'Perhaps,' replied Edward. 'That's a generous thought, old man.' He understood that Shelley wanted no impediment to Claire's leaving Pisa before the news reached her, but he also knew that Jane liked her privacy. Even though he was the most considerate of husbands, the thought of living actually on the sea ... Edward was even more passionate about boats than Shelley, if that were possible.

Jane gave a small, resigned smile. 'It will be a squash, but I suppose we might manage.' She was clearly uncomfortable but trying to be loyal to the Shelleys.

'Of course we can all cope with a tight fit,' laughed Claire, who would not be there for the whole time and would be the first to complain, thought Mary irritatedly. Then she immediately felt guilty because of Claire's impending blow.

Shelley accepted more tea from a fresh pot brought in and said, slowly, as if thinking it through: 'It sounds to me that if we don't get this one we will be stuck in Pisa or the hills for the summer and we all had our hearts set on being by the sea. So, I think we should attempt to secure this place. Let's see. What about Mary going tomorrow to negotiate with the owners. Claire, you can go with her to show her where to go. She can take Percy and the nurse. I will stay to supervise the furniture and so will Edward and Jane and their children. It will be too expensive for too many of us to put up at inns. We'll come on in the next couple of days.'

Shelley did that well, Mary thought.

'Will Mary be able to cope?' asked Claire, sweetly.

'What on earth do you mean?' Mary snapped, then took another deep breath.

Claire carefully removed a crumb from her pink muslin. She seemed to dress herself vey well on her allowance. She looked up at Mary from under her lashes. 'You have seemed somewhat unwell this last week, since I arrived.'

Shelley and Mary exchanged a glance, from which Shelley received clear instructions.

'Sharp-eyed Claire! I'm delighted to tell you all that clever Maie is preparing to deliver us a new child.' He got up to go and stand behind Mary, put his hands on her shoulders and kiss the top of her head. She put her hands up to grasp his. Edward and Jane were all smiles and congratulations. Claire added hers, not sure which she felt more, smugness or jealousy, and trying to show neither.

'As you in particular know, Claire, Mary is often very unwell at this early stage. That's one reason I want you to accompany her, to help her.' Oh, clever, clever Shelley, thought Mary. 'I will also ask Trelawney to go with you both, in case there are any difficulties that require his strength or protection.' Even more clever Shelley. Trelawney would act as a buffer between her and Claire. Shelley understood that Mary was even less able to tolerate her step-sister when pregnant, and the tension made her even more ill. Trelawney liked Claire. Ever a man for danger.

# 3

'Sometimes realities took ghostly shapes; and it was
impossible for one's blood not to curdle at the perception
of an evident mixture of what we knew to be true, with
the visionary semblance of all that we feared ...'

*The Last Man,* Mary Shelley

'I hate living here, at Magni.'

It was a rare moment of peace on Shelley's boat, gently drifting
a mile or two from the shore. Mary lay with her head on his lap and
shut her eyes.

'This beautiful place gives me the utmost misery,' she murmured,
sadly. 'I know if I were writing about it in a novel I would certainly
describe the scenery as idyllic, with its vines and walnut and ilex
wood-covered promontories, those castles rising above little towns
and the islands and bays stretching to the west. Then there are the
sunsets and the moonrise, the stars, all things of wondrous beauty.
Except that to me it feels wild, dirty and full of danger. I long for
something more civilised and safe. '

'Yet I love it here.' Shelley was equally sad. 'The sense of the
beauty in the unformed, the possibility of redemption.'

'Look, even our house, perched there over the bay, seems exposed
and vulnerable to every evil force of nature.'

'Evil is only where we see it, Mary. Can't you try to be content?'

'It's fine for you. You let Jane and her guitar sooth your senses,
with smiles and songs. You have your little boat, you fish with Edward
for hours, and you can bathe and frolic every evening with the whole
disgusting, filthy population of the village as they flock into the sea.'

'But it is quiet, and at least Claire is too subdued after losing
Allegra to disturb you.'

'Oh she disturbs me all right. It is three years tomorrow since we lost William. She didn't understand the strength of my feelings then, when I lost a child whom I had cared for every day. Now you would think no one has ever had a grief to match hers, losing a child she wasn't even allowed to see. And she bears up so well.'

Mary knew that her heavy irony was mean-spirited. For the past month she had been so much the slave of misery in some form or other, that she had lost the memory of joy as a prisoner loses memory of the clarity of open sky. Her perspective had become narrow and dark and full of foreboding. The luxury of having Shelley to herself for a few hours was like a shaft of sunlight which shows the prisoner his degradation, and his failure.

'I am sorry, my dearest. My nerves are so wound up. I'm sharp with you. The others think I am unfeeling and cold. They think I make you unhappy and … and I suppose I do.' The tears which had been small rivulets on her cheeks, burst their banks and her shoulder shook. 'I'm so sick, sick in body because of this new child inside me, sick in mind with the fear of bringing a new, vulnerable creature into the world. I'm so full of foreboding now that Percy is close to his three years' birthday. William was three when he was taken from us.'

'Maie, I will always look after you and Percy. I will keep him safe, I promise.' He stroked her hair and the gentle rhythm matched that of the waves. 'Pecksie, I know, I really do, how difficult it has been for you. I know Clara and William are always with you – but it must not spoil the love and trust between us. I know you miss the bustle and sociability of Pisa. Yes, you do, don't deny it,' as she tried to shake her head. 'And it's so hard for anyone to visit us, it's a boat trip or a bumpy horse ride down the mountain track. Consider, though. You are with child, and even back in society you would be the Doormouse again, because you are tired and constantly sick. So better to be here, with good friends, just for the summer. Most of all, I need you Mary, my best Mary. With me. My spirit feels cold without your soul's warmth.'

'I know.' She sat up and looked across the bay at the pretty white roofs of Lerici. 'It is worse this time, though. I have such forebodings of disaster. I have had dreams where I am alone with one child. I am in agony whenever you and Percy are out of my sight. I can't lift my spirit out of the mire. I don't have an appetite for writing and I feel total want of inspiration.'

'Doormouse, in one month you will be twenty-five. Look what you have achieved. You astonish me, what you take on, what you have learnt. What a good mother you are. What you can endure. Your writing has astounded the world. On my good days I still have hopes of what we can do if we continue to love and learn together. We may still transform the world. Especially now I am out of the daily influence of Byron.'

His words and his touch worked a little magic, enough to lift her failing spirits for an hour, but on shore there would still be the crowded living conditions and the isolation of Casa Magni to deal with, and Mary would still silently scream to leave. They rowed back and Shelley helped her to clamber awkwardly out of the boat onto the sand front of the house. A servant came out to tie up the little vessel alongside the sailing ship, the Don Juan, that had recently been delivered by Trelawney and Captain Roberts. Shelley paused to run his hand lovingly along it's wooden side.

'I'll take you upstairs then find Edward for a sail. It will be a perfect evening. Just a light breeze.' He stood with no coat, no tie, rolled trousers and pale skin slightly reddened by the sun, and glanced at her. He felt uncomfortable as she unsympathetically considered his wild appearance. 'Remember, Trelawney is coming tomorrow. He'll cheer you!'

Inside, Jane was tight-lipped and pale. Her usual soft and languid stance had hardened into a stiff back and rigid jaw. This, for Jane, was evidence of a maelstrom of discontent. She stood waiting for them, standing behind a chair and gripping the top. When she spoke though, her voice was as controlled and gently melodic as ever, except that she blushed, melting hotly into the pink lace that trimmed her muslin.

'Mary, dear. I do wish you would talk to the cook. I went down to the kitchen to speak to her because little Janey felt ill after eating strawberries and I saw that they have completely muddled our saucepans and some of mine were missing!'

Mary was taken aback. She wanted to burst out laughing, but a look at Jane's solemn face made her bring the corner of her shawl across her mouth in semblance of a cough. It was hard to reconcile the Jane who sang for them in the evening with sweet sensitivity, sitting angelically on the verandah brushed by the last shafts of sunlight, with a Jane who cared deeply about saucepans.

A glance for help to Shelley was of no use. He was busily slipping past into his room to avoid arbitration.

'Jane, dear,' she soothed, putting her hand over Jane's tiny one. 'Please don't worry. I promise that when we leave I will ensure all of your own saucepans go with you. I know you have a care for how your food is prepared.'

'Yes, well.' Jane, usually the conciliator, was smiling with relief. Jane's world was simple and clear. The surface of her lake always glistened with sunlight or rippled with breezes and was only occasionally disturbed by storms. Agitation in the depths or turbulence above rarely troubled her.

Claire had come into the room during their exchange. Because the villa was small, there was only one public central room and little privacy. It opened directly onto the terrace facing the sea and all the main bedrooms opened off it. Though it was a large room, the furniture of both the Shelleys' and the Williams' apartments in Pisa — all of which had been painstakingly ferried in by boat — jostled for precedence in the room. They had used screens to try to separate sitting and dining areas but it felt oppressive compared to the open vista seen through the glass doors. Both Mary's and Shelley's rooms, which faced the sea, doubled as their studies. Jane and Edward had back bedrooms on the same floor. The children, servants and any visitors occupied the lower floors. There were few private conversations or activities possible unless two people overtly left the main room together through one of the bedroom doors.

'Of course, Mary, you wouldn't understand how Jane feels,' said Claire, who had heard it all. 'Your head occupies too high a realm!' Jane innocently accepted a complicit smile from Claire. Two artistic spirits. 'Will you take a walk, Jane, to enjoy the late afternoon breeze?'

As they left, Mary felt a wave of nausea and retreated to her room, She collapsed onto her bed.

I have imagined the dangers of man assuming the role of God, but is it not more true that we all want God to be in our own particular image? Right now I want a vengeful God who would punish Claire for her schemes to appropriate Jane.

A wave of guilt was a reminder that Claire had recently had a taste of Hell.

It felt strange to want to be in Jane's good books, but everyone did. She was certainly superficial, and even with a husband who aspired to join the ranks of the published, she rarely read or joined in a political conversation. She never seemed to feel the need to apologise for this, or to envy others their skills. Jane just was, and this quality of composedness was like a deep calm bay. If one needed to drop anchor, it was the ideal place. She did not seem to recognise Claire's manipulations. She took her friendship at face value It was nail-bitingly frustrating, but impossible to point out.

Days of continuous sickness kept Mary confined to her room with a bucket. 'I shall not move,' she said to Shelley and to Jane, who was all solicitude. 'I will keep this baby inside me. I will.' She drank only milk or wine. No food would stay down, not even the chicken soup Jane instructed the cook to make. She clung to Shelley's hand for strength, and he sat for long hours reading to her, until she fell asleep, exhausted, only to be woken by the next wave of nausea. Once or twice he carried her down to the sea and immersed her three times like a penitent for the curative properties of the salt water.

'Hold me tight,' said Mary. 'We neither of us can swim.'

'I would drown with you or drown myself, but never let you drown alone. There is no world without you.'

Shelley became too anxious to be able to sleep. The benefits of the sea and the tranquility that had buoyed him evaporated. When he lay by Mary it was hard to know which of them was the most pale or drained.

Pounding, drumming, clashing, twanging. The world became a thirty-day symphony of discord in three movements. Piano to forte, mezze forte, crescendo.

First there was clatter along the terrace, then a banging of doors in the house and Mary's door was flung open by Jane, wild-eyed.

'Shelley, where's Shelley? I saw him. I saw him. I did. Where is he?'

Trelawney came up behind her and took her by her shoulders, which were shaking.

'Sit here with Mary, my dear, I will find him.' He led her gently to a chair by Mary.

'What happened?' Mary tried to sit up.

'Nothing, I … No, it is stupid.'

'Tell me.'

'He was walking along the terrace, in shirtsleeves. That way.' She pointed to the right. 'Then just a second later I saw him go the same way again.'

'He was pacing.'

'No, he had not come back in between. I do not imagine things, Mary. You know that.' Jane squeezed her brows trying to force out the pus of fancy. 'Then he didn't come back at all and I thought he must have fallen over the end. So we went to look and there was no-one there. My heart stopped as I looked over the railing, but there was nobody below. Nothing. Nothing at all.' She stared at Mary, waiting for an explanation.

Just then the large brawny, bearded Trelawny came into the room dragging an out-of-breath Shelley behind him like a schoolboy off for a whipping. Jane sagged in her chair and began to sob huge, relieved sobs.

'What is it?' asked Shelley, puzzled anxious. 'What on earth …?'

'Have you been on the terrace this afternoon?' Trelawney demanded.

'No, I've been on the Don Juan all morning with Edward. We got back at two and have been working on the sail since.'

'Are you sure?'

'Of course I'm sure. What is this about?'

So they told him. Mary and Shelley did not doubt that this portent had meaning, in spite of the backtracking reassurances of Jane — a headache, the sun through the window — and the practical, none of this nonsense, affirmations of Trelawney. They came to no satisfactory conclusion, except to feel that it was not a good omen. They obsessively did the Sortes Virgiliae until they fell asleep over their copy of the Aeneid.

Next, a bell ringing at almost dawn in Mary's room brought the maid, Shelley, Jane and Claire. Shelley saw Mary in her newly red nightgown, staring, diminished, foetal. Mimicking the shape of the wetly glistening mass between her legs. The women pushed him out of the door, and the maid ran for rags and hot water. He banged on Trelawney's door and sent him, half-dressed and hatless, to fetch the doctor from Viareggio and to stop at the ice-works at Pietrasanta to ask for an urgent delivery. 'Pay what you must to get it sent now. Bribe someone. Anything.'

As he went back to Mary's room, the maid was coming out with blood-soaked bundles. 'Keep it safe.' He was barely audible. 'I will deal with it later.'

Jane and Claire had lifted Mary's legs on pillows but there was still a steady trickle. Jane was pressing her brow with a vinegar soaked cloth. Shelley sat by her head. 'Get brandy.' He had a notion that she must not be allowed to pass into a faint. 'Eau de cologne, too. We have some?'

She seemed to be fading before his eyes. She spoke to him through dry lips and her voice was paper thin.

'I feel content, my love. Not apprehensive at all. I could go now if it were not for leaving you, and Percy.'

'No, no, no! Above all, stay with me.' If he could command her life spirit with the force of his will, he would do so. 'It would be a misfortune I could not endure, to lose you.' He thought of the prussic acid he had asked Trelawney to procure for him in Leghorn. His escape route prepared. It supported him over the next nightmarish hours as Mary drifted close to unconsciousness, drawn back by all his powers of persuasion. He talked to her of plans, of books still to read, of Percy. He read her heroic passages from *The Odyssey*, and funny passages from Peacock's farces. Claire and Jane brought them tea and brandy and tended to the cloths to stem the bleeding, but it didn't stop. At two o'clock they heard the servants pulling up a boat onto the beach filled with ice panniers wrapped in hay. Shelley went onto the terrace and called for them to bring them up to Mary's room.

'We must wait for the doctor,' said Claire, and Jane agreed.

'If he comes by road he could be another hour, maybe two. We can't wait. Send for the copper bath,' he said, with unusual authority. 'It is my decision.'

With the help of the servants they filled the copper bath with cold water and threw in chunks of ice. Shelley lifted Mary into it in her nightgown and she gasped with the shock, but was too lost to the world to feel the full pain of the freezing water. Shelley cradled her head and watched the thin stream of blood that coiled to the surface, until it stopped.

Finally a scream at midnight. Mary's door was flung open and Shelley stared at her wide-eyed, clutching his head on both sides as if he would wrench it from his body. Screaming again and again.

'Shelley, Shelley, wake up! Stop it, my love. Wake up!' Mary tried to make herself heard, but he seemed locked in a private hell. She made a supreme effort to get up, her legs barely supporting her so soon after her miscarriage. She tottered out of the room across to Jane William's door, collapsing onto her knees as she grasped the handle. Jane's astonished face appeared in the opening and Mary almost fell through into her room. 'It's Shelley,' she gasped, as Edward appeared and helped her to sit on their bed. 'Edward, he's out of control. See if you can calm him, please!'

As Edward crossed the dining hall towards Mary's room, the screaming had already stopped, and soon, as Mary and Jane strained to hear, there came the steady murmur of voices.

'Help me back to him, Jane, please.'

They found Shelley, dazed and trembling, lying on Mary's bed.

'Come, embrace me,' he whispered, and held out his arms for her to join him. The others left and closed the door behind them.

'You had a nightmare. What was it about? Do you remember?' She wrapped her arms around him to keep out the spirits of the night.

'It was a vision. A horrible vision. One of my worst.'

'You screamed so loudly, you frightened me.'

'Screamed? I did not scream.' He looked puzzled, irritated. 'I was in bed, and I clearly saw Jane and Edward come into my room, all bloodied and bruised, bones sticking through their skin, with Edward the worst, almost carried by Jane. He groaned in pain and told me to get up and flee, for the sea had come up and was flooding the house and it was about to collapse. So I went to the window and saw that it was true. The tide was as high as the terrace and was about to overwhelm us. In the spray I saw an image of myself with my hands around your throat, so I rushed into your room to prove your safety and when I saw you in bed, I was rooted to the spot, unable to move. Then you got out of bed and the vision vanished.' Or you woke up, thought Mary.

'What does it mean, Mary? I am scared.'

'Don't worry. It is that your nerves are splintered. We have just lost another child. You nearly lost me. It is understandable.' She hugged him more tightly. 'Stay here. Try to sleep.'

'You don't understand. It is not the first. I haven't wanted to worry you. Twice I have met a figure of myself walking towards me on the terrace. It comes from the south end and seems to melt as it gets close to me. The last time it called: *how long do you mean to be content?* as it faded.'

Mary felt a cold chill, but forced her voice to be matter of fact. 'It is the same thing. How hard we have to try to overcome misfortune. Endless misfortune it seems. I felt the same sense of doom before I lost this baby. You have always had visions when you are troubled or unwell. This is no different.'

'Mostly our forebodings have proved true.' He fought to keep his eyes open, scared of the unconscious world. 'In any case, this time Jane saw it too, and she is never hysterical.'

Though he could not fight sleep any longer, it was nearly dawn before Mary herself succumbed. She had found no rational conclusion to her labyrinthine imaginings. What could this all mean? The baby has been lost. The worst had already happened.

# 4

'I felt, that we were enchained to the car of fate, over whose coursers we had no control. We could no longer say, This we will do, and this we will leave undone. A mightier power than the human was at hand to destroy our plans or to achieve the work we avoided.'

*The Last Man,* Mary Shelley

'Don't go!' She clung to his sleeve! 'Please don't go!'

'Mary, dearest love, I have to.' For the hundredth time, it seemed, Shelley released her grasp with such sympathy that it was not obvious how much he longed to be gone.

'I can't let Hunt arrive and not be met. I have to take him to Byron myself, you know that. One wrong word and the whole arrangement could collapse. I would love you to be able to come ...'

'And I am so anxious to see Marianne and know how she has survived the long sea journey ...'

'You are still far too weak. You can barely crawl to the terrace.'

'Byron will hate the noisy Hunt brood, all six of them.'

'Another reason I have to be there to smooth things over. It will not be above a week, I hope.'

'A week! What could happen in a week! I will be so miserable without you in this horrible, isolated place. Suppose something happened to Percy, or he was taken ill. A day up a mountain track by horseback or a half day on the sea if the wind's right, if we need help. And just us women here. These local menservants are such savages. Even their jargon is disgusting.'

She was working herself up to hysterical pitch again.

He quickly took her by the shoulders and tried to lock eyes with her. She thought, his teeth are getting worse. 'Please, Mary, try not to be so sad. I hate to go and leave you like this.'

A last embrace.

Her door clicked shut and another opened in the pit of her stomach that allowed the exodus of hope and reason. Panic rushed in to fill the void. Fists, eyes clenched. *Be reasonable. Be reasonable. Be reasonable.*

The door opened again and Claire stood there. 'You are being unreasonable.'

Mary pushed past her onto the terrace and clung to the rail. Below, Shelley and the boy were about to push out the rowboat. Edward was already on board. 'Shelley!' A peregrine falcon swooped mercilessly into a flock of gulls and the anguished shriek of the prey mingled with Mary's own cry. Shelley looked up. He gestured to the others to wait and bounded back up the stairs that led to the terrace. She took his collar in her hands and pulled his face to hers, until they almost touched.

'If you are not back in a week, I will take Percy and go to Pisa, where I have friends and I have doctors. I will,' she said fiercely, tears shining.

'Now, now. I will be back home soon, I promise. We must go or we will miss the fine westward breeze.'

'This is not home.'

'Where you are, Mary.'

He ran back down to the waiting boat, past the falcon which had dropped its prey to the ground and was absorbed in its destruction.

Two days later, a little stronger in body if not in soul, Mary paced the terrace in the evening in nightgown and shawl, interrogating the sea, while Claire and Jane walked on the shore. She could not be still. She read to Percy in the afternoon. She wrote to Shelley, insisting that while he was at Pisa he should look for a house they could move to, maybe in the countryside at Pugnano and reminding him of his promise to be back in a week. She felt oppressed by the other women: Jane, so perfectly prepared to make the best of Casa Magni for Edward's pleasure and Claire, delightedly drawing comparisons with Mary's inability to do so for Shelley.

On Thursday there was a letter from Shelley in Pisa. Poor Marianne had arrived so sick that he called in Dr. Vacca, who pronounced her not long for this world. He said Hunt's fragile spirits seemed to crumble under this final blow. Theresa's family, the Gambas, had been exiled from Tuscany, and Byron insisted he would go with them — somewhere: America, Switzerland, Genoa, or Lucca — and issued conflicting orders every day to his bemused friends and servants. This put Hunt in greater despair, since he had arrived with no money, and Byron was too preoccupied to give him any sensible decisions about the fate of the new journal. She could see Shelley, she could picture him beset at every turn, trying to offer comfort to everyone and unravel the chaos. Now she was mortified that her two letters to him had been so despairing and so demanding.

On Saturday there was letter from Edward to Jane. He was at the port, waiting for Shelley to arrive from Pisa, before they could return. He said that if Shelley had not come by Monday, he would return by himself in a felucca. His anxiety to see Jane was enough for him to abandon Shelley. It would be Tuesday evening at the latest.

On Monday it was stormy all day and on Tuesday there was rain. Two motionless, wind-blown Cassandras manned the ramparts, scanning the bay in spite of the weather, clutching each other's hand to suppress their private prophesies of doom from each other.

Wednesday brought feluccas in on a fair wind and reports that Shelley and Edward had sailed on Monday. Impossible, they said to each other.

Thursday was another fair day but there was no sign of their boat, the Don Juan. Jane declared she would be rowed to Leghorn the next day.

'Wait for the letters at midday,' said Mary, not prepared to give way to fears of illness or, at best, customs disputes delaying them.

'I shall go. We have never been apart this long. He would not stay without word,' said Jane, pale but insistent. Mary knew she would have to go, too.

Friday morning produced a high swell, so no boat could leave. It also produced a letter from Hunt to Shelley, which Mary opened, feeling justified by her anxiety:

*"Pray write to tell us how you got home, for they say that you had bad weather after you sailed Monday, and we are anxious."*

'It is all over,' said Jane, quietly. Mary tried to suppress her own panic by reassuring Jane. It gave her strength.

'No, we don't know yet what has happened, but we must find out. We will go over to Lerici, then take a post to Pisa. Hunt is there. I am not sure if Byron is. Someone there will know what has happened to them.'

At Lerici they were told that no accident had been reported, but they were not reassured and looked for the next post to Pisa. There was only one place left inside but they were so wild-eyed and distraught that a kind young man gave up his seat to them and rode on the back.

It was Saturday at one a.m. when the coach drew up to Casa Lanfranchi. Jane had never met the Hunts and agreed to wait while Mary tried to wake Hunt to find out what he knew. Theresa Guiccioli, whose maid opened the door to Mary's hammering, said she had never seen anyone more like a ghost, incandescent and pale. She crossed herself and shrieked before summoning Byron. Neither of them knew anything other than that Shelley and Williams had sailed on Monday. Mary refused to let them wake Hunt. She couldn't bear to see him for the first time after four years when she was in such distress and in no state to sympathise with his troubles. It was better to keep up the momentum and go to Leghorn and look for Trelawney, who was at the port working on Byron's boat.

On Saturday at two a.m. their coach arrived at Leghorn, and they collapsed fully clothed onto the beds at the first inn that showed a light. Not knowing where Trelawney was staying, at dawn they rose and asked at inn after inn until they found him, and he was summoned. As he started down the stairs he saw them at the bottom, looking up at him, haggard, their hair loose and uncombed under their bonnets, their clothes crumpled. His face became as pale as theirs.

'What has become of Shelley and Edward?' demanded Mary.

'Dear Trelawney, help us,' cried Jane, and they each clung to one of his robust seaman's arms as if they were life rafts.

'Come into the parlour, Mary, Jane.' He shepherded them into the little room and called the servants for tea and bread in spite of their insistence that they could not take anything.

'Shelley and Williams were here Monday morning. They bought food and paper and boat supplies in the town. Shelley found a copy of Pliny the Elder that he had long desired. They aimed to set off at midday. Captain Roberts was worried that a storm was brewing and tried to persuade them to wait a day, but at that moment the sky was clear and the wind fair. Williams could not wait to get back to you, my dear,' he smiled at Jane, 'and Shelley spoke of his promise to you, Mary, to stay no more than a week. *I am overdue by a day*, he said. *Mary will not forgive me another.* He was optimistic that all would be fine. You know how he cannot be gainsaid in that mood. So they set off. About three the storm came up and Captain Roberts went up the watchtower to look for them through the glass. He saw them about ten miles out taking in their topsails, and then the rain was too heavy to see anymore. We waited, thinking they may return here, but when they didn't, we assumed they had managed to continue to you at Casa Magni. I was about to set out for there today, to confirm their safe arrival.'

Trelawney was a man of action and a consummate gentleman. Even had he not admired Shelley and considered him a friend, the two distressed ladies would have driven him to the heights of chivalry.

'We must not despair,' he soothed, with more confidence than he truly felt. 'They could have been driven anywhere along the coast or even over to Corsica. Even now they might be trying to persuade a Corsican peasant to dry their clothes and repair their ship.' A look at their faces told him this tone was too light-hearted. 'If you will permit me to leave you for a short while, I will find a courier to go along the coast between here and Spezia, to ask at each of the watchtowers if anything has been seen or found. I think it best if you both take a carriage back to your house, in case they manage to return by another route. I will come with you. You cannot go alone.' They protested but were grateful to let him take control. Mary, whose terror had so far overcome the weakness that still afflicted her from her loss of blood, felt suddenly as if the pegs that had held her on shore were pulled way and she were sliding into a watery abyss.

'I will be an hour or two,' said Trelawney. 'Try to rest.' But Mary was already asleep, her head falling onto the arm of the chair.

By nine o'clock they were in a coach bound for Lerici. The route took them close to the coast at Viareggio, and they decided to detour to the town to see if there were any news. The coastguard told them that a little boat had been swept ashore a few miles up the coast. He described it as made of thin planks stitched together. They had also found a water cask which sounded like the ones they had taken with them. As they continued on to Casa Magni, Mary engaged all of her imagination to construct scenarios that would deny her worst fears. They had thrown the small boat out to lighten their load. The cask had got swept over in the storm. It proved they had got so far, perhaps beyond the storm. They had got close to the coast, come ashore on the small boat and were wandering somewhere on the coast. Pictures rotated in her head as if she were standing in a manic diorama until she felt unable to breathe. And always the rhythmic jolting of the carriage pounded the unsuppressable thought. Shelley can't swim.

The last leg of the journey was crossing the bay from Lerici in a rowboat. A fiesta was in full swing in a fishing village on the shore as they rowed by. There were lights, torches, laughing, dancing on the sands and singing. It continued all the next week, a jarring counterpoint to their long silent wait for news from the messengers.

They sat each day in candlelight, the curtains drawn against the sight of the sea. Uneaten meals lay on the sideboard. The sirocco wind regularly banged in the shutters at night, or was it gentle Jane's head drumming against her wooden bedhead? Mary woke from a doze drenched in sweat from the heat of July, or was it from the vision of Shelley underwater, wild hair floating upwards as he sank slowly, smiling reassuringly at her, illuminated in wavering shafts of sunlight from the world above, and holding out his hands that, struggle as she might, she could never quite touch.

Little Percy ran into the gloom. 'Mamma, perché è buio?' How can I tell him why and where it is dark? The easiest answer. 'I have a headache, little maschio. Come here to me.' He climbed eagerly into her lap.

'When is daddy home? We're going fish.' Nodding. She saw the certainty in those big serious blue eyes with Shelley's lashes. Shelley had — has — such plans for you.

'Soon, my love.'

Come back, Shelley, and I will go anywhere with you.

Come back, Shelley, and I will live in this woebegone place forever if that is what you want, and never complain.

Come back, Shelley, and I will endure the pain of giving you many more children.

Claire was silent. For once there was no barb, no insult, no accusation or insinuation that would do. Trelawney was a muzzled beast in a cage, pacing the beach, watching for messengers and sails, making forays along the coast on horse-back, frustrated beyond words at being able to do nothing, but obliged by a sense of chivalry not to leave the women alone to face what might come. Finally he and they could stand it no longer and he set off for Leghorn to see what more he might do or find out.

# 5

'He was an elemental spirit imprisoned
here, but free and happy now.'

*Letter to Thomas Medwin, 30*

'How will I survive? How in this wide world will I survive without
you, Jane? No-one else really knows what it's been like.'

Jane turned from her packing up of her jewellery box to see Mary
standing in the doorway, clinging to the lintel as if she could restrain
her from going away by keeping her doorway anchored to the floor.
Jane went over and took her hands and the two young women moved
to sit together on the edge of the bed, still gripping tightly.

'Oh, Jane.' Mary could say nothing else. There was too much to
say. Without Jane, the last, horrible month would be locked inside
the theatre of her mind, replaying endlessly to an audience of one.

Only Jane had shared the moment when all emotion had been
hollowed out by the sight of Trelawney returning from Leghorn, his
news written in his face. There was no longer any doubt. Shelley's
body had been washed up on the beach at Viareggio, and Williams'
a little further down the coast. They had begged to be taken to the
bodies, but Trelawney was adamant. He would deal with it all. He
praised the dead men to the skies, and told Mary what a genius
Shelley had been and how she and Jane, both women weakened as
they were by grief, could not stand the strain. They now had their
children to consider and he had the servants bring the orphans to
their mothers as he spoke. The authorities were being difficult about
reclaiming the bodies because of the quarantine laws which forbade
any contact with them. Mary wanted Shelley buried near William
in Rome, but Trelawney pointed out that the red tape would be
more than her nerves could stand. The bodies had been battered and
bruised by the sea. They should remember them as they had been, not
have a vile image to constantly reappear in their nightmares. He did

not tell them that the bodies, when they were washed ashore, were so eaten away that there was little flesh to identify them. Williams had been recognised by his monogrammed neckerchief and his boots, but Shelley had been identified only by the volume of Plutarch in one pocket and Keats in the other.

Eventually Trelawney had got permission from the authorities to burn the bodies on the beach and take Shelley's ashes to be interred in Rome. Jane wanted to be able to take Edward's ashes to England. Mary thought an Hellenic cremation a fitting and heroic funeral. She wanted above all for Shelley to be done sufficient honour and no-one but Trelawney could have had the sense of romance that upheld his dignity. Byron was for letting the bodies stay unremarked, buried in the sand, but Trelawney arranged it all and took Byron and Hunt to Viareggio to attend the farewell.

Although a man of action, Trelawney's description of the day was sufficiently detailed and poetic to satisfy Mary. She could clearly see the deserted beach, distant islands like dashes of colour on the sparkling blue canvas of the Mediterranean, with a thick wood of sand-blown, twisted trunks behind and the Apennines beyond; the soldiers and health officers standing deferentially some distance away on the hot sand; Trelawney landing the iron furnace from the boat and piling the driftwood high; the corpses dug up from their temporary grave under the sand and lowered onto the pyre; the metal becoming white hot; the friends sprinkling wine and oil and frankincense on the bodies — more wine, as Trelawney said, than Shelley had drunk in his lifetime; the flames that flickered high and unrestrained, shimmering silvery in the hot air with the energy of Shelley's spirit; Trelawney burning his hand and risking quarantine to snatch Shelley's unburnt heart from the embers.

Trelawney did not recount how Byron had disgustedly compared the bodies to the rotting carcass of a sheep, and had insisted they try the strength of the waves that had claimed their friends by swimming a mile out to sea while the fire cooled, and how he had been taken with vomiting and had to be rescued.

So now it was time for Jane to go back to her relatives in England, since she had no other means of support for herself or her children. The women would longer be able to share their grief. More than that, no-one would understand their shared, unspoken guilt, unspoken even between each other. Both knew that their men had left Leghorn in haste to return to them; for Jane, because Edward could not bear to be away from her; for Mary, because of her threats and importuning.

Mary still gripped Jane's hands in panic and desolation, before getting up and pacing around the room, picking up half-sorted books off a pile, stroking the silk of a gown laid out on the bed. Jane had seen this pattern in Mary over the last few weeks. Her days were spent in tearless restlessness. She would start reading, or copying or writing but could not settle at anything. She would start on walks only to return for a forgotten glove or scarf and then give up on the idea of going out. No discussion lasted for more than a few sentences before her eyes glazed over or she found she had to go to the kitchen or to see Percy. Her dressing took an hour because she could not decide what to wear and changed several times before being prepared to leave her room. Jane heard her sobbing at night. Jane's own grieving was of a quieter kind. She spent long hours sitting silently in corners, pretending to be ready to be part of the world, if it needed her.

'The others think me cold, Jane. I have become a silent imitation of myself. I appear to be strong, to be rational and I do not show enough emotion to please those who measure pain by violent demonstrations. But I can't let go in front of them. Hunt thinks I was cold to Shelley and made him unhappy because Shelley confided in him how angry and miserable I was those last days at Magni. I think he must have said something to Mrs. Mason, too, in Pisa, because she has shown little sympathy to me and is more concerned about Claire.'

'Did you feel Claire might have stayed with you in Italy to comfort you?'

Mary laughed and it became an hysterical giggle. 'Claire? Come now, Jane. Even your good nature could not pretend that Claire has been any comfort to me! She thinks me cold, too, because she is the last person I can break down in front of. Besides I am dependent on Byron for a living, to copy for him and to write articles for *The Liberal*, and he would not have Claire near.'

The only glimmer of relief in this horror was that there was no longer any necessity to pretend with Claire. The threads that bound her to Mary's domain had loosened and been washed away with Shelley. Had she nevertheless expected Claire to comfort her? No, Claire herself had felt she needed comfort. She declared to all who would listen that she was lonely, bereft, abandoned. Her income from Shelley had been abruptly terminated and there was now no daughter to keep her in Italy. In Pisa, while they waited to leave for Genoa, she had stayed with Mrs Mason, who had tried to get an income for her from Byron. When rebuffed, she had recommended that Claire join her brother in Vienna. Of course, the gossip did not stop, and Claire deserting Mary was seen as proof that she had been part of the household only to fulfil Shelley's desires. There was now only a formal cordiality between the step-sisters . Mary repressed a sudden, sickening realisation that had Shelley lived, Claire might have gone to Vienna anyway, and she would have had him to herself at last. She had given Claire money for the journey. Claire thought it too little, but she stopped herself from complaining. She knew that Shelley had provided for her in his will and, for however long it took to get the money, she needed Mary's goodwill.

'At least you have Byron and Tre,' said Jane.

'I am so grateful to Trelawney. When he comes I can talk about my beloved Shelley and he eulogises him to me and I remember how blessed I am to have had him even for only nine years. And he stirs my determination to publish all of his works to a wide public. He does the same for Edward, does he not? He thought him a fine, kind fellow. After you and then me, he was his greatest admirer.'

Jane let show a little of her despair.

'In England I will have no-one to talk to about him, except to describe him to my children. My family did not know him and his family hates me.'

'Go and see Hogg. Take my letter. You will find in him a sympathetic ear.'

'And you have Byron to talk about Shelley with, surely?'

'He has been good to me, giving me work copying the latest cantos of his poem, *Don Juan*, and coming to live near us. I have done a small service, I think, finding the Casa Saluzzi for him and his entourage and this Casa Negroto for me and the Hunts. But he is not nice to Hunt and he is not enthusiastic about *The Liberal*. I have to keep him interested in it because Shelley felt responsible for Hunt. And I feel responsible for Marianne. She is still ill, and I don't think she could travel far if they had to leave Italy.

'You know, Jane, I find it hard to talk to Albe. Every time he speaks I remember the discussions and disputes he and Shelley had long into the night at the Villa Diodoti in Geneva and I expect every time to hear dear Shelley's voice answering him.'

Jane nodded sadly, with understanding. 'I cannot bear to look at the sea any more. It seems cruel that it should be so carefree, so unfeeling, going about its usual business as if it were not guilty of murder.'

The long silence was broken only by the sounds of the children playing a game with a ball beneath the window. Mary went over to stare out at them and thought that it was as if she were seeing them through the wrong end of a telescope.

'You are only twenty-four, Jane, and I am still five and twenty. We have so many years left to be bitter.'

She thought she saw a tall figure run with a stooping gait and open arms towards little Percy, but then a cloud moved across the sun and the vision disappeared. This was all she now had of Shelley, her dreams and her hallucinations.

Mary turned back to Jane. 'I must not stop you from packing any more.' She smiled. 'I feel stronger now. This is for the best. I must stay here until there is some agreement with Sir Timothy Shelley about the fate of me and my child. Byron was right to recommend it, and he is doing his best to get a settlement for me from the old man.' She gave a sardonic grin. 'Though I think Theresa is less happy. She is an Italian and can be jealous of even a pathetic creature like me!'

She shrugged and started to leave, but Jane caught her arm. 'What about your father?'

Mary groaned and clasped her head. 'Oh Jane, he drives me mad. He worried poor Shelley half to death ...' She stopped and closed her eyes and caught her breath. 'He worried me and Shelley constantly for money, and the only thing he could write to me was that now I would be on the same level as him, suffering as much because I would be just as anxious about money as him. No condolences. Nothing.' She shook her head. 'Then in the next letter he's praising my talent and telling me that I have the ability to earn my living through my writing! And goodness knows I need encouragement. It has always been Shelley who has believed in me and I studied to be worthy of him. Now it is even more important to me. Study and work on my writing are the air that I breath now. That, and the well-being of my child.'

The next day she bade a tearful goodbye to Jane and her children, and she remembered saying goodbye to Claire at the coaching station a week ago. Claire had left in an ill humour, because no family could be found that was traveling to Vienna to accompany her, so she had to travel alone. She had kissed Mary and reminded her to write as soon as she knew anything about Sir Timothy. After all, she had said, the old man is nearly seventy, he can't go on for long! Just as her last bags were being loaded and the drivers were whipping up the horses, she had leant out of the window.

'Oh, Mary, I have such a good idea, about how I can make some money and not worry you any more! I have a story I have almost finished. I will send it to you and you can finish it for me, and get it published under your name — well, I mean, as "The Author of Frankenstein"!'

# EPILOGUE

London September 1823

Since I must live, how would I pass the day,
How meet with fewest tears the morning's ray
How sleep with calmest dreams, how find delights,
As fireflies gleam through interlunar nights?
First let me call on thee, lost as thou art
Thy name aye fills my sense, thy love my heart.

*The Choice*, Mary Shelley, 1823

The curtain rose and Mary gripped the hand of Jane who was sitting on her left, as Mr Wallack, playing Frankenstein, made his entrance.

'He looks suitably full of hope and expectation,' whispered Mary to Hogg, on her right.

The set on the stage of the English Opera House showed a study with a staircase to Frankenstein's laboratory above. At the end of the first act Frankenstein went into his laboratory and dramatically exclaimed *"It lives!"* clearly showing that he was consumed with horror and terror. The Demon then emerged from the workshop door wreathed in black smoke and leapt down onto the stage. His skin had been made to look a slimy yellow, his eyes were painted into black caverns, his hair was long and wild and he was wrapped in a sheet. He approached Frankenstein with gestures of conciliation, but Frankenstein retreated. The Demon chased him, seized him and threw him violently on the floor amid drum rolls and sounds of thunder, before uttering an unearthly gurgle and disappearing through a casement window as the curtain fell.

There were shrieks and screams as the ladies in the audience took in the full menace of the creature. Two fainted and the ushers, stationed in the aisles for just such an eventuality, were at hand with smelling salts.

'Do you think it is the dark painted lines on Mr. Cooke, depicting barely covered sinew, the blacked hollow eyes, or the fact that he is half naked, that so exercises the ladies' sensibilities?' whispered Mary to Jane, who giggled.

In the dress circle bar of the English Opera House, at the end of the second act, Hogg asked: 'Well, what do you think of your creation brought to life on the stage, Mary?'

'They have taken great liberties with the story, having Henry, not Victor, fall in love with Elizabeth, but I find I don't mind at all. The spirit of the book is there, and I like it that they use the Monster's fondness for music to show his moods.

'It is on its twenty-third night — a great success — and "The Author of Frankenstein" is a minor celebrity!

'My father has had a reprint made of the novel because of it and it's selling well. But thank goodness only a few of the literary world know who the author really is. Sir Timothy Shelley seems unlikely to contribute anything to Percy's support unless I give him up to strangers, which I will never do. He still blames me for Shelley's disgrace. To have me paraded as an authoress would horrify him, though I still live in hope. After all, that's one of the reasons we've finally left Italy, to be here and try to influence him. He certainly would offer nothing if we were in Italy. Anyway, at the moment my work has to be our source of income. So as my novel, *Valperga*, was published in February under the name 'Author of Frankenstein', perhaps it will sell more copies as a result of this play. Maybe more journals will take my stories and articles as well.'

'I'm sure they will,' agreed Hogg. 'Your father told me that Charles Lamb said he thought your novel was the most extraordinary realisation of the idea of an unnatural being that had ever been created. He has, apparently, recommended you as an author to the proprietors of the *London Magazine*.'

Hogg looked at her quite proudly, even proprietorially. He and she were both thinking of the time, eight years ago, when he had tried to seduce Mary, with Shelley's tacit consent. Shelley's ideal communities, thought Mary. The world had not been ready, and neither was I, if I am honest. Anyway, Hogg could expect there to be no repeat of that. I am as much married to Shelley now as when he was alive. No man will ever replace him. He read her eyes and transferred his gaze to Jane. Yes, Jane could be for you, thought

Mary. Jane needs security and you are a good lawyer. She is the ideal women to reassure an insecure man.

'I've been back in London for two days and already it feels as if the blue skies of Italy were a dream. Smoke and dirt, and ugly accents. Nothing has changed. You are the same Hogg! Longer whiskers, and a little grey, perhaps?' She smiled at him.

He looked up at her. She had forgotten how short he was. 'You have grown prettier, Mary,' he said gallantly. 'From your face, no-one would know the catalogue of your misfortunes. I must admit that I thought life would be easier for you and Percy if you stayed in Italy, outside of the poisonous atmosphere of England and the criticism of Shelley's ideas and way of life which clings to his memory.'

'It is going to be the work of my life to bring his poems and his ideas to the public,' replied Mary, eagerly. 'Everyone must learn about his real character, and see his vision for the future of humanity. I intend to publish his complete works, with explanations, as well as his biography, if Sir Timothy does not forbid it.

'In any case, it was all changing in Italy. Byron has been persuaded to go to Greece to bolster the Greek independence movement in their struggle against the Turks. He will join Prince Mavrocordato, who is leading the forces there. I think he will enjoy war better than peace. Already he is buying arms to take. Without action he gets irritable and is wonderfully mercurial and mean. He quarrels with Hunt over money and I am caught in the crossfire. By going to Greece he can abandon his small wars with both Theresa Guiccioli and Hunt, for a larger one, which will gain more praise and admiration. Trelawney is going off with Albe on his Greek adventure, too. I do hope that they both keep safe. Dear Tre. It's mainly through his steady generosity that I was able to come back.

'I heard that Trelawney wanted to marry Claire,' said Hogg, with a sideways look at Mary that asked for more fat to flesh out the gossip.

'Claire said that Trelawney likes excitement and she wants a quiet life, which is not a sentiment that rings very true to me,' said Mary. 'But she also said — and I quote from a letter of hers so it is no slander — *that he is full of fine feeling and has no principle, but I am full of fine principles but never had a feeling in my life.* Which is amazingly perspicacious for Claire.'

'In any case,' added Jane quickly, to soften the antagonism in Mary's voice, 'Claire has always been against marriage on principle. Although I do wonder, after she was so ill in Vienna, and the Viennese authorities made such objections to her because of her connection to the subversive, Shelley, if she didn't regret her decision.'

'Oh, but this is the latest — have you heard, Jane? — she has fallen in with a Russian Countess and gone to St. Petersburg as companion and governess to her daughters. Mrs. Godwin is beside herself. She prates at me endlessly: *who knows when we shall see her again? And the weather! She is so used to the climate of Italy. You know she is frail; she swears she will die at thirty-seven; she will not survive a Russian winter.*' Mary made a grimace. She wondered, not for the last time in her life, why Claire should be made her problem.

A week will probably be the length of my tolerance of staying in my father's house, thought Mary. He is insufferable about his own financial worries and has little sympathy for mine. And it had not taken Mrs. Godwin's thorns long to emerge from beneath the soft bark. The only brightness at the Godwins' was being reacquainted with her little half-brother William, now grown up to eighteen. She savoured his youthful ebullience, but reflected, sadly, that Shelley had been barely a year older when she first met him, and was also full of the enthusiasm of youth and plans for their future.

Mary decided she would begin the search for a house of her own the very next day. Perhaps near Jane. This thought lifted her spirits and she smiled at Jane. 'At least the grey skies of England are lightened by your gaiety of character. Even subdued and swathed in black, you can lift my spirits.'

Jane shook her head modestly. 'You still have many friends here. Last week Hogg and I were visiting the Gisbournes in Bryanstone Square and they were asking particularly about the Hunts.'

'Marianne had a successful confinement — a little boy. Vincent Leigh. It is intolerably vain of Hunt to give all of his children, even the girls, his own name as a middle name. I'm not sure if he thinks it a joke! I had to stay with Marianne until she was stronger because she speaks no Italian, and her English servant had run off. Vacca was wrong in his prognosis of her death to Shelley in those last days and she is mending, slowly. So the Hunts stay at Genoa for the moment, and Hunt is trying to manage another edition of *The Liberal*, but I am not sure of its success. He has finally become enamoured of Italy — he complained much at the beginning — but Marianne may be lonely now I have left. There are no other English people to talk to, although even I have not been much company this last year. I have been solitary, a perpetual mourner. Hunt was inclined to be kind if I was in want, but I am glad not to be a burden on them now Albe has left. They are considering moving to Florence, but I suspect we may see them back here soon, even though they live so much more cheaply in Italy.'

'I am glad to hear that Marianne is getting better,' smiled Jane.

'And what of the Gisbournes? Will we visit them tomorrow, Jane?'

'Yes. They are not too cheerful. They think they may have to move to Penzance or somewhere equally far away to eek out their income. And Henry is finding it hard to get permanent work as an engineer. He is talking of the opportunities in South Africa, which does not please Mrs. Gisbourne, as you may imagine. He has a lovely fiancé, though — Amelia.'

One survivor from Claire, thought Mary. Another was Peacock, happily settled working for the East India Company, and living with his Welsh wife Jane by the Thames at Lower Halliford in Surrey. It was thirty miles further down the river from Marlow, but Mary suspected that his lifestyle, when she visited, would painfully remind her of the year they had all spent in that village. She wondered: if Claire had married Peacock, would she have ever settled for such a quiet, rural life? Would they all have gone to Italy, had it not been necessary to take Allegra to Byron? Clara might still be alive. And William.

Jane looked closely at Mary, whose eyes had become glazed, and said, 'I am anxious to see little Percy again. Almost four! He must have grown so!'

Mary rallied. 'And he wants nothing more than to see your little ones again. We have been working on his English this past year and he does not sound so much like a little Italian now. I am even teaching him to read, using my mother's texts. He is such good company.'

'And what will you write next, Mary?' Hogg asked.

'I have an idea for a novel about the end of the world. Fitting, don't you think? I am calling it *The Last Man*! It suits my mood. In Italy I have sometimes felt as if I were a sole survivor of the Pisan community that Shelley loved.'

'And how does the world end?'

'With a plague. And with the flaws in human nature.'

The bell rang for the third act, and they re-entered the auditorium. Back in her seat, she was surrounded by the darkness and thunder on stage as Frankenstein now pursued the Monster. In the theatre of her mind, though, she was remembering the thunder during those long days of unnatural darkness at the Villa Diodati in Geneva, when the end of the world had become a topic of discussion.

It had been a good decision to come back, she thought. In spite of the difficulties, and in spite of missing the beauty of Tuscany, I think I may regain some of my powers of imagination. There will be the company of old friends, and there is Jane, and there is music to be enjoyed.

I will make Shelley the model for my main character in my new novel. Someone who has the power to bring reason and justice, and inspiration when all seems desolate. What might he have done had he lived? His work and Percy will be his legacy. In my darkest days, after losing Clara and William, I never once wondered what I would have been without him. When I hated Claire the most, I only ever wanted her absence, not his. From the young, untested, unenlightened girl in the churchyard I am become this fragile, weather-beaten shell that carefully hoards all the pains and pleasures of the past nine years. And it has not been destroyed.

The avalanche of the final scene rumbled down the mountain to engulf Frankenstein and the Monster. The audience enjoyed this last tragedy and the curtain fell to loud applause and cheers.

*I may dream of grand ideas — I may see scenes which may enchant me — I may think either of the past, or the future, such as I would have it — or I will arrange in magnificent procession and gorgeous array some wondrous tale of combinations of man's thoughts and passions ... this is strange vanity–but I am not vain–I would cherish such thoughts as those that may best egg me on to endeavour — but there is another dearer still — to gain some affinity to thee, my lost one–Will you not aid me to deserve you?*

Mary Shelley *Journal. December 1822*

# Mary Shelley–List of Works*

## Novels and travel works

*History of a Six Weeks' Tour through a Part of France, Switzerland, Germany, and Holland: with Letters Descriptive of a Sail round the Lake of Geneva, and of the Glaciers of Chamouni* London: T. Hookham, Jun.; and C. and J. Ollier, 1817

*Frankenstein; Or, The Modern Prometheus* 3 vols. London: Printed for Lackington, Hughes, Harding, Mayor, & Jones, 1818

*Valperga: Or, the Life and Adventures of Castruccio, Prince of Lucca* 3 vols. London: Printed for G. and W. B. Whittaker, 1823

*The Last Man* 3 vols. London: Henry Colburn, 1826

*The Fortunes of Perkin Warbeck, A Romance* 3 vols. London: Henry Colburn and Richard Bentley, 1830

*Lodore* 3 vols. London: Richard Bentley, 1835

*Falkner. A Novel* 3 vols. London: Saunders and Otley, 1837

*Rambles in Germany and Italy, in 1840, 1842, and 1843* 2 vols. London: Edward Moxon, 1844

*Mathilda* Ed. Elizabeth Nitchie. Chapel Hill: University of North Carolina Press, 1959.(Posthumous)

*Maurice or the Fisher's Cot,* Ed. Claire Tomalin: The University of Chicago Press 1998 .(Posthumous)

## Published stories and essays

"A Tale of the Passions, or, the Death of Despina". *The Liberal* 1 (1822): 289–325.

"The Bride of Modern Italy". *The London Magazine* 9 (1824): 351–363.

"Lacy de Vere". *Forget Me Not* for 1827.

"The Convent of Chailot". *The Keepsake for MDCCCXXVIII.*

---

* Does not contain unpublished works or some newly attributed.

"The Sisters of Albano". *The Keepsake for MDCCCXXIX.* 1828.
"Ferdinando Eboli. A Tale". *The Keepsake for MDCCCXXIX.* 1828.
"The Mourner". *The Keepsake for MDCCCXXX.*, 1829.
"The Evil Eye. A Tale". *The Keepsake for MDCCCXXX*, 1829.
"The False Rhyme". *The Keepsake for MDCCCXXX.*, 1829.
"The Swiss Peasant". *The Keepsake for MDCCCXXXI.*, 1830.
"Transformation". *The Keepsake for MDCCCXXXI.* 1831.
"The Dream, A Tale". *The Keepsake for MDCCCXXXII.* 1831.
"The Pole". *The Court Magazine and Belle Assemblée.* 1832
"The Brother and Sister, An Italian Story". *The Keepsake for MDCCCXXXIII.* 1832.
"The Invisible Girl". *The Keepsake for MDCCCXXXIII.* 1832.
"The Mortal Immortal". *The Keepsake for MDCCCXXXIV.* 1833.
"The Elder Son". *Heath's Book of Beauty. 1835.* 1834.
"The Trial of Love". *The Keepsake for MDCCCXXXV.* 1834
"The Parvenue". *The Keepsake for MDCCCXXXVII.* 1836.
"The Pilgrims". *The Keepsake for MDCCCXXXVIII ...,* 1837.
"Euphrasia, a A Tale of Greece". *The Keepsake for MDCCCXXXIX* 1838.

**Edited works**

Percy Bysshe Shelley. *Posthumous Poems of Percy Bysshe Shelley.* London: John and Henry L Hunt, 1824
Percy Bysshe Shelley. *The Poetical Works of Percy Bysshe Shelley,* Mrs. Shelle,y ed. London: Edward Moxon, 1840
Percy Bysshe Shelley. *Essays, Letters from Abroad, Translations and Fragments, By Percy Bysshe Shelley,* Mrs. Shelley ed. London: Edward Moxon, 1840

**Biographies**

*Lives of the Most Eminent Literary and Scientific Men of Italy Spain and Portugal,* Volume III: Vol 88 of the Cabinet of Biography, ed

Rev. Dionysius Lardner (Lardner's Cabinet Cyclopedia). London, Longman Orme, Brown, Green and Longman, 1837

*Lives of the Most Eminent Literary and Scientific Men of France,* Volume I and II: Vol 102 and 103 of the Cabinet of Biography, ed Rev. Dionysius Lardner (Lardner's Cabinet Cyclopedia). London, Longman Orme, Brown, Green and Longman, 1837

# Percy Bysshe Shelley–
# List of major works

## 1810-1814

The Wandering Jew (published 1877)
Zastrozzi
Original Poetry by Victor and Cazire
Posthumous Fragments of Margaret Nicholson: Being Poems
Found Amongst the Papers of That Noted Female Who Attempted
the Life of the King in 1786
St. Irvyne; or, The Rosicrucian
A Vindication of Natural Diet (essay)
The Necessity of Atheism (essay)
The Devil's Walk: A Ballad
Queen Mab: A Philosophical Poem

## 1814 -1816

A Refutation of Deism: In a Dialogue
To Mary Wollstonecraft Godwin
Mutability
On Death
On Life (essay)
On a Future State (essay)
A Summer Evening Churchyard
Feelings of a Republican on the Fall of Bonaparte
Alastor, or The Spirit of Solitude
To Wordsworth
The Daemon of the World
Mont Blanc
## 1817

Hymn to Intellectual Beauty
Laon and Cythna; or, The Revolution of the Golden City: A
Vision of the Nineteenth Century
The Revolt of Islam, A Poem, in Twelve Cantos
Ozymandias
Marianne's Dream
To Constantia, Singing
To The Lord Chancellor
To William Shelley
On Fanny Godwin

**1818**

The Banquet (or The Symposium) by Plato, translation from
Greek
Rosalind and Helen: A Modern Eclogue
Lines Written Among the Euganean Hills
On Love (Essay)

**1819**

The Cenci, A Tragedy, in Five Acts
Ode to the West Wind (text)
The Masque of Anarchy
Men of England
England in 1819
A Philosophical View of Reform (published in 1920)
Julian and Maddalo: A Conversation

**1820**

Peter Bell the Third (published in 1839)
Prometheus Unbound, A Lyrical Drama, in Four Acts
To a Skylark
The Cloud

Oedipus Tyrannus; Or, Swellfoot The Tyrant: A Tragedy in Two Acts

The Witch of Atlas (published in 1824)

**1821**

Adonaïs

Hellas, A Lyrical Drama

Ion by Plato, translation from Greek into English

A Defence of Poetry (first published in 1840)

Epipsychidion

**1822**

The Triumph of Life (unfinished, published in 1824)

The Magnetic Lady to her Patient

'To Jane:The Invitation

To Jane:the Recollection

With a guitar, To Jane

Lines Written in the Bay of Lerici

# Select Bibliography

Armstrong, Margaret W., ed. 1940. *Trelawny: A Man's Life*. New York: The Macmillan company.

Bennett, B. T. (Ed.) 1980. *The Letters of Mary Wollstonecraft Shelley*. Vol 1 *A Part of the Elect*. Baltimore: The John Hopkins University Press.

Blunden, Edmund, ed. 1925. *Shelley and Keats as They Struck Their Contemporaries: Notes Partly from Manuscript Sources*. London: Beaumont.

Brewer, William D. 1994. The Shelley-Byron Conversation. Gainesville, FL: University Press of Florida.

Brewer, William D. 2001. The Mental Anatomies of William Godwin and Mary Shelley. Madison, NJ: Fairleigh Dickinson University Press.

Brinkley, Robert, "Documenting Revision: Shelley's Lake Geneva

Brown, Ford K. 1926. *The Life of William Godwin*. London: J. M. Dent & Sons, Ltd.

Buss, Helen M., D. L. MacDonald, and Anne McWhir, eds. 2001. *Mary Wollstonecraft and Mary Shelley: Writing Lives*. Waterloo, Ont.: Wilfrid Laurier University Press.

Butler, M. 1994. *Mary Shelley Frankenstein or the Modern Prometheus: the 1818 Text*. Oxford: Oxford University Press.

Cameron, K. N. (Ed.) 1973. *Romantic Rebels: Essays on Shelley and his Circle*. Cambridge, Massachusetts: Harvard University Press

Cameron. K. N. (1961). Shelley and his Circle. The Carl H. Pforzheimer Library. Cambridge, Massacuetts: Harvard University Press. Vols 1-5

Church, Richard. 1928. *Mary Shelley*. New York: Viking Press.

Clair, William St. 1989. *The Godwins and the Shelleys: The Biography of a Family*. New York: W. W. Norton.

Cline, C. L. 1952. *Byron, Shelley, and Their Pisan Circle*. 1st ed. Cambridge: Harvard University Press.

Crane, David. 1999. *Lord Byron"s Jackal: A Life of Edward John Trelawny*. New York: Four Walls Eight Windows.

Diary and the Dialogue with Byron in History of a Six Weeks' Tour", in *Keats– Shelley Journal*, 39 (1990), pp. 66–82.

Dowden, Edward. 1887. *The Life of Percy Bysshe Shelley*. vol. 1, London: Kegan Paul, Trench.

Feldman, P. R. & Kilvert, D. S. (Eds.) 1995. The Journals of Mary Shelley: 1814-1844. Baltimore: John Hopkins University Press.

Fisch, Audrey A., Anne K. Mellor, and Esther H. Schor, eds. 1993. *The Other Mary Shelley: Beyond Frankenstein*. New York: Oxford University Press.

Glover, A.S.B. (Ed.) Shelley: Selected Poetry, Prose and Letters. London, The Nonesuch Press

Gordon, Armistead C. 1926. *Allegra: The Story of Byron and Miss Clairmont*. New York: Minton, Balch & Company.

Hill, Alan G. and Ernest De Selincourt, eds. 2000. *The Letters of William and Dorothy Wordsworth*. Oxford, England: Clarendon Press.

Hillary, C. B. Find Date . Essays and Letters by Percy Bysshe Shelley. London, The Walter Scott Publishing Co.

Hotson, Leslie, ed. 1930. *Shelley's Lost Letters to Harriet*. London: Faber & Faber Limited. Retrieved May 31, 2012 (http://www.questia.com/PM.qst?a=o&d=5448410).

Hunt, L. 1949. *The Autobiography of Leigh Hunt*. London: Cresset Press.

Ingpen, R. (Ed.) 1972. The Letters of Percy Bysshe Shelley. Vol II. London: Sir Isaac Pitman & Sons Ltd

Ingpen, Roger, ed. 1903. *The Autobiography of Leigh Hunt: With Reminiscences of Friends and Contemporaries, and with Thornton Hunt's Introduction and Postscript*. Westminster, England: A. Constable & Co.

Johnson, Claudia L., ed. 2002. *The Cambridge Companion to Mary Wollstonecraft*. Cambridge, England: Cambridge University Press.

Jones, F. L (Ed.) 1951. Maria Gisborne & Edward E. Williams : Shelley's friends, Their Journals and Letters. Norman : University of Oklohoma Press.

King-Hele, Desmond. 1960. *Shelley: The Man and the Poet.* New York: Thomas Yoseloff.

Leigh Hunt and the London Literary Scene: A Reception History of His Major Works, 1805-1828; Wordsworth Circle, Vol. 37, 2006

Lovell, Ernest J. . 1962. *Captain Medwin, Friend of Byron and Shelley.* Austin, TX: University of Texas Press. Retrieved May 31, 2012 (http://www.questia.com/PM.qst?a=o&d=3501673).

MacCarthy, F. (2003). Byron: Life and Legend. Croydon, Faber & Faber.

Marchand L, ed. *Byron's Letters and Journals,* 13 vols, (London: John Murray, 1973–81), vol. 5, p. 162.

Mayne, Ethel Colburn. 1924. *Byron.* New York: Charles Scribner's Sons.

McAleer, Edward C. 1958. *The Sensitive Plant: A Life of Lady Mount Cashell.* Chapel Hill, NC: University of North Carolina Press.

McMahan, A. B. 1907. *With Shelley in Italy: a Selection of the Poems and Letters of Percy Bysshe Shelley.* London : Fisher Unwin.

Monkhouse, Cosmo. 1893. *Life of Leigh Hunt.* London: W. Scott, Ltd.

Monro, D. H. 1953. *Godwin's Moral Philosophy: An Interpretation of William Godwin.* London: Oxford University Press.

Moore, Thomas, and George Gordon Byron. 1835. *The Works of Lord Byron: With His Letters and Journals, and His Life.* vol. 1, London: John Murray.

Nitchie, Elizabeth. 1970. *Mary Shelley: Author of "Frankenstein".* Westport, CT: Greenwood Press.

Norman, Sylva, ed. 1934. *After Shelley: The Letters of Thomas Jefferson Hogg to Jane Williams.* London: Oxford University Press.

Norman, Sylva. 1954. *Flight of the Skylark: The Development of Shelley's Reputation.* 1st ed. Norman, OK: University of Oklahoma Press.

Peck, Walter Edwin. 1927. *Shelley: His Life and Work.* vol. 1 & 2, Boston: Houghton Mifflin. Retrieved May 31, 2012

Gittings R & Manton, J., *Claire Clairmont and the Shelleys, 1798–1879* (Oxford and New York: Oxford University Press, 1992),

Reiman Donald, H, (Ed.) (1973). Shelley and his Circle. The Carl H. Pforzheimer Library. Cambridge, Massacusetts: Harvard University Press. Vols 6-10

Robinson, C. E. *Frankenstein or The Modern Prometheus: The Original Two Volume Novel of 1816-1827 from the Budleian Library Manuscripts by Mary Wollstonecraft Shelley (with Percy Bysshe Shelley).* New York: Vintage Books

Scott S., W. ed 1948. *New Shelley Letters.* London: Bodley Head.

Shelley, M. 2009. Frankenstein or the Modern Prometheus. Camberwell, Vic.:Penguin Books.

Shelley, Mary Wollstonecraft. 2000. *Valperga, Or, the Life and Adventures of Castruccio, Prince of Lucca.* Edited by Stuart Curran. New York: Oxford University.

Shelley, Mary. 1994. *The Last Man.* Edited by Morton D. Paley. Oxford: Oxford University Press.

Stocking, M. K. (1968). *The Journals of Claire Clairmont.* Cambridge, Massachusetts: Harvard University Press.

*Stocking, M. K. (1995).* The Clairmont Correspondence: Letters of Claire Clairmont, Charles Clairmont, and Fanny Imlay Godwin, Vol 1: 1808-1834. Baltimore: Johns Hopkins University Press. (Add in Vol 2 if necessary)

Todd, J. 2007. Death of the Maidens: Fanny Wollstonecraft and the Shelley Circle.Berkley: Counterpoint

White, N. I. (1940). *Shelley.* Vol II. New York: Alfred A Knopf.

White, Newman I., Frederick L. Jones, and Kenneth N. Cameron. 1951. *An*

William St Clair *The Godwins and the Shelleys: The Biography of a Family* (London: Faber, 1989)seven

# Thanks and Acknowledgements

Writing this book has been a challenging journey of scholarship and self-discovery. I'm not sure it would have ever been finished without the support and encouragement of my husband Steve and my beautiful children Joanna, Jessica and Tim.

Equally, there has been invaluable input from many friends and colleagues who enthusiastically believed in the project, read countless drafts, guided me around essential sites such as Marlow and Pisa, and delivered 'don't give up' homilies at all the appropriate moments. In particular I would like to thank Jenny Quinn, Wendy Mellor, Julia Brooke, Lyn Fergusson, Susie Simkins, Maria Arrigo and Sue Bell.

A special debt of gratitude is also owed to my editor, Catherine Hammond, without whose patient and motivational input over three years, this work might never have been completed.

I would also like to acknowledge the important contributions of Bodleian Museum and the Carl H. Pforzheimer Collection at the New York Public Library in providing access to original documents. The staff of the Mitchell Library in Sydney, in particular Helen Banacek, provided invaluable support for my research, both in terms of accessing materials and providing a haven for scholarship.